# AND SO IT BE

"Everything all right?" asked Athgar.

"Svetlana is expecting a baby," replied Natalia.

"And is this a good thing?"

"Of course. Why would you think otherwise?"

"I worry the family might attempt to kidnap her child like they did with Oswyn."

At the mention of her name, their daughter perked up. "Did you say Auntie Svetlana's having a baby?"

Athgar raised an eyebrow. "Auntie Svetlana?"

"Well," said Natalia, "she's like a sister to me. What else would she call her?"

Oswyn strolled over, placing her hands on her hips. "You didn't answer the question."

"Now, now," admonished Athgar. "Is that any way to speak to your mother?"

She stared at her feet. "No. Sorry."

"Apology accepted," said Natalia. "To answer your question, yes. Auntie Svetlana is expecting a baby."

"Can we go visit her?"

"We must finish here first, so it'll be a few days before we leave."

Oswyn, never the type to stick around for explanations, ran off. "Agar! We're going to see a baby!"

Natalia chuckled. "I haven't the heart to tell her how long a pregnancy takes."

"I'll take care of it," offered Skora. The old woman followed in Oswyn's wake, showing remarkable speed for a person her age.

"We'd best get going," said Athgar. "The vard won't be happy to be kept waiting."

# ALSO BY PAUL J BENNETT

**Heir to the Crown Series**

Servant of the Crown

Sword of the Crown

Mercerian Tales: Stories of the Past

Heart of the Crown

Shadow of the Crown

Mercerian Tales: The Call of Magic

Fate of the Crown

Burden of the Crown

Mercerian Tales: The Making of a Man

Defender of the Crown

Fury of the Crown

Mercerian Tales: Honour Thy Ancestors

War of the Crown

Triumph of the Crown

Mercerian Tales: Into the Forge

Guardian of the Crown

Enemy of the Crown

Peril of the Crown

Mercerian Tales: The Spark of Change

**Power Ascending Series**

Tempered Steel: Prequel

Temple Knight | Warrior Knight

Temple Captain | Warrior Lord

Temple Commander | Warrior Prince

Temple General | Warrior King

**The Frozen Flame Series**

Awakening - Prequels

Ashes | Embers | Flames | Inferno

MAELSTROM | VORTEX | TORRENT | CATACLYSM

THE DUALITY OF MAGIC SERIES - COMING SPRING 2025

VOICES FROM THE PAST

**THE CHRONICLES OF CYRIC**

INTO THE MAELSTROM: PREQUEL

MIDWINTER MURDER

THE BEAST OF BRUNHAUSEN

A PLAGUE ON ZEIDERBRUCH

# CATACLYSM

## THE FROZEN FLAME: BOOK EIGHT

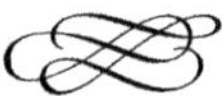

PAUL J BENNETT

First Edition: February 2024

ePub ISBN: 978-1-990073-75-5
Mobi ISBN: 978-1-990073-76-2
Print ISBN: 978-1-990073-78-6
Smashwords ISBN: 978-1-990073-77-9

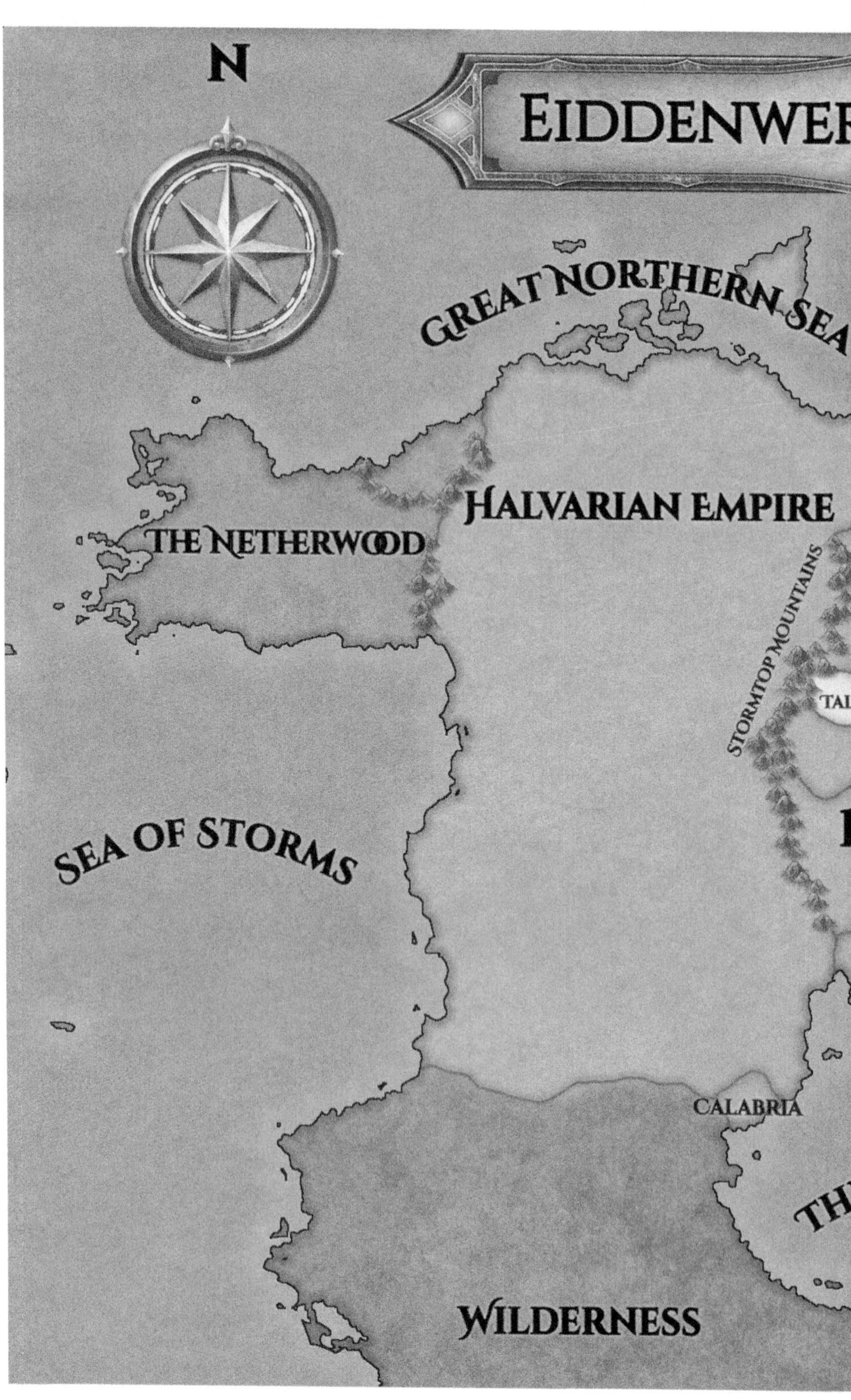

N
EIDDENWER
GREAT NORTHERN SEA
HALVARIAN EMPIRE
THE NETHERWOOD
STORMTOP MOUNTAINS
SEA OF STORMS
CALABRIA
WILDERNESS

HE - 1110 SR
RUZHINA
KARSLEV
ZARAN
REINWICK
KIENENSTADT
ABELARD
ANDOVER
EIDOLON
CARLINGEN
BRAYMOOR
WILDERNESS
ARNSFELD
BEORWIC
OSTROVA
ZALISTA
THERENGIA
KRAGEN-TOR
RUNEWALD
GREY SPIRE MOUNTAINS
HADENFELD
HOLSTEAD
KRIEGHOFF
TTY KINGDOMS
THE WILDLANDS
HIMMERING SEA
THE PIRATE COAST
THE GREAT SEA

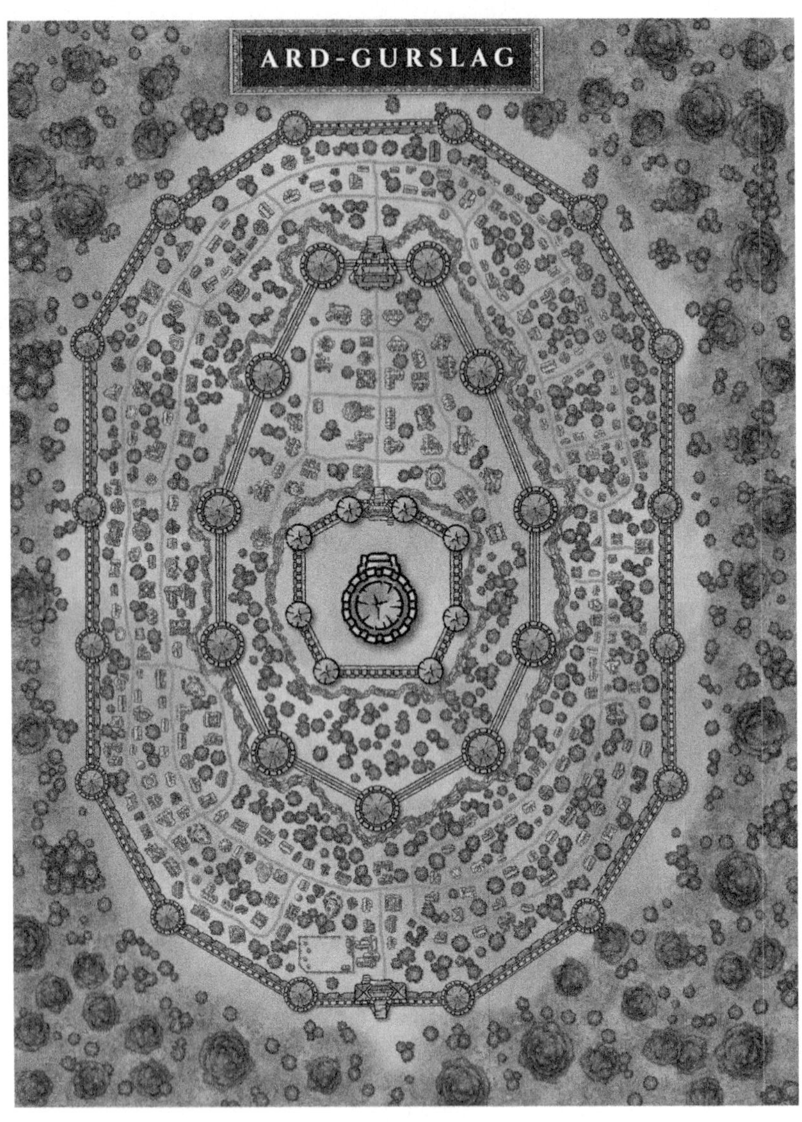


*City of Ard-Gurslag*

# THE HALLS OF THE KING

## SPRING 1110 SR* (*SAINTS RECKONING)

Farin Greybeard, Vard of Kragen-Tor, stroked his beard, staring at his visitors. He'd ruled for over a decade, but before that, he'd developed a loathing for Humans as the Guildmaster of the Warriors Guild. Now, the High Thane of Therengia stood before him with his entourage, which included not only Humans but Orcs and even a Dwarf. "You say you come here in peace, yet you've expanded your borders at an alarming rate. How long before you seek to annex my lands?"

"Appearances can be deceiving," replied Athgar. "I shan't deny that our borders have grown over the last few years, but none of that was our doing."

"Then who is responsible?"

Belgast pushed himself to the forefront. "With all due respect, Majesty, I vouch for everything the High Thane claims."

Farin's gaze fell on the Dwarf. "Perhaps you'd care to explain how you arrived at your present position of power?"

"Most certainly. It started with the Church of the Saints, or rather, the Temple Knights of Saint Cunar, who initiated a crusade against the eastern lands. We weren't called Therengia then, but the Humans there were the descendants of the Old Kingdom. We defeated their invasion, leading to the knights abandoning the City of Ebenstadt, leaving it under the influence of brigands, necessitating firm action on our part."

"So you took it upon yourselves to conquer the city?"

"We did, Majesty. Thinking us weak, the Kingdom of Novarsk launched an invasion, but it, too, met with a similar fate, leading to their surrender."

"And then you just absorbed Novarsk?"

"We intended to restore their monarchy, but it quickly became apparent they couldn't be trusted, and thus, a governor was named to rule over the kingdom."

"I see," said Farin. "Yet, if I'm not mistaken, the expansion didn't end there."

"No," replied Belgast. "It didn't. Upon returning from the west, we came across a… well, there's no quick way to explain this. The Kingdom of Carlingen was threatened with invasion, and we intervened on behalf of King Maksim, neutralizing the threat. Though we didn't ask for it, Ostrova ceded us a portion of their eastern lands, which, I might add, were little more than wilderness. Thus, our borders now reach as far as King Maksim's lands. I assure you, however, that none of this was planned; it just happened."

"This sounds a little far-fetched to me. I'm tempted to tie you up between the Pillars of Truth and verify your story."

Belgast grinned. "You're more than welcome to do so, Your Majesty, but you know as well as I, it won't change my story."

Farin barked out a laugh. "It's been years since you were at court, Lord Belgast, but I am not so old that I cannot admit when I have been outwitted. I will accept your explanation and listen to the proposal your High Thane wishes to discuss."

"You are most gracious, Majesty," said Athgar. "My intention in coming here is to secure a lasting peace with Kragen-Tor and assure you we bear no interest in claiming your lands. Quite the opposite, in fact. We are willing to take steps to ensure no one else tries to deprive you of them."

"What are you proposing?"

"A treaty of mutual defence."

"You are more likely to be attacked than us," replied the vard.

"True, yet Belgast tells me you've had issues with both Zalista and Novarsk."

"You are correct, but how can I trust you? According to Belgast, Novarsk is now part of your empire. Perhaps I'd be wiser to worry about Therengia on our border than Zalista?"

Kargen moved up to stand beside Athgar. "I am Kargen, Chieftain of the Red Hand. May I speak, Majesty?"

"You may."

"Clearly, you distrust Humans, but would you take the word of another Elder Race? Therengia is not only a land of Humans, but also where Humans and Orcs live in peace and harmony. My tribe is but one of four now living under the banner of Therengia."

"Don't Orcs reside in the lands of Humans elsewhere on the Continent?"

"They do, Majesty, but Therengia is the only place where they participate in the ruling of the realm."

"How do your people contribute?"

"The chieftain and shaman of each tribe sit on the ruling council of Therengia, with status equal to the Humans."

"Most impressive," said Vard Farin, "yet a mutual defence pact works to your advantage more than mine. We are but one city, whereas you rule over many more. And there's your heritage, which sets the majority of the Petty Kingdoms against you. How do you propose we overcome these obstacles?"

"We would come to your aid if threatened," replied Athgar, "and in return, we ask that you help those areas of our land within a reasonable distance of Kragen-Tor."

"And what do you consider a reasonable distance?"

"Those details can be discussed later, providing you agree in principle."

The vard sat back, stroking his beard once again. "I shall give this considerable thought, but before I decide, I must confer with my advisors."

Athgar bowed slightly. "Of course, Majesty."

Natalia stared into the bowl as the words of power issued from her lips. The water rippled, then the image of Svetlana appeared.

"Greetings," said the Queen of Carlingen. "How are the negotiations in Kragen-Tor?"

"Progressing slowly. Belgast believes the vard will come round to our way of thinking but admits Dwarves take their time making decisions. How are things there?"

"We are doing well," replied Svetlana. "We completed the casting circle in the Palace, and I've already used it to travel to Beorwic and back, as has Katrin, making it much easier for her to report on their progress in future. You'll need to commit it to memory the next time you visit."

"Speaking of Beorwic, how is that shaping up?"

"The Stone Crusher Orcs you arranged for have been most useful in clearing away hundreds of years' worth of forest growth, uncovering much of the ancient city. Unfortunately, there's little left save for the foundations, but there's enough rubble to meld into fresh stones."

Natalia smiled. "The advantage of having masters of earth at hand. How goes the reconstruction?"

"Under Katrin's supervision, they've begun work on new housing close to the stone pillars, and there's no shortage of volunteers for just about every Therengian in Carlingen offered to help. We can't pay them; we haven't the funds, but in exchange for their assistance, they'll get title to a plot of land."

"And how fares the City of Carlingen?"

"It's calmed down considerably. Temple Captain Cordelia sends her regards, by the way. She assumed temporary command of the town watch while we reorganized."

"Town watch?"

"Yes, an amalgamation of the various groups who patrolled the city during the recent crisis. We've properly equipped them, and the Temple Knights are giving them some much-needed training in weapons."

"You've certainly been busy," said Natalia. "How are you doing?"

"Our finances are no longer an issue."

"No. I mean, how are YOU doing? You look a little worn out."

"I'm fine, all things considered."

Even through the magic image, Natalia noticed her blush. "What is it you're not telling me?"

Svetlana beamed. "I'm expecting."

"Congratulations! That's wonderful news. When did you discover this?"

"I've suspected it for some time, but the Royal Physician confirmed it last week. Any advice on what to expect?"

"Yes. Don't be alarmed if you find yourself unable to cast. It's only a temporary loss, so you needn't worry."

"And will my child be capable of using magic?"

"You're from a long line of Stormwinds, so that's possible. However, it's not guaranteed, particularly as we know nothing about your husband's history with magic."

"I shall be glad for a child, magic or not. I was merely curious."

"How does Maksim feel about it?"

"He's ecstatic."

"As he should be." Natalia paused. "Perhaps I'll visit you once we're done here."

"You'd be more than welcome. Shall I meet you in Beorwic?"

"No. I'll meet with Katrin and have her bring us to Carlingen from there. I wouldn't suggest using your magic for the next few months, especially the frozen arch spell. You might find yourself suddenly without the power to return."

"I shall wait for you here, then. Any idea when to expect your arrival?"

"That depends on the stubbornness of Dwarves, but I doubt it'll be for a few days, possibly even a week. I'll contact you at the next prearranged time to make further arrangements."

"Anything else you'd care to pass on?"

"Actually, yes," said Natalia. "I recently heard from Galina that Reinwick and Andover are finally working together. They have big plans concerning their alliance, and both sent emissaries to Eidolon. Hopefully, we'll soon see their alliance growing even stronger."

"Do you think they'll be successful?"

"I'm hoping so, but we've heard rumours of a Stormwind there, so it'll be an uphill battle."

"Any word on Halvaria?"

"No. Captain Grazynia said the Great Northern Sea has been relatively peaceful." A shadow loomed over Natalia, and she looked up to see Athgar.

"Sorry to interrupt," he said, "but we've been summoned back to the king's presence."

"He's a vard," called out Belgast. "You must remember that. You don't want to upset him."

"I stand corrected."

"I'd best say goodbye," said Natalia. "I'll talk to you next week, as scheduled." She waved her hand over the bowl and dismissed her spell, returning it to a simple water container.

"Everything all right?" asked Athgar.

"Svetlana is expecting a baby."

"And is this a good thing?"

"Of course. Why would you think otherwise?"

"I worry the family might attempt to kidnap her child like they did with Oswyn."

At the mention of her name, their daughter perked up. "Did you say Auntie Svetlana's having a baby?"

Athgar raised an eyebrow. "Auntie Svetlana?"

"Well," said Natalia, "she's like a sister to me. What else would she call her?"

Oswyn strolled over, placing her hands on her hips. "You didn't answer the question."

"Now, now," admonished Athgar. "Is that any way to speak to your mother?"

She stared at her feet. "No. Sorry."

"Apology accepted," said Natalia. "To answer your question, yes. Auntie Svetlana is expecting a baby."

"Can we go visit her?"

"We must finish here first, so it'll be a few days before we leave."

Oswyn, never the type to stick around for explanations, ran off. "Agar! We're going to see a baby!"

Natalia chuckled. "I haven't the heart to tell her how long a pregnancy takes."

"I'll take care of it," offered Skora. The old woman followed in Oswyn's wake, showing remarkable speed for a person her age.

"We'd best get going," said Athgar. "The vard won't be happy to be kept waiting."

Athgar and Natalia led the way, with Kargen and Shaluhk behind them. Belgast, an expert in Dwarf customs, followed along, ready to answer any questions that might arise.

The King's Hall was the largest room in Kragen-Tor, with the Pillars of Truth anchoring one end and the vard's throne at the other. Befitting a Lord of Stone, Farin's throne sat on a raised platform, allowing him to look down on any seeking his judgement. While it worked well when those concerned were Dwarves, these taller Humans and Orcs left him with a more level gaze.

Athgar bowed deeply. "Majesty, we come at your bidding. Have you made a decision regarding our proposal?"

The Dwarven vard swept his gaze over his visitors. "I consulted with my advisors, discussing the matter at great length."

"That doesn't bode well," muttered Belgast.

"While there is merit in your idea, other issues demand our attention at this precise time."

Natalia straightened her back. "Might I ask what those issues are?"

"As you no doubt surmised, the bulk of our trade is with the Human Kingdom of Zalista, which lies to our north. We used to get along well with them, but their new king decided his treasury was low and imposed an additional tariff on our trade goods. We've discussed sending a delegate to his court to resolve the issue, but we've recently received reports His Majesty is casting a greedy eye south, to our mountain home."

"Surely you don't think he'll attack?"

"Why attack when he can starve us out? He's not after the city, just the gold filling our coffers."

"What sort of exports do you refer to?"

"A variety of things," replied Farin, "but mostly finished goods, particularly worked metal."

"Does that include weapons?"

The vard nodded. "It does. Ironic that the very weapons we sold them could be used against us."

"I'm sorry," said Athgar. "I thought you said they wouldn't attack?"

"And they won't, but they can use their army to seal off the roads. Without trade, this city will starve."

"If I might be so bold," offered Natalia, "those items you spoke of would be most welcome in Therengia."

"Would they, now? What tariff would you impose on us?"

"None."

"None?"

"We require goods," she continued, "and in exchange, we offer you the opportunity to purchase goods from us. If my information is accurate, you import large quantities of food, particularly grain. Is this true?"

"It is."

"Then we only ask that, in return for accepting your goods, you pay a reasonable price for ours."

"Which would be?"

"In that, I must defer to our Minister of Finance."

"Who is?"

"Belgast Ridgehand, with whom I believe you have a history."

Belgast sputtered, "M-me? Minister of Finance? Since when?"

"Since now," said Natalia, "assuming the High Thane is in agreement?"

Athgar quickly nodded.

"I accept the position," replied Belgast, "but perhaps next time you intend to spring something like that on me, you might give some advanced warning."

The vard cleared his throat, garnering everyone's attention. "That is most agreeable. Am I to understand you require weapons and armour as well?"

Belgast stepped closer. "We do, Majesty, particularly armour, which would need to be Human-sized as we don't have a substantial Dwarven population."

"And do your Orcs wear armour?"

"Not currently, but it's worth considering in the future. Presently, our best warriors are clad only in mail."

The vard snorted. "Mail? That's rather archaic. Most of the Continent employs plate armour, at least for their knights, if not their footmen."

"We employ no knights, Majesty. Merely a Thane Guard, although admittedly, that is now comprised of four companies."

"And your archers?"

"Our Therengian archers use bows, but they pale in comparison to the warbows of the Orcs."

Farin rubbed his hands together. "Well, that's something we can help you with." He rose from his throne, which caught his guards by surprise.

Those on either side made to advance, but he halted them with a raised hand. He approached Athgar, standing before him in a pose much like what Oswyn had used earlier.

He thrust out his meaty hand. "We have an agreement, at least in principle. I shall work out the details with Belgast."

Athgar cemented the deal. "I look forward to our two realms working closer, Majesty."

"Enough of this Majesty nonsense. We are equals, you and I. Let's dispense with the formalities and use our given names."

"Of course."

Farin turned to face Natalia and bowed. "You honour us with your presence, Lady Stormwind. I am well-aware of your family's history regarding the mages of Karslev, but you may rest assured, we shall not hold it against you."

"Did you know they are working with Halvaria?" said Natalia.

The vard shrugged his shoulders. "It doesn't surprise me. There is far too much conflict amongst the Petty Kingdoms for it to be a coincidence. I've always suspected someone was behind it. Now you've put a face to it. Interestingly enough, I received a letter from Ruzhina just before you arrived."

"Might I ask its nature?"

"They wished to send an emissary to my court. I refused them, but I expect they'll try again."

"If you want to stop them from asking again, tell them of our agreement."

"Won't that upset them?"

"Doubtless it will," replied Natalia, "but their influence has weakened, and they are no longer the power they used to be."

"I'm curious," said Athgar. "How are you so well-informed about the politics of the Petty Kingdoms?"

Farin smiled. "One of my closest friends is the Guildmaster of the Smiths Guild, whose members travel the length and breadth of the Continent. As they go about their business, they hear things which they pass on to me."

"Anything we should know about?"

"Nothing I can think of, but I shall be sure to let you know if I hear of any plans to attack Therengia."

"Thank you. That is most generous."

"Not at all. It's the least I can do, considering our new trade agreement. Since it will take a few weeks to work out the details with Belgast, will the rest of you return home?"

"Natalia and I are travelling to Carlingen to visit a good friend of ours who is expecting her first child."

"We are returning home," replied Kargen. "There are tribe matters that need attending to. Will you take Oswyn with you to Carlingen?"

"I doubt she'd accept anything else."

"Would you consider taking Agar with you?"

"It would be our pleasure."

# BEORWIC

## SPRING 1110 SR

The ice columns continued to build, and as the spell progressed, they joined at the top, forming an arch.

"It's ready," announced Natalia.

"Me first!" yelled Oswyn, running through the opening.

Agar raced towards the arch. "I should go after her before she gets lost in the ruins." The Orc youngling stepped through.

"Shall I follow?" asked Skora.

"Go whenever you like," replied Natalia. "Don't worry. There are plenty of people on the other side, so there's no danger."

The old woman approached the arch, peering through. "It's quite remarkable. The landscape is completely different there."

"Beorwic is hundreds of miles away, on the southern border of Carlingen."

"I'm aware of that, but to see it up close is disorienting."

"You'll get used to it."

"I thought we were going to Carlingen?"

"Eventually," said Natalia, "but the magic circle there is new, so I haven't committed it to memory yet."

"Another circle? Is there no limit to how many you can memorize?"

"It varies with each individual, but according to the instructors at the Volstrum, it's not unreasonable for a mage to learn ten or more. They don't usually teach this to students; it's more of an advanced spell."

"Then how did you find out about it?"

"We were taught about a Fire Magic spell called ring of fire, but it amounts to the same thing. In both cases, you can only travel to a known location."

"Wait a moment," said Athgar. "Didn't you tell me you created a frozen arch to escape the Palace grounds in Andover?"

"I did, but I made that up on the spot."

"As you did in Beorwic?"

"Exactly. Since leaving the Volstrum, I understand magic with greater clarity, and I have you to thank for that."

"Me?"

"You opened my eyes to another way of envisioning magic, one allowing me to reach past the limitations of my training."

"You should thank the Orcs for that, not me."

She smiled. "No. You taught me to find my inner spark—not that it's a spark, in my case, more like a comforting pool of water."

"I'm happy to have been of help."

"Pardon me for interrupting," said Skora, "but shouldn't we be stepping through this arch before it begins to melt? It is made of ice, you know."

"Yes, of course," said Athgar. "You may proceed."

Skora stepped through, and then Athgar held out his hand for Natalia. She, in turn, moved up to stand before the opening, grasping his hand firmly.

They stepped through together, the air now more humid, not to mention warmer, for Kragen-Tor was up in the mountains, whereas Beorwic stood astride a river.

Their first visit to the ancient Therengian city had been nearly nine months ago when the Ostrovan army threatened an invasion of Carlingen, but relations had cooled considerably in the interim. King Eugene, the ruler there, claimed he'd been unaware of the plot and, in compensation, ceded the eastern portion of his kingdom to Therengia to avoid a war, allowing Carlingen to finally have an ally on their border. Athgar spurred on the region's development, for with new villages came roads and an abundance of volunteers willing to settle the area.

The sound of hammering greeted their ears, for the once-deserted streets of Beorwic were coming back to life. A nearby guard watched them emerge from the gateway but didn't challenge them as Natalia dismissed the spell. They stood at the base of the ancient stone gateway built under the supervision of some long-forgotten mage, but she preferred the term standing stones.

Oswyn ran towards them, pulling a familiar girl by the hand. "Look who I found!"

"Good to see you, Greta," said Natalia. "How do you like your new home?"

"I much prefer it to the court of Andover."

"Is Katrin nearby?"

"Yes. She's overseeing the construction of the great hall."

"Not a keep?"

"No," replied Greta. "Considering most here are Therengian, we thought it best to emulate their ways."

"We? Are you one of her advisors now?"

The girl straightened. "Of course. Come. I'll take you to her."

She proceeded down a now-cleared roadway. Cobblestones had been laid here in the past, but centuries of abandonment resulted in it being covered by a forest intent on reclaiming its terrain. However, with the reintroduction of people, they'd removed some obstructions, starting with this particular road.

Athgar marvelled at the progress made in such a short period. The Stone Crushers lent some of their masters of earth to reshape the stone walls abandoned long ago, and the influx of Therengians from Carlingen had led to the building of many sturdy wooden houses. More people would continue coming over time, but it already felt like a city, albeit sparsely populated.

They encountered Katrin by the riverbank, watching a group of men rolling barrels off a boat onto a newly rebuilt dock.

"I hope we're not interrupting?" asked Natalia.

Katrin turned, and they hugged. "I wasn't expecting you for another week. How did it go in Kragen-Tor?"

"Splendidly, thanks to Belgast, but there are still a few details to settle. We're headed to Carlingen. I believe you have access to their magic circle?"

"I do," replied Katrin. "When did you wish to travel?"

"There's no hurry. This is purely a personal visit. We wanted to look around Beorwic, if that's all right with you?"

"By all means. Would you like me to show you around, or do you prefer to wander?"

"I don't want to drag you away from anything important, but when you're able, I'd appreciate an update on your progress here."

"What do you want to know?"

"Let's start with all these people. Just how many are living here?"

"That depends entirely on what you mean by living? Close to five hundred consider this place their permanent home, while the rest seek work and, I expect, will move on as summer arrives. Most come via boat, but whenever Svetlana or I use magic to travel here, we bring a few more."

"I assume you've had no shortage of volunteers."

"You are correct," said Katrin. "The bigger issue for us is finding people with the skills necessary to get this town started. Cutting timbers is relatively easy, and even building houses isn't too difficult, but we require merchants and traders."

Athgar scanned the area, noting the occasional mail-clad warrior, reminding him of Herulf, the Therengian he'd found in Reinwick. When they'd returned to Runewald last fall, Herulf elected to remain in Beorwic, in command of the local fyrd. He looked back at Katrin. "How is Herulf?"

He detected a slight blush on her cheeks. "He's doing well."

"She's sweet on him," offered Greta. "I keep telling her he feels the same, but she doesn't believe me."

"Give it time," said Natalia. "Athgar and I didn't quite see eye to eye when we first met."

"That's because you almost killed me," he replied.

"Not on purpose."

Athgar winked at Greta. "That's just one of the stranger mating habits of Water Mages."

The girl laughed. "While you're here, I have a question."

"Ask away."

"If Herulf and Katrin had a child, would it have grey eyes?"

"It would," said Athgar. "Only one parent with grey eyes is needed to ensure a child is similarly blessed."

"So they'd be Therengian?"

"Look around you," replied Natalia. "What do you see?"

"Therengians, Orcs, and even a few non-Therengians like you. Why?"

"You're as much a Therengian as Athgar, regardless of your eye colour."

"But I've never set foot in Therengia. I live in Carlingen with Katrin."

"Yes, but that doesn't matter."

"She's right," added Athgar. "And I'm the High Thane, so I ought to know. You're not about to argue with me, are you?"

Greta shook her head.

"Good. Then it's all settled. Perhaps you'd care to familiarize Agar and Oswyn with the area?"

"I would be happy to. Where are they?"

Athgar pointed. "Over there by Skora, I imagine."

She ran off.

"Ah, the passion of youth. I remember it well."

Katrin laughed. "You're not that old yourself."

"It's not age that wears on me; it's responsibility. Perhaps I should give up the position of High Thane and become a simple hunter?"

"We both know you could never do that," offered Natalia. "You've too much of a desire to see the land prosper."

"Guilty as charged."

"Come with me," said Katrin. "There's something I want to show you." She led them upstream, away from the docks. "As you know, Carlingen's tiny fleet was hardly ever used. However, as we explored the ruins, we discovered what appears to be an old shipbuilding facility. Maksim suggested it might prove useful to rebuild it. If Beorwic is half as successful as we hope, we'll experience a vast increase in river traffic."

"Has he given up all thought of a navy?" asked Athgar.

"He's agreed to help fund the Temple Fleet, and they, in return, will keep our waters free of pirates and such. He considered building more like the *Bergannon,* but he'd prefer the merchant ships be in the hands of individuals."

"Ah, yes," said Athgar. "The *Bergannon.* If I recall, it was not the steadiest of ships."

"True enough, but it got you to Ruzhina."

"Does it still sail?"

"It does," said Katrin. "It's been wintering up in Carlingen, although I suppose by now, they've seen fit to return it to the water and outfit it for shipping. Svetlana can tell you more."

She paused as they emerged into a small clearing. "We discovered stone beneath the river sediment, and after digging down, we found what's left of a channel excavated centuries ago." She moved inland. "About a hundred paces this way, you'll see a shallow depression, which we believe was an artificial bay they floated their boats into."

"Do we even know what kind of boats the Old Kingdom used?" asked Natalia.

Athgar shrugged his shoulders. "Don't look at me. You know more about that than I do."

"We can make some deductions," said Katrin. "Many older boats in use on the Great Northern Sea are open-topped vessels, carrying a crew of only a couple. They struggle at sea but would serve us well on the rivers. Scholars suggest they're based on old Therengian designs, and after looking through our discoveries here, I'm inclined to agree."

Natalia wandered around the clearing. "I think you're correct. This was definitely connected to the river in the past."

"Now that you're here, I wonder if I haven't got this wrong. You don't suppose it could be a temple dedicated to Akosia, do you?"

"No," replied Athgar. "On our last visit, Belgast discovered the Temple of Tauril, which is more like a theatre. This place is completely different, so your earlier deduction is more likely the case. Not that it matters. Whoever built this has long since moved on to the Afterlife."

"If you really want to know," said Natalia, "Shaluhk can visit and speak with the Ancestors."

"It's nothing that needs immediate attention," replied Katrin. "Merely idle speculation on my part."

"Anything else you've discovered?"

"Additional evidence that Orcs and Therengians lived side by side, but that's hardly surprising. We also uncovered what remains of a city wall, or at least part of one. I can't quite decide whether it was under construction when the city was attacked or destroyed by whoever defeated them."

"Unfortunately, we don't know who defeated them," said Athgar. "All we know is that they were Human, but not which kingdom."

"It wouldn't matter much anyway," said Natalia. "The Successor States rose and fell in a very short time; the vast majority of the Petty Kingdoms didn't evolve until nearly a century after the fall of the Old Kingdom. There are exceptions, but they are mainly to the west."

"What about Ruzhina? Were they considered a Successor State?"

"The instructors at the Volstrum always claimed it was founded before the Old Kingdom, but I have my doubts. What do you think, Katrin?"

"I tend to agree. The evidence indicates it was founded while the Old Kingdom was at its height rather than earlier. However, it wasn't much of a power in the Continent until the Stormwinds founded the school. At least that's the Volstrum's belief."

"Interesting," said Athgar, "but don't they have a line of kings stretching back centuries?"

"They do," replied Katrin, "but records predating the Old Kingdom's fall are rare. Scholars claim they can trace the king's ancestry for over eight centuries, but the written records are much more recent. I believe most of that lineage was written well after the fact, likely invented to support the Crown's assertion that it's one of the oldest Royal lines on the Continent."

"So they just made things up?"

"That's a simpler way of saying it."

"Perhaps I should invent a history of my own," suggested Athgar.

"You wouldn't be the first ruler."

"I was only joking."

"I wasn't," said Katrin. "I'd estimate at least half the ruling families of the Petty Kingdoms did exactly that, or someone in their ancestry did. Kings have done a great many questionable things to secure their Thrones."

"I never took you for such a scholar."

"I was always good when it came to history. Unfortunately, my magical abilities lagged behind. That's how I became one of the Disgraced."

"You know I don't like that term," said Natalia. "There is no disgrace in taking time to learn magic."

"The family didn't see it that way."

"No, they didn't, and that's their loss. Now, let's change the subject to more pleasant things. How has your casting progressed? Has Svetlana kept up with your instruction?"

"She has, though we meet less often than we used to."

"You've learned the frozen arch spell, or else you wouldn't be able to travel back and forth to Carlingen."

"I have, although admittedly, it took a long time. It's the most difficult spell I've ever attempted."

"And now you've mastered it. We shall have to take you back to Therengia so you can commit the circle of stones to memory, and then you can visit us whenever you want."

"I'd like that."

"How has Greta been?"

"Aside from teasing me about Herulf, she's wonderful."

"Has she been making friends?"

"She has," replied Katrin. "The Therengians who came from Carlingen brought their families, and the children often go into the woods to gather berries and mushrooms to supplement our food. An Orc hunter or two escorts them, but you'd be surprised at what they find."

"And she enjoys that?"

"She does. In a manner of speaking, she's become their unofficial leader, although I suppose that's my fault for setting an example."

"Well," said Athgar, "you're doing an excellent job of it here."

Katrin beamed. "Thank you. Svetlana tells me Beorwic is the only place in Carlingen that's prospering."

"Not the other barons?"

"They're doing reasonably well, but their efforts have met with only limited success so far."

"Why do you suppose that is?"

"Those who come here are excited to begin a new life, while the same can't be said of those heading to Adlinschlot or Raketsk. There's also the matter of their work ethic."

"I'm not sure I follow," said Athgar.

"Therengians usually come from families who've worked the land for generations and are committed to working hard to build their homes. These others I speak of are mostly descendants of treasure seekers who came to Carlingen. As a result, they wish to make their coins with the least amount of effort possible. They're not as interested in settling down as in making enough to return to what they perceive as a more civilized land. That doesn't exactly provide the barons with the best choice of workers. The king should encourage more farmers to travel to Carlingen and settle the countryside."

"I shall bring that to his attention the next time I see him."

"Good luck with that."

"That's an odd thing to say."

"I've raised the matter several times, but he's too busy to do anything about it. What he really needs is some decent advisors."

# CARLINGEN

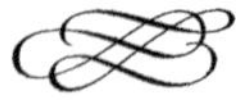

## SPRING 1110 SR

Katrin closed her eyes, concentrating on her spell. The air tingled as the frozen arch formed, and then the image beyond changed, revealing the casting circle in Carlingen.

"Very good," said Natalia, hanging on to her daughter's hand. "I see Svetlana's lessons have borne fruit."

"They have. Not that we've had much time, though it's slightly easier now the circle is complete." She walked through the archway, beckoning the others to follow.

They stepped into a large stone room, Agar being the last after Skora. A wall on one side held three stained-glass windows reaching to the high ceiling, but the outside was so smeared with salt it was difficult to decipher what the scenes depicted.

"Where are we?" asked Athgar.

Katrin smiled. "We're in the old Temple of Saint Mathew, built several centuries ago, but they replaced it with a newer, larger temple about eighty years ago."

"How far are we from the Palace?"

"Quite close. The main temple doors originally led out to the street, but once they made it part of the Palace, they closed it in, and now there's a walkway attached directly to the eastern side."

"They should have guards posted here."

"I'm sure they will, eventually, but Svetlana and I are the only ones who've committed this circle to memory."

Athgar knelt, examining the floor. "This looks like gold inlay."

"It is," replied Natalia. "Gold is one of the few metals that retains and amplifies magic."

"There are others?"

"Silver, though not as efficiently, and then there's godstone, or skymetal, as some call it. It's the most powerful of all metals."

"We have some of that in Runewald."

"You do?" asked Katrin. "Why haven't you used it?"

"That's easier said than done," replied Natalia. "It requires a smith with enough skill to work it, not to mention a hotter forge."

"And you know this how, exactly?"

Natalia chuckled. "Belgast keeps pestering me about it."

"And it's not ours," said Athgar. "By all rights, it belongs to the Orcs of the Red Hand, as we found it in their territory."

"It is being saved," added Agar. "My mother says that one day it may be needed."

"Let me make sure I understand this," said Katrin. "You have skymetal, but you've put it away in storage somewhere?"

"That's about it," replied Athgar. "Why?"

"They say that stuff is worth a king's ransom. How much do you have?"

"According to Belgast, there's enough to make a weapon or two and a couple of rings if we use it sparingly."

"Sparingly? Whatever does that mean?"

"That's beyond my understanding," said Athgar. "I'll be the first to admit I know little of smithing."

"Have you considered selling it?"

"And see it used against us? I don't think Kargen would agree to that."

"But it could fill your coffers."

"There's more to life than filling chests with coins."

"I suppose that's one way of looking at it."

"Much as I enjoy admiring this circle," said Natalia, "shouldn't we leave here and visit Svetlana to pay our respects?"

"Yes," replied Katrin. "Of course."

Svetlana sat before the fire, her feet up on a footstool.

The door opened, and Oswyn charged in, full of excitement, running towards the queen, then stopped short, her eyes scanning the room. "Where's the baby?"

"In my belly," replied Svetlana. There was no denying the look of disappointment on the child's face. "Cheer up. It'll be here soon enough, and then you can meet your new cousin."

"Will it be a boy or a girl?"

"We'll have to wait and see."

Agar entered next, followed by the rest.

"There you are, Oswyn," said the young Orc. "You must learn not to run off like that."

Athgar chuckled. "When has she ever listened to reason?"

"Actually," said Skora, "she's often well-behaved of late. I like to think Agar's manners are rubbing off on her."

Natalia moved to stand before Svetlana. She bent down, hugged her, then stepped back, taking in her appearance. "How are you feeling?"

"Tired, but that's more to do with recent events than this child of mine."

"Why? What's happened?"

"There's been a development, one that I daresay has the potential for far-reaching consequences. I'd elaborate, but that's best left for the king." Svetlana reached out. "Help me up, will you?"

Natalia pulled her to her feet.

"Thank you. Now, follow me, and I'll bring you to see Maksim."

"Shall I take the youngsters to their rooms?" suggested Skora.

"Yes," replied Athgar. "I think that best for now."

"We've put you in the same rooms as last time," said Svetlana. "You know the way?"

"I shall manage, Majesty. Thank you."

Skora chased Oswyn and Agar from the room, their footfalls echoing in the Palace halls, forcing Natalia to smile. "It won't be long before it's your own child making those sounds."

"It'll be some months yet, but I must confess, I'm looking forward to it. Now, where were we?"

"You were taking us to see the king?"

"Oh yes. You must forgive me. I am quite absent-minded of late. I suppose it comes from being pregnant."

"Perhaps I should ask Shaluhk to check on you?"

Svetlana waved away the offer. "I'm fine. Come with me, and let's see if we can't find that husband of mine."

They followed her through the Palace's labyrinthine corridors, finally emerging in the great hall. King Maksim sat on his throne, focused on a man in front of him, a merchant by the look of him.

"What's this?" whispered Athgar.

"He holds a common court once a week where people from all walks of life come seeking his counsel."

They watched the merchant back up, then bow. "Thank you, Your

Majesty. You've been most gracious." The fellow turned, and one of Maksim's servants escorted him out. The king scanned the room: a small knot of people stood ready to bring their appeals to him, but then he beheld his new visitors.

"Lord Athgar," he called out, "and Lady Natalia. I must say, this is a pleasant surprise. When did you arrive?"

"We came by way of Beorwic," replied Natalia, "and only just set foot within the Palace."

"No doubt my lovely wife told you of recent events?"

"I have not," said Svetlana. "I felt it best it come from your lips, sire."

The king rose, then suddenly turned to those waiting to see him. "My apologies, gentle folk, but I have urgent business with these visitors. To make amends, I'll hold a common court again tomorrow. Give your names to my clerk, and I shall ensure you are seen first thing in the morning." Maksim moved towards the door. "Come. Let us find more comfortable surroundings for a discussion."

He took his wife's hand and led her back into the hallway. They eventually arrived at a small room similar to where they'd found Svetlana.

Maksim nodded at a servant waiting at the door. "Get us some drinks, will you?"

"Of course, sire." The man disappeared while everyone else took a seat.

"How are things back in Therengia?"

"Peaceful," replied Athgar. "The people of Novarsk have calmed down in recent months."

"Are they accepting of your rule?"

"The merchants are prospering once more, while the common folk have full bellies. What more could anyone ask for?"

"I wish it were that simple," said the king. "Which brings me to our current… well, I hate to call it a problem. Perhaps I should refer to it as a situation?"

"That being?"

"Before I explain that, let me tell you a story. Prior to your departure, you suggested I contact King Yulakov of Ruzhina. To that end, I took quill to parchment and wrote to him. Much to my surprise, he replied quickly, and thus, we began exchanging correspondence on a regular basis. Now, this is where it gets interesting. Yulakov is a new king, and many of his letters sought advice on ruling, as I've been a king far longer than he, but lately, I've begun to suspect there was something more to his enquiries. His most recent letter seems to confirm that suspicion."

He waited as a servant entered, distributing drinks, and then he took a sip of wine before continuing. "Let me provide some background on the

King of Ruzhina before going into the specifics. Yulakov the Seventh, his father, was unwell but believed the healers of Karslev could keep him alive for years. Sadly, he passed on about a year ago, and the current king was crowned Yulakov the Eighth."

He took another sip of wine as he mulled things over. "From his earlier letters, he obviously distrusted the Stormwinds, and later on, he hinted they'd held a great deal of influence at his father's court. I soon came to the realization he wished to be free of the 'clinging atmosphere of the Karslev court', as he put it."

"He didn't want to be king?" asked Katrin.

"He embraces his role of king but hates the influence the family exerts over his kingdom. His most recent letter suggests we meet in person to discuss 'matters pursuant to the effective rule of kings'. Quite the mouthful, but clearly a cry for help."

"Very interesting," said Natalia. "Where does he propose you meet?"

"In Abelard, if you can believe it."

"A logical choice. The family knows Carlingen is no longer under their influence, whereas Abelard likely still has a Stormwind at court."

"Precisely my thought," said Svetlana. "That's why I suggested you and Athgar travel to Abelard with Maksim."

"To what end?"

"If Yulakov is truly interested in removing the Stormwinds, he'll need help. Who better than you two to advise him on what's possible?"

"Yes," added Maksim. "Now, there's every possibility this might be some elaborate plot by the family, but I can't ignore the fellow's plight. I plan to travel to Abelard, with or without you. However, your company would be greatly appreciated, even if only in an advisory capacity."

"Are you certain that's what he truly wants?" asked Athgar.

"That's just it," said Maksim. "I won't know for a certainty until I meet with him."

"What does your gut tell you?"

"My gut?"

"Yes. You must have some inner feeling about this, or else you wouldn't have brought it up. Does your heart tell you to trust King Yulakov?"

"It does," replied Maksim.

"Good, then it's worth considering. What do you think, Natalia?"

"The family is willing to use deceit to achieve their goals, but this doesn't sound like something they'd orchestrate. I would agree with His Majesty's interpretation and say it's an honest desire on Yulakov's part to rid his court of the family's influence."

"And this whole business about travelling to Abelard?"

"Even though the family would have a presence there, that doesn't guarantee one of them would attend the meeting. It could be an attempt to break free of their control, and if that's true, I want to be there."

"Then it's settled," said Athgar. "We'll join you. When do you intend to leave?"

"The *Bergannon* is in port," replied the king. "I thought we might delay its departure until the end of the week."

"Are you sure that's enough time to inform Yulakov of our plans?"

"He's already sailed."

"How did he know you'd accept his offer?"

"He likely didn't," said Maksim. "He's visiting Abelard to strengthen trade between them and Ruzhina. The meeting between us was meant to take advantage of an already planned trip."

"How soon can we leave?" asked Natalia.

"The ship can be loaded and ready to sail by morning."

"Are there any Temple Ships in port?"

"The *Formidable* is here. Why?"

"Travelling aboard a ship of the order is far safer, and although you've already stated you trust King Yulakov, there's still the possibility the family could have intercepted his correspondence. If so, I wouldn't put it past them to attempt an attack at sea."

Svetlana gasped. "Surely they wouldn't go so far as to attack the king?"

"Wouldn't they? It wouldn't be the first time they've interfered in the politics of the Petty Kingdoms, and I might remind you, they tried to abduct Oswyn. I don't imagine they believe anything is too extreme if it furthers their aims or those of the empire."

"And will the Temple Knights of Saint Agnes agree to take you?"

"I believe so," replied Natalia. "We've worked together in the past, and it serves their interests, especially considering that King Maksim contributes funds to support their fleet."

"Will they be enough?"

"*Formidable* is a warship captured from the Halvarians. As such, it's a difficult target to attack, especially for the smaller vessels Ruzhina employs, and that's not accounting for its complement of knights."

"How do you know all this?" asked Svetlana.

"Temple Captain Cordelia and I have been exchanging letters. When we were last here, I broached the subject of her order sending knights to Therengia. Her superiors saw fit to give her the responsibility of negotiating the terms under which they would operate."

"But she's only a Temple Captain."

"True, but if her order expands into our lands, she'd be promoted to

Temple Commander. After all, she already has a working relationship with us."

"In that case," said Maksim, "I have no objections to travelling aboard the Temple Ship if you can arrange it."

"I shall travel there directly," replied Natalia.

Papers littered Temple Commander Cordelia's desk. "You must excuse the mess," she said, "but we took over the Cunar commandery after they left, and we've been busy bringing it up to our standards."

"How interesting," replied Natalia. "Does that mean your command is expanding?"

"It is. Sorry, I can't tell you all the details, but certain kingdoms in the Petty Kingdoms ordered our knights to leave their lands. As a result, they are being relocated to more accommodating realms, which includes Carlingen."

"There's plenty of open space in Therengia."

Cordelia smiled. "We'll get there, eventually, but I have my hands full dealing with all this."

"Your order works closely with the Temple Knights of Saint Mathew, yes?"

"Of course. Why?"

"Temple Captain Yaromir commands their order in Ebenstadt, our largest city. If you're willing, I'm sure he'd be amenable to making arrangements on your behalf."

"I shall write to him. You say his name was Yaromir?"

"Yes, and he's not only a Temple Captain, he's also one of the three who rule over the city."

"A strange position for a Temple Knight."

"True," said Natalia, "but his responsibility is mostly confined to keeping the streets safe and overseeing the defences, both of which he is well-versed in."

"Is there a commandery in Ebenstadt?"

"Yes. An older building the Cunars vacated when they abandoned the city. Yaromir keeps his own knights there at present, but he hasn't the numbers to fill it, so he'd most likely turn it over to your order in exchange for something more suitable to his numbers. I'd offer to build you a new commandery, but such things take time, and it appears that's a luxury you don't currently possess."

"You have certainly piqued my interest."

"I can use magic to take you there once we return from Abelard, and then you can see it for yourself."

"You're headed to Abelard?"

"Yes," said Natalia. "That's why I'm here. King Yulakov of Ruzhina offered to meet King Maksim in Abelard. I wondered if we might prevail upon the Temple Fleet to provide us with a ship."

"When would you want to leave?"

"As soon as possible. Word is, Yulakov is already on his way."

"Abelard is one of the kingdoms that ordered us expelled. I could use the opportunity to meet with my fellow sisters and arrange for their transportation."

"Couldn't the Temple Fleet do that?"

"The Temple Fleet consists of warships, not merchants, and it's not so much the knights who create the problem; it's their horses."

"So that means you're coming with us?"

"Yes, providing that doesn't cause undue hardship?"

"Not at all," said Natalia. "Not at all."

# FORMIDABLE

## SPRING 1110 SR

Natalia stood on the docks, staring at the *Formidable*. Originally, gold leaf had decorated its stern, but the Temple Knights removed that, replacing it with scarlet paint, which better represented their order. The modification made the ship more intimidating, proving highly effective in dissuading pirates in recent years.

"Is that the ship we're going on?" asked Oswyn, glancing up at her mother. "It doesn't look very big."

"It's one of the larger vessels afloat on the Great Northern Sea."

"Why don't they build them bigger?"

"Building a ship, especially that size, takes a lot of work, and few shipbuilders could construct one similar, let alone something larger."

"Are they bigger in the south?"

"They are," replied Cordelia. "On the Shimmering Sea, the Holy Fleet has five-masted behemoths. Down there, the sea is more forgiving, but their flagship, the *Triumphant*, would never withstand the pounding of the Great Northern Sea."

The Temple Knight turned to walk away, but Oswyn wasn't finished with the conversation. "What's a flagship?"

"The ship the admiral uses to command the rest of the fleet."

"And is the *Formidable* a flagship?"

"No," replied the Temple Captain. "That is her sister ship, the *Fearless*."

"They both start with an 'F'."

"They do. We named them that way to remind us the ships are similar. We call them sister ships."

"And do they have any other sisters?"

"Yes, two. Aside from the *Furious*, there's the *Faithful* and the *Fervent*."

Agar moved up to stand before Cordelia. "How long did it take to build the *Formidable?*"

"I'm afraid I couldn't tell you. We captured it from the Halvarian Empire, as we did its sister ships."

"But you made changes to it, did you not?"

"We did. A process that took three months."

"Why so long?"

Cordelia grinned. "The empire is not known for keeping its ships in good order. Every ship we've captured required months of repairs, which doesn't include any battle damage."

"So many questions," said Athgar. "It's a wonder we get anything done."

Agar looked at his uncle. "I only ask to understand."

"And there's nothing wrong with that. I was referring to Oswyn's endless series of enquiries."

The Orc youngling nodded. "She never ceases. Sometimes, I think she could speak for an entire day without tiring." As he was about to expand on this, he noticed activity farther up the dock. "The king is coming."

They all turned to see Maksim, escorted by six warriors. Svetlana would remain in Carlingen, handling the Royal Duties in the king's absence. She'd agreed without hesitation, for despite being a Water Mage, the thought of putting out to sea reminded her how unsteady her stomach was of late.

"Majesty," said Cordelia. "It's nice to see you out of the Palace for a change."

The king smiled. "Yes. It's not often I have an opportunity to appreciate the great outdoors." He took a deep breath and then shivered, for the northern wind still bore a chill. "I trust everyone is in good spirits this morning?"

"Indeed," said Natalia. She nodded towards the Temple Ship. "That's the *Formidable*. The ship's boat is on the way to pick us up."

"Who commands her?"

"Captain Valeria," replied Cordelia, "a seasoned veteran. Under her command, the *Formidable* chased down over a dozen pirates last year alone."

"I trust none will be threatening us on this trip?"

"One would hope not, Majesty, but if they do, they'll have to contend with the *Formidable's* fighting complement."

They fell quiet, watching the ship's boat draw closer until it bumped against the dock. The men leaped out to secure the boarding plank, then tied the boat to the pier. The Temple Knight in charge disembarked and bowed before the king. "Your Majesty. My name is Sister Denise, and I have the honour of taking you to *Formidable*."

"Thank you," said Maksim. He stepped into the boat, nearly losing his balance as it rocked. One of his guards moved swiftly to steady him, and then the king took a seat. The others followed him, with Sister Denise taking the last position in the rear before giving the order to push off.

"This is exciting," said Oswyn as the boat departed the docks.

Natalia closed her eyes, sensing the calm of the sea. Water Mages were always like this around water, and for the briefest of moments, she wished she lived on the coast, surrounded by the element that infused her with such peace. The feeling passed as Athgar placed his hand on hers. He and Oswyn were her home, and she'd live anywhere to be with them.

"Thoughts?" he said.

"I was enjoying the feeling of being surrounded by water."

"You miss it, don't you?"

She nodded. "Now that I've studied the circle in Carlingen, I can visit anytime."

"Do you feel that?" said Oswyn.

"Feel what?" asked her father.

"There's something beneath us."

Athgar looked over the side of the boat, spotting a dark shape swimming under them. His first thought was to loose a fire bolt, but the water would make that ineffective.

"Relax," said Sister Denise, sensing his panic. "It's just a seal."

It broke the surface and rolled onto its back, its flippers striking the water.

"He's waving," said Oswyn. "I think he likes us."

"I doubt that," replied the knight, "but if you keep an eye on the sea, you might spot a whale or a dolphin. They're considered good omens."

"Omens?" said the king. "I never took you Temple Knights for superstitious folk."

"We follow the teachings of Saint Agnes," she replied, "but only a fool sets out to sea without the blessing of Akosia."

"Akosia?"

"The Goddess of the Sea," offered Natalia, "although some prefer to call her the Goddess of Water. I suppose it depends on where you live."

The king was taken aback. "Are you suggesting these people worship pagan gods?"

"Do they not do so in Carlingen?"

"I suppose I hadn't really considered it."

"You have Therengians in your city," said Athgar. "Did you assume they all worshipped the Saints?"

"My apologies. It wasn't my intent to insult. I was merely surprised a member of a religious fighting order would openly admit to receiving the blessing of a pagan goddess."

"The old religion persists in many realms of the Continent."

"Indeed," agreed Cordelia. "And the Church of the Saints teaches us to accept their worship."

The king frowned. "I was unaware this trip would be a lesson in religion."

"It wasn't meant to be," replied Natalia, "but it's best to avoid the subject while we're in Abelard, just to be safe."

As the boat bumped against the *Formidable's* hull, an oarsman reached out to steady the rope ladder hanging there to accommodate their boarding.

"What's the custom regarding who climbs up first?" asked Maksim. "I'm at a loss without Svetlana to advise me."

"That depends," replied Natalia. "A king would typically board first, but certain monarchs insist their bodyguards ensure the way is safe."

"I hardly think a Temple Ship could be considered hostile, but maybe Sister Cordelia should lead us?"

Cordelia nodded. "I shall be delighted, Majesty." She climbed the ladder effortlessly, then leaned over the side. "You may come when ready, Majesty."

Maksim grasped the ropes, but before he set foot on a rung, a wave shifted the boat, and he lost his balance. Without Athgar's quick actions, he'd have fallen into the water between the boat and the *Formidable.*

The king paused, gathered his courage, and then attempted another climb, successfully navigating the ascent. Standing on the deck, he watched his guards follow one at a time.

Agar moved to the side of the boat, gazing up at the massive hull of the Temple Ship. "This does not feel natural," he said. "It is far too unsteady."

"Nonsense," replied Athgar. "You'll get used to it, and it doesn't look half as bad once you're up on its deck."

"I would feel better ashore."

"It helps if you try to think of the *Formidable* as an oversized umak."

"But it has no paddles."

"True, but it has sails, which means you don't need to row." Athgar turned towards Oswyn, but rather than concentrating on boarding the ship, she stared across the water with a blissful expression.

"She senses the water," said Natalia, "far more than I at her age." A splash drew the child's attention, and her mother looked in the direction of Oswyn's gaze to where a seal poked his head up. It swam closer until just out of reach, then rolled over, diving beneath the surface.

"He likes me," said Oswyn.

Athgar smiled, then shifted his attention to Agar, who'd just begun climbing up to the *Formidable*. "You're next, Skora. Then the rest of us will follow."

The old woman grasped the ropes so tightly her knuckles turned white. She was obviously nervous, but to her credit, she forced herself to climb and soon disappeared over the ship's railing.

Sister Denise stood. "Your daughter is a little young to handle a rope ladder. It might be best if one of you carried her, or, if you prefer, we can lower a rope with a seat on it."

"I'll manage." Athgar nodded at Natalia, who guided Oswyn over to her father. He knelt, allowing her to wrap her arms around his neck so he could carry her, piggyback style. "Hold on tight," he said, then began climbing.

He felt the rise and fall of the waves even as his feet moved from rung to rung. The railing was just above him as two Temple Knights grasped his arms, hauling him onto the deck. Oswyn cheered, then let go of her father's neck, sliding down his back until she was on the wooden planking.

"That was fun!" she shouted. "Can we do it again?"

"Later," said Athgar, "once we arrive at our destination." He looked around the ship. "I don't believe I've travelled on a ship this size before."

Natalia came up behind him, having just climbed up herself. "Nonsense. The *Bergannon* was bigger."

"Well, it was certainly rounder, but this one looks longer."

"That's because is it," declared a voice of authority. "Allow me to introduce myself. I'm Captain Valeria, commander of the Temple Ship *Formidable*."

"Pleased to meet you, Captain. I'm— "

"I know exactly who you are, my lord. His Majesty King Maksim introduced each of you."

"You don't seem pleased to have us aboard."

"This is a warship, and while I'm prepared to transport people of import, I can't say I'm happy with the idea of children being placed in danger."

"Danger? We're sailing friendly waters, aren't we?"

"That's the theory, but the Great Northern Sea remains plagued by ongoing challenges—sudden storms, pirate attacks, or something far worse."

"Worse?"

"Inevitably, the Halvarian Empire will shift its attention eastward once more, deploying their warships. If that happens, my crew shall be far too busy to watch over children."

"Rest assured," replied Athgar, "if that does occur, both children will be looked after."

The captain stared back, then nodded. "I shall take you at your word. Now, you must excuse me. I have things to attend to."

He waited until she was out of earshot. "I don't think she likes us."

"That's because she doesn't know us," said Natalia.

"You'd think she'd be happy to have a powerful Water Mage sailing with them."

"Perhaps the king didn't see fit to mention my magical prowess? Do you think I should speak with her?"

Athgar nodded towards the stern of the ship. "It looks as if Cordelia beat you to it." He watched as the two knights exchanged words, and then Captain Valeria joined the two mages.

"I must offer you my apologies," she said. "His Majesty failed to mention you were no longer in the employ of the Stormwinds."

"I thought Captain Grazynia would've informed you of our part in helping Reinwick?"

"We captains spend the majority of our time at sea, so our paths haven't crossed for months. Doubtless, I shall learn of your exploits when I return to Temple Bay, but that won't be for some weeks."

"We accept your apology," added Natalia. "My magic is at your disposal, should you wish it."

"Thank you," said Valeria. "That is a most generous offer."

"Might I enquire about the route we'll be taking?"

"We sail west until we come across Braymoor, then follow the coast. With a good wind, we'll reach Kienenstadt by the end of the week."

"That soon?"

"The *Formidable* is a fast ship, and the currents are in our favour. I should warn you that if we encounter a ship in distress, it is our sworn duty to assist, which could still mean battle."

"And if that occurs, my husband and I would happily assist."

"Your husband?"

"Yes. He's a master of flame, what you refer to as a Fire Mage."

Captain Valeria grinned. "The king has once again failed to inform me of your capabilities. I trust he won't get carried away with his magic?"

"That's highly unlikely since the Orcs trained him. He's also well-versed in battle, including ship-to-ship actions, so he knows to be careful with his spells."

"Good to hear, but let's hope we're allowed a peaceful trip, shall we?"

"I couldn't have said it better myself."

. . .

The water of the Great Northern Sea remained calm throughout their voyage as if Akosia herself watched over them. Oswyn took to standing by the railing each day, searching for signs of whales or dolphins. Occasionally, a ship passed by them, either a fishing vessel or a merchant heading east. However, there was little interaction aside from dipping their flags to acknowledge the Temple Ship.

The coast of Braymoor was as windswept as Carlingen, giving the place a bleakness that matched its reputation. Years ago, the Prince of Braymoor had backed a plot to overthrow the King of Abelard, culminating in the Battle of Krosnicht. The king retained his Throne, and Braymoor never recovered from the expense.

Athgar watched the coast as they sailed past, wondering who'd choose to live in such a desolate place.

As if sensing his mood, Agar moved to stand beside him, leaning on the railing. "That land looks to be poor hunting."

"I was just thinking the same thing."

"Will Abelard be any different?"

"I expect so," said Athgar. "According to Natalia, Abelard is a thriving realm and one of the richer Petty Kingdoms."

"Do they accept Orcs amongst them?"

"That I can't tell you, but don't worry, we won't let anything happen to you."

"Perhaps it would have been better for me to return to Runewald with my parents?"

"And miss all the excitement? I think not. Besides, your father would be the first to tell you to enjoy your travels."

"Even when my people are not welcome?"

"My people remain persecuted in numerous kingdoms," replied Athgar, "but without action, there can be no change. You and I are of a type, Agar. We strive to help those in need. The key is knowing how and when."

"So, in the meantime, we watch and learn?"

"That's exactly what we do. Your mother has taught you well." Athgar paused, savouring the fresh air. "When this is all over, we should dedicate more time to nurturing your inner spark. Have you been practicing your meditations?"

"I have, although I have been unable to bring it forth as magic."

"That's understandable, considering your age, but don't worry, it'll come soon enough, and when it does, I'm sure you'll be ready for it."

"What does a master of flame do?"

Athgar looked at him questioningly until nodding. "That's right. You're too young to remember Artoch. A master of flame manipulates the power of fire to benefit the tribe."

"Is that all?" asked Agar.

"You make it sound unimportant. Would you say the same of your mother?"

"Of course not. She is a shaman and acts as a moderator within the tribe."

"As does a master of flame. We are much more than spellcasters. We are also protectors of the tribe, just as masters of earth protect the Stone Crushers or masters of the air protect the Cloud Hunters. You might say we're an integral part of the tribe."

"I understand that, but will I have the choice to pursue my own path, or will I be compelled into a life of service?"

"No one will force you to do anything, Agar. Free will is at the very core of who we are."

"You are a Human."

"I may not have your green skin, but I am every bit a member of the Red Hand as you are or Natalia is."

"And Oswyn?"

"She, too, is a member of the tribe; the Ancestors willed it. Why, her very name means Orc friend."

"Will she undergo the ordeal?"

"I expect so, but as a Human, she matures slower than you. She'll likely be sixteen before she's ready, perhaps even older."

"Then I shall do my best to ensure she is ready when the time comes."

"I have no doubt you will," said Athgar. "You two share an extraordinary bond that can weather even the most difficult times."

"You believe difficult times are coming?"

"We live in an age of great changes, which often proves challenging to the unprepared. We can prepare you two for the future, but no one can predict what it will bring."

# ARRIVAL

## SPRING 1110 SR

Kienenstadt was situated at the mouth of a river, and over the centuries, successive kings had built a massive breakwater, forming a large harbour on the western side. *Formidable* sailed into this harbour, dropping anchor amongst the dozens of ships present.

"Impressive," said Agar. "Never have I seen so many ships in one place before."

"Hardly surprising," replied Skora. "You've only seen ships at Carlingen, and there's not much traffic there."

"Have you seen more?"

The old woman laughed. "Me? I spent my life amongst the forests of Athelwald. When would I have seen ships?"

"How are you so knowledgeable about them, then?"

"I have ears, don't I? You can learn much more from listening than talking."

"So I should remain silent?"

"No, of course not. It's healthy to ask questions." A small boat rowed past, its occupants staring at the Orc youngling. "What are you looking at? Mind your own business!" yelled Skora. "The nerve of some people."

"I should expect such things," said Agar.

"Nonsense. There's no excuse for bad manners."

"The people of the Continent fear Orcs."

"Only because they don't know any."

"Trouble?" called out Athgar. He came over beside them. "Let me guess —curious onlookers?"

Agar looked at his uncle. "Why do the men of the Continent hate us so?"

"I can think of two main reasons. The first is your appearance. Your green skin and much wider shoulders intimidate the average Human."

"And the other?"

"These people fear the Old Kingdom's return, and we know that Orcs and Therengians worked together at its height. To the average folk, you represent their worst nightmares; we all do."

"They fear what they do not understand."

"Exactly. Of course, that goes for us Therengians too. One glimpse of my grey eyes causes all sorts of problems. It certainly did in Reinwick."

"How do we deal with that?"

"By sticking together."

"When do we go ashore?"

"Not for some time yet. King Maksim sent one of his men to report to the Royal Palace, and then I expect he'll go ashore to pay his respects to King Rordan."

"What about the rest of us?"

"We stay on the *Formidable*. Officially, we're not here and don't want our presence announced at court. Instead, we'll wait for Yulakov to approach us."

"And then we will meet him?"

"That's the plan," replied Athgar, "although I can't say where or when."

"Would he come aboard our ship?"

"I doubt it. If anyone in Ruzhina discovered he'd boarded a Temple Ship, the family would confront him."

"Why would they do that?"

"The family is likely keeping a close watch on their new king, the better to control him. There's no love lost between them and the Temple Knights."

"So the family would pursue retribution against their king?"

"Yes, though no one knows what form that might take. We don't have a good idea of how tight their grip over King Yulakov is."

"He managed to arrange a meeting with Maksim."

"That's very astute," said Athgar. "Are you certain there isn't a full-grown Orc lurking in that youngling body of yours?"

"I spend much of my time listening to my parents' discussions."

"You couldn't have a finer example."

Natalia stared out over the water as she stood on the *Formidable's* bow, her daughter at her side, the mere presence of the sea a comforting embrace.

"Look, Mama," said Oswyn. "A seal. Is it the same one we saw when we started?"

"It's doubtful, but anything is possible." Natalia stared down into the water, reaching out with her magic. She felt the presence of the seal, but there was something else, a power drawing it to the ship, and she realized her daughter's innate magic had attracted it. "Remarkable."

Footsteps echoed off the planking, and she turned to see Cordelia.

"I hope I'm not interrupting," said the Temple Captain.

"Not at all. We were just enjoying the view."

"You'll pardon me if I prefer land. I've had some unpleasant experiences on ships."

"Understood. Is there a reason you're here?"

"There is. I'm going ashore shortly, and I wondered if I might prevail upon you to accompany me."

"To visit the local commandery?"

"Yes. That's right."

"I hardly believe I can bring anything to the table."

"On the contrary," said Cordelia. "In your capacity as Warmaster of Therengia, you represent a safe haven for our order."

"Safe haven? Isn't your order respected across the length and breadth of the Continent? I've heard you've faced challenges recently, but aren't there many kingdoms that would still welcome you?"

"There would be if not for the Temple Knights of Saint Cunar. I probably shouldn't be telling you this, but the fighting orders have collapsed."

"Collapsed? What does that mean, exactly?"

"The Council of Peers ordered us to disband."

"Why?"

"It's far too long a story to discuss right now. Suffice it to say, someone in the Antonine wished to eliminate most of the fighting orders, amalgamating them all into the Temple Knights of Saint Cunar."

"Except for the sisters?"

"Naturally."

"So you operate in defiance of Church doctrine?"

"That about sums it up, yes."

Natalia shrugged. "The Church of the Saints doesn't possess any influence in Therengia. Regardless of your order's legal position, we'd still love to have you."

"Thank you. That's a great weight off my shoulders. Does that mean you'll come to the commandery with me?"

"I will, providing you have no objection to me bringing Oswyn?"

"Are you certain you want to subject her to that sort of scrutiny?"

"Are you suggesting the Cunars might interfere with your removal of the Temple Knights?"

"You saw how the Cunars treated us in Carlingen. I'm told worse has happened here."

"They demanded you turn over your commandery," said Natalia. "How much worse could it get?"

"I've received reports they've interfered with our knights while they were out attempting to fulfill their duties."

"What manner of interference are we talking about?"

"Actively blocking their way. It's led to several tense encounters, but so far, no bloodshed. At least not according to the last message I received."

"That being the case, I'd best leave Oswyn here. When do you wish to depart?"

"I just need to retrieve some correspondence. Captain Valeria has a boat waiting."

"That was fast."

"Not really," said Cordelia. "It only just returned from dropping off King Maksim's messenger."

Natalia waved at Oswyn as the boat pulled away from the *Formidable*. The day was clear, the water calm, yet her senses remained on high alert. Did something lurk beneath the surface, or was her mind playing tricks on her?

The boatswain barked out an order, and the crew dug their oars into the sea. Cordelia sat in the bow, watching the docks grow closer. From Natalia's vantage point, she couldn't help but notice the Temple Captain's hand resting on the hilt of her sword. Was Cordelia that worried violence might erupt? She and Athgar had certainly experienced more than their fair share of conflict with the Cunars. Her thoughts strayed to what Cordelia had told her about the Church. It was clear to her that the family engineered the fall of the Temple Knights. How soon before they exploited the situation and launched a full-scale invasion of the Continent? She found herself cursing the family and all it had done.

The boat finally bumped up against the dock. Cordelia stepped ashore, Natalia soon following.

"This way," said the Temple Captain.

"Are they expecting us?"

"No. This was more of a spur-of-the-moment decision. The local commandery was instructed to stockpile supplies for a long journey, but they intended to sail to Carlingen, not ride for Therengia." She surveyed the ships in the harbour. "I hope the Temple Captain here hired some of those."

"Only time will tell. How far is the commandery?"

Cordelia dug out a scrap of paper, perused it, and then looked inland.

"According to these instructions, it's two streets south, just past the Temple of Saint Mathew."

"Lead on."

They made their way inshore, where the buildings were close together, making for narrow streets. It reminded Natalia of Ebenstadt, though it felt less welcoming and more maze-like. Cordelia led them up a flight of steps, and then they were amongst the taller buildings signifying the merchant district.

"Tell me," said Natalia. "How many sisters are gathered here?"

"As far as I know, only the one company. Why?"

"Just doing some mental calculations. A company consists of fifty knights at full strength, although I suppose that varies from city to city. There's also the matter of spare mounts to consider."

"Consider for what?"

"Transportation, of course. If everything goes as planned, this company can be in Therengia by nightfall."

"How?"

"I know a spell called frozen arch," said Natalia, "which allows me to open a portal to the standing stones near Ebenstadt, then your fellow sisters can ride through."

"But that's hundreds of miles away."

"It is, but the arch remains in place as long as I keep feeding it. Once the spell is cast, maintaining it is only a slight drain on my power."

"Where are these stones?"

"In the middle of the wilderness, but the Orcs who watch over them can escort your knights to the city."

"But none of them know Orcish."

"I shall speak with them myself."

"Are you intending to travel with them?"

"Only long enough for a chat with whoever is present."

"Won't that drain your power?"

Natalia smiled. "Those stones sit upon a power node, and I learned how to harness that power in Beorwic. I'm not aiming to create a flood this time, so there's no real risk except making me a little tired."

"In that case, I accept your offer."

"Good."

Cordelia led them around a corner, and then there was the commandery, a trio of Cunars standing guard outside, causing the new arrivals to slow their pace. "This doesn't look promising."

"Let me handle this," said Natalia.

"With magic?"

"No, at least not initially. If my suspicions are correct, I may be able to flaunt my family name, convincing them to leave us alone."

"I'll let you do the talking, then."

They continued advancing until a Cunar called out a challenge. "You there," he said. "What is your business here?"

"We are here to arrange for the evacuation of the commandery," replied Natalia.

"Oh yes? And who might you be?"

"Does the name Valentina Stormwind sound familiar?"

The fellow shuddered. "My apologies, Mistress." His eyes flicked to Cordelia, wearing a scarlet surcoat and sash identifying her as a Temple Captain of Saint Agnes. "We were ordered to bar entry or access to any of her order."

"That makes it a little difficult for them to abandon the commandery, don't you think?"

"It is not my place to question orders, Mistress."

"Then I suggest you stand aside, or I'll be forced to report you to your superiors."

The Cunar backed away, bowing slightly. "My apologies."

"That's better. Now come, Captain Cordelia, and let's rid this city of your scarlet-clad sisters."

They approached the door and knocked. A Temple Knight of Saint Agnes opened it, ready to rebuke their captors, but the words died in her throat at the sight of a Temple Captain.

"My pardon, Captain. We had no idea we had visitors."

"Where is your captain?" asked Cordelia.

"In her office. Shall I escort you there?"

"Remain at your post. I know the way." As all commanderies on the Continent were constructed using the same plan, they soon stood before the local captain's office.

"Come in," said a voice.

"How did you know we were here?" replied Cordelia.

"The door is not so thick that I can't hear footsteps."

Cordelia opened the door, and behind the desk sat the Temple Captain, her sable hair tinged by a considerable quantity of grey. "I'm Temple Captain Gabriel. I assume you're Temple Captain Cordelia?"

"I am, and this is Lady Natalia Stormwind."

"Stormwind? I've heard little that endears that name to me."

"Natalia is the exception. She's actively working to lessen the Stormwinds' influence."

"Is she indeed? How can you be certain?"

"She is the Warmaster of Therengia, and we've worked together before."

"Therengia, you say? How interesting. To what do I owe the pleasure of this visit?"

"I am here to arrange the transport of your company," replied Cordelia.

"Arrangements were made for us to board ships and sail for Carlingen."

"Pardon me if I'm speaking out of turn," said Natalia, "but I have a much faster option."

"Which is?"

"I'll use my magic to open a portal to the east, which your knights can pass through."

"To Carlingen?"

"No, Therengia. You'd then have to ride north to Ebenstadt, where you'd take up permanent residence."

"I understood we'd be going to Carlingen."

"Those plans have always been in flux," replied Cordelia, "and I decided to accept the warmaster's offer."

"I am the senior captain," said Gabriel.

"Perhaps, but I've been appointed as regional commander."

"That is highly unusual."

"As are the times we live in."

"My question," said Natalia, "is how long do your knights need to prepare to travel?"

"That depends on what they should bring."

"The trip from the Standing Stones to Ebenstadt is several days. Any food you can carry would be useful. Arrangements will be made for the city to support you upon your arrival."

"Before we leave, the matter of seniority needs to be addressed."

"The High Thane of Therengia has already accepted Captain Cordelia as the order's representative. I speak with some authority when I say he won't budge on this matter."

"How can you be so certain?"

"He's my husband," replied Natalia. "Now, how soon can your knights assemble?"

"Some are stranded in town. Other than those, they need time to don armour and mount their warhorses."

"And supplies?"

"Each knight carries a week's worth of hardtack, but we expected the ships to provide water."

"We have hunters deployed at the stone pillars who can advise you where to find streams along the way."

"Hunters?"

"Yes," said Cordelia. "Orcs. I hope that won't be a problem?"

"Greenskins? How are we to trust them?"

"I've fought beside them before. Give them a chance, and you'll find they're not too different from us Humans."

"This gets worse and worse."

"How so?" asked Natalia. "We're offering you a safe haven in a city where Cunars have no presence. We are also aware of your standing with the Church."

"And?"

"And nothing. It matters not one whit to the High Thane or the rest of the Thane's Council."

"What's in it for you?"

"Me, personally? Nothing, but your presence in the streets of Ebenstadt will help keep the peace and stabilize the region. There is also room for expansion, as we now find ourselves in possession of cities in the Therengian Province of Novarsk who require similar aid."

"I still need to recover the rest of my knights, which won't be easy to accomplish with the Cunars outside our gates."

"Where are they?"

"Temporarily holed up at a local inn called the Magpie. Their horses are being cared for by the Temple Knights of Saint Mathew."

"Weren't all the orders disbanded?"

"They were," replied Gabriel, "but the Mathews here offer no opposition to the Cunars, so they were left alone."

"Cordelia and I will see what we can do about bringing these sisters home. While you're waiting, I suggest you gather whatever goods you wish to take from this commandery. I suspect it will be some years before your order returns."

"We need wagons for that."

"Then I shall add it to the list."

"What makes you believe the Cunars will allow you to deliver them to us?"

"I can be very persuasive when the occasion calls for it."

# SECRETS

## SPRING 1110 SR

Darkness had fallen by the time Natalia and Cordelia returned from the city. Oswyn immediately ran into her mother's arms, and even Agar smiled at their touching reunion.

"I was beginning to wonder what happened to you," said Athgar.

"There were some difficulties," replied Natalia. "The Cunars are not keen to allow anyone access to the Agnesite commandery."

"That must have been frustrating."

"It was," added Cordelia, "but Natalia came up with a remarkable solution."

"Do tell."

"I'll get to that shortly," replied Natalia. "Anything interesting happen here during our absence?"

"As a matter of fact, yes. Maksim went ashore as a guest of King Rordan. He sent word back that Yulakov is in Kienenstadt and that he's arranging a private meeting."

"Any idea where that's taking place?"

"Not yet, although he hinted it might be one of the king's many country estates. Further details will follow on the morrow. Until then, all we can do is wait."

Natalia shifted her gaze to Agar. "And how have you been? Not bored, I hope?"

"Not in the least," replied the Orc. "The Temple Knights have been telling me about their rich history. It is most fascinating."

"Does this mean you intend to take up vows as a Holy warrior?"

Agar laughed. "No. Their ways are not ours, although I am very interested in their training methods."

"Even aboard ships?"

"Perhaps one day, Orcs will sail the seas and help keep the peace."

"They'd be most welcome," said Cordelia. "As it stands now, maintaining a fleet of ships is expensive."

"And yet," said Natalia, "your fleet prospers."

"It does, primarily due to the generosity of the kingdoms sitting astride the Great Northern Sea. Supporting us allows them to pay a fraction of the cost of maintaining their own fleet of ships while still safeguarding their merchants."

"I sense a but," said Athgar.

"Several kingdoms rebuffed our offer, Abelard being one of them."

"Yet here we are."

"Officially, we are here to see our Temple Knights out of Abelard. Most know nothing of our true intentions."

"Which are?"

"Bringing you to this secret meeting with Yulakov."

"And here I thought you only had the best interests of the order at heart."

"I hope your endeavours here benefit all of us."

"As do I," replied Athgar.

"I'm curious," said Natalia. "Did Maksim indicate when he and Yulakov will meet?"

"He said we should be ready on short notice, so I expect it to be soon. Why?"

"I'm afraid my efforts on behalf of the Temple Knights will require my attention for another day at least."

"I can handle Yulakov. You finish up here."

"I'll take Oswyn with me, providing Agar doesn't mind meeting another king?"

"I should be honoured," replied the Orc, "but what about Skora?"

"She can accompany me," said Natalia, "or, if she prefers, remain here on the *Formidable*."

"She'd enjoy the rest, I'm sure," said Athgar. "I'll leave word with her once we know where we're going, allowing you to follow if you feel so inclined."

"Oh, most definitely; I just don't have a sense of how long I'll be."

"I'll try not to discuss anything important in your absence."

"Nonsense. You're the High Thane and more than capable of making decisions without me."

"True, but I value your insight."

"For the present, rely on Agar."

The Orc visibly straightened. "I shall do my best to advise him with all the wisdom of the Ancestors."

Morning arrived far too early, and with it, a carriage conspicuously waiting on the docks. It wasn't until someone sent a messenger boat out to the *Formidable* that they realized it was there to take Athgar to his meeting with Maksim and Yulakov. He bade Natalia and Oswyn goodbye, and then he and Agar climbed into the ship's boat for the trip ashore.

"There are warriors on the docks," noted the Orc.

"Likely an escort," replied Athgar, "although I'm surprised they're not wearing the king's colours."

"You know King Rordan's colours?"

"No, but none of those men are dressed alike and wear no surcoats. Highly unusual, to say the least."

"Do you think we are in danger?"

"No, but I'm certain there's more to this story. We'll need to wait till we're closer to discover what that might be."

They sat in silence until the boat was tied off to the docks and then walked towards the carriage.

One of the warriors moved to intercept them. "Are you Lord Athgar?"

"I am. Who wants to know?"

"My pardon, my lord. My name is Captain Dorkin. I have the honour of providing your escort today."

"These men are yours?"

"Yes. They're all members of the Grim Defenders."

"Who are they?"

"Mercenaries," the fellow replied. "At the risk of sounding arrogant, we've quite the storied career. We helped repel an invasion of Erlingen back in ninety-five."

"The name means nothing to me."

"One of our most esteemed members now sits upon the Throne of Hadenfeld."

"Yes. I've heard of that realm before. Where is it, precisely?"

Dorkin shrugged. "I don't rightly know. I'm told it's one of the middle kingdoms." He was about to say more, but then Agar joined them, leaving the mercenary's mouth hanging wide open. "You brought an Orc?"

"Yes," said Athgar. "This is Agar, son of Kargen. His father is the Chieftain of the Red Hand."

"Is that somehow notable?"

"He's travelling with the Thane of Therengia, which speaks for itself."

"Yes, of course. My pardon, my lord. It is, my lord, isn't it? I'm not sure how to address a High Thane."

"Lord will do fine," said Athgar. "How did you come to be our escort?"

Dorkin straightened, pride filling his voice. "We were hired by His Majesty, King Maksim of Carlingen."

"And where are you to conduct us?"

"One of King Rordan's estates, half a morning's travel to the west."

Athgar studied his escort. "Ten men, including a captain. Are you expecting trouble?"

"One can never tell, especially given recent events."

"What recent events?"

"I'm afraid politics is not my strength, my lord."

"Yet you've heard something."

"I have."

"Then out with it."

"It's only rumours, Lord. Little more than gossip."

"I'll be the judge of that."

"They say war is brewing."

"That's nothing new," said Athgar. "They've been predicting a Continent-wide war for years."

"True, but this time, it's different."

"Different, how?"

Dorkin lowered his voice. "They say we can no longer rely on the Holy Army to protect us."

"When have they ever protected us?"

"I beg your pardon?"

"Many praise the Holy Army as a force for the greater good, yet when did they ever step up to protect the people of the Petty Kingdoms?"

"What about Arnsfeld, or Reinwick?"

"Those were individual orders, not the Holy Army."

"Then what about the Crusades?"

Athgar took a step towards the man. "You dare to talk to me of the Crusades? They were an abomination, a campaign of terror against my people! They did nothing to bring peace to the Continent. They only made things worse."

"My apologies," said Dorkin. "I didn't mean to upset you. As I said earlier, politics is not one of my strengths."

"No, it's my fault. I pushed you to reveal what you'd heard." The mercenary looked uncomfortable, and Athgar couldn't blame him. He changed the subject. "Is this our carriage?"

"Yes, my lord." Dorkin moved to open the door, allowing them to climb inside.

"Most interesting," said Agar. "These seats are so soft. Are all carriages made like this?"

"I wouldn't know," replied Athgar. "This is not something I do very often. At a guess, though, I'd say this is more comfortable than most."

"Because it is larger?"

"No, because a king hired it."

Natalia led Oswyn to a chair in the Magpie, an unremarkable inn as far as such things went. "You wait here," she said. "We need to speak to those knights." Seven knights of Saint Agnes stood at the bar, silently watching them.

Both Natalia and the Temple Captain approached. "I am familiar with your circumstances," began Cordelia, "but you may rest assured we have a plan to get you back inside the commandery, along with your horses."

"What good will that do us?" asked one. "The Cunars will still be guarding the only way out."

"Not so. Allow me to introduce Natalia Stormwind. She is the Warmaster of Therengia, as well as being an accomplished Water Mage."

"Water Mage? How does that help?"

Cordelia nodded, allowing Natalia to take centre stage.

"When Temple Captain Cordelia said I was accomplished, she only told half the story. I am considered one of the most powerful casters on the entire Continent. I've spent my lifetime honing my skills, and amongst my retinue of incantations is a spell so powerful, I can quickly whisk you and your sisters off to safety, but to do that, I need you all assembled in one place."

"How does that help us return to the commandery?"

"You shall see. The first step is to don your armour, then go to the Mathewite commandery and retrieve your horses. You'll rendezvous back here at the Magpie, where supply wagons will be waiting."

"Listen carefully," added Cordelia. "No one must know what we're up to, which means you must avoid trouble wherever possible, particularly with the Cunars."

The knight persisted. "And then?"

"We'll take a circuitous route to the rear of the commandery to avoid arousing suspicion."

"But there's no entrance there."

"True," replied Natalia, "but to use my spell, I must have sight of both you and the destination."

"I'm not sure I understand what you mean?"

"She means," added Cordelia, "she'll be on the commandery roof, which gives her a view of the alley and the courtyard."

"Yes," continued Natalia. "Once everyone is in place, I'll cast my spell, and then an arch made of ice will appear in front of you. When I tell you it's complete, you must enter it in single file. It will lead you into the courtyard."

She scanned the room, ensuring all were paying attention. "It's important you ride through the arch as quickly as possible. The spell will consume a considerable amount of my power to hold it open long enough for all of you to go through, including the wagons. Once you rejoin your fellow Temple Knights, we can move on to the next step."

"Which is?"

"After I recover my strength, we'll repeat the process. Only this time, the destination will be much farther away."

"You're going to Therengia," added Cordelia, "but I'll go through first. Our allies wait on the other side, but I must warn you not to panic, for they are Orcs."

"Friendly Orcs," said Natalia. "Members of the four tribes living in Therengia."

A knight in the back raised her hand.

"Yes? You have a question, Sister…?"

"Karis. What if the Cunars try to stop us?"

"The arch will appear in front of you. If they try to interfere, you must do everything possible to enter it."

"Even if we have to fight?"

"Yes," replied Cordelia. "We're taking a great risk here, but the rewards are well worth it. Any more questions?"

The room fell silent.

"Prepare for battle," called out Cordelia.

The knights nodded, then left the inn.

"Battle?" said Natalia. "Let's hope it doesn't come to that."

"It wasn't meant literally. The expression is merely the order to don armour. It originally meant to attend to prayers, then don armour, but things have evolved considerably since then."

"A curious tradition."

"Don't your people have their own traditions?"

"Yes, we do, although I'm unsure if you're referring to Therengia or the Stormwinds?"

"Whichever you prefer."

"It appears you are a diplomat and a warrior. You'll do well as a regional commander."

"Let's not count our blessings quite yet. Many things could still go wrong."

The carriage slowed considerably, and then Agar leaned out the window.

"See anything?" asked Athgar.

"An enormous building made of stone."

"How big?"

"Nearly the size of the Palace in Carlingen."

"That must be the estate where we'll meet King Yulakov."

Outside the carriage, Dorkin gave a yell, and then they rolled to a stop. Agar sat back as a servant ran up and placed a small step below the door. Once opened, the well-dressed man bowed. "Lord Athgar, you bless us with your presence." The man's face drained of all colour when he noticed Agar staring down at him.

Athgar chuckled. "This is Agar, son of Chief Kargen of the Red Hand. He comes representing the Orcs of Therengia."

"I do?" whispered Agar.

"Hush now. Do not speak out of turn."

The servant recovered quickly. "Greetings to both of you. If you allow me, I will escort you behind the estate, where you'll find both Their Majesties awaiting you."

Athgar stepped down, scanning the area. "Why are we so far from the manor?"

"King Rordan felt it best you make a less-public entry, my lord. It is believed the Stormwinds may have ears amongst the servants."

"How do we know those ears don't include yours?"

"I must protest, my lord. The king himself hand-picked me for this."

"And is King Rordan in attendance?"

"No. The meeting is intended for the benefit of King Yulakov."

"Then by all means, take us to them."

They were led into the woods, following a pathway that meandered considerably. Eventually, they cleared the trees, coming upon the back of the estate. Within a small patio, located beside a stone-lined pond far from the manor house, sat two men, one unmistakably King Maksim, while warriors surrounded them, staring outward.

"Lord Athgar is here, Majesties," called out their guide. "Along with Master Agar of the Red Hand."

"Come. Join us," said Maksim. "Allow me to introduce Yulakov the Eighth, King of Ruzhina."

Athgar saw a man of thirty-five years of age or so, with short, black hair and a clean face, save for a miserable attempt at a moustache. "Your Majesty," he said. "It is an honour to meet you."

"Before we begin," replied Yulakov, "do I address you as Majesty, or is there another honorific you prefer? I'm afraid I'm not well-versed in Therengian customs."

"Athgar will do, or lord."

"Lord, it shall be." He snapped his fingers, and a servant came bearing an additional goblet. "Some wine?"

"That would be nice. Thank you."

The King of Ruzhina stared at Agar. "So this is an Orc. How fascinating."

"I am Agar, son of Kargen, Chieftain of the Red Hand."

"So I've been informed. It is an honour to meet someone of such import. Can I fetch you something to drink?"

"I am fine, thank you."

"My son is around here somewhere. He's about your size; perhaps you'd like to meet him?"

"I would."

Yulakov turned to Athgar. "If that meets with your approval?"

"By all means."

"Yakim, find him and tell him he has a visitor."

A guard nodded. "Yes, sire."

Athgar watched the fellow head up to the manor house.

"I'm glad you could make it," said Yulakov.

"I thought you intended to meet with Maksim, not me."

"That was originally the plan, but upon hearing the High Thane of Therengia was in Abelard, I knew I must meet you."

"Ruzhina and Therengia are hardly on good terms."

"That's precisely why I wanted to speak to you."

"I'm listening."

Yulakov took a sip of his wine while he gathered his thoughts. "You and I have the same problem."

"Which is?"

"The Stormwinds. I'm aware of your wife's break from the family, and Saints know how much I loathe them. They are a blight on my court, a clinging fungus I can't wash my hands of."

"Then dismiss them," said Athgar.

“If only it were that simple. They have massive amounts of gold at their disposal and are not above using that wealth to prevail.”

“Are you suggesting they bought their way into your court?”

“Bought, cajoled, even threatened. There’s no end to their methods.”

“What precisely are you proposing?”

“I want you to invade Ruzhina.”

# PLOTTING

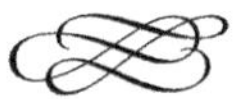

## SPRING 1110 SR

Natalia slowed, still clutching Oswyn's hand. Behind her, Cordelia led the seven Temple Knights who'd been refused entry to their commandery, along with a pair of empty wagons. They walked the horses, an action that reduced the noise drastically.

Their route had kept them far from the Cunar Commandery, and they now approached the rear of their own, which consisted of nothing but an alley, barely wide enough for the wagons.

Natalia halted, raising her arm to signify the rest should do likewise. "Hold them here," she said to Cordelia. "Oswyn and I will enter the commandery. Then hopefully, you'll soon see me up there." She pointed at the rooftop.

"It's a pity we don't have a back door," replied the Temple Captain. "Then again, if we did, the Cunars would be there too."

"Let's go, Oswyn," said Natalia. She headed back the way they'd come.

"Where are we going, Mama? Aren't we going to the front door?"

"We are, but we're going to come from a different direction to avoid raising suspicion. Now remember, not a word about the sister knights, you understand?"

"I do," replied the little girl.

They retraced their steps three blocks before turning right, cutting across another two blocks before heading towards the commandery. Five Temple Knights of Saint Cunar were there, one watching their horses while the other four guarded the entrance to the building. Natalia's approach soon caught their attention, as did the presence of Oswyn.

"What do we have here?" said the oldest knight.

"I am here on Stormwind business," she replied.

"Oh yes? What business might that be?"

"That is none of your concern."

"Isn't it? We received strict instructions to prohibit any entry or exit, especially today."

"And do those instructions include Stormwinds?"

The fellow paused. "Not precisely, but this young girl is a different matter."

"This girl is the key to this entire operation."

The knight laughed. "A child? That's absurd."

"I'm not laughing."

He sobered. "My apologies, Mistress, but it will become dangerous in short order."

"All the more reason you must admit us."

"The assault is to commence soon."

"Not if I can't get inside." She lowered her voice. "Who do you think will open that door for you?"

"Why do you need the child?"

"Are you familiar with blood magic?"

He paled. "She's meant to be a sacrifice?"

Natalia nodded, her ruse complete.

"You may pass," said the knight, turning to his men. "Let her through."

Moments later, she was knocking at the door. A small view port slid aside, and after a look of recognition, the door opened, admitting them both.

Natalia waited until the door closed behind them before speaking. "They're planning an assault for some time today. Alert the Temple Captain and ask her to ready everyone in the courtyard."

"They're already assembled," replied the knight. "Was that not the plan all along?"

Natalia managed a smile. "In my haste to ensure everything was prepared, I neglected to arrange the time. Where is Temple Captain Gabriel?"

"In the courtyard, with the other knights. Shall I take you to her?"

"I know the way."

She picked up Oswyn and went through the commandery, emerging into the open-topped courtyard in the centre of the building. Half the knights stood by their horses, the Temple Captain at their head.

At the sight of Natalia, Gabriel dismounted. "I assume everything went well?"

"You might say that. Your missing knights are in the alley out back. It's a pity you don't have windows there."

"It wouldn't be easy to defend if we did."

"I need to get to the roof."

"I'll take you there myself. You can leave the girl here." She nodded towards the other knights. "They'll look after her."

Natalia knelt, placing her daughter on her feet. "You remain here, Oswyn, and keep out of the way of the Temple Knights."

"Are you going to use your magic, Mama?"

"I am. Soon, you'll see an ice arch materialize. Make sure you stay far away from it."

"I will. I promise."

"Good girl. Now, I must go, sweetie. Mama has work to do." Natalia forced herself to look away. "The roof?"

"Yes," said Gabriel. "This way."

They entered the commandery, heading towards the stairs, and guilt nearly overwhelmed Natalia. Bringing Oswyn here had been a mistake, possibly jeopardizing her life. Why hadn't she left her daughter aboard the *Formidable* with Skora?

They soon reached the second floor, passing by the Temple Captain's office, then down a long corridor leading to a small set of stairs.

"This is the only entrance to the roof," explained Gabriel. "It's a bell tower, but we have no use for one here in the city."

Natalia ascended the stairs, then paused. "There's no bell."

"There never was, but the design used by all commanderies was established long ago, and the order prefers consistency."

The bell tower proved only marginally taller than the commandery's peaked roof, making it relatively simple to climb onto the top of the building.

"Can't you cast your spell from here?" asked Gabriel.

"No. Without a clear view of the alley, I won't be able to anchor the other end of the arch." Natalia took a step, which proved more difficult than she expected. "Why is the roof so steep?"

"To prevent the accumulation of snow. I'm told commanderies in the south have flat roofs."

"Just my luck."

"Do you need help?"

"No," said Natalia. "You'd best return to the others; you might be needed." She edged out farther until she straddled the roof's peak, the courtyard on her right, while the alleyway beckoned her from the left. She closed her eyes and concentrated on her magic, feeling it build within her as the words of power tumbled from her lips.

Two frosty pillars formed in the courtyard, and then their tops joined, making an arch. With the anchor point in place, Natalia directed her focus to the alleyway.

A shout from below caught her attention as a group of grey-clad men approached from the side of the commandery. There was no mistaking their allegiance, for although their surcoats were a lighter grey, they bore the emblem of Saint Cunar. Natalia had seen them before at the Battle of the Standing Stones and recognized them for what they were: initiates hoping to earn full admittance to the order. She wanted to shout a warning but couldn't break her concentration without cancelling her spell.

Seeing the threat, Cordelia ordered her command, small as it was, into the fray. Natalia felt the power building within her, bursting to get out. She focused on a portion of the alleyway, allowing the second set of pillars to form.

The shouts grew more urgent, but she ignored them, a difficult thing to do, especially as sounds of fighting erupted. To save the Temple Knights of Saint Agnes, she must continue her spell. The icy pillars in the alleyway grew until the top finally materialized. She felt a slight surge of power as the two arches connected, then shifted her focus to the melee below.

Cordelia and her seven sisters had rushed into the initiates of Saint Cunar. They'd make quick work of them but initiates seldom fought far from full-fledged knights. When the younger men fell back, others wearing darker surcoats over plate armour replaced them.

"Get the wagons through," shouted Natalia.

The wagon drivers, mesmerized by the conflict, snapped out of their paralysis, urging their horses onward. The first draft animals paused when they reached the arch, but then the sight of the courtyard stole their attention, and they stepped through without further delay.

Natalia felt the drain of holding the arches open, but it was manageable. The commandery walls echoed with shouts coming from the courtyard as Temple Captain Gabriel led a group of her sisters through the arches and into the alleyway.

The mounted Temple Knights of Saint Agnes charged into the fray. The initiates broke first, fleeing from the alleyway while the full-fledged Cunars fell back to form a defensive line.

Cordelia's group charged towards the arch, passing through without incident. Temple Captain Gabriel, however, seemed to be taunting her enemies. Upon her command, her knights rushed forward only to turn around at the last moment, riding for the archway.

The Cunars, sensing they were about to escape, chased after them, but it was too late. As soon as the last horse went through the arch, Natalia released her hold on it, the frozen arches fracturing into chunks of ice that immediately started melting in the sun. After ensuring all was well in the courtyard, Natalia returned to the old bell tower via the rooftop.

"That was impressive," said Gabriel as Natalia reappeared in the courtyard. "I had no idea Water Mages were so powerful. Can you all do that?"

"No," replied Natalia. "The frozen arch is a carefully guarded secret. Only the most powerful of the family's casters are allowed access to it."

"Yet they taught it to you."

"On the contrary—I stole it."

"You mean you learned it without them knowing?"

"No. I pilfered it from their inner sanctum, where they store their most powerful spells."

"Does that mean they can no longer employ it themselves?"

"Not quite," said Natalia. "It's still possible for someone who already knows the spell to teach it, but I doubt there's too many of those."

"Why is that?"

"It requires a great deal of magical potential to cast it."

Oswyn ran over and jumped into her mother's arms, giving her a big hug.

"What happens now?" asked Gabriel.

"Mama rests," said Oswyn.

"She's right," added Natalia. "I must regain my strength before I can send you to Therengia."

"How much time do you need?"

She looked skyward, where the sun hung near its zenith. "I should be ready by mid-afternoon, providing there's somewhere quiet I can lie down."

"You can use my quarters."

"I'll make sure Mama sleeps," insisted Oswyn.

Ogda arched his stiff back. Even for an Orc, he was big, and as a hunter, he was not accustomed to remaining stationary all day. Still, he was tasked with guarding the standing stones and took the responsibility seriously. He looked around, spotting fellow members of the Black Axes. Each tribe took turns guarding the structure and knew its importance to their security.

He yawned, struggling to stay awake in the drowsy afternoon sun. All he wanted to do was go and lie down for a little nap, but then he felt something, a tingle in the air that suddenly jolted him wide awake.

*"Prepare yourselves,"* he called out in the language of his people. *"Someone is using magic!"*

A slight chill crept through the area, and then two ice pillars formed before his eyes. He backed up, readying his axe for whatever might be coming.

The air grew progressively colder as the top of the arch formed. The space between the pillars glowed, and then he was looking at a large group of mounted warriors. Before he could issue another warning, a familiar figure moved to stand in the archway.

*"Lady Nat-Alia,"* he said. *"We received no warning that you would be using your magic."*

*"Ogda,"* she replied in the Orcish tongue. *"It has been some time since last we met. I apologize for the inconvenience, but I need your help."*

*"I am yours to command, Warmaster."*

Natalia stepped to one side, allowing him a good view of those behind her. *"These are Temple Knights of Saint Agnes. I need someone to guide them to Ebenstadt. Once they arrive, Temple Captain Yaromir will take care of them."*

*"It shall be as you wish, Warmaster. You may send them through whenever they are ready."*

"What did he say?" asked Gabriel.

"The Orc I spoke to is named Ogda," replied Natalia. "He'll arrange for someone to guide you to Ebenstadt."

"How will we understand him?"

"He speaks our language, just not very well."

"Well enough to guide us?"

Natalia forced a smile. "Yes, but let me make one thing clear, Temple Captain. The Orcs are our allies: you are to make no threatening actions towards them. Is that understood?"

Gabriel clearly wanted to object but held her tongue.

"Listen carefully," added Cordelia. "Our presence in Ebenstadt is an important step for our order. You must do all you can to maintain the peace, not antagonize our new friends."

"I understand."

"Good," said Natalia. "Then you may begin sending your Temple Knights through the arch."

They watched as the sisters rode in single file, Gabriel leading the way.

"I hope she won't cause problems," said Cordelia.

"So do I," replied Natalia, "or it's likely to become a bloodbath, and it won't be the Orcs who suffer."

"Perhaps I should go myself?"

"No. You can't. You're needed back in Carlingen."

"We're a long way from Carlingen."

"For now, but once we're done in Abelard, it'll be a simple matter of stepping through another arch."

"To the circle in the Palace?"

"You know about that?"

"It costs a fortune to build and requires the hands of skilled tradesmen. Do you honestly believe they could keep that a secret?"

"No. I suppose not."

The courtyard began to clear as more and more knights rode through the arch.

"We truly are living in a new age, aren't we?" said Cordelia.

"I imagine every generation believes that."

"Yes, but consider all that's happened in the past decade. The Temple Fleet in the north, a reborn Therengia, the Church's conflict with the fighting orders. The list goes on and on."

"When the Old Kingdom was torn apart, it threw the Continent into chaos," said Natalia, "but it survived. You speak of changes, yet everything you mentioned is positive if you look at it in the right light."

"I'm not sure my order would view it that way."

"Wouldn't they? You are now freed from the restrictions the Council of Peers placed upon you. Restrictions that stopped you from fulfilling your vows to protect others."

"I suppose that's one way of looking at it."

"Mama is smart," offered Oswyn.

"She certainly is."

The last of the knights rode through, and then the two wagons moved forward, ready to make the trip.

"So what of us?" asked Cordelia. "Do we walk out of the commandery as if nothing's happened?"

"Not with Cunars waiting outside," said Natalia.

"Then how do we leave?"

"While on the roof earlier, I noticed a building across the street with a flat rooftop. I thought we might use another arch to get to it."

"And then walk away?"

"That's the general idea, yes."

"To where?"

"To the *Formidable*."

"Didn't you want to catch up to Athgar?"

"I did," said Natalia, "but it's too late in the day to join him, so I'll have to content myself with waiting."

"If you're looking for something to do, I wouldn't mind learning Orc, or do we call it Orcish?"

"Either will do, although I'm surprised you'd take an interest."

"Though I'm only a Temple Captain, I've been appointed regional commander, which now includes Therengia. Since the population there includes Orcs, I think it in my best interest to learn more about them, don't you?"

"I do, and for the record, I believe you'll make a marvellous Temple Commander. Once this mess here is all cleared up, I'll take you to Runewald to meet all the important people."

"Like Uncle Kargen," said Oswyn, "and Auntie Shaluhk."

Cordelia knelt, putting her head at the child's eye level. "I've already met them. They came to Carlingen, remember?"

"Oh yes. I forgot." A grin spread across her face. "But you didn't meet Laruhk!"

"Laruhk?"

"Shaluhk's brother," offered Natalia. "They're twins, actually. He commands the tuskers."

"What are tuskers?"

"They're big," said Oswyn. "Even bigger than your horses, and the Orcs ride them and use extra-long spears."

"Truly?"

"Yes," replied Natalia. "They're native to the region. The Stone Crushers employ their magic to communicate with them."

A pounding noise reverberated through the courtyard.

"Someone's knocking," said Cordelia. "It appears the Cunars brought a ram to take down the door."

"Then we'd best be off," replied Natalia.

# DISCUSSION

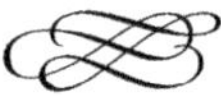

SPRING 1110 SR

Athgar sat back, grappling with the implications of Yulakov's words. Was the man speaking in jest, or did he truly wish Therengia to invade his home? Perhaps he was mad?

The King of Ruzhina leaned forward as if reading his mind. "I'm not mad, though doubtless some would claim otherwise."

"You just asked me to invade Ruzhina. Surely, you didn't expect an immediate response. A request of that magnitude requires time to digest."

"It surprised me too," said Maksim. "When he asked to meet you, he did not mention this."

"You must pardon all this secrecy," said Yulakov. "I couldn't risk my plans becoming public knowledge."

"I understand," said Athgar. "One whiff of this, and the family would be all over you. You'd be lucky to survive the day."

"I've managed to outsmart them so far, or at least I hope I have."

"But there's got to be more to this than asking us to invade?"

"Naturally. Since the death of my father, I've spent a great deal of time learning just how insidious the Stormwinds are—your wife excepted, of course. I was aware of them growing up, but as the heir to the Crown, much was shielded from me. Imagine my surprise when I was named king only to learn I was nothing more than a figurehead."

He took a sip of wine before he continued. "Now, when I say I want you to invade, I'm not talking about you taking over, merely liberating us from their influence." He locked eyes with Athgar. "I need you to destroy the Volstrum to break the Stormwinds' hold on my kingdom."

"Couldn't you do that yourself? You are the king."

"King, I might be," said Yulakov, "but I would be foolish to put my army's loyalty to the test."

"So you invite a foreign army to do your dirty work for you?"

"It wouldn't be only you. There are a few companies whose loyalty I can rely on, just not enough to get the job done."

"Pardon me for saying so," interjected Maksim, "but this sounds like a fool's errand. Even if Therengia pulled together a large enough army, they'd still need to get it to Karslev. Which means either assembling a vast fleet to transport them or marching through Zaran, and we all know the dangers of that."

"I hadn't considered that," said Yulakov. "Couldn't they march farther east and avoid Zaran altogether?"

"And how would we navigate?" replied Athgar. "We know absolutely nothing about that area or the dangers lurking there. Marching an army is a different beast entirely from leading an exploration party. There's also be the problem of getting supply wagons through the wilderness."

"Could you not hunt as you go?"

"For what? We don't even know if there's suitable game in the area. For that matter, we have no idea of what type of terrain we'd encounter."

"It would be forest, surely?"

"Would it? There's no guarantee of that. If you travelled to Therengia, you might assume it was a heavily forested region, but go to the southern border, and you'd find the Grey Spire Mountains. What if we discovered something similar east of Zaran? That would put an abrupt end to this entire campaign."

Yulakov sank back into his chair. "Then it appears I am doomed to live under the endless influence of the Stormwinds."

Agar entered the room, leaving his escort, the warrior Yakim, outside. A well-dressed youth stood by the fireplace, staring at the flames.

"Be careful," said Agar. "Fire has a hypnotic effect."

As the youth turned to face him, his scowl vanished at the sight of an Orc. No more than ten years of age, his mop of black hair was cut short in the same style as his father's. His clothes were made of the finest cloth, and even in this brief meeting, he projected a sense of entitlement.

"Who are you?" he asked, his voice betraying mild annoyance.

"I am Agar, son of Kargen."

"You speak our language?"

"How else would I be able to answer your questions."

"There's no need to be impertinent. My father is a king."

"And mine, the Chieftain of the Red Hand. Shall I take offence at your words, or do we consider the matter of little consequence?"

The youth stepped closer, stopping within arm's reach. "My apologies. I did not mean to offend. I am Prince Piotr of Ruzhina. What brings you here, Agar?"

"I come in the company of Athgar, High Thane of Therengia."

"Is he in the habit of travelling with children?"

"He is my uncle."

"I didn't think half-Orcs were possible."

"As far as I know, they are not, but Athgar is like a brother to my father. Thus, I refer to him as Uncle. Have you no similar customs where you are from?"

"I have no close friends, and neither does my father."

"Yet you must have a mother?"

"We do not speak of her," said Piotr. "She died when I was very young."

"I am sorry."

"What of your own mother? Does she still live?"

"She does. She is Shaluhk, Shaman of the Red Hand."

"Shaman? What's that?"

"You would refer to her as a Life Mage."

"Does that mean she makes sick people better?"

"Usually, though there are some things even a gifted healer cannot do."

"Meaning?"

"Magic cannot keep the ravages of time at bay."

"You are well-spoken for a child," said Piotr.

"I could say the same of you."

"How old are you?"

"I am almost seven, but in Human terms, I am closer to eleven."

"I'm not sure I understand?"

"We Orcs mature faster than Humans."

"I wish I would age faster."

"Be careful what you wish for," said Agar. "We might come of age sooner, but our lifespans are shorter."

"How much shorter?"

"I hope to see my thirtieth year."

"And what do you do when you're not being the chieftain's son?"

"I am proficient with the axe and bow, though there is still room for improvement. In addition, there are my ongoing attempts to master the spark within me."

"What does that mean?"

"I have been marked by fire. In time, I shall become a master of flame."

"Is that the same as a Fire Mage?"

"Yes, although I am led to understand there are significant differences in how the magic is approached."

"Fascinating. I've met Water Mages at court, but I've not seen any demonstration of their magic."

"We also have a Water Mage. Several, in fact: amongst them, our warmaster."

"I assume that's akin to a general?"

"Yes."

"And how powerful is he?"

"The warmaster is Nat-Alia Stormwind."

Piotr frowned. "Oh, one of those. You are as cursed as we are."

"Not so. She fights against the Volstrum, not for it. If she had her way, she would see them wiped from the face of the Continent."

"That is my father's wish, also, but I fear it will never be more than a dream. They are too powerful."

"They have been defeated before," said Agar, "and they shall be again."

"That's news to me. I thought them invincible."

"Stormwind Manor was burned to the ground."

"That was an accident—a careless tending of a fireplace."

"It was not. Athgar and Nat-Alia were there, along with others."

"Why are you telling me this?"

"So that you do not despair," replied Agar. "The Stormwinds are powerful, but their days are numbered."

Athgar sipped his drink, a dark ale their host graciously provided. While not as good as the stuff back home, it wasn't terrible.

"I sympathize with your plight," said Maksim, breaking the silence, "but Athgar is right; it's too difficult. Even with the Temple Fleet's full support, we could only transport a few hundred warriors to the shores of Ruzhina. That's nowhere near the numbers we'd need to break their hold."

"Give me some time to consider it," replied Athgar. "With the help of my warmaster, we might find a solution."

"You have something in mind?" asked Yulakov.

"Merely a glimmer of an idea at the moment, but it has the potential to grow into something worth considering."

"How long would you need?"

"A day, maybe two?" replied Athgar. "It depends on whether or not my wife has concluded her business in the city."

"Then might I suggest we reconvene in two days?"

"Here?"

"Yes, unless you have a preference for another location?"

"No. Here would be most acceptable."

"Might we speak of other matters?" asked Maksim. "Trade, perhaps? I doubt that would bring the ire of the Stormwinds."

"Ordinarily, I'd agree," replied Yulakov, "but the family's recent rebuffs at your hands might suggest otherwise. There's also the matter of Carlingen offering financial support to the Temple Fleet."

"There must be something we can agree on that won't incur the Stormwinds' wrath?"

"What about Zaran?" asked Athgar.

"Zaran?" said Yulakov. "That is nothing more than a dense wilderness. A fellow named Karzik tried to settle it about a century ago, but he and his men were never seen again."

"There are rumours of terrible creatures living there. Do you know about them?"

"Any time someone disappears, stories surface of horrible creatures rending people from limb to limb. Naturally, no one lives to tell of these horrors, which is convenient from a storyteller's perspective."

"So you believe them to be false?"

"Don't you? Oh, I'm certain dangerous creatures live in the wilds; that's true of any unmapped region, but I doubt it's anything like the stories."

"Ever heard of a tusker?" asked Athgar.

"I can't say I have. What are they?"

"Massive creatures, twice the size of a horse."

"You're exaggerating, surely?"

"I assure you I'm not. The Orcs back in Therengia learned to ride them."

"Truly?" asked Yulakov.

"I've seen it with my own eyes. Of course, their masters of earth communicate with the beasts."

"Masters of earth?"

"What you call an Earth Mage."

"Just how prevalent is magic in Therengia?"

"There is a history of it amongst the Orc tribes."

"But not the people?"

Athgar frowned. "The Orcs are people."

"You know what I mean."

"Amongst my own people, magic is rare, but we have quite a few Humans who wield magic between us and our allies. Not as many as the Volstrum, but add the Orcs, and we could give them a serious challenge."

"Are you implying you can compete with the family?"

"We already did in Karslev."

"What's this, now?"

"Surely you heard?" said Athgar. "Stormwind Manor was destroyed by fire."

"That was you?" replied Yulakov. "They told me it was an accident."

"Of course they did. The last thing the family wants is to admit it suffered a loss. That was also where we discovered the family supports Halvaria."

"The empire? Why hasn't anyone mentioned this to me before?"

"I imagine the family went to great pains to suppress this. Do you honestly believe they'd admit they're attempting to overthrow the Petty Kingdoms? They would lose their places in courts across the Continent."

"Are you saying the Stormwinds control Halvaria or that they are working in league with them?"

"Possibly both. We recovered notes written in Illiana Stormwind's hand that revealed a connection. They didn't go into the specifics but left no doubt about their ultimate goal—the complete conquest of the Continent."

"But why would they even consider the idea?"

"It's all about power," replied Athgar. "If they control whoever rules, they can do whatever they want."

"Such as?"

"They could carry out their breeding programs in peace."

"Breeding programs? What are you talking about?"

"Did they not tell you their practices?" said Athgar. "They force their most powerful graduates into siring children. They believe that by selective breeding, they can raise generations of extremely powerful mages."

"And does it work?"

"Natalia appears to be a shining example that it does. Of course, she left the family before they forced her into coupling."

"Yet," said Yulakov, "I'm led to believe she has a daughter."

"She does, or rather we do. I'm the father."

"There's irony in that," said Maksim. "Here they are trying to match up powerful mages to further the future of magic, and she's done the very thing they tried to force on her."

"Natalia and I were never forced into anything!"

"No, of course not," said Yulakov. "I'm sure he didn't mean to infer you were. I value free will, which is why I want the Stormwinds gone from my court."

Athgar shook his head. "I doubt an invasion would be able to accomplish that. If anything, it would unite your people behind the family."

"You make an excellent point."

"There has to be an alternative," said Maksim. "Can't you order them to leave?"

"Saints, no," replied Yulakov. "If I did that, I would soon find myself overthrown."

"Really?" said Athgar. "That surprises me. I would think you'd be more popular amongst the commoners."

"And perhaps I am, but the family controls the narrative. If they portrayed me in an unfavourable light, there's no end to the trouble they might cause, not to mention their magic. I could become the victim of a hailstorm or whatever they use to eliminate problem makers."

Maksim set his cup down on the table. "Athgar and Natalia helped me throw off the yoke of the family. I'm confident they can do the same for you."

"High praise from a fellow king, yet our circumstances are quite different. In Carlingen, you only had to deal with a single Stormwind, whereas I am inundated with them at every turn."

"How many are at your court?"

"On an ongoing basis? Only three are permanent, but others come and go as they please. I warrant that since becoming king, I've dealt with at least twenty: everything from initiates to the grand mistress herself."

"Grand mistress?" said Athgar. "Do you mean Marakhova?"

"Of course. Is there another?"

"One can never be certain when the family's politics are concerned."

"And when you say they're at court," asked Maksim, "what precisely do they do?"

"My father saw fit to appoint a man named Veris Stormwind as his military advisor. Unfortunately, that gave him unfettered access to the Army of Ruzhina, allowing them to extend their influence on its officers, the effects of which were quickly felt."

"Did your father not fear them?"

"No. Quite the reverse," said Yulakov. "He welcomed them. I think he was cowed by their power and influence, and why wouldn't he be? According to them, they have a presence in every court of the Petty Kingdoms, or at least the important ones."

"You mentioned there were three Stormwinds?"

"Yes, that's right. Shortly before my coronation, Yaleva became the treasurer, and Irinushka's been at court for as long as I can remember."

"And what does she do?"

"She is the Royal Chancellor. As such, she presides over matters of law."

"Pardon me for saying so," said Athgar, "but couldn't you replace them? You are the king after all."

"A fact I am well-aware of, but it's not that simple. These three Stormwinds control the courts, the army, and the treasury. Without them, the realm would be thrown into chaos."

"Yet you seek to destroy the family's power base. Wouldn't that leave you in precisely the same position?"

"Granted, it would, but with the family's power broken, I could rebuild the kingdom."

"I wouldn't be so certain of that," said Athgar. "In my experience, the Stormwinds can be spiteful when things don't go their way. Still, I can't argue with your reasoning."

"The important question," said Maksim, "is how we proceed from this point forward. If invading is not possible, what other options do we have?"

"Political pressure?" offered Yulakov. "The family's influence is on the wane. Perhaps I could use that to dismiss these three from their positions?"

"No," said Athgar. "You've already indicated you fear repercussions, and if we don't break the family first, you're inviting trouble. Any way you look at it, we need to destroy the Volstrum."

"The Volstrum is just a building," said Maksim.

"No. It's much more than that—it's the symbol of their power over the Continent and is the root of our problem."

"What you say makes sense," said Yulakov, "but the Volstrum is packed with mages. Why, there must be hundreds within its walls."

"Students, perhaps, but from what Natalia told me, I doubt there are many instructors."

"Even a student can use magic."

"Only those who underwent the unleashing, and even then, only a few become battle mages. The vast majority will have little option but to avoid the fight."

"Assuming that's true, it's primarily an issue of getting an army into the Volstrum, but how can that be done when the very family we wish to destroy commands my troops?"

"That," said Athgar, "is the root of our problem."

# PLANNING

## SPRING 1110 SR

Natalia watched the boat bearing Athgar draw closer.

"About time you showed up," she called out.

"It's been a long day," he replied, "and it's not over yet."

Agar stood up in the bow, clutching a rope. As the boat bumped against the larger ship's hull, he tossed it to one of the *Formidable's* crew. Moments later, they were pulled into place, and then the young Orc grasped hold of the rope and quickly hauled himself up onto the deck.

"That was quite adept," said Natalia.

"Where is Oswyn?"

"Below decks, fast asleep, or at least she was. Knowing her, she's heard your return and is even now coming to greet you."

Athgar climbed up onto the ship.

"What did King Yulakov want?" she asked.

"He wants us to invade Ruzhina."

"Invade? Surely you jest?"

"I'm afraid not," replied Athgar. "He wants to escape the Stormwinds' influence and feels an invasion is the only method to accomplish that."

"It sounds more like a trap to me. Do you trust him?"

"You know, I think I do. He strikes me as a ruler who wants to better the lives of his subjects. A difficult job, given his circumstances. How familiar are you with the politics of Ruzhina?"

"I'm no expert," replied Natalia, "but even I know the family has a firm grip on the Crown."

"That's basically what he said."

"And how did you respond to his request to invade?"

“That it’s not practical. Attacking the Volstrum would require a huge army, but the only method of transportation is either by ship or traversing the wilds of Zaran, neither of which is particularly feasible. Even if the entire Temple Fleet agreed, they couldn’t carry the required number of warriors. And as for Zaran, we’d be fools to try marching an army through that terrain, especially without reliable maps.”

“Was that the end of the discussion?”

“Not the end,” said Athgar, “but we moved on to other topics. He has three Stormwinds at his court, each holding a position of considerable power.”

“Let me guess: the chancellor, the treasurer, and the marshal?”

“More or less. He referred to the last individual as a military advisor, but how did you know?”

“It’s a strategy they taught at the Volstrum, though it was always discussed in the third person. Far be it for the family to admit they used the tactic themselves.”

“Anything else you can tell me about their strategies?”

“Only that they’ll have eyes and ears throughout the Royal Palace.”

“How?” asked Athgar.

“The family has a vast treasury they can pull from, and bribery is a proven method of keeping one’s finger on the pulse of the kingdom.”

“So there is truly no way to defeat the Volstrum?”

Natalia smiled. “Had you asked me that yesterday, I might be inclined to agree, but recent events have given me food for thought.”

“Why? What’s happened?”

“I used my frozen arch to send all the Temple Knights to Therengia.”

“All of them?”

“Yes,” replied Natalia, “except for Cordelia. She has responsibilities in Carlingen to attend to.”

“Isn’t that spell draining, even for someone as powerful as you?”

“It would have been had I not connected to the standing stones back home. Like those in Beorwic, they tap into the magical energy flowing beneath the Continent. Once I connected, it was a simple matter of directing that energy towards the arch rather than having it flow through me.”

“You must teach me that trick sometime.”

“I don’t think it would do you any good. The stones only affect spells targeting them, and as far as I’m aware, you haven’t learned the ring of fire.”

“It’s difficult to learn without someone to teach me, and I doubt there’s any Sartellians who’d volunteer.”

She chuckled. "Most definitely not. Now, before I talk more about my idea, tell me about yours?"

"What makes you think I have a plan?"

"I know you. You've been mulling this over ever since Yulakov mentioned it."

"I thought we could use magic to bring our army to Carlingen, then march up the coast, using ships to supply us from the sea. What do you think?"

"The idea has merit, but I have a much more practical suggestion."

"Care to share?"

Cordelia chose that exact moment to wander over to them. "What are you two up to?"

"Just discussing strategy," replied Natalia. "The King of Ruzhina wants Therengia to invade his country and displace the Stormwinds."

"Displace?"

"My choice of words. His Majesty is intent on destroying their power base."

"How does he propose you accomplish that?"

"By using our army to destroy the Volstrum."

"Is it really that simple?"

"No," said Natalia. "Hence our discussion of strategy."

"How many warriors would you need?"

"That's difficult to answer."

"It is," agreed Athgar. "We're looking at two or three thousand, but getting them there is the problem. Shipping that many by sea is nearly impossible, and travelling through unexplored forest is not the wisest strategy. What are your thoughts on the matter?"

"Could you use Natalia's magic to get them there?"

Natalia smiled. "Precisely what I was thinking."

Athgar shook his head. "I know you committed the magic circle in the Volstrum to memory, but it's not large enough to hold an army."

"Although I like the element of surprise that appearing in the Volstrum would give us, we still have the problem of supplies. The more men we bring, the more food we'll require for an extended fight."

"Then we take the building quickly."

"The Volstrum would be difficult to capture quickly. Its architecture is specifically built to withstand attack. That's not to say we couldn't use the circle to help secure an entrance, however."

"So what do you propose?"

"We take a small contingent and cross Zaran. Then once we're in

Ruzhina, I use my magic to open a frozen arch to the standing stones in Therengia, where our army will be waiting."

"The wilderness is a dangerous place."

"Not for the likes of Athgar. He thrives in such places as do the Orcs. I imagine Kargen would be quite taken with the idea."

"He most definitely would," agreed Athgar. "Even if you wanted to, you couldn't stop him from coming with us. Shaluhk, either."

"Still," said Cordelia, "there's a big difference between a company of knights and an entire army."

"There is," replied Natalia, "and that's where Katrin and Svetlana come in. My first spell would bring them through, then they can open their own arches."

"Wouldn't they need to be familiar with these standing stones in Therengia?"

"They would. Some preparation is required, but I doubt that would prove too difficult. The bigger issue is bringing tuskers through, for they'd require a larger arch."

"Might I suggest Temple Knights in their stead? It's not as if tuskers would prove effective within the halls of the Volstrum."

"You'd be willing to commit your knights to such an endeavour?"

"Yes," said Cordelia. "The time has come for us to take a more active role in defending the Petty Kingdoms."

"But Ruzhina is a Petty Kingdom," said Athgar.

"True, but we have known for some time now they've been working with Halvaria, which makes them our enemy as well as yours."

"In that case, I accept your offer, although, at this point, I'm not certain who will comprise the rest of this expedition."

"I'm sure Captain Valeria would let you use her cabin if you need somewhere private to discuss it. Shall I ask?"

"Yes, but if your knights are assisting, your presence is requested."

Later that night, they gathered around a lantern, peering down at a rough map of the area. Captain Valeria had graciously lent them the use of her cabin, but the quarters were so tight they struggled to fit around the table.

"This map," explained Natalia, "is a crude representation of the Great Northern Sea's eastern reaches. You can see the problem we face. Ruzhina has no neighbours, save for Zaran, and any approach involves a lengthy trek through unknown and, by all accounts, dangerous terrain."

"Dangerous in what sense?" asked Cordelia. "I hope you'll pardon my ignorance, but I'm still relatively new to this area."

"The area to the east is unexplored wilderness," replied Athgar.

"And Zaran?"

"That's another story entirely. It's also wilderness but with a grisly history. A fellow calling himself King Karzik sailed from Carlingen with a fleet of ships, intent on landing on Zaran's coast and claiming the area, but he was never heard from again."

"When was this?" asked Cordelia.

"About a century ago. Passing ships sighted debris on the shore and evidence that survivors went inland, but nothing more."

"Fascinating. Is there a chance any of them could have survived?"

"After a century?" replied Natalia. "That'd be pushing their luck."

"Could they have left children?"

"Had they women in the expedition, yes, but I'm afraid it was composed entirely of men."

"An odd way to begin a kingdom, isn't it?"

"I imagine he intended to bring women after establishing a foothold, but that was predicated on them surviving the initial trip."

"And we have no idea what happened to them?"

"None whatsoever," replied Natalia. "It's one of life's great mysteries, at least in the eastern kingdoms."

"Do we know how many ships he took?"

"Six, though we are unaware of the size or the number of men Karzik brought with him. Carlingen might have records, but before now, it's only been of cursory interest to us."

"It bears looking into," said Cordelia. "If you intend to mount your own expedition, you may encounter the same threats."

"True," said Athgar, "though I would think they were worn down by a combination of sickness and the local wildlife. We'll be travelling with a shaman, and both Kargen and I are hunters, which lessens the danger somewhat."

"And you're confident you can navigate that terrain?"

"I am. My intention would be to follow the river that defines the eastern border of Zaran."

"Not along the coast?"

"It's possible, but a passing ship might spot us. It also means we're travelling overland, slowing us down. Instead, I suggest we go by umak, which is better suited to river travel."

"Umak?" said Cordelia.

"Yes, the small river craft of the Orcs. If you recall, we used them last year when travelling to Carlingen's southern border."

"Yes, of course."

"You don't approve?" said Natalia.

"I'm concerned for your safety, but you know better than I what to expect. Perhaps we should focus on the army, specifically the number of men you intend to employ in Ruzhina?"

"You're the one from Ruzhina, Natalia," said Athgar. "How many warriors do you think they have at their disposal?"

"The family keeps a tight grip on the king's court, and a large army would threaten that. Furthermore, Ruzhina lacks neighbours, at least any that could threaten invasion. It would surprise me if they even have a thousand men, most of which would be in Porovka, their primary port."

"That makes sense. It's the most probable invasion route, though no one would be so foolish as to attempt it."

"Yet despite that, we are planning the same thing."

"What is our precise objective?" asked Cordelia. "Are we to conquer the entire kingdom or merely capture the Volstrum?"

"We don't know yet," said Athgar. "Yulakov wants the family defeated, so I imagine that includes the Volstrum."

"Have they no other strongholds?"

"We honestly don't know. We burned down Stormwind Manor two years ago, but I expect their matriarch found an alternate home by now."

"And there's nothing else?"

"I suppose we could include Zurkutsk."

"Which is?"

"A mine where they use forced labour to dig out magerite."

"And what, precisely, is that?"

Natalia held out her ring. "Magerite changes colour based on the magical energy of the person wearing it. You'll note mine is an intense blue." She removed it, setting it on the table, and it soon turned to a much paler shade.

"Remarkable."

"This is blue magerite, which works with Water Mages. There's also a red version that indicates potential with Fire Magic."

Cordelia looked at Athgar. "I assume you wear one of those?"

"No. I'm not interested in such things, although I spent some time in the mine."

"Truly?"

"Yes. I was held there as a prisoner for a while."

"And where is Zurkutsk?" asked Cordelia.

"East of Karslev, their capital."

"Then I suggest that's where we start."

"Might I ask why?" said Athgar.

"Taking that mine would give us a base to operate from, a secure position where we could mass our troops before marching on Karslev."

"I like the way you think," said Natalia.

Cordelia smiled. "How many men do you need to capture the mine?"

"Not many," replied Athgar, "though I suspect they've increased the garrison since my incarceration."

"A hundred, perhaps?"

"Likely less. The mine still needs to remain profitable, and too many warriors would quickly negate any income."

"So we attack with an initial force of, say, two hundred?"

"That sounds about right."

"I recommend you take a company of Temple Knights to secure the surrounding area, then go in with a combination of foot and archers. Against those numbers, the local guards will likely surrender. Does that sound reasonable to you?"

"It does," said Natalia.

"How long must your gate remain open for all those people to pass through?"

"I possess enough power, if that's what you're asking."

"It's not power I'm worried about; it's time. They'll need to march to the standing stones first, won't they?"

"They would," said Athgar. "But they can set up a camp there while we travel through Zaran. How long did it take for the Temple Knights to go through your arch?"

"I see your point," replied Natalia. "Moving that many might consume half the morning."

"Yes," said Cordelia, "during which we'd be more vulnerable. I suggest we pick a spot a few miles from Zurkutsk to assemble without fear of discovery."

"You impress me yet again," said Natalia. "Your training has given you a solid foundation in strategy and tactics. Either that, or you're just naturally gifted."

"No. My background was raising horses, not organizing a military campaign. All that I picked up at the Antonine during my training as a Temple Captain."

"So we capture the mine," said Athgar, "then assemble the rest of the army."

"Which is to be how many warriors?" asked Cordelia.

"As to actual numbers," said Natalia, "I recommend the majority be foot soldiers. They'll be assaulting the Volstrum, which is not the best location for deploying archers."

"Agreed," said Athgar. "And when we do get inside, we'll need to use mages alongside our warriors, or else all those Stormwinds will overpower us."

"How many mages do you have?" asked Cordelia.

"At last count, nearly twenty."

"That many? How is that even possible?"

"There's Natalia and me, as well as Svetlana and Katrin, providing they agree to participate. Then there are four Orc tribes in Therengia, each with two or three spellcasters, and that's not including their shamans."

"I had no idea Therengia had grown so powerful. You probably possess more mages than any realm on the Continent, except for the empire itself."

"Indeed," said Natalia. "I just hope we can still make that boast once this is over."

# A DEAL IS STRUCK

## SPRING 1110 SR

Athgar dozed in the carriage as it journeyed westward. Natalia was wide awake, as was Cordelia, for the Temple Captain had been invited to accompany them. Oswyn remained aboard *Formidable,* under Skora's watchful eye, but Agar was eager to learn what the King of Ruzhina might make of their plans.

"Tell me, Agar," said Natalia. "What is your impression of Yulakov?"

"He seemed eager for his home to be cleansed of the family," replied the Orc.

"Did you believe him honest in that desire?"

"If he was lying, I saw none of it in his face."

"Were you with them the entire time?"

"No," replied Agar. "We all met outside, and then I went indoors, where I found Prince Piotr. The two of us spent the remainder of the day in the manor."

"And the King of Abelard wasn't in attendance?"

"That was by design," said Athgar.

Natalia smiled. "I thought you were asleep."

"I was, but it's difficult to remain so when everyone around me is talking." He gazed out the window. "Where are we?"

"We should be arriving soon," said Agar. "Yesterday, we met up where the road turns slightly."

"You remember that?"

"I am an Orc—the shape of trees is as recognizable to me as buildings are to you Humans. Does the forest not look familiar, Uncle?"

"Uncle?" said Cordelia.

"Yes," replied Agar. "Athgar and my father are tribe brothers."

"Couldn't the same be said for every member of the Red Hand?"

"Tribe brothers are more than being members of the same tribe."

The carriage slowed, interrupting the youngling's lesson in Orcish culture.

"We are here," he announced.

The door opened, revealing a very startled Yakim. It wasn't the presence of Natalia that made him freeze—it was the armour-clad Temple Captain.

"Greetings," said Athgar, ignoring the fellow's surprise. "As you can see, I returned, bringing two of my closest advisors."

The guard recovered quickly. "Of course, my lord. If you'll follow me, I'll show you to Their Majesties."

"Is King Maksim still here?"

"Indeed, Lord. He availed himself of King Yulakov's invitation to remain at the manor house last night."

"Wasn't the idea to keep some distance from the building to avoid spies?"

Yakim shrugged. "I'm afraid I can't comment on such things. If you come with me, my lord, I shall be pleased to escort you."

"Of course." Athgar stepped from the carriage, waiting for the others. "Allow me to introduce my wife, Natalia Stormwind, and Temple Captain Cordelia of the Temple Knights of Saint Agnes. Agar, you've already met."

"I shall be sure to announce you all once we've found His Majesty."

Yakim led them down the path they'd taken yesterday. King Yulakov waited in the same chair as the previous visit, making it look like he hadn't moved. King Maksim sat nearby, smiling when he noticed Natalia had joined Athgar this time, and young Prince Piotr nodded at Agar.

Yakim introduced everyone, and they all found seats. Natalia moved a chair to sit beside her husband.

Piotr rose and wandered over to Agar. "Do you want to visit the practice yard? They have archery targets."

"I am afraid I did not bring my bow," replied the Orc.

"You can use one of ours. Come. I'm interested to see how good you are."

Agar looked at his uncle.

"Go ahead. Enjoy yourself," said Athgar. "We won't leave without you."

The two younger members of the group ran off.

"Ah," said Yulakov. "The passion of youth. I wish we could call upon that same sense of urgency in our later years."

"Later years?" said Natalia. "You and Athgar are not far apart in age. Are you suggesting you're both getting old?"

"Rather than referring to years, should I refer to the weight of responsibility that wears on us both? Would that be more acceptable?"

"It would indeed."

"I must admit," continued Yulakov, "I'm a little surprised to see you in the company of a Temple Captain. Might I ask why you brought her?"

"Cordelia has extensive military knowledge," replied Athgar. "Between the three of us, we may have a possible solution to your problem."

"You have my full attention."

"When we spoke yesterday, the likelihood of sending an army to Ruzhina was not an option. I've since been persuaded that such a thing is possible."

"Might I ask what caused you to change your mind?"

"The application of magic," offered Natalia.

"How so?"

"Let's just say that amongst the many mages of Therengia, we have the ability to move large numbers of warriors in short order. I won't bore you with details, but a military campaign against the Volstrum is now a distinct possibility."

"How do you intend to carry out this campaign?"

"I would rather not say, Majesty. It's best if you remain ignorant of the actual details to protect our army from discovery until we're in a position to act."

Yulakov nodded. "A wise precaution, considering how corrupt my court has become. I shall trust that you have a plan we can count on. When would we begin?"

"We must discuss some details before we proceed," replied Athgar. "While I'm not opposed to destroying the Stormwinds, we need assurances that this is not an elaborate ploy to lure us into a trap."

"I assure you it's not."

"That," said Natalia, "is precisely what you would claim if it were."

"What is it you're asking for?"

"We'll get to that shortly. First, I'd like a clearer picture of the forces at your disposal. How big is the Army of Ruzhina?"

"The last time I checked, it numbered some eleven hundred men, but I need to speak to my military advisor to give you a more accurate count."

"That would be Veris Stormwind," noted Maksim. "Not the most trustworthy source."

"I must admit I hadn't considered that, but you have a good point."

"Let's see," said Natalia. "Eleven hundred equates to roughly twenty-two companies. I assume the bulk of those are in Porovka?"

"Yes," replied Yulakov. "How did you know?"

"It's the most logical place to billet them, which affords us an advantage since I imagine it would take two or three days' march for them to reach Karslev. Speaking of the capital, how large is the garrison there?"

"Five companies."

"And how many do you consider loyal to you?"

"I might remind you," added Athgar, "you claimed some companies would support you."

"I did," said Yulakov, "but only two of those are in Karslev. There's one in Porovka and another in the northeast."

"What's in the northeast?" asked Cordelia.

"Nothing more than rumours, I hope, but we must do our best to be responsive to the people's needs. They asked for our help, so we sent a company to keep the area safe."

"What is the nature of these rumours?"

"I hesitate to even mention them."

"Please do," said Natalia. "It may prove valuable to our cause, even if you consider it trivial."

"If you must know, there are rumours concerning the Kingdom of Shadows. These stories resurface every few years and cause a mild panic."

"I'm sorry," said Cordelia. "What in the name of the Saints is the Kingdom of Shadows?"

"I've heard of that," said Athgar. "According to legend, a woman named Vicavia lost her child to a fever. In her grief, she turned to dark magic, attempting to recover what had been taken from her. She reportedly kidnapped children to conduct horrible experiments in her quest to reanimate the dead."

"That's right," added Yulakov. "Even now, the peasants swear she walks the streets at night, seeking wayward children to spirit away."

"Yes. That matches up with what Anushka told me. There's also stories of strange half-Human creatures wandering out of the forest, striking fear into everyone."

"That is what they say, although I haven't seen any actual bodies."

"Then why send men?" asked Cordelia.

"To placate the nobles. The last thing I need are malicious rumours spreading and stirring up panic over the entire kingdom."

"Tell me," said Natalia. "Was there ever an actual mage named Vicavia?"

Yulakov looked surprised. "I never said she was a mage."

"She reportedly studied Necromancy. How else would someone reanimate the dead?"

"I hadn't considered that. To answer your question, yes, there are historical records concerning a woman named Vicavia. If I recall, she was an Enchantress who disappeared some two centuries ago."

"And did she have a child?"

"If she did, we have no record of it."

"I'm curious," said Natalia. "How is it you are familiar with her details? I would think her background of trifling interest."

"Ordinarily, I'd agree," said Yulakov, "but folk tales were a particular penchant of my father's, and the Kingdom of Shadows was one of his favourites. It's a pity he's no longer with us, for he could talk on the subject for days."

"I still don't see the connection," said Cordelia. "I understand this woman's disappearance, even the tales told to frighten children, but where does the term 'Kingdom of Shadows' come from?"

"Ah," said Yulakov. "That's a more recent invention. People believe she rules over a kingdom of… we're not sure what exactly, but whatever you call them, they're apparently not very nice."

"Where is the Kingdom of Shadows located?"

"East of Ruzhina, hidden away somewhere in the unexplored wilderness."

"Oh great," said the Temple Captain. "Just what we needed, another complication."

Natalia shook her head. "I hardly think a tale meant to frighten children will pose a threat to us."

"It's not the stories that bother me; it's the thought that something unexpected might upset our plans."

"It's always a gamble when a realm marches to war."

"To clarify," added Yulakov, "I sent my men northeast not because of a perceived threat but because their presence will calm the locals."

"Is there anything else we should know?"

"The Volstrum is a heavily fortified building. Have you siege equipment?"

"No," replied Natalia. "We have something better."

"That being?"

"I'd rather not say. Let's return to the garrison of Karslev, shall we? Does it include cavalry?"

"It does," replied Yulakov, "but nothing that rivals Temple Knights."

"Meaning?"

"They are what you would consider light cavalry, more suited to keeping peace in the streets than fighting a pitched battle."

"Any archers?"

"One company of crossbowmen, though they seldom have a need to leave their billets. The bulk of the garrison are footmen."

"And how are they equipped?"

"Padded gambesons and mail coifs, along with helmets. They are trained in various polearms but carry clubs to deal with unruly citizens while about their duties."

"Don't get me wrong," said Cordelia. "This is all important information, but where do the mages come into play? Do they assign Water Mages to each company, or do they carry out independent patrols?"

"No Water Mages are in the Army of Ruzhina," said Yulakov. "Magic is the exclusive right of the family."

"And do they patrol the street on a regular basis?"

"No. They leave that to the army."

"I can confirm that," said Natalia. "Members of the Volstrum are duty bound to defend the building with their lives, if necessary."

"At least they'll all be in one place," said Athgar.

"I'm afraid it's much more complicated than that."

"Oh? What am I missing?"

"If you recall," explained Natalia, "Katrin's parents resided in Karslev, and they were both mages. What we haven't considered is the students' parents. Admittedly, they won't all live in Karslev, but a good portion will, and some of those will be Sartellians, so we'll need to be prepared for them."

"Sartellians? But they're Fire Mages," said Cordelia. "I assumed they'd all be in Korascajan?"

"They are trained there but live throughout the areas controlled by the family. The parentage of Stormwinds and Sartellians is credited with producing powerful mages. Thus, we'll find many in Karslev, giving their all to increase the family's presence through reproduction."

"That's a polite way of saying forced breeding," offered Athgar.

Cordelia shook her head. "I have no words to describe my revulsion at the thought."

"Now you understand what we're up against," said Yulakov. "I've said it before, and I'll say it again: the family is a blight on the Continent and must be wiped out."

"Quite," agreed Natalia. "Now, let's revisit what we touched on earlier, a guarantee this is no trap."

"Is my word not enough?"

"With all due respect, no. If you were an agent of the family, you would lie to further their aims."

"Then what would you have me do?"

"Give us your son."

"I beg your pardon?"

"You heard me," said Natalia. "Hand over your son as a hostage to ensure your good behaviour. Should you lead us into a trap, his life will be forfeit."

Yulakov paled. "You can't possibly mean that?"

"Can't I? The last time I was in Ruzhina, the family took my husband from me and threatened to kill him, thus forcing me to do their bidding. Wouldn't you do the same if your child's life was in danger?"

"But... but... he's my heir! I can't return home without him. What would everyone say?"

"I can think of several things," said Natalia, "which is why you'll inform them you've left him in the care of King Rordan of Abelard."

"Why would I do that?"

"It is the custom in the Petty Kingdoms to send one's son and heir to another king's court to acquire a better knowledge of the workings of the nobility."

"I'd suggest saying you sent him to Carlingen," offered Maksim, "but I'm afraid that would raise too many suspicions. Everyone knows we're not on friendly terms with the family these days."

"Agreed," said Yulakov, "but the family has contacts in Rordan's court. It wouldn't take them long to realize he was elsewhere."

"I think you overestimate their interest," said Natalia. "You return to Karslev acting the dutiful king, and I doubt they'll even consider it a problem."

"Perhaps, but sooner or later—"

"We'll already have marched by then," said Athgar, "and they'd still need to send messengers to Abelard to confirm their suspicions."

"How can you possibly be marching so soon?"

"You forget," said Athgar. "We have mages. We'll be back in Therengia before you even set foot on your ship. By the time you're in Porovka, we'll be halfway to Ruzhina ourselves."

"But you still need to organize an entire army."

"There are people back home who can do that, leaving us to concentrate on an overall strategy: a strategy, I might add, that we've already given considerable thought to."

"How do I know you'll treat my son well?"

"Why wouldn't we? We aim to be your allies, Majesty, not your enemy. Turn on us, though, and you'll be making a huge mistake."

"Couldn't the same be said of the Stormwinds?"

"It could," replied Natalia, "but if you succumb to their influence now, you'll never be rid of them. It's your choice, Majesty. Nothing is stopping you from backing out of this idea right now. Say the word, and we shall pretend this meeting never occurred."

They waited as Yulakov weighed his options. The man clearly fought with his conscience, torn between his love for his son and his duty to his people. "I accept your terms," he finally said. "I shall offer up my son as a guarantee that I mean no ill will."

"And we, in turn, will ensure he's well-cared for."

Yulakov turned to his right-hand man. "Yakim, go fetch him, would you?"

"Of course, Majesty." The warrior dutifully left.

"I understand how hard this decision was," said Natalia, "but ultimately, it secures the future of Ruzhina."

"Are you absolutely certain you can defeat them? If not, my entire family is in jeopardy."

"Nothing is guaranteed in war, but we wouldn't undertake an expedition of this nature if we didn't believe it had every possibility of success. I must caution you, though. The likelihood of casualties on both sides is high."

"It will be worth it if we can break their stranglehold on the Continent."

"Destroying the Volstrum doesn't guarantee that. They'll still have mages at courts across the Petty Kingdoms."

"True," said Yulakov, "but once the news spreads that they've been pushed out of Ruzhina, their days of influence will be at an end. After all, of what value are advisors who can't protect their own home?"

"Let's hope you're right," replied Athgar. "The Continent would be a far better place without their interference."

"I wish it were that simple," said Cordelia, "but history has proven that when one person is removed from power, another steps up to replace them."

"Then let us hope that whoever does has the Petty Kingdoms' best interests in mind."

# RETURN

## SPRING 1110 SR

The carriage hit a rut, causing those inside to bump into each other.

"The roads here are atrocious," said Piotr. The young prince was in a sour mood, hardly surprising given his new status as a hostage. He looked at Athgar. "Is it like this in Therengia?"

"I'm afraid so, though if you prefer the city, you'd probably enjoy Ebenstadt."

"Is that where you're taking me?"

"No. You'll be joining us in Runewald."

"Runewald? It sounds like a dung heap."

"You should learn to be more gracious towards your hosts."

"Hosts? More like captors."

"Now, now," chided Natalia. "Your father agreed to this."

"I still don't understand why."

"Your father wishes to crush the power of the Stormwinds; to do that, he needs our help."

"What has that got to do with me?"

"You are the guarantee that we're not being lured into a trap."

"So I am a prisoner!" declared Piotr.

"We prefer to think of you as a guest. You'll be perfectly safe amongst us. Who knows, you might even learn something."

"Do not worry," said Agar. "I will look out for you."

The prince settled back in his seat. "Do you have a palace in Runewald?"

"No, but there is a great hut where important people gather."

"What important people?"

"The Thane's Council," said Natalia, "which includes the chieftains and shamans of the four tribes."

"Shouldn't that be the High Thane's Council?"

Athgar chuckled. "He has a point. Perhaps we should rename it?"

"You should proclaim yourself king," continued Piotr, "then the other Petty Kingdoms would take you seriously."

"I am the Ruler of Therengia, chosen by the people I rule on behalf of."

"Are you not feared?"

"Is that what you think makes a great ruler?"

"That's how things are done in the Petty Kingdoms."

"That's not our way," replied Athgar.

"That's likely why the Old Kingdom died."

"You hold a lot of opinions concerning politics. Is it a particular interest of yours?"

"My father wanted to give me a good education, so he employed some of the Continent's greatest minds to teach me."

"That must have cost him quite a bit."

"You have no idea."

"Be honest, now," said Natalia. "What do you think of the Stormwinds?"

Piotr shrugged. "They are a constant presence at court. Aside from that, I have no opinion."

"Are you aware of your father's distaste for them?"

"I am, though I fail to see why he views them as a threat. Do they not ensure the safety of Ruzhina by their very presence?"

"They do," replied Natalia, "but if you knew them as we do, you might better understand the threat they pose."

"Then explain it to me."

"Have you heard of Halvaria?"

"Of course," said Piotr. "Everyone on the Continent's heard of the empire. Why? What do they have to do with the Stormwinds?"

"The two are inextricably linked."

"How?"

"The Stormwinds supply powerful mages to Halvaria and may even rule over them."

"Are you suggesting they are working towards conquering the Petty Kingdoms? That makes no sense. They would be helping in the loss of Ruzhina as well."

"We have proof."

"What proof?"

"A letter in the hand of Illiana Stormwind herself."

"Who is?"

"The matriarch of the family, but she died some time ago."

"Yet you managed to discover this great secret? It all sounds a little too convenient to me. A pity she's no longer alive to confirm the details of this so-called letter."

"You don't have to believe us if you feel otherwise inclined," said Natalia, "but you should at least look at the facts before making a decision."

"What facts?"

"The family orchestrated the war between Reinwick and Andover," replied Cordelia. "Their cousins, the Sartellians, were complicit in the attack on Arnsfeld, not to mention plotting to build a fleet in Carlingen to confront the Temple Fleet."

"I had no idea," said Piotr. "My lessons didn't include such things."

"And who taught you history?" asked Natalia.

"A woman by the name of Yeleva Stormwind."

"Are you sure you don't mean Yaleva?"

"No. That is her twin sister."

"Do you suppose that explains why you were never taught those things?"

"Admittedly, yes."

The carriage slowed.

"Something's wrong," said Athgar.

Cordelia gazed out the window. "It seems we're back in Kienenstadt."

"Yes," agreed Natalia. "I can sense the sea, but why have we slowed?"

The carriage drew to a stop, and then Captain Dorkin appeared at the door, providing the answer. "My apologies, my lord, ladies, but there is a disturbance up ahead."

"What kind of disturbance?" asked Athgar.

"Nothing more than a disagreement, I assure you. I'm certain it will soon be resolved."

"Yet it's enough to halt our carriage. Are you suggesting there might be danger hereabouts?"

The fellow stared off, focused on what was transpiring ahead of them.

"What precisely is happening?" demanded Athgar.

"Church business."

"When has that ever stopped traffic?" Athgar put an edge to his voice. "What is going on here?"

"A group of Temple Knights have taken someone into custody, my lord."

"Temple Knights?" said Cordelia. "They wouldn't happen to be Cunars, would they?"

"They would indeed," replied the warrior. "Were it anyone else, we would intervene, but only a fool attempts to thwart the wishes of a Cunar."

"Who did they arrest?"

"I wouldn't know, my lady."

"I'm not a lady; I'm a Temple Captain."

"Then perhaps you'd see fit to intervene on the king's behalf?"

"With pleasure." Cordelia opened the door and climbed out.

"Hold on," said Natalia. "These are Cunars you're talking about. It's best if we're there to back you up." She, too, exited.

"We'd best all go, then," said Athgar. "Agar, you and Prince Piotr stay behind us."

"Finally," said the prince. "Something interesting!" They followed the others out of the carriage, heading towards the disturbance. A group of six grey-clad knights held three men under armed guard.

"What's going on here?" called out Cordelia.

A Temple Knight turned to face her. "This is none of your business, Captain. Be on your way."

"I'll be on my way once you've explained yourself."

"You have no right to make demands. You are outcasts in the eyes of the Church. If it were up to me, the lot of you would be in irons. Now begone, before I change my mind."

"Careful," warned Natalia. "You are speaking to a regional commander."

"This is none of your concern," said the Cunar.

"Why are these men under arrest?"

"They stepped outside their responsibility to the Church."

"Wait!" Cordelia moved closer. "I recognize them. They're crew members from the *Formidable*."

"Which is why I placed them under arrest. They violated Church law."

"They most certainly have not."

"The *Formidable* is now under the Holy Fleet's command."

"Since when?"

"It has been since your order was ordered disbanded."

Natalia took a step forward. "That ship is under the protection of Reinwick, Carlingen, and Therengia. Would you so callously risk war over this?"

"Who are you that believes they can order around Temple Knights?"

She straightened her back, allowing her magic to build within. "Release these men immediately, or I will be forced to take action."

The fellow sneered. "Oh yes? And what will you do—give me a stern talking to?"

She looked at Athgar. "You heard him. He wouldn't listen."

"It's his own fault," he replied. "Do what you must."

"What's happening?" asked Piotr.

"Quiet!" snapped Agar. "You are about to witness the might of Nat-Alia's magic."

Words of power emanated from Natalia's lips as the air grew colder, and then she stepped forward, placing a hand against the knight's chest. Frost expanded from the point of contact, rapidly spreading to encompass the entire breastplate. The fellow's beard iced up, and then a cracking noise rent the air.

The knight backed up, staring down at where his armour had split. One of his companions stepped closer, his hand on the hilt of his sword, but Athgar let loose with a spell of his own, a fire streak that struck the ground right in front of the Cunar.

"This can go one of two ways," Athgar warned. "Either you turn these men over to us and be on your way, or you experience first-hand the effects of magic on bare flesh. Which will it be, gentlemen?"

"You are a fool if you believe we'll hand them over."

Natalia frowned. "I was afraid you'd say something like that. Oh well. It wasn't as if we didn't warn you." She thrust her hands towards the ground before her, ice erupting from her fingers to splatter the ground and then crawl towards the Cunars. So mesmerizing was the sight that the two of them stood watching as the ice-encased their boots, trapping them in place.

Their leader drew his sword and raised it, intending to strike at Natalia. Athgar saw the movement and brought forth his inner spark. Flames leaped up the blade, which glowed, growing hotter by the moment. The Temple Knight grinned, convinced it would only add to the strength of his attack, but then reality settled in as his gauntlet heated up, smoke emanating from it. He dropped his weapon and clutched his hand but refused to cry out in pain, instead backing up and grimacing.

Cordelia moved amongst them, physically grabbing a knight's arm and removing it from his prisoner. "These men are with me."

Athgar took another step, fire erupting from his palms. Rather than loose it at them, he stood in place, allowing the flames to fly up into the afternoon sky. "Leave!" he commanded. "Now!"

They abandoned their frozen colleagues who were desperately trying to free their feet.

"It seems they left you," said Cordelia. "If we release you, will you join them or try something foolish and force us to kill you?"

"We shall leave. We promise."

"Natalia, if you would be so kind?"

A wave of her hand dismissed the spell. The ice soon began to melt, and then their boots pulled free. True to their word, the remaining pair of Temple Knights withdrew.

"They'll be back," said Cordelia.

"Then we'd best get aboard *Formidable* with all haste."

. . .

"I must thank you," said Captain Valeria, looking over the guard rail. "I wasn't expecting those men to be arrested."

"It was my pleasure," replied Natalia. "I trust you have no more people ashore?"

"None at all unless you include King Maksim. You don't think he's in danger, do you?"

"I doubt even a Cunar would have the gall to arrest a king, especially a guest of King Rordan. I expect he'll return sometime this evening or tomorrow morning. I trust that works well with your plans?"

"I was instructed to provide transportation for His Majesty. Until that task is complete, I have no other duties."

"In that case, you'll be pleased to know we will no longer require your services after tomorrow."

"Don't you want to return to Carlingen?"

"Yes," said Natalia, "but I'll use my magic to get us there. My only stipulation is you'll need to drop us somewhere along the coast so I can cast my spell."

"And that will take you to Carlingen?"

"Yes, and even farther, if necessary."

"And what of Cordelia?" Both of them turned to the Temple Captain.

"I shall accompany them to Carlingen, at least for now, but I'll need to follow along to Therengia if the order is to assist in this madcap scheme."

"Madcap?" said Natalia. "I prefer to think of it as a well-reasoned strategy."

Cordelia laughed. "And it might be, eventually, but may I remind you, it's still in the planning phase. Although we discussed capturing the mine, we have yet to devise a strategy for attacking the Volstrum."

"A valid point, but not insurmountable. I have several ideas, but I'd rather not mention them until I've consulted with the Stone Crushers."

"They're Earth Mages, aren't they?"

"Masters of earth, to be more precise, but you have the right idea. I'm hoping they might have some ideas on how we could break into the Volstrum."

"Have they done anything like this before?"

"They helped us capture Ebenstadt five years ago, but in that instance, they created a tunnel beneath the city walls. I doubt that tactic would work with the Volstrum."

"Why is that?"

"The building has subterranean levels, and rock is more difficult for them to manipulate than dirt."

"Is there no other way to gain entry?"

"Several, but there's more to defeating the family than just getting into the building."

"There is?"

"The Volstrum is an immense structure, and though I'm familiar with the general layout, I spent most of my time in the classrooms."

"Why is that?"

"I was a student there in my youth, but when I returned as an instructor, I was a prisoner. Each day after teaching, they took me back to Stormwind Manor. Galina knows the layout better, as she taught there for years."

"Galina?"

"Yes. A fellow student now working against the family from the safety of Reinwick."

"Interesting," said Cordelia. "Do you think she'd consider joining the expedition?"

"I shall certainly extend the offer, but it's a long way for her to travel."

"Can't she use the same spell as you?"

"She can, but she's never seen the casting circle in Carlingen or the standing stones in Therengia."

"Why does that matter?"

"To use a frozen arch, the caster must be familiar with the destination, which requires intense study."

"We could bring her by ship," offered Valeria. "I can take *Formidable* directly to Korvoran since I'm no longer needed here."

"An excellent idea," said Natalia. "I'm due to contact her tomorrow. I'll let her know you're on your way."

"Won't that cost us valuable time?" said Cordelia.

"Not really. Assembling the army will take time, and we won't require her knowledge until just before the attack commences. We'll need to familiarize her with the standing stones back home, along with Svetlana and Katrin, but that shouldn't take too long."

"Remarkable," said Captain Valeria. "I was aware of magic, but I never knew it could be used to travel to distant lands. Is there any limit to the distance a mage can go?"

"In a manner of speaking, yes," said Natalia. "Mages draw on magical energy from within themselves. We learn to hold more of this power as time passes, but it demands discipline and practice."

"Yet you can travel all the way to Carlingen. That's quite the distance?"

"That's nothing," said Cordelia. "The arch she opened to Therengia spanned over a thousand miles."

"That was different," replied Natalia. "I had the help of standing stones, which allows me to tap into the ley lines."

Valeria looked around the deck. "Couldn't you cast this frozen arch spell aboard the ship?"

"Much as I'd like to, I'm afraid that's out of the question."

"Why is that?"

"Once the arch forms, it's immovable until I dispel it. Even the gentle rocking of the waves would cause problems."

"How is that a problem?"

"If I cast the spell here, it would become an immovable force. The arch would remain in place as the ship rises on a swell, damaging the vessel."

"But the arch would be destroyed, surely?"

"It would," replied Natalia, "but in the process, your decking would be damaged, and it could also affect those using the arch. They might be transported to some random location, possibly thousands of miles from their intended destination. Of course, that's assuming they're not killed outright. In any case, I'd rather not take that chance."

"Something's happening ashore," said Cordelia. On the dock, a group of Cunars were busy climbing into a longboat.

"Fools," said Natalia. "Will they never learn?"

"Look," called out Valeria. "King Maksim is farther down the dock. I recognize the carriage, not to mention his escort."

They watched as His Majesty climbed out of the carriage. Thankfully, they'd halted several hundred yards away from the Cunars, allowing them to board the *Formidable's* boat without delay. The boat's crew dipped their oars, propelling the king towards the Temple Ship.

The Cunars ignored them, filling up their boat with Temple Knights. They pushed away from the dock, dug in their own oars, determined to row out to the *Formidable*.

"To arms!" called out Captain Valeria.

"That won't be necessary," said Natalia. "If you'll allow me, I'll take care of them."

"By all means."

Natalia closed her eyes, digging deep within herself. A flood of power came forth as if water were rising within her, and then she snapped her eyes open and pointed at the sea in front of the Cunar Knights. The air buzzed like a swarm of bees had been released, and then the water turned frosty. Ice appeared, crawling towards the Cunars like a shark after its prey.

The small boat stopped as it bumped up against the ice. Soon, the entire vessel was surrounded.

"There," said Natalia. "That should hold them awhile. Now, let's get King Maksim aboard, shall we? It's time we left port."

# LOGISTICS

## SPRING 1110 SR

"Are you certain about this?" Wynfrith leaned on the table to emphasize her words. "This is a risky undertaking that could easily end in disaster." She looked at the others who'd gathered for the meeting.

Athgar and Natalia had assembled everyone in Ebenstadt to discuss their plans prior to going home to Runewald. It had been difficult to arrange, but now all the Thanes of Therengia sat at the table, along with the four Orc chieftains and their shamans. The Temple Captains of both Saint Agnes and Saint Mathew rounded things out.

Natalia had hoped everyone would support their plans for the attack on the Volstrum, but some voiced disagreement about how, or even if, the campaign should commence. "I doubt we'll see another opportunity like this again. If we don't act while we have the advantage, we will never be rid of them."

"I agree," said Belgast. He'd returned from Kragen-Tor with grand news, for the vard had agreed to Athgar's proposal. Even as they gathered here, the first wagons of Dwarven goods were headed to Therengia.

"You would," said Stanislav, "but you're not the one doing the fighting."

"I resent that. I'm no coward."

"And I'm not saying you are, merely that we've lost many fine people because of our military campaigns. Successful we may have been, but at a grim cost."

"War is brutal," said Yaromir, "but if we are unwilling to fight for what we believe in, we only perpetuate the evils of the past."

"Well said," added Temple Captain Gabriel. "I say we confront them now before they use their power to assist in the empire's conquest of the Petty Kingdoms."

Natalia turned to Kargen. "What do you think?"

The Orc chieftain studied those seated at the table, finally resting his gaze on Shaluhk, who nodded slightly. "We are at a turning point in history. As the Temple Captain indicates, if we do nothing, we risk the empire seizing control of the entire Continent. Our people did not fare well under their rule."

"How could you possibly know that?" asked Gabriel.

"Our shamans can communicate over long distances."

"What do you mean by 'our people did not fare well'?"

"They were exterminated, or at least we assume they were. Contact with the tribes in Halvaria ceased centuries ago. We have no alternative but to end this while we still possess the strength to resist."

Wynfrith nodded. "I still hold reservations, but if the majority feels it necessary, then so be it."

"Good," replied Athgar. "Now we've dealt with that, let's talk about specifics. What is the state of our army?"

"It is as strong as it's ever been," replied Natalia. "More than capable of supporting this endeavour."

"That begs the question of how many warriors we need."

"What are your thoughts?"

"Thanks to Temple Captain Cordelia," said Athgar, "we have the commitment of two companies of her knights. In addition, I suggest all four companies of the Thane Guard, along with a decent number of archers."

"Arrows won't be much use in the Volstrum," warned Yaromir.

"True, but the Army of Ruzhina might force us into a battle before we arrive."

"I have consulted with the other tribes," said Kargen, "and they agreed to commit an equal number of Orcs, along with two companies of warbows."

"Will that be enough?" asked Stanislav. "The Volstrum was always well-protected whenever I visited."

"That is where we come in," said Zharuhl, Chieftain of the Stone Crushers. "Rather than attack at an entrance, our masters of the earth will make short work of their stone walls. We shall be in amongst them before they realize what is happening."

"A good strategy," said Yaromir, "but I'm more concerned about what happens once you're inside. The Stormwinds are powerful mages, and we need to neutralize their magic, not to mention worrying about any family members residing in the city."

"Arrows can take down any mage," said Natalia. "Remember, a mage is deadly one-on-one, but hit them with numbers, and we'll overwhelm them."

"We're looking at what..." said Stanislav. "Eight hundred warriors?"

"We could certainly take more," replied Athgar, "but bring too many, and they'll end up getting in one another's way."

"True, but that should give us enough to secure the perimeter. The last thing we need is the mages who live outside the Volstrum descending upon us while it's under attack."

"Would they respect Temple Knights?"

"I doubt it. The knights have no presence in Karslev, or the rest of Ruzhina, for that matter."

"That makes sense," replied Natalia. "They're allied with Halvaria, and the fighting orders are the sworn enemies of the empire."

"Whether they recognize our orders or not," said Cordelia, "they'll be hesitant to take on heavily armoured knights."

"The family can be fickle," offered Stanislav. "I'd be willing to bet there's a good chance many would avoid getting involved until they see which way the wind's blowing. The key to this is finishing them off quickly before they organize themselves."

"Precisely," said Natalia. "Which is why we must maintain the element of surprise."

"I'll deal with organizing the army," offered Wynfrith, "but you should give some careful consideration as to who will accompany you on the journey there."

"We've already discussed that. Athgar and I will proceed upriver with Kargen and Shaluhk."

"Using umaks?"

"That's the plan, yes."

"I can't say I fancy the idea of our High Thane undertaking such a perilous journey without protection, let alone our warmaster or the Chieftain of the Red Hand."

"We are the best ones equipped for the journey," replied Shaluhk. "Yes, it is risky, but a smaller group travels faster than a large one."

"And if you run into danger?"

"We have a powerful Water Mage with us. It is difficult to conceive of anything that would prove too much for Nat-Alia, not to mention Athgar's Fire Magic."

Stanislav wasn't convinced. "I might remind you an entire expedition disappeared into Zaran, and naught has been seen of them since."

"That was a century ago," said Athgar. "And unlike King Karzik, we have experience surviving in the wilderness."

"Yes," added Shaluhk, "and we can always return home using Nat-Alia's magic if necessary. Do not worry. We will proceed with extreme caution."

"Just out of curiosity," said Belgast, "how do you intend to navigate?"

"I have given that much thought," replied Kargen. "The Zaran River that forms the region's eastern border joins up with the Windrush, the very same river on which Beorwic lies. We follow that downstream until we find where they converge, then head upriver. If the river veers off target or stops before we arrive in Ruzhina, we shall abandon it and travel directly north."

"A smart strategy," said Stanislav. "We know there's a river forming Ruzhina's southern border. What we don't understand is what lies south of it. What if wild tuskers are about, or even worse creatures?"

"Worse?" said Belgast. "What could possibly be worse?"

"I might remind you that until you ran into tuskers, you didn't know they existed. There could be all manner of beasts in the area we're unfamiliar with."

"They're more than capable of dealing with whatever comes their way."

"What we really need to know," said Wynfrith, "is how long it will take you to get to Ruzhina? We can't keep eight hundred souls camped by the standing stones forever. They'd eat up all their supplies."

"I shall be in daily contact with Voruhn," said Shaluhk. "Once we cross the river that borders Ruzhina, the army should travel to the standing stones. Prior to that, I suggest they camp in Runewald, which is reasonably close by."

"Raleth will command the Thane Guard," said Athgar. "All four companies worth, and I want Hilwyth to command the fyrd's archers." He turned to Kargen. "Who will command the Orcs in
your absence?"

"Kragor," the chieftain replied.

"Not Laruhk?"

"Laruhk is a fine leader, but he commands the tuskers. In my absence, I also need him in Runewald to act as chieftain."

"I assume," said Yaromir, "that Temple Captain Cordelia will command the Temple Knights?"

"Yes," replied Athgar. "I suggest the masters of magic be organized under Voruhn, providing that causes no offence?"

"I am in agreement," said Kargen. "Her responsibility will be to ensure all our spellcasters are ready to travel once Nat-Alia activates the frozen arch."

"Then it appears we've covered every detail. If we think of anything else during our travels, Shaluhk will advise you."

"What about the actual attack?" asked Cordelia.

"There's no sense worrying about that until we reach Ruzhina."

"I would suggest the cavalry go through the arch first so they can spread out and secure the area."

"Certainly," agreed Athgar, "but I'd like Kragor's warbows next in line. We might need them if any dangerous creatures are in the area. In regards to the rest, I'll leave the order up to Raleth."

Wynfrith stood. "I shall issue the orders unless you want to see to them yourself?"

"No. I'm far too busy preparing for our trip. I trust you to do what's needed."

"Then I suggest we let the High Thane have some privacy." She looked around the room, daring any to object. "Well… don't just sit there. Be about your business!"

Everyone filed out save for Athgar, Natalia, Kargen, and Shaluhk. Athgar waited until the door closed to turn to his wife. "I'm concerned we won't have enough spellcasters."

"Aside from Shaluhk and myself, we have three shamans, three masters of earth, and one master of air. That's more than sufficient to bring down a wall or two of the Volstrum."

"Yes, but they can field scores of Water Mages."

"I estimate less than fifteen are battle mages, and they will be the most experienced ones there. Fortunately, except for the dining halls and dormitories, most of the Volstrum consists of a series of corridors."

"Wouldn't that make it easier to defend?"

"You might believe so, but the relatively confined area makes it easier for warriors to close with their opponents. Remember, it takes time to cast a spell, time in which an opponent can get within melee range. You must also remember no mages will be wearing armour, which makes them easy prey should our people get close enough."

"Is Marakhova a battle mage?"

"She is," replied Natalia, "and likely the most powerful caster we'll find ourselves up against. She'll have a variety of spells at her disposal, so we must keep an eye out for her. There's also the possibility she might flee at the first signs of danger."

"What of guards?" asked Athgar.

"In all probability, they'll be the biggest obstacle. They're intimately familiar with the layout of the Volstrum, not to mention fanatically loyal to the family. I doubt they have as much experience as our people, but I don't want to underestimate them."

"Agreed. We did that last time, and it didn't turn out so well."

"We escaped, didn't we?"

"We did, but we lost too many in the process. I prefer not to repeat the mistakes of our past."

"Then we shall take great care."

"This Volstrum," said Shaluhk. "I assume the walls are thick?"

"So I'm told," replied Natalia, "though I've never really noticed. I spent most of my time within the walls, not examining them."

"With the help of the other shamans, I shall endeavour to ascertain their defences."

"How will you do that?" asked Athgar.

"Thanks to Khurlig, I have memories of spells from the past. I can use them to travel into the spirit realm and walk amongst them."

"Yes," added Kargen. "We used it to learn of Ostrova's plans last autumn. It was as if we were ghosts."

"I'm not convinced," said Athgar. "Wouldn't the family set magical wards against such things?"

"Wards?" replied Natalia. "The spirit realm is not easily blocked, and besides, the family doesn't employ Life Mages."

"Not even for healing their students?"

"They may have some in Halvaria, but as far as I'm aware, none in Karslev."

"How would you know if there were?"

"During my time there, a student made a mistake while casting ice shards. She ended up losing a leg, but then the wound festered, and she died of a fever. I can't imagine that happening if they had a Life Mage, not when a student represents years of investment."

"You talked of Life Mages and Water Mages," said Kargen, "but we must also consider the possibility that Sartellians may be present, which means our people might end up facing Fire Magic."

"We considered that but can do little to prevent it from happening. Still, even an accomplished Fire Mage can be killed by an axe. We also have the advantage that we can heal our injured."

"We shall have plenty of time to refine our strategy once we are underway," said Shaluhk. "The trip through Zaran is a lengthy one."

"I assume we'll take only one umak?" asked Athgar.

"I originally thought two in case one got damaged, but after careful consideration, we are safer all together."

"Agreed," said Kargen. "I arranged for one to be ready for us in Runewald. Will we use a frozen arch to take us to Beorwic?"

"Yes," replied Natalia. "Then we'll make our way down the Carlsrun."

"The Carlsrun?"

"Their name for the Windrush River."

"How original," said Athgar. "I suppose by that logic, the river at Beorwic should be referred to as Beorsrun?"

"I don't believe they've given it a name," said Natalia, "but now that you mention it, I'll suggest that to King Maksim. Oh, and before you ask, Carlsrun is named after the city's founder, a fellow named Carl Dotterfeld—the city, too, for that matter."

"Didn't Svetlana say he was a drunkard and a wastrel? It seems history has a way of forgetting things like that."

"You are too nice," said Kargen, suppressing a laugh. "If you want something named after you, my friend, you need to become closer with your darker instincts."

"No, thank you," replied Athgar. "I don't want a river named after me, or a city, for that matter. I'm more than happy just being Natalia's husband."

"And the High Thane," added Shaluhk. "Not to mention a powerful master of flame in your own right.

"Yes. Well, let's not get carried away. I'm trying to remain humble. Any more praises, and my helmet will no longer fit."

Natalia stood. "Come along, Shaluhk. You and I should gather the children while our bondmates ready the horses."

"Don't forget Prince Piotr," said Athgar. "Agar's keen to show him Runewald, although I have a feeling our young princeling will not be impressed."

"Have you arranged extra horses?"

"I have. I considered a carriage for His Highness, but something tells me he would see that as beneath him."

Kargen grinned. "Are you suggesting he is... What is the expression?"

"Full of himself?" suggested Shaluhk.

"Yes, a most interesting term. What else, I wonder, might someone be full of if not himself?"

"Dung springs to mind," said Athgar.

"Now, now," chided Natalia. "We should be more charitable. Piotr has his flaws, but that's not his fault; he's a victim of his upbringing. The Volstrum taught us such attitudes are common amongst the nobility throughout the Petty Kingdoms."

"It is a wonder they've lasted so long."

"I agree," said Kargen. "Such an attitude would not endear a chieftain to his tribe."

"True," said Athgar. "Then again, Gorlag was the Chieftain of the Red Hand, and I don't recall him being much different."

"You speak the truth, my friend, but thankfully, our people had the sense to be rid of him."

“Only after I fought him.”

“I am not speaking of the fight; I refer to the events that succeeded it. If you recall, the tribe banished Gorlag.”

“I wonder whatever happened to him?”

“We shall likely never know,” said Shaluhk.

# UNDERWAY

## SPRING 1110 SR

Kargen stepped through the frozen arch, then waited as Natalia followed. Behind them came Athgar and Shaluhk, carrying the umak over their heads.

The familiar face of Herulf greeted them. He was now captain of the Beorwic fyrd, small though it was, and took pride in ensuring they were properly trained. "Aelfric, Wulfwyn," he called out. "Come, take the umak."

Athgar lowered the boat to the ground. "Thank you. I appreciate the help." He studied the two warriors. "Are these members of the fyrd?"

"They are. What do you think?"

"You've found them mailed coats. Are they all armoured alike?"

"Regrettably, no," replied Herulf. "Only six currently, but the armourers in Carlingen are working on more."

"Good to hear. You know Kargen and Shaluhk?"

"I do, Lord. We met last autumn in the capital." He peered around behind the new arrivals, watching the frozen arch collapse. "No children this time?"

"No," replied Natalia. "The trip through Zaran is far too dangerous. They're back in Runewald, under Skora's watchful eye."

"So, the rumours are true," said Herulf. "You're heading north."

"That's why we brought the umak. It's likely the safest method of travel."

"We've been gathering supplies for you, but no one would say where you were travelling. Some speculated you might be headed west."

"West?" said Athgar. "Why would we go west?"

"They thought you were going to explore the rest of Carlingen's southern border, looking for signs of encroachment by the Ostrovans."

"Their king ceded land to Therengia. I doubt he's in a position to make problems with our new ally."

"In that case, please follow Aelfric and Wulfwyn. They'll lead you to the docks."

"You're not coming?"

"I must find Katrin first. She'll be eager to speak with you before you leave." At this, he bowed his head, then disappeared amongst the buildings.

Natalia chuckled. "He could have sent anyone to get Katrin."

"Then why didn't he?"

"Need you ask? Did you not notice the blush on his cheeks when he mentioned her name?"

"Oh yes. That's right. Greta mentioned it the last time we were here. You don't suppose they've done anything about it?"

"That's hardly our business," she replied. "Although it's nice that Katrin might have found someone to share her life with—other than Greta, of course."

"Come," said Shaluhk. "We must follow the umak before it disappears from our view."

They followed the two warriors down the street, eventually arriving at the new docks, where they set the umak down on the wooden planking beside several neatly piled sacks.

"Are those our supplies?" asked Athgar.

"They are, Lord," replied Wulfwyn. "You've got a month's supply of food, though you'll need to locate your own water. I suppose that's easy enough considering you're travelling on a river, but you might want to bear that in mind if you find yourself heading inland."

"Water won't be a problem," replied Natalia. "I can provide us with fresh water, thanks to my magic." She moved closer, opening and then peering into a sack. "What's in here?"

"Mostly charc, but there's also hard bread."

"I'm not familiar with either of those."

"Charc is dried meat," said Athgar. "It derives its name from its resemblance to charcoal. According to Tonfer Garul, it was a common travel ration back in the days of the Old Kingdom."

"How does it taste?"

"Admittedly, it's a bit chewy but has the advantage of lasting for months. I would caution you, however, to drink lots of water when you eat it, or else your mouth tends to dry out."

"Curious. I don't remember learning anything about it at the Volstrum."

"Does that surprise you? It's not as if the family tells their students about the Old Kingdom. When we met, you'd never even heard of a Therengian."

She smiled. "And now, here I am, embracing that very culture. The Continent would be a better place if we all learned more about one another."

"Agreed, although the history of the Petty Kingdoms makes that difficult."

"Ah, there you are," came Katrin's voice. "I wondered when the four of you might show up." She greeted Natalia with a hug, then stood back. "You look ready to conquer the world."

"And by that," said Natalia, "she means we're not wearing courtly clothes. It might interest you to know, Katrin, this is what we wear on a daily basis back home."

Herulf came up to stand beside Katrin, with Greta soon joining them.

"I hope you didn't mean to leave without saying goodbye," said the girl.

"We wouldn't dare," replied Natalia, "but now everyone's here, we must be off."

Kargen dragged the boat towards the river, letting it slide into the water, then he transferred the sacks into the boat.

"I will take the stern," offered Kargen. "You sit in the front, Shaluhk, and Athgar and Natalia can sit in the middle. We will change positions later in the day to conserve our strength."

"Wise words," said Shaluhk. She climbed into the umak, then steadied it against the dock while Natalia and Athgar took their seats.

"Farewell," said Natalia. "Shaluhk will send daily reports to Voruhn, keeping you informed of our progress."

"I'll be ready," promised Katrin. "You take care of yourselves."

Athgar pushed off, and the umak drifted farther into the river, the current taking them downstream, Kargen steering with his paddle.

Natalia watched the southern bank as they proceeded along the river. "It's hard to believe all that land belongs to us now."

"It is," agreed Kargen. "According to Zharuhl, the game is plentiful here, the perfect area for a tribe to settle."

"Do you think he'll bring the Stone Crushers here?"

"No. Their home is in Khasrahk. They have a history there, but there are other tribes interested in coming east."

"Indeed," said Shaluhk. "They seek a place where Humans will not drive them away."

"They're more than welcome in Therengia," said Athgar.

"So I informed them, but it is not easy to move an entire tribe, particularly when they must traverse Human lands to get here."

"Interesting," said Natalia. "When this is all over, perhaps I shall travel the Petty Kingdoms and offer to bring them here, using my magic."

"You mean we," said Athgar. "I wouldn't want you to do that all by yourself."

"You're the High Thane of Therengia; you can't wander all over the Continent looking for Orcs."

"Why not? That's basically what we've been doing these last few years."

Natalia chuckled. "So it is, but there are other things to consider."

"Such as?"

"The majority of Petty Kingdoms want to eradicate Orcs from the Continent."

"Even more reason to do it. The kings will get full access to their lands while the Orcs settle into new homes in Therengia. It's a victory for both the Humans and the Orcs."

"I wish it were that simple," said Kargen, "but much like the Red Hand, some will choose to remain in their ancestral lands. We cannot force people to abandon their homes."

"You're right. I hadn't considered that. Still, as High Thane, I could try convincing the local rulers to accept the presence of the tribes within their borders? It certainly worked for the Ashwalkers."

"It bears further consideration."

"Tell me," said Shaluhk. "What do you think awaits us in Zaran?"

"That's an excellent question," replied Athgar. "I imagine it's mostly thick forest, so expect the usual: bears, wolves, perhaps even a tusker or two, but if we stick to the river, we should be safe enough."

"What a short memory you have," said Natalia. "The last time we undertook a trip down a river, we encountered a wyvern, and don't forget the river serpent."

"True, but you're a much more accomplished mage now, as am I. Speaking of our last trip, you don't think you could convince another beaver to guide us, do you? I imagine this would be their type of terrain."

"I can't ask a creature to leave their home—it's just not right. I will, however, attempt to speak to some of the local inhabitants once we're on the Zaran River. That might give us some insight about what we could come up against."

Shaluhk sighed. "It is peaceful here. I look forward to the day when we can finally live without fear of someone coveting our land."

"We'll get there in time," said Natalia.

They all fell silent, settling into a steady rhythm with their paddles.

. . .

They came ashore each night to camp, the terrain offering ample fuel for the fire. It was a surreal experience, for there they were, quite literally, in the middle of nowhere, with nothing to occupy their days save for the company of friends and endless paddling. They each took turns, and by Kargen's reckoning, they made close to thirty miles a day. Last summer, he and Shaluhk had travelled upstream from Carlingen to Beorwic in just over a ten-day. This time, they chose a more leisurely approach, conserving their strength for the wilds of Zaran.

When they reached the point where the Zaran River joined the Windrush, they came across their first difficulty. The Zaran was narrow here, with a much faster current than the river it emptied into, making it challenging to navigate upstream. All four paddled, but the water proved too swift. In desperation, they headed ashore, resting after their exertions.

"I hope the entire river isn't like this," said Natalia, "or it will take forever to reach Ruzhina."

"I imagine the river widens once we are farther upstream," replied Kargen. "Back in Ord-Kurgad, the river that formed the border with Krieghoff was similar."

"How did you deal with it there?"

"We carried the umak and any supplies we needed overland."

"How far do you think we would need to travel?"

"I am unable to say."

"Perhaps your magic might help, Nat-Alia," suggested Shaluhk. "Any local creatures would have knowledge of the river's behaviour."

"What a wonderful idea. I shall cast my spell and see what responds." She waded ankle-deep into the river, ensuring her footing was secure lest she be swept away. Closing her eyes, she called on her magic, seeking out what animals were in the area.

Anticipating the spell might take a while, Athgar found a fallen log to rest on. He had only just sat when he noticed a large, dark shadow beneath the river's surface moving deliberately towards Natalia. He opened his mouth to shout a warning, but before he uttered so much as a single word, she turned towards the shape, moving deeper into the river until she was waist-deep.

The shadow nudged her, and then she plunged her face into the water for the count of five, resurfaced, took a breath, and submerged her face again. However, this time, she held her breath longer before coming back up. She shook her head, sending water everywhere before making her way back to Athgar.

"Everything all right?" he called out.

"Yes, it is," she replied. "I was having a pleasant conversation with Satira."

"Who is?"

"I believe you would call her a sea cow, although the term river cow might be more appropriate. They're common in the southern reaches of the Continent, but I'm surprised to see her this far north."

"What did Satira have to say? Does she find the current strong?"

"She does," said Natalia, "although she is strong enough to swim against it. Don't worry, though. The river is wider upstream with a corresponding reduction in speed."

"How far upstream?" asked Kargen.

"From her description, a thousand paces or so."

"Does she know why the current is so strong?"

"Yes. There's a pair of rocks protruding on either side of the river, constricting its passage. Once we get past those, the current eases considerably."

"Athgar and I will scout the area and find the easiest route. You two remain here and watch the supplies. I do not want anything to happen to them."

Athgar strung his bow, then followed Kargen into the trees.

"They should not be gone long," said Shaluhk. "It does not look too difficult to traverse, and they only need to follow the riverbank."

"Still," said Natalia. "We don't know what animals are hereabouts."

"Kargen is an experienced hunter, while Athgar is a powerful master of flame. Little here could threaten them."

"How can you be so certain?"

"Your friend, Satira, would not be in the area if danger threatened."

"What a remarkably keen observation. I wish you'd been with us in Abelard."

"How was Agar on your trip?"

"He spent the bulk of his time with Athgar, but from what I saw of him, he seems to be growing up to resemble his father in terms of being inquisitive, yet I sense your influence in his wisdom. It's remarkable to see it in one so young."

"I often find myself wondering what he will do with his life," said Shaluhk. "I know he will master his inner spark, but I worry he has an unsettled heart."

"Unsettled?"

"Yes. I believe you call it wanderlust. A most curious term, but one that fits him perfectly. He wants to travel the Continent, experiencing life in all its glory. I keep telling him that is dangerous for an Orc, but he does not seem to care."

"I wonder where he gets that from?" asked Natalia.

"I do not know for certain, but I suspect it is a result of recent events. Many have come to Therengia from distant lands, filling his head with tales of strange customs and wondrous places. He wants to experience that himself."

"You don't think he'd run away, do you?"

"No. He understands the dangers of being untrained in the mastery of flame and is committed to learning to control it. Regardless, he won't leave until he passes his ordeal, which is still a few years away."

"He'll wait a little longer than that, I think."

"Why do you say that?" asked Shaluhk.

"Unless I miss my guess, he'll wait until Oswyn comes of age."

"Then they will run away together?"

"Don't think of it as running away," said Natalia. "They simply desire their own adventures. I'm sure, once they're older, they'll keep each other safe."

"They grow up so fast."

"They do. It seems like only yesterday I gave birth, and now Oswyn is running around, itching to try out her bow. I hope she's not too much for Skora."

"Skora helped raise Athgar and his sister. Oswyn is easier in comparison."

"That's mostly due to Agar. She adores him."

"As she should of an older brother."

"We're back," called out Athgar.

"So soon?" said Natalia.

He emerged from the forest. "There's a rough path following the bank of the river."

"A path? Are you suggesting someone lives around here?"

"No. Likely animals local to the region have followed the same route to the river for water, wearing down the underbrush till there's a track."

Kargen soon joined them, slinging the bags of supplies over his shoulder. "It will take several trips to get everything upstream."

"Then it is best you and I do the bulk of the carrying," said Shaluhk. "Now grab those paddles, bondmate mine, and let us be about our business."

# UP THE RIVER

## SPRING 1110 SR

By Athgar's reckoning, they'd travelled fifty or sixty miles up the Zaran River, yet the land had changed little; the forest seeming endless on both sides. At the end of each day, they sought out a small clearing, pulled the umak from the water, and rested for the night.

Nothing seemed out of the ordinary on the fourth day when they came ashore to make camp, but as Shaluhk began working on a fire, she suddenly froze.

"We are being watched," she said.

Kargen drew his axe, then cast his gaze around the area. "By what?"

"I do not know, but I cannot shake the feeling we are not alone."

"What does your magic tell you?"

Shaluhk stood, moved back from the fire, and then turned away from the flames. Words of power tumbled from her lips, her eyes glowing with an inner light, and then she scanned the camp's perimeter.

"What do you see?" said Kargen. "Is something there?"

Shaluhk visibly relaxed. "Do not be alarmed. It is only wolves."

"How many?" asked Athgar.

"Eleven."

"That's hardly comforting. Wolves are dangerous, especially in packs."

"Some tribes raise wolves to aid in the hunt," said Shaluhk. "A master of wolves cares for them."

"Is that a mage of some kind?"

"No. Merely someone skilled in their care."

"But none of our tribes do that."

"No, but far to the west, the Orcs of the Black Arrow do. Their chieftain is also their master of wolves."

"That's strange, isn't it? I would think the role of chieftain enough for anyone."

"It usually is, but his bondmate is a ghostwalker, and wolves are known to calm the spirits of the dead."

"Ghostwalker?" said Natalia. "What's that?"

"On rare occasions, an Orc is born who exists between the land of the living and the spirit realm. They are marked by snow-white hair and a pale complexion, able to see spirits without the aid of magic. Zhura, bondmate to Urgon, is one such individual."

"Is this how they learned wolves calm the spirits?"

"It is."

"If that is so," said Kargen, "then what spirits require calming in Zaran?"

"The presence of wolves does not mean spirits are amongst us."

"Then why are they watching us?" asked Athgar.

"They are likely drawn by the sounds of our voices."

"Couldn't that mean they're here to eat us?"

"No," replied Shaluhk. "They are merely curious, which is a good sign."

"It is?"

"Yes. They would flee at the first hint of danger. Their very presence tells me there is no threat."

"Other than the wolves," Athgar reminded her.

"I have never known you to show a fear of wolves."

"That's because I've never been surrounded by an entire pack."

"I never said we were surrounded."

"So, they're all bunched together?"

"No," replied Shaluhk. "They do have us surrounded, but up until now, I had not indicated it."

"Just to be safe, I'll use one of my spells." Athgar dug deep, drawing on his inner spark. He held out his hands, spreading his fingers, and then tiny flames flew forth to float around the camp's perimeter.

"That's interesting," said Natalia. "I don't believe I'm familiar with that one. What is it?"

"It's called fire watch, taught to me by the Ashwalkers."

"I assume the spell is meant to illuminate the perimeter?"

"Oh, it does much more than that. Watch." Athgar moved closer to a flame, causing it to flare. He then backed up, and it returned to its original level. "Each flame detects movement nearby, brightening in proportion to its proximity and size."

"And if they become very bright?"

"Then we should run."

"How long does it last?"

"That depends on the caster. With no disturbances, they'll last all night, but the brighter they burn, the sooner they extinguish. In addition, a less-experienced master of flame would only be able to produce one or two, whereas I've managed ten."

"I'm impressed," said Natalia. "Any other spells you've been hiding?"

"I can't give away all my secrets. How would I maintain my air of mystery?"

"Interesting," said Kargen. "All three of you have become exceptionally powerful since we met. Perhaps I should have taken up magic myself?"

"Is there magic in your family?"

"No, which is just as well. I much prefer being a hunter."

"I suggest we get some sleep," said Shaluhk. "The wolves will alert us should anything dangerous appear."

"How do you know that?" asked Athgar. "Have you taken up speaking to animals now?"

Shaluhk shook her head. "The pack is gathering in preparation for sleep. Should danger threaten, those left awake will alert the others. I am certain their growls would be sufficient to awaken us." With that, she lay down, using a rolled-up blanket as a pillow.

"Good enough for me," said Kargen, joining her.

Athgar wasn't convinced. "I'll stay up a little longer, just to be certain."

Dawn came far too early for Athgar's liking. It was his own fault; he'd been so suspicious of the wolves, he'd stayed up half the night. However, he needn't have bothered, for with the coming of daylight, it was clear nothing had disturbed his fire watch and entered the camp.

They ate sparingly, keenly aware they had no idea how long they would be travelling for. They could hunt should it prove necessary, or Natalia could cast a frozen portal and send someone through to retrieve food from back home, but such things would only delay their progress.

They continued upriver, and at various points along the way, the trees grew so thick their branches covered the river completely, throwing them into shadows.

The water here took on an unpleasant smell, that of rotting vegetation, and patches of the river, particularly on either bank, grew thick with green algae. Rather than drink from the river, Natalia used her magic to create fresh water.

Late in the afternoon, they spotted a large shape floating ahead of them.

Rather than risk encountering anything dangerous, they paddled to the bank, pulling the umak ashore. Then, taking care to remain as quiet as possible, they walked along the riverbank, attempting to get a better view of whatever it might be.

They'd gone no more than two hundred paces when Natalia halted them. "It's a body."

"What kind of body?" asked Athgar.

"An animal, but it's mostly below the surface."

"Interesting," said Shaluhk. "I suggest we investigate it further. We should try to determine what it is and, even more importantly, what killed it."

"Agreed," said Kargen. "There may be a large predator in the area, and we can't afford to be surprised."

"We'll need the umak," said Athgar. "The river's too deep here."

"I could freeze it," offered Natalia. "Then we could walk over to it."

Kargen shook his head. "No. That would freeze it in place, and we may need to roll it over to identify it. Let me swim to it instead. I'll attach a rope, and then we can drag it to shore."

"Before you go, I'll cast a spell that allows you to breathe underwater, just in case."

"In case of what?" said Athgar.

"We don't know what killed it. There's a distinct possibility it could be something in the water."

"Please cast your spell," said Kargen.

Natalia reached out, placing her hand on the Orc's shoulder. After a few brief words of power escaped her lips, she withdrew it. "There," she said. "You're ready."

"I feel no different."

"That's because the magic doesn't work while you're surrounded by air. Once you're in the water, you'll feel different. I should warn you, though, your body won't enjoy the prospect of breathing underwater. My advice is to dip your head and force yourself to breathe."

"I agree," said Athgar. "It worked for me off the Teeth of Karamir."

"I do not believe I know that story," said Kargen.

"Now is not the time for tales," warned Natalia. "The spell has a limited duration, so you'd best get swimming."

Without any further discussion, Kargen looped a coil of rope over his shoulder, then waded into the water, picking a spot free of algae. As soon as he was waist-deep, he ducked his head under, remaining in place as he accustomed himself to the strange sensation of breathing water.

His hand broke the surface, waving briefly, then he was swimming out to the carcass, his head remaining fully submerged. The others watched him intently, worried, lest something in the water prove dangerous.

Kargen emerged closer to the body. "It is large," he shouted, "but the corpse has started to rot, making it difficult to identify. I shall dive under it and try to find the head." He disappeared beneath the surface once more.

"This does not bode well," said Shaluhk. "There are few creatures Kargen might describe as large, and all of them are dangerous."

Her bondmate surfaced once more, shaking his head. He unwound the rope, then dove again.

"He is coming back now," said Shaluhk.

A dark shape approached, and then Kargen stood up, the other end of the rope firmly in his grasp. "I cannot be certain, but I think that is the body of a tusker."

"That bodes ill," said Shaluhk. "What manner of beast could kill such a creature?"

"Could it have been felled by magic?" asked Athgar.

"We shall soon find out," said Kargen. "Take up the rope and help me haul it to the riverbank where we can examine it better."

They easily dragged the body through the deeper water, but as it drew closer, it hit the bottom of the river, and no amount of pulling made a difference.

"Close enough," said Shaluhk, wading into the waist-deep water by the body. Athgar and Kargen soon joined her, but Natalia remained ashore, watching for any signs of danger.

"Definitely a tusker," announced Athgar. "Looks like it got into a fight."

"With another tusker?" called out Natalia.

"No. Something with claws."

"Indeed," added Kargen. "And by the size of these marks, it was large."

"We once ran into a wyvern; could that be what attacked this creature?"

"I do not believe so. Wyverns sting with their tail and then bite. Their claws are not capable of penetrating the skin of a tusker."

"A dragon?" suggested Natalia.

"That is certainly a possibility, although I am led to believe they live in the mountains, and we have seen no signs of such terrain."

"True," added Shaluhk, "but the thick forest here blocks our view of almost everything. If we gained some height, it might improve our view of the surrounding terrain."

"I wonder," said Athgar. "Could a weapon have made these marks?"

"What weapon could pierce skin that thick? From our own experience, we know spears have minimal effect on such beasts."

"Yet Kargen felled one!"

"Only with help," replied Shaluhk, "and that beast was smaller than this." She looked at her bondmate. "I did not intend to belittle your accomplishments, but whatever killed this tusker is significantly more powerful than anything we have encountered before."

"We once came across a river snake," said Athgar. "Could that have done it?"

"Possibly," replied Natalia. "They use constriction as their primary method of attack. Are there any signs the body was crushed?"

"Not that I can see," said Shaluhk.

"Can we determine how old the body is?"

"I would guess between three and five days. Anything less, and it would be lying on the bottom of the river. If it were older, the flesh would be more decayed."

"I wish it were longer," said Athgar. "Whatever was responsible might still be hereabouts. After all, why leave an area with plentiful food?"

"I do not believe it was killed for food," replied Kargen. "There are no signs that any flesh was removed."

"Then why kill it?"

Kargen shrugged. "Perhaps it stumbled into another creature's territory or threatened its young."

"Agreed. Now, did the attack come from the air or from ground level?"

"Just out of curiosity," said Natalia, "how do you know it wasn't attacked from the water?"

"The legs are mostly intact, as is the underbelly, which are the obvious targets for a river creature."

"I agree," said Kargen. "The claw marks could be made from something airborne, but perhaps the attacker was taller?"

"Either way, I'm not eager to meet whatever did this."

"Nor am I," added Shaluhk. "I suggest the safest way to proceed is by remaining in the umak and keeping a close eye on the riverbanks and the sky."

"I second that," said Natalia.

"Have you any magic that might give us warning of an attack?"

"I'm afraid not. How about you, Athgar? Any more surprises lurking beneath your cloak of mystery?"

Her husband laughed. "No. If I knew how, I could conjure a phoenix, but they possess no mind of their own. In any case, the Ashwalkers didn't have that in their collection of spells."

"And your fire watch?"

"It's stationary, I'm afraid. We'll have to rely on good old-fashioned eyes to warn us of any danger."

"Not so," said Kargen. "We also have ears, not to mention noses."

"A good point," replied Athgar. "What about summoning another water mammal?"

"It's worth a try," said Natalia. She moved upstream a few paces and closed her eyes, seeking her inner peace, then called it forth, letting the words of power flow through her in a steady stream. The call went out, but she felt no response, only emptiness as if the river were dead. Her eyes snapped open.

"Locate anything?" asked Athgar.

"No," she replied. "Nothing at all. To the best of my knowledge, no creatures in the area are capable of responding to my call."

"That might have something to do with the dead tusker."

"No. It would dissuade other predators, but river life should carry on. This is most unusual."

"Something has scared them off," declared Shaluhk. "Something dangerous."

"Strange," said Athgar. "I thought we determined the threat didn't come from the water. Wouldn't that suggest the river was safe from attack?"

"We found the tusker's body floating in the water. Whatever attacked must be large enough that the river's depth was no barrier, or the tusker ran into the river after being attacked, then died of its wounds."

"I don't suppose you could talk to its spirit?"

"No," replied Shaluhk. "I can only communicate with Orc Ancestors."

"Are you certain?"

"I have never tried anything else, but it stands to reason that I must understand its language to speak with a spirit. Perhaps if I were a master of earth, it might be another matter. But if that were true, I would not be able to call the spirit in the first place."

"This is making my head spin," said Kargen. "Let us be on our way. The sooner we leave here, the better."

They returned to the umak and pushed it out into the river. The forest surrounding them was quiet, uncomfortably so, reminding Athgar of the legends of Zaran. If the stories were true, hundreds had disappeared here, and he held no desire to be counted amongst their number.

They proceeded in silence, alert for any signs of danger. Every single sound drew their attention, from a snapping twig to the rushing water, to such an extent that an unease overwhelmed them.

The sun grew lower in the sky, and they found themselves travelling into ever-deepening shadows. Usually, they would search for a spot to camp, but the oppressive atmosphere drove them to keep paddling well past nightfall.

Athgar conjured forth a magical flame to light the way, the green fire floating above his hand. It allowed them to see the immediate area, but the shadows it produced on the thick trees lining the riverbank only made them much more nervous.

Time ceased to have any meaning as they paddled through the night. The view of the sky here was limited to a narrow stretch directly overhead, making navigation by stars impossible. Instead, they could only follow the river, wherever it led them.

# WATERFALL

SPRING 1110 SR

Kargen paused mid-stroke. "Do you hear that?"

"Unless I'm mistaken," said Natalia, "that's a waterfall."

The rumbling sound increased as they paddled harder. The river turned slightly to the right, and before them appeared a massive cascade that fell from a cliff high above: a two-hundred-foot drop from an escarpment that ran as far as the eye could see.

"It appears our way is blocked," said Athgar. "I don't fancy the idea of carting the umak up there, not to mention our supplies."

"There is another way," said Natalia. "Pull over to the left bank, and let me take a closer look."

Shaluhk, sitting in the rear this day, steered them to shore. They were soon on dry land, their eyes glued to the sight before them.

"Well?" said Athgar. "What are you thinking?"

"There's a flat area of rock at the top, on the right-hand side. Do you see it?"

"I do, but how does it help us?"

"If I can get up there, I can cast a frozen arch spell."

"I'm not certain that will do anything. We're trying to get up a waterfall, not go home."

"When we were in Andover, I used the spell to escape the Royal Palace. I need only see the target area to connect to it with an arch."

"Couldn't you cast it from here?"

"No. I need to see the anchor point, and we're too low relative to the source of the falls. If I can get up there, connecting that flat area to this spot here would be simple. Who's the best climber?"

"Kargen," said Shaluhk. "He was known as the tree snake in his youth."

"Then he and I will make the ascent."

"Shouldn't we all go?" asked Athgar.

"No. Someone needs to watch our supplies. The last thing we need is to get to the top only to discover a wild animal ransacked our camp."

"What animal? We haven't seen hide nor hair of anything since we found that carcass."

"True," replied Shaluhk, "but the tusker came from somewhere, and I doubt it fell down that waterfall."

"A good point, but Natalia's never climbed anything like that before."

"I shall go first," offered Kargen, "then lower a rope for Nat-Alia to use."

"You'll need a lot more rope than we have."

"Then we will do it in stages. I see some ledges here and there that should suffice for a resting space for Nat-Alia while I ascend to the next section."

"And what should we do in the meantime?"

"Fret," said Shaluhk. "It is what all bondmates do when their loved one is in jeopardy. We will also watch for any signs of danger. Remember, we still do not know what killed that tusker."

Kargen pointed. "We will start there, at that mass of rubble at the bottom of the gorge that forms a ramp. Thereafter, we will be climbing an almost vertical cliff face."

"This would be an ideal time for a spell of scrying," said Natalia. "Too bad we don't have an Enchanter with us."

"Have we ever actually met one?" asked Athgar. "I remember Fire and Water Mages, and we suspected Air Mages were at work off the coast of Corassus, but I can't recall anyone capable of casting enchantments."

"Nor I, which is a pity, considering Greta's potential in that field. Hopefully, we can seek one out once we've dealt with the Volstrum. That doesn't help us at this particular moment, but it's always good to keep an eye on the future."

"I know of tribes who practice such magic," said Shaluhk. "The Night Dreamers come to mind, but even they are in far-off Talyria."

"Then perhaps, when this is all over, we'll visit them."

"Agreed," said Kargen, "but we should concentrate on the task at hand, which is getting up that cliff face. Come, Nat-Alia. It is time we start climbing."

Athgar leaned against the umak, watching as Kargen and Natalia traversed the steep, rocky slope. It demanded their utmost attention to keep a stable footing, but their progress was relatively swift. They rested as they reached the base of the cliff, Natalia turning to wave back at Athgar and Shaluhk.

"What do you suppose they will find up there?" asked Shaluhk.

"Nothing good, I'll wager. This entire area feels so…"

"So, what?"

"I was going to say primitive. It's as though it's lain untouched for thousands of years."

"It likely has. Most of the eastern lands are untrodden, and I know of no one who ventured this far north and returned to tell of it."

Athgar's gaze turned eastward, though nothing was there save for thick forest. "I wonder what strange sights lay undiscovered. Until we came to Therengia, we had never seen a tusker. I suppose even stranger beasts might exist farther out in the unexplored regions."

"We shall likely never know," said Shaluhk, "but perhaps future generations will travel there, seeking to unlock whatever mysteries lurk within."

Kargen climbed the cliff face, digging in with fingers to grasp small crevices in the rock. He progressed swiftly but needed to locate a ledge for Natalia to rest. He glanced over his shoulder, judging the distance down to her. Any farther, and he would lack the rope to pull her up. He looked to either side, searching for a suitable position. He moved to the right, feeling the lip of a ledge, and hauled himself onto it and sat, dangling his legs over the edge as he caught his breath.

He leaned over, waving, catching Natalia's attention. "I found a ledge," he shouted. "Give me a chance to rest, and then I shall lower the rope." She waved back in reply. Kargen was only half the way up, but it gave him a good view of the area, not that there was much to see. On either side of the river, trees stretched to the horizon. With the cliff blocking his view north, anything could be up there, from mountains to ancient fortresses. Would he reach the top only to come face to face with creatures even larger than a tusker?

Kargen shook it off, then stood, removing the rope from his shoulder. He tied one end around his waist before lowering the other to Natalia. She waited until it was unrolled, then began climbing, quickly pulling herself up the rope, and soon took Kargen's proffered hand to join him on the ledge. "That was easier than I imagined," she said.

"Perhaps, but it will only get worse. The cliff above has a slight overhang. The next time you climb, the rope will hang free rather than against the rock wall." He gathered up the rope and looped it around his neck and shoulder. "It is time for me to climb again." With that, he was scrambling up the stone wall, finding handholds in the tiniest crevices.

"I am curious," said Shaluhk. "What else did you learn from the Ashwalkers?"

"You know most of it," replied Athgar. "The ability to resist fire and the fire watch spell." He paused momentarily. "Oh yes. There was something else: a ball of fire that could be tossed back and forth, building in intensity and a spell you set in place like a ward."

"And what does it do?"

"It sends a flame skyward if anything large comes close. The Ashwalkers used them to mark their territory."

"I would think such a spell would have limited usefulness."

"What makes you say that?"

"Look around you," said Shaluhk. "Much of this forest is dry. A flame such as you describe could rapidly grow to engulf the entire area."

"I hadn't considered that. Fortunately, their new home in the Thornwood isn't nearly as dense as it is here."

"You have surpassed the teachings of Artoch. These spells you learned were not known to him."

"You yourself have unlocked unknown magic."

"Yes, the result of retaining Khurlig's memories after her possession. Now that I have had time to sift through them, I realize how deep her knowledge of life and death was."

"I should think that makes you the most powerful shaman in all of Eiddenwerthe."

"Do not confuse knowledge with power. Yes, I have Khurlig's memories, but that does not strengthen my magic; it merely unlocks long-forgotten spells. Power is measured by the ability of a mage to control the energy within. By that measure, Nat-Alia is the most powerful mage to ever exist, as evidenced by her mastery of the ley lines."

"Do you know of any shamans who rival your own abilities?"

"Laghul and Voruhn possess a more limited collection of spells but are as powerful as I am. If we expand our search outside Therengia, then I would say Aubrey is the most powerful I know, though she is a Life Mage, not a shaman."

"She's the Human from the west, isn't she?"

"She is. I hope to meet her one day, for the exchange of information would be most rewarding."

Athgar glanced up at the waterfall. Natalia was three-quarters of the way up the cliff face, sitting with her legs dangling over a ledge while Kargen climbed the last stretch. "It won't be long now," he mused, "then we can continue our journey."

"What is that?" said Shaluhk.

"I don't see anything."

"There," she replied, pointing eastward.

In the distance, a tiny speck glided high up in the air. As it grew closer, Athgar noticed flapping wings. "What in the name of the Gods is that?"

"Whatever it is, it is huge."

Athgar looked back to the cliff face where Kargen had neared the top while Natalia watched him from below. He knew he shouldn't worry, for they had plenty of time to complete their climb before the distant flier drew close, but something nagged at him. He returned his gaze to the intruder. "There's something odd about it," he said, "but I can't figure out what."

"I noticed it too," said Shaluhk. "It is closing remarkably fast, far faster than I would expect."

The creature turned, flying parallel to them. In form, it was not too dissimilar to the rygaurs Athgar and Natalia had encountered in the south, but on a substantially larger scale. Even from this distance, they could make out its dog-like head attached to a body that stretched out, ending in a snakelike tail. A fin running down its back made it look even more serpentine, and when it screeched, it revealed rows of teeth.

"I don't like the sound of that," said Athgar.

It flew above the river, heading south before turning west to cross over the waterway, then turned north. Another screech echoed off the cliff face, and the creature began a shallow dive, aiming straight for Kargen.

"Look out!" yelled Athgar, but the waterfall made it impossible for the Orc to hear his warning. He looked skyward once more, finding it hard to focus on the creature, for the air surrounding it writhed with dark smoke as if it had flown directly out of the Underworld. With a final flap of its membranous wings, it plummeted towards the top of the cliff.

Kargen had climbed to the top and was in the midst of lowering the rope to Natalia, so he didn't see the approaching horror until it was almost upon him, but he reacted fast, dropping to the ground as its claws reached for him.

The thing flew directly overhead, missing his head by a finger's breadth, then continued following the river northward, eventually disappearing around a bend.

A surge of relief ran through Athgar. He rushed forward to the base of the slope, calling out to Natalia, but she had already begun climbing the last length of rope. Fearful the creature might return, he searched the sky, finding nothing. Then, he caught sight of Shaluhk pointing skyward and followed her gaze to spot the creature flying south incredibly fast.

He pointed at it as he called on his inner spark. Flames shot out from his fingertips, climbing skyward, but he'd miscalculated the beast's speed in his haste, and his attack missed.

Onward, it rushed at an astonishing speed, flying straight up before it flipped around and dove back down, heading straight for the waterfall.

Athgar readied another streak of fire, aiming directly in its path, but it swerved to the left at the last moment, displaying remarkable agility.

He considered stringing his bow, but the beast flew so fast it would be long gone before he could nock an arrow. He lifted his arms, ready to cast again, but the creature was too close to Natalia.

She was halfway up when its massive claws plucked her from the rope, and then the creature was flying west, paralleling the cliff face with Natalia clutched in its grasp.

Athgar watched in horror as it climbed into the air, its powerful wings flapping, each stroke taking her farther away. Athgar dared not cast a spell for fear of hitting his wife, yet what else could he do, simply watch her carted off as food?

Kargen had strung his warbow, an arrow flying from the top of the cliff, striking the tail, but it did not slow it down. The creature flew on, the arrow now a mere decoration.

---

Natalia struggled to breathe, one arm crushed against her by the massive claw, the other reaching out, desperate to pry herself loose.

Blood flowed freely from her left arm even as it pressed into her side. The creature's talons had reached out, one cutting deeply into flesh, the other tearing her from her position on the rope. Now she was hurtling upward, its vice-like grip crushing her lungs.

She fought to remain conscious but grew more light-headed as the blood pumped out of her veins. Was this how it all ended, carried aloft by a strange beast, never to be seen again? Her heart went out to Athgar, flooding her with a desire to live. She closed her eyes, trying to cast a spell, but a wave of intense pain invaded her concentration. Her life was bleeding out, her strength diminishing with every breath.

She weakly raised her hand, grasping the creature's leg as she had the mage hunter, Nikolai, all those years ago. Her power built, and the soothing embrace of her magic enveloped her as it poured out. Her fingers turned frosty, ice creeping out, spreading over the creature's leg and down its foot, the air turning frigid as the talons froze over.

As frost turned to ice, the creature let out a horrific wail. The talons released their prey, sending chunks of ice flying, and then Natalia was falling, staring up in shock at the massive beast above her.

---

Athgar held his breath as Natalia fell, unable to turn away from the horrific sight of her plummeting hundreds of feet, building up speed as she tumbled through the air.

He glanced at Shaluhk to see her running for the river, not understanding why. He struggled to think of anything he could do to save her, even contemplated using his magic to spare her the pain of death, but he could do nothing except watch, mesmerized as she struck the river, her limbs hanging loose, her head lolling to one side, and a plume of water exploded upwards.

# LOSS

SPRING 1110 SR

Pain. Searing, burning agony. Natalia's flesh was on fire, a pain unlike anything she'd ever experienced. Was this the Underworld, where she would spend an eternity writhing in anguish? She tried moving her limbs, but they wouldn't respond. Her heart pounded, and she felt her life draining away.

In desperation, she called out, but no sound emerged. She forced her eyes open to see Athgar staring down at her, dripping wet. She needed to tell him how much she loved him before death claimed her, but only a tormented scream escaped her lips.

---

Shaluhk's hands glowed as she gently placed them on Natalia, the colour bleeding into her broken body, illuminating her many injuries.

"Will she live?" said Athgar.

"Although her wounds are grievous, I can heal the flesh, but there is something more." She nodded at the claw marks on Natalia's arm. The flesh was torn, and beneath the wound, something festered, turning the flesh putrid as it spread.

"What is it?"

"Necrotic rot," replied Shaluhk. "I have never seen it before, but the memories of Khurlig know it well."

"Can you cure it?"

She shook her head. "It is spreading too fast. If it reaches her heart, it will kill her."

"There must be something we can do?"

"Ready your axe, for you must sever the limb before it spreads further."

Horror filled Athgar's face as he stared back. "Surely not?"

"A limb I can regenerate, but even the most powerful shamans cannot bring back the dead." She looked at Natalia, whose eyes flicked around in fear. "I shall put her to sleep. It is best she is not awake for this." Power built within Shaluhk, and then she touched Natalia's forehead, and she went limp. "Your axe. Now!"

Athgar pulled forth his axe, his hands shaking as he held it overhead.

"You must cut here," said Shaluhk. "Halfway between the elbow and the shoulder. Do you understand?"

He nodded, too shocked to give words to his fears.

Shaluhk pulled Natalia's arm out straight. "Sever it in one blow and be quick about it before it is too late."

The axe came down with all the strength Athgar could muster. He'd cleaved through countless enemy warriors in battle with nary a thought, but this was by far the worst thing he'd ever been forced to do. The blade struck, making a clean cut, blood spurting forth from the stump. Bile rose in his throat, and he turned away, expelling the contents of his stomach.

Behind him, magic poured out of Shaluhk, but he couldn't bear to watch. He retched again and again until it felt like his stomach had turned inside out, then a hand grasped his shoulder.

"It is done," said Shaluhk.

He looked past the Orc to see Natalia lying peacefully in slumber.

"Will she survive?"

"Yes. Her spirit is strong, but she lost much blood and will need to rest."

"And her arm?"

"The spell of regeneration takes time to work. If you recall, when you and Kargen were badly burned back in Ord-Kurgad, it was nearly a ten-day before your flesh healed."

"We should never have come here."

"We all knew the risk, Nat-Alia included."

"Will she be able to use her magic?"

"Yes, though her casting will be hampered until her arm is fully restored. Has she ever cast a spell one-handed?"

"I believe so. Why?"

"She can likely still do so, although I suspect the frozen arch will not be possible. Spells of that power require concentration, and a weakened limb would prove most distracting."

"Then it looks like we're stuck here for a while."

Shaluhk nodded. "Now, let us make her comfortable. Her body needs to recover."

Kargen returned from the top of the cliff, though he had little to tell them. The plateau above was similar to the river below, thick with trees and silence.

"Even the birds have abandoned the area," he mused. "Could that thing have chased them away?"

"There is something far darker within that forest," replied Shaluhk. "I can sense it."

"Perhaps it is time to reconsider our plan."

"No. Natalia would want us to carry on."

"And we will," replied Kargen, "once she fully recovers, but I worry there might be worse things ahead."

"What did you make of that monstrosity?" asked Athgar.

Kargen mulled it over. "I believe it killed the tusker."

"Did it, though? We saw no sign of necrotic rot on the carcass."

"Perhaps we did," said Shaluhk. "If you recall, the body was rotting."

"All bodies rot, eventually."

"True, but what if the tusker was a fresher kill than we thought, the rot making it appear older?"

"Is that sort of thing common?" asked Athgar. "How does such a creature survive without being killed by its own venom?"

"It is not venom," said Shaluhk. "Necrotic rot is only found amongst the animated dead."

"Are you suggesting that creature wasn't alive?"

"That is the most logical explanation."

"How would it come to be in the wilderness?"

"That," said Kargen, "is an excellent question. I do not know much about the living dead, but I surmise they are not naturally born."

"You are correct," replied Shaluhk. "Creatures of that ilk are created by acts of Necromancy. The spirit realm has creatures with similar powers, but they cannot enter the world of the living without a bridge into our world."

"That tends to support the rumours of Vicavia delving into forbidden magic."

"It does."

"We're too far south for Vicavia," said Athgar. "She's supposed to live off the eastern border of Ruzhina."

"Perhaps her domain is larger than we realized?" offered Kargen. "It is possible we were given false information."

"Or this creature escaped captivity," said Shaluhk. "It has no natural predators to fear and could find plenty of food to sustain it."

"Do the living dead still need food?"

"It expends strength to survive, so it makes sense it must replace that energy. It would likely not eat in the traditional sense but would absorb the life force of its victims. The dead tusker supports that since its flesh, though rotting, remained relatively intact. If you recall, we saw no signs of bite marks, only the raking of claws."

"You're right," said Athgar. "Now tell me, do creatures like that reproduce?"

"Not as far as I know," replied Shaluhk. "There is also no truth to stories about their victims becoming living dead, at least from Khurlig's memories."

"Still, it proves a Necromancer is out there or was at one time."

"You raise a valid concern. A Necromancer either created or summoned this creature, but we have no evidence of how long it has been in existence. With plentiful sources of energy nearby, this creature could live for centuries."

"I'm not sure if that's reassuring or not."

"We can discuss this later," said Kargen. "It will soon be dark, and if we are to be here a ten-day, then we should build ourselves a campfire."

"You two gather wood," said Shaluhk. "I shall check on Nat-Alia before I contact Voruhn to inform her of what has transpired."

They dragged the umak farther into the woods, hiding it lest the creature return, then built a campfire. Athgar cast his fire watch spell, but it did little to calm their nerves. It was an eerie sensation, being in the thick of a forest with no signs of life, running water the only sound besides their movement.

After a restless night, they set about building a shelter for Natalia. Collapsed trunks and rotting branches strewn about the forest floor provided them with all they needed. They built a frame of wood, tying it together with plant fibres that Shaluhk twisted into a thin rope. They collected greenery to create a roof, resulting in a small hut that could hold all four, if necessary, though it would be crowded.

They kept the fire outside, for Athgar cast his spell of warmth on everyone. Instead, it became the focal point of their camp, chasing away the shadows when darkness descended.

Natalia finally awoke that evening, her complexion even paler than usual. After a second day of rest and another regeneration spell, Natalia got up and gingerly moved around the camp. She was not ready to continue their journey but was on the mend.

Kargen explored the area, though he kept to the forest rather than expose himself to a threat from above. The cliff remained an obstacle, but over the next few days, he searched its base, looking for an easier way up. He discovered a place where the trees grew right against the cliff edge, offering more protection from airborne threats. With Shaluhk's help, they fashioned additional lengths of rope, enough to pull Natalia up to the top once she was fully recovered. Then she only needed to move closer to the edge of the falls, where she could cast her frozen arch.

The days wore on, and after a week, signs of life returned to the area. The birds appeared first, no longer scared by the strange creature that had attacked them. Whatever it was had gone off seeking greener pastures.

Shaluhk's magic did its job, and by the morning of the ninth day, she cast her final regeneration spell. Natalia flexed her fingers, looking in wonder at the newly restored limb.

"It feels stiff," she remarked, "as if it's been out in the cold."

"The muscles are like those of a newborn, requiring attention to develop further. Try casting something."

Natalia closed her eyes, digging deep to summon her inner power. Moments later, she snapped them open and pointed at a distant tree. A large spike of ice flew from her fingertips, missing the target by a few paces. "My power is still intact, but I've lost my accuracy."

"That will return once the muscles are restored to their former strength. I suggest you practice casting as much as possible, as it will help your body adjust to the change."

"I can't thank you enough for saving me, Shaluhk. I thought I was dead."

"I could not let my tribe-sister die here, in the middle of nowhere, but you should be thanking Athgar, not me. He pulled you from the river."

"Without your healing, I would have perished."

"And without him, you would have drowned. I could not pull you from the river, for I am not a good swimmer."

"I shall keep that in mind."

Athgar and Kargen wandered into camp carrying the body of a deer.

"What's this, now?" said Natalia.

Athgar grinned. "It seems larger prey has returned to the region." He paused as he looked at her arm. "How does it feel?"

"A little stiff, but I'll get used to it."

"Good," added Kargen. "Then we can soon continue on our way."

"Today?"

"No," replied the Orc. "We have a deer to cut up and prepare for travel. Tomorrow, perhaps?" He looked at his bondmate.

"Tomorrow will be fine," replied Shaluhk.

"Good. Athgar and I will prepare this, and then we shall have a feast to celebrate the occasion."

They set off the next day, making it a full ten-day since Natalia's injury, just as Shaluhk predicted. Rather than split up, they hid the umak, then proceeded up the cliff, using the new path Kargen had discovered.

Natalia stood at the lip of the cliff, looking upriver, seeking a place to act as an anchor point for her spell. She soon found a large, flat rock, around five paces wide. Her attention then turned to the river below them, picking out a section of the riverbank clear of trees.

Athgar came up beside her. "Are you certain you're up to this?"

"I'd better be," she replied, "or we'll be stuck up the river without an umak." She chuckled, the first sign of mirth she'd displayed since her injury. "It's funny. Being here, in the middle of nowhere, just the four of us."

"In what way?"

"It sounds like a joke. Three mages and a hunter walk into the wilderness. I suppose I'm still waiting to see what the punchline is."

"We don't need to continue. We can return to Runewald, and no one will complain."

"No," she said. "We must see this through—I have to see this through. The family has been my private nightmare for far too long. I want Oswyn to grow up without having to constantly look over her shoulder. She can't do that when the Volstrum is out there, searching for her."

"What can I do to help?"

"Stand behind me and hold on to my waist, like you do when we're at sea."

"You're that unsteady?"

"I find it hard to explain. It's as if my body is no longer accustomed to the weight of my arm, and it's throwing me off balance. Don't worry. I won't fall, but even a wobble might send my magic careening off target."

"And if you do miss?"

She laughed. "This doesn't require a fine degree of accuracy. As long as the arch opens up somewhere near the river down there, it's fine."

"You cast," said Kargen. "Shaluhk and I will go through and retrieve the umak." The two Orcs moved over to the flat rock in anticipation. "You may begin whenever you wish."

Natalia concentrated on her target, bringing forth the magic from within. A sense of power flushed through her as if water rushed through her veins, then two pillars of ice formed in front of the Orcs. She kept up the effort until the top of the arch finished forming.

With the first arch complete, she turned towards the bottom of the falls, tracing the river downstream until she spotted the selected point for the other arch. More power poured forth, and then the ground below frosted five paces to the right of her intended target. Part of her rebelled at the thought she'd missed her intended focal point, but she was thankful it ended up in the general vicinity. Instead of recasting, she poured more energy into the spell and was rewarded by the arch of ice taking form. She felt the connection between the two end points take hold, knowing it would no longer require her full concentration to maintain it.

Kargen and Shaluhk entered the frozen arch on the cliff face, reappearing below at the side of the river. They'd loaded the supplies into the umak, so they only needed to drag the boat back with them.

Athgar watched with avid interest. It was one thing to step through the arch and quite another to witness it in operation. It defied all reason, for half the umak was down below while the other half was at the top of the cliff, exiting the portal.

"We are finished," called out Kargen.

Natalia released her hold on her spell, the two archways shattering into chunks of ice.

"How do you feel?" asked Athgar.

"A little tired," she replied. "My arm is sore from the strain of casting, but at least it worked."

"You'll be back to normal in no time."

"Let us get the umak into the river," said Shaluhk. "The sooner we're away from this place, the better."

They dragged the umak upriver and then placed it in the water. Kargen held it steady as they all climbed in, then pushed them out, pulling himself in at the last moment. The current grabbed the boat, dragging it back towards the waterfall, and then they all dug in with the paddles.

The sounds of nature were more pronounced here, and Natalia even spotted some fish. Insects buzzed, birds chirped, and the occasional sound of scurrying feet revealed plentiful wildlife.

Natalia still had one weak arm, but the rest paddled almost continuously, trying to put as much distance between them and the waterfall as possible. As night approached, they stopped at a small clearing and soon had a fire going to ward off the darkness.

Natalia sat before the fire, listening to the sounds of nature. "It's nice here," she said. "There's a sense of peace I haven't felt since we left Carlingen."

"We should still remain alert," warned Kargen. "There is no telling what dangers lurk in these parts."

# THE BRIDGE

## SPRING 1110 SR

The terrain changed as they continued, the forest giving way to cliffs on either side of the river, leaving them nowhere to go but through the bottom of the gorge.

"I don't like this," said Athgar, peering up at the giant walls of stone. "This terrain looks like a place a dragon would inhabit."

"Dragons don't exist anymore," said Natalia. "We learned all about them at the Volstrum."

"Yes, they do," insisted Shaluhk.

They turned to her in surprise.

"Belgast is full of stories," said Athgar, "but that's a far cry from them being real."

"A dragon named Melethandil helped our friends to the west, and two more dragons were at that same battle."

"Where did these dragons come from?"

"The Kurathian Isles," replied Shaluhk. "The princes who rule there pride themselves on raising them."

Athgar gazed skyward. "I felt safer not knowing that."

"We are safe from dragons on the river."

"What makes you so certain?"

"They are large creatures with massive wingspans; the cliffs on either side would prove too restrictive."

"Still, that doesn't preclude an attack by something else. I might remind you that wyverns are smaller and more than capable of killing us."

"This is not like you, Athgar," said Kargen. "I have never known you to show such fear."

"I'm sorry. Natalia's injury has me on edge. It reminded me how fragile life is."

"That is understandable. To ease your fears, I suggest one of us always watches the sky."

They continued along the gorge, slowing their paddling to conserve strength. It felt like the cliffs were pressing in on them, for the farther they went, the closer the rock walls came to the river's edge. The channel narrowed until they could reach out on either side and touch the walls with the end of their paddles.

"I see something," Natalia called out.

Athgar looked skyward, expecting it to swoop down on them. "I don't see anything."

"No. Look ahead." She pointed to where a thin line stretched across the top of the gorge. As they advanced, it became apparent someone had built a rope bridge spanning the gap. They halted the umak, Kargen reaching out to steady them against the left-hand cliff face.

"The question is," said Athgar, "who built it?"

"The logical deduction," replied Shaluhk, "would be Karzik and his men, which seems to prove they survived."

"Perhaps," said Natalia, "but why this far east? The coast would have been a better place for him to build his empire."

"I can think of several reasons," replied Kargen. "Chief of which is game. Perhaps the coastal regions made for poor hunting?"

"Or they found something here," offered Athgar. "Something worth remaining for."

"Such as?"

"Gold springs to mind. Of course, if that were true, I would have expected them to return home. There's not much point in mining gold if you can't use it."

"We need a better look at that bridge," said Natalia. "We can speculate all we want, but without proof, that's all it is." She turned to Kargen. "Feel like climbing another cliff?"

"Someone needs to develop a spell for climbing," replied Athgar.

"There is one used by Enchanters. Unfortunately, none of us can cast it."

"I will climb it," offered Kargen, "and we still have that extra rope Shaluhk made. My main concern is where Nat-Alia will create the archway in the gorge. You need land to anchor the spell, do you not?"

"I do, but I think I have the solution." She called on her inner magic, then reached over the side of the umak, dipping her hand in the river. The water thickened with frost, then ice formed, quickly spreading to both banks, locking the umak in place.

"How long will that last?"

"I only need to reinforce it occasionally so it won't melt. Once you're atop the cliff, lower the rope, and I'll re-freeze the river, then climb up and join you. It should hold until then."

"And when we decide to continue upriver?"

Natalia smiled. "I don't need to touch the water to freeze it—I just need to see it."

Shaluhk chuckled. "Up you go, Tree Snake, but be careful. We do not know what might lie atop the cliffs."

"I shall be cautious," said Kargen. He stepped onto the ice and examined the rock wall until he found his path of ascent. He wedged his fingers into the stone and hauled himself upwards.

"Useful skill that," said Athgar. "Perhaps I should learn how to climb?"

"Why?" replied Natalia. "Runewald is flat, hardly the terrain requiring such skills."

"Yes. I suppose that's true."

Kargen reached over the top, grabbed the edge, and hauled himself upwards enough to see. The bridge was several hundred paces to the right, but the land atop the gorge was uneven, with scattered rocks and occasional clumps of trees, a much different sight from what they'd experienced so far. He saw no signs of danger, so he pulled himself up and looked around, getting a better view of the area.

Not far to the south, a sturdy tree root stuck out of the ground, emerging from between a large, cracked rock. He tied off one end of the rope before he lowered the other down the cliff face, careful not to let it hit anyone.

The snap of a twig grabbed his attention, and he twisted around. Nothing was in sight, but he couldn't help feeling someone, or something, was watching him. He let go of the rope, then drew his warbow and nocked an arrow.

He knelt, searching for signs of tracks, but found none on the hard stone. Any number of creatures could inhabit terrain like this, but that was beyond Kargen's experience. They'd crossed the Grey Spire Mountains, but that had been with an entire tribe whose very numbers scared off anything dangerous. He quietly moved up to the closest knot of trees, listening for any movement.

A low growl erupted from the shadows, and then something moved. Kargen caught a brief glimpse of a large cat racing off to the north and then relaxed. He was safe, at least for the moment. He carefully examined the copse of trees lest another predator lay in hiding, but his fear proved unfounded. He returned to the cliff face to find Natalia waiting for him.

"Trouble?" she asked, noting his bow.

"Just an animal," he replied. "It fled when I came close, but I saw no other signs of danger."

"Then I shall create my frozen arch."

Kargen moved closer, gazing northward. From his new vantage point, he saw large posts erected on either side of the gorge, from which ropes hung, supporting the bridge. It was a curious construction, unlike anything he had seen before, yet its design made sense.

He felt a slight drop in temperature as Natalia called forth her first arch. She then stepped closer to the cliff edge to cast her second. He knew when it was complete, for the upper arch revealed Athgar and Shaluhk standing by the river. They dragged the umak through, and then Natalia dismissed the spell.

Kargen moved closer, grabbing the bow of the boat and dragging it towards the copse of trees. "We shall hide it over there"—he pointed—"then we can go investigate that bridge."

They stowed the boat and headed north, following the edge of the gorge. The bridge looked sturdy, with two massive wooden poles sank into the stone on either side, thick ropes stretching across between them, and additional, smaller lines supporting the wooden planks.

Shaluhk stopped to examine the larger, upright poles. "Magic was at play here," she said. "See where the stone was softened to allow the wood to be anchored?"

"Earth Magic," agreed Natalia. "I don't recall the stories of Karzik including mages, do you?"

"No. Someone else must be responsible for building this bridge."

"I agree," added Athgar. "And whoever built it knew what they were doing. This isn't the work of primitive people, not if they're sinking timbers into the rock."

"Primitive?" said Kargen. "Who is to say what is primitive? Amongst the Humans of the Continent, Orcs are seen as primitive, yet we possess magic."

"You're right. My own people are considered primitive amongst the cities of the Petty Kingdoms. I meant to say that whoever built this knows a thing or two about bridge construction."

"On that, we agree." Kargen glanced westward. "There is a trail heading in that direction, but the prevalence of weeds indicates it is seldom used."

"Weeds?" replied Natalia. "Amongst the rocks? How strange. This bears further investigation." She moved away from the bridge, stooping to examine the ground. "Look here," she said at last. "Someone has taken pains to lay fitted stones, but over the years, dirt has hidden them. This is a road."

"Who builds a road in the middle of nowhere?"

"Something of importance lies to the west, important enough to warrant a road. It also indicates the presence of trade at some point in the past."

"So which way do we go—across the bridge to the east or farther west?"

"I suggest west," replied Shaluhk. "The coast is that way, and civilization tends to be found near water."

"True," said Natalia, "but for all we know, there could be an entire sea to the east."

"There are no recent tracks," said Athgar. "Whoever built this road is long gone. What about calling on the Ancestors?"

Shaluhk shook her head. "I doubt anyone died here, and judging from the state of this road, it has been centuries since this path was trodden."

"It worked in Beorwic."

"Yes, but Beorwic lay dormant for only a few centuries; the state of this area suggests much longer."

"Then how is the rope still intact?"

"I can answer that," said Natalia. "A spell of preservation; an enchantment typically used to preserve food, but it'll work on rope and timber just as well. It also means whoever built the bridge had Enchanters in addition to Earth Mages."

"The mystery deepens."

"The Volstrum has no history of this area before the founding of Ruzhina, and even then, records are scarce."

"Yet there are stories," said Athgar. "Vicavia being one, though that was alleged to take place much farther north. Could the family have kept this information hidden? After all, they had to get their Water Magic from somewhere?"

"It's a distinct possibility," replied Natalia. "I never had full access to the Volstrum, and it's a massive place. It wouldn't be difficult to conceal something like that."

"But they let you into the Baroshka, didn't they?"

"They did, but it's a spell repository, not a library of history. Once we take it over, we can search for such a place, but its possible existence has no bearing on our decision here."

"The evidence suggests a fallen civilization," said Kargen. "I doubt we will find anything except ruins. Could this be an old Therengian outpost?"

"No," replied Athgar. "It's too old and too far north from what I've learned. Then again, the existence of Beorwic surprised us, so we can't dismiss the possibility, except for the age thing."

"I agree with Shaluhk," said Kargen. "My vote would be for us to explore westward."

"Me too," added Natalia, walking off in that direction.

"Don't I get a vote?" asked Athgar.

They all stopped to look at him. "Of course," said Shaluhk, "but three of us voted to go west."

"And I'm in agreement with that; it's just nice to be asked."

"Come," said Natalia, holding out her hand. "Let us walk together."

The beginning of the trail was easy to follow, but then the rocky ground ended, replaced by a lush forest, more akin to what they'd experienced in the first part of their travels upriver, slowing their progress considerably. It wasn't that they couldn't navigate through the woods, it was keeping the ancient roadway in sight, and there was the umak, which they'd left hidden amongst the trees. They needed to be able to find their way back if they hoped to retrieve it.

As the sky darkened, they made camp. To save time, Athgar used his magic to get a fire going, then set his fire watch to alert him of any signs of danger. Shaluhk dug out their food and handed it around.

"I'm not complaining about this," said Athgar, "but it would be nice to have fresh meat instead of this cured stuff."

"This cured 'stuff', as you call it, is light," said Kargen. "Would you rather carry around the carcass of that deer for days on end?"

"No, but it'd be great to have some variety. I'd even take a stonecake if there was one to be had. Perhaps we should convince Belgast to set up a Dwarven bakery back in Runewald or at least sell us the recipe?"

"The mountain folk guard their secrets," said Kargen. "I doubt they would part with the recipe." He paused, then turned to Shaluhk. "Do you think Elves made this road?"

"It is ancient," she replied, "perhaps even dating back to the Great War."

"I've heard that mentioned before," said Athgar. "Wasn't that the war between the Elves and the Orcs?"

"It was. In those days, both our races lived in cities. Even the Ancestors do not remember how it started, but it ended with our cities destroyed and our people scattered to the ends of the Continent."

"And no Orc cities survived?"

"No."

"And the Elves?"

"They won the war, but at a heavy cost, for their numbers were so depleted that they were unable to resist the spread of Humanity. Their cities were also destroyed during the war, but some survived, or so we have been told. We know an Elven realm survives in the west, that of the Darkwood, but I am unaware of others. If this road leads to an Elven city, then we are in considerable danger."

"Even after all this time?"

"Even so," said Shaluhk. "The Great War was a brutal conflict, with both sides refusing offers of surrender. If the descendants of those Elves live in this area, they will kill us on sight, at least Kargen and I. I have no idea how they might treat Humans."

"Then we shall proceed with caution," said Natalia. "I suggest Athgar and I take the lead. Hopefully, that will make them think twice about outright killing us."

"It just occurred to me," said Athgar, "that the phoenix spell would be particularly useful right about now. I don't suppose the Volstrum would have it hidden in their Baroshka?"

"No. Those are all Water Magic spells. To find that, you'd have to travel to Korascajan."

"Is it anything like the Volstrum?"

"I wouldn't know," replied Natalia. "I've never been there. They're both schools, but the Sartellians control Korascajan, and they're rumoured to guard their secrets closer than Dwarves."

"But you've met Sartellians before—we both have—only you've interacted with them more."

"They're people, much like us, but driven with a passion for controlling others. There's also a strong rivalry between them and the Stormwinds."

"How does that matter to us?"

"There's a good chance they may sit by and watch us dismantle the Volstrum."

"I find that surprising."

"Do you?" asked Natalia. "You shouldn't—it's all about power. With the Stormwinds out of the way, the Sartellians' reach becomes all the stronger. There are, however, more important matters to consider for the time being, chief amongst them how to deal with Elves should we encounter them. I don't suppose anyone here speaks their language?"

"They speak the ancient tongue," replied Shaluhk, "much as our Ancestors did. It is an archaic form of Orc, although they will have developed their own dialect if we are any indication."

"Of course," said Athgar, "that presupposes they'd hold off on killing us long enough for you or Kargen to get any words out."

"Then we shall rely on Kargen and your hunting skills to avoid being surprised. Elves are notoriously gifted in the woodland skills, so you must take great care."

"I will." He took a bite of his dried meat, mulling things over as he chewed it. The magical flames guarding the camp's perimeter roared to life, interrupting him.

# CAPTURED

## SPRING 1110 SR

Seven hulking, armoured figures entered the clearing, holding spears with wicked-looking blades affixed. Athgar went to draw his axe, but an arrow thudded into the ground beside him. He turned to see six more warriors lurking in the shadows of the trees.

One of the spear wielders held up his hand, an order for his warriors to hold. He then removed his helmet, revealing the face of an Orc. Ignoring both Athgar and Natalia, his gaze settled on Kargen.

"*Who are you?*" he demanded in the tongue of the Orcs.

"*I am Kargen, Chieftain of the Red Hand, and this is Shaluhk, my bondmate.*"

"*What strange manner of speaking you have. From what city do you hail?*"

"*We were born in Ord-Kurgad, but that village was destroyed years ago. We now call Runewald, in the Kingdom of Therengia, our home.*"

"*This name means nothing to me. Who is your king?*"

"*I suppose that would be me,*" offered Athgar, "*although I prefer the title of High Thane.*"

The Orc looked at him in shock. "*You speak our language?*"

"*We all do,*" replied Natalia. "*Our people live side by side in peace and harmony.*"

"*Who might you be?*" asked Kargen.

"*I am Garag, First Glaive of Ard-Gurslag.*"

"*Greetings, Garag. May the blessings of the Ancestors be upon you.*"

"*Ancestors? Do not speak of them; they abandoned us long ago.*"

"*Can your shamans not contact them?*"

"*Shamans? They are the stuff of legends.*"

*"I am a shaman,"* said Shaluhk, *"and I assure you, the Ancestors always answer my call. Have you no healers?"*

*"Healers, yes, but they possess no magic. Rather, they are skilled in medicine."* His eyes flicked to Athgar and Natalia. *"The punishment for outsiders entering our land is death."*

*"Do not be so eager to kill your kin."*

*"Kin? They are Humans!"*

*"They are members of the Red Hand,"* replied Kargen. *"Athgar is our master of flame, taught by the great master Artoch, and Nat-Alia is a master of water. Surely your laws do not pronounce a death sentence on fellow tribe members?"*

*"You have given me much to consider,"* replied Garag. *"Such decisions are not to be taken lightly. I shall bring you all back to Ard-Gurslag and present you to Urgash."*

*"Is that your chieftain?"*

*"No. Our queen."*

*"Then take us to see her, and we shall plead our case in her presence."*

*"As you wish. This way."* Garag turned and walked away, his warriors falling in behind him. The archers waited for Kargen's party to follow, then brought up the rear.

"Did you note their armour?" said Kargen, switching to the Human tongue. "It matches that worn by the warriors Shaluhk summoned at the Battle of the Standing Stones. Do you understand what that means?"

"Indeed," replied Shaluhk. "These Orcs are from one of the lost cities."

"How can you be so certain?" asked Athgar.

"The very name, Ard-Gurslag, means 'Fortress City of Gurslag' in our tongue. However, the term 'Ard' is no longer used, for we have no cities, or fortresses, for that matter."

Kargen switched back to Orc. *"How far away is the city?"*

*"We shall be there before the sunsets tomorrow,"* replied Garag.

*"And this queen of yours, Urgash, what is she like?"*

*"I do not understand your question. She is our queen and rules over us. What more is there to know?"*

*"Might I ask how long she has ruled?"*

*"Close to twenty winters. She inherited the Throne from her father."*

*"You do not elect your leaders?"*

*"Elect?"* said their host. *"What strange method of governance is that?"*

*"Our leaders, myself included, are chosen by the tribe. Even our High Thane is chosen thusly."*

*"Your customs are strange, but then again, we thought ourselves the only Orcs who survived the great purge."*

*"You refer to the war with the Elves?"*

*"You know of it?"* asked Garag.

*"We do indeed,"* replied Kargen. *"The forest folk destroyed our biggest cities, driving our people to the far reaches of the Continent. We call it the Great War. My people are descended from those survivors."*

*"And do the Elves now control the Continent?"*

*"No,"* replied Shaluhk. *"While they destroyed your cities, their victory cost them dearly. When Humans arrived on the Continent, the Elves were powerless to oppose them."*

*"Humans are weak,"* said Garag. *"When they enter our lands, we execute them."* He glanced at Athgar and Natalia. *"I am still undecided whether we should consider your friends tribe members."* He shrugged. *"In truth, it is unimportant since I will not be deciding your fate."*

*"If you do not speak with the Ancestors,"* said Kargen, *"who do you worship?"*

*"The Gods. Particularly Hraka, who gave us life."*

*"I am familiar with him as he is the God of Fire in addition to creating Orcs."*

*"You tell me what I already know."*

*"That was meant to inform my companions,"* declared Kargen, *"not you."*

*"My apologies, Chief Kargen. I meant no disrespect."*

*"Pardon my saying so,"* said Athgar, *"but you're awfully forthcoming for someone who captured us. I would think you'd be less informative about your city."*

*"I have no reason to hide our existence. Either the queen accepts you, or you will be put to death, in which case, the knowledge dies with you."*

*"Hardly the most reassuring of answers."*

Garag stopped suddenly, causing the entire column to halt. He turned, then moved to stand before Athgar. Their eyes met, but neither blinked.

*"You are no ordinary Human,"* said the Orc. *"Others of your race have come to this land, but there is something different about you."* He paused, tilting his head. *"You do not fear us."*

*"I am a member of the Red Hand and a master of flame. I am also a Therengian."*

*"I do not know what that is."*

*"It was a great kingdom,"* explained Kargen, *"ruling over a large portion of the Continent centuries ago."*

*"Why would that be of interest to us?"*

*"In the Old Kingdom, as we now call it, Orcs and Therengians worked side by side, something we do again in the Kingdom of Therengia reborn."*

*"Again, you talk of Therengians. Are they not Humans?"*

*"Look at Athgar again, and you will notice his grey eyes. It is a mark of his race."*

*"I have met few Humans before; how am I to understand such distinctions?"*

*"Yet you know what they are."*

"*Of course*," said Garag. "*We keep records of the past. Your intrusion onto our land is not the first, although it is the first to consist of Orcs.*"

"*Wait a moment*," said Athgar. "*Did you say you've met other Humans?*"

"*I have. When I received my first command, my task was to patrol our land. One day, we ran across signs of intrusion—footprints, abandoned firepits, that sort of thing. We were responsible for tracking down the intruders and punishing them for their crimes. After two days of searching, we found them. They put up a valiant fight, but in the end, we defeated them.*"

"*Why kill them? Why not take them prisoner?*"

"*To what end? The security of Ard-Gurslag relies on keeping its location secret. We will not risk outsiders discovering our city.*"

"*But when people disappear without a trace, it inspires others to search for them.*"

"*You have not lived our history*," said Garag, "*so I will forgive your ignorance. We survived two thousand years by hiding our existence. Would you have us expose ourselves to the threat of attack once more?*"

"*The Great War has ended*," said Kargen, "*and with it, the threat of an Elven attack. The woodland folk are scattered, much as we are, and no longer pose a threat to you.*"

"*And what about these Humans? Can you honestly tell me they would not see us as a danger and invade our lands?*"

"*You are set in your ways, so I will not argue the point. Hopefully, your queen will be more accepting of change.*"

Garag grinned, baring his teeth. "*I would not hold much hope for such if I were you. She is fair in all things yet is not one to ignore precedence.*"

"*Meaning?*"

"*The death penalty for outsiders is part of our history. I doubt she will abandon the practice, but you are more than welcome to try to convince her otherwise.*"

Kargen switched to the common tongue. "It seems our hosts are likely to be inflexible when it comes to killing outsiders."

"A pity," replied Natalia. "I'd prefer not to demonstrate my magic to prove a point."

"That point being?"

"That we deserve to live."

They travelled late into the afternoon, then Garag called a halt. Being surrounded by ancient, armoured Orcs left them feeling uneasy. Shaluhk had used her magic to conjure warriors of the past, but those were indistinct and ghostly in appearance, while these warriors were living beings.

They kept to themselves, not engaging with their Orcish hosts. Had they wished, they could have escaped into the forest, but Athgar held out hope they could reach an understanding with the queen.

"*Garag,*" said Shaluhk, reverting to her native tongue. "*How much farther to your city?*"

"*We shall be there before dark. It lies atop a big hill, surrounded by three sets of walls, each higher than the one below. You will know it once you set eyes on it.*"

"*I am surprised we have not seen it yet.*"

Their host chuckled. "*You will not see it until you are almost at its gate, for magic protects it.*"

"*What sort of magic hides a city?*"

"*You would have to ask Morgal; he looks after such things.*"

"*Morgal? Is he an Enchanter?*"

"*Why would you ask that?*"

"*We came across a rope bridge with a spell of preservation cast upon it.*"

"*I know the bridge of which you speak. It has not been used for centuries and is not Morgal's work.*"

"*But you have now confirmed he is an Enchanter.*"

Garag grinned. "*You are clever, I give you that. Are all shamans so gifted in the arts of deduction?*"

"*It varies from tribe to tribe, but in addition to being healers, we shamans are neutral arbitrators. As such, we must know how to sort truth from lies.*"

"*An interesting skill which would be useful in the queen's presence.*"

"*Are you suggesting your queen would lie?*"

"*The queen? No, but the elite of our society are another matter. There is an old saying that a lie is easier to bear than an unpleasant truth. I fear that concept has been taken to heart by many with the monarch's ear.*"

"*Has she no bondmate to aid her?*"

"*He died some time ago, a victim of his advanced years. It is not our practice to bond with another.*"

"*A custom we share,*" said Shaluhk.

"*Then you know the heavy burden such a loss brings with it. Our queen is alone, surrounded by those seeking to enrich their positions and influence.*"

"*That is a trait common amongst the Human realms. Athgar and Nat-Alia have dealt with it on many occasions.*"

"*Then perhaps it is good we found them.*"

"*Earlier, you introduced yourself as First Glaive—is that your rank or a title?*"

"*Both,*" replied Garag. "*The First Glaive commands the muster of Ard-Gurslag, although it has not marched in nearly two thousand years.*"

"*Muster?*"

"*Yes, every able-bodied Orc is expected to train once a ten-day in either *polearms or bows. This responsibility is ingrained into the minds of all Orcs at a very young age."*

*"Have you no hunters?"*

*"We do, but likely not as many as your people. We farm the land, which provides us with more food than hunting ever could. Beneath the city lie the food caverns."*

*"You grow food underground?"*

*"In the abandoned levels of the mines, illuminated day and night by our Enchanters' magic. If the queen permits it, I shall arrange for you and your companions to be shown the wonders of our city."*

*"That would be most appreciated."*

*"We have rested long enough,"* said Garag. *"We should be on our way."*

As the journey continued, the Orcs of Ard-Gurslag quickened their pace, becoming more animated, talking amongst themselves about loved ones and favourite pastimes.

They stopped on a treeless hill that gave them a commanding view of the countryside, a rare thing with the preponderance of trees nearby. Despite claims they were close, there were no sightings of the Orc city, roads, or any other signs of civilization.

Athgar suspected they would camp here for the night, then continue on to Ard-Gurslag in the morning, but to his surprise, they halted only long enough for Garag to form his warriors into a proper column. The First Glaive then took the lead, heading back into the forest with the rest of his detachment following in pairs. Kargen and Shaluhk came next, with Athgar and Natalia bringing up the rear.

"This is confusing," said Athgar. "Where's the city? Could it be underground?"

"Doubtful," replied Kargen. "If these Orcs are anything like the Red Hand, they'll enjoy the sun on their skin. I suspect it will be more a case of hiding the city in plain sight."

"It is true," added Shaluhk. "According to Garag, they use an enchantment to mask the city from its enemies."

"How does one mask an entire city?" asked Athgar. He turned to Natalia. "You're the expert. What do you think?"

"There's an enchantment that allows people to blend into their surroundings, but I've never heard of it being used on such a massive scale."

"How does that work? Do they paint the walls of the city green to make it look like trees?"

"No," replied Natalia. "Blend is an interesting spell. As an outsider, you would see the blended object as belonging amongst its surroundings, thus drawing no further interest. I know it's a tough concept to get your head around, but I assure you, it works."

"That would be useful in a battle."

"It would, but only for a short duration. Any acts of aggression nullify its effects, including casting spells. We learned all about it at the Volstrum as part of our training as battle mages."

"Yet," said Athgar, "the students there were Water Mages."

"True, but blend could be used to infiltrate a camp with the intent to murder one of our own; thus, we learned techniques to counter it."

"Which are?"

"A detection of magic does the trick."

"How would that work?"

"If observing a blended individual, to my eyes, they would glow with a pale light, assuming I cast a spell of detection."

"But no one else would notice?"

"No," replied Natalia. "Hence the danger. Thankfully, Enchanters are rare, so it's seldom a possibility."

"If you cast your spell of detection now, would you be able to tell if the city was blended?"

"Most likely, but it would be risky. Our hosts are already mistrustful of Humans. If they see me casting, they might react with violence."

"Best not try, then," said Athgar.

"On that, we are in complete agreement."

As the warriors synchronized their footsteps, the forest parted to reveal an immense wall with a gatehouse in the middle. Athgar was stunned. The city before them was easily as large as Ebenstadt, consisting of three sets of walls, each progressively higher on the hill upon which Ard-Gurslag sat.

"Walls within walls," muttered Athgar. "I'd hate to have to attack this place. It would be next to impossible to conquer."

"Look," said Natalia, pointing to the top of the hill where a massive tower rose above the rest of the city. "That must be where the enchantment is held."

The group halted as Garag waited for the city gates to open. He disappeared into the guardhouse, then returned, ordering his warriors to continue marching.

"The towers on this lower level are all red," noted Athgar.

"Likely the type of stone used to construct them," replied Natalia.

"But not the walls? Could it be another enchantment?"

"If you'd asked me that two days ago, I would've said unlikely, but it appears the traditional rules of magic don't apply here."

"Tradition rules?" replied Athgar. "You taught me there's no such thing."

Natalia looked at her husband and smiled. "I learned that from you. The one thing I've discovered about magic these last few years is there are no rules. If you can imagine it, you can conceivably bring it about through magic."

"Then let's hope this queen of theirs doesn't imagine us being executed."

# ARD-GURSLAG

## SPRING 1110 SR

They cleared the gatehouse and entered the city, the road continuing towards the hill before branching left and right, presumably wrapping around the inner walls. The dwellings packed into Ard-Gurslag looked nothing like the ones found in Orc villages throughout the Continent. Instead, these buildings were made of wooden planks with cedar shingles, painted in various bright colours.

The townsfolk stopped to watch as the group marched by, focusing their gazes on the Humans. Athgar noticed no signs of hatred, only curiosity, younglings even halting mid-play to stare at the unexpected visitors.

Garag led them to the left, revealing more buildings, as they circumnavigated the base of the hill in what Athgar thought of as the outer ring. To his right lay the next ring of towers, each topped with a blue roof. It was odd to see peaked roofs on towers, for in Ebenstadt, they were flat, the better to accommodate archers.

He glanced at the Orc archer in front of him, who'd slung his bow onto his back. Compared to Kargen's great warbow, it was a crude weapon, and it took him a moment to realize why. The terrain here was vastly different from back home. Between that and the thick underbrush, it only made sense that their bows be easy to carry, even if limited in range.

Athgar shifted his gaze to the polearm-wielding Orcs. Garag had called himself a glaive, and it was easy to see why, for the weapons they carried were precisely that, single-edged blades mounted on poles only slightly taller than their wielders. It took immense strength to handle such a weapon, but he had no doubt the Orcs could do them justice.

The road ahead bent to the north, leading to many places of business for customers lined up to purchase goods from open windows. To his mind, it was a strange way to do business, but no one appeared to care.

They crossed through the city, red towers on their left, blue on the other side, until the road once more curved, this time to the east. They approached the extreme opposite end from where they'd entered, but instead of another exit, a ramp on the right led up to a smaller gate set in the wall with the blue turrets.

Garag halted his command. *"This leads to the inner city. The most powerful of Ard-Gurslag call this place home, so we must mind our manners."* He looked directly at Athgar, then Natalia. *"Humans have never set foot in the inner city. I have no idea how you will be received. Do you understand?"*

*"We do,"* replied Natalia.

*"Good. Then let us finish this before word of your arrival beats us to the Royal Council Chambers."*

*"That is not likely,"* said Kargen. *"We marched all the way through the inner city. Someone will have alerted Her Majesty of our arrival. That is what you call your queen, isn't it? Her Majesty?"*

*"We prefer the term Greatness,"* said Garag, *"but I doubt she will argue the point."* He marched everyone up the ramp, stopping at the large, iron-bound doors flanked by two flat-topped towers.

A sentinel appeared at the top of one, barely looking at who'd approached before issuing a challenge. *"Who seeks admittance to the inner city?"*

*"I do,"* replied their guide. *"Garag, First Glaive of Ard-Gurslag."* He delivered the line with a boredom that suggested both were going through the motions.

*"And who is with you?"*

*"My warriors, along with four outsiders."*

The guard on the wall suddenly grew more attentive. *"Outsiders? You have made this day considerably more interesting."*

*"Will you let us in or simply gawk, Krogal? We should not keep the queen waiting."*

*"Yes, of course. One moment, and I will open the gate."* The fellow disappeared from the top of the tower. They waited an inordinately long time before the twin gates swung wide to reveal the inner city. The buildings here were larger than those they'd walked past but bore the same strange assortment of colours, making for a vibrant display. Athgar could only imagine what it looked like on a sunny day, with light streaming from above.

Garag led them through the opening, then along a straight road paved with flattened stones. At the far end stood a final gatehouse leading into the inner keep and the home of the great tower which dominated the place, though its base was hidden by this new gate.

The population was less dense, with few onlookers remarking on the group as it passed. Those watching them were adorned with jewellery, including torcs, rings, and bracelets, while their attire was similar to the rest of the population, simple tunics or robes, though woven of much finer cloth. The vibrant colours led Athgar to wonder if more magic wasn't at play.

Houses lined the main thoroughfare, though a few businesses were on side streets, for Orcs emerged carrying goods. Merchants pushed wagons, bringing their wares to the wealthy rather than expecting them to visit the more modest environs of the common folk.

Several Orcs called out to Garag as he passed, but the fellow ignored them, concentrating instead on his destination. As they advanced, the Palace gates were blocked by six heavily armoured Orcs bearing glaives similar to those wielded by Garag's warriors, but these blades were heavily adorned with filigree depicting the Gods.

"*The queen awaits you,*" said the leader of this new group, though he didn't deign to introduce himself. "*Your warriors will remain here. The rest will follow me.*"

Garag dismissed his command before he turned to Athgar's group. "*You heard him. You will soon be in the presence of Her Greatness. She does not suffer insolence.*"

"*Understood,*" replied Kargen. "*I promise we will be on our best behaviour.*"

"*Lead on,*" said Garag, speaking to their new guide.

They passed through the gatehouse, and before them stood the base of the tower, a massive structure, the largest in the entire city, even without accounting for its height.

"Interesting," said Natalia in the Human tongue. "It appears the entire Palace is held within this one tower."

"How many floors do you reckon there are?" asked Athgar.

"Were this a Human tower, I would estimate at least a dozen, but their interior architecture may differ from what we're accustomed to."

"*Quiet,*" snapped Garag. "*You are in the great tower. Such chattering is considered unseemly, especially given you speak the language of outsiders.*"

"*My apologies,*" said Natalia, reverting to Orcish. "*I shall be more mindful in the future.*"

They were escorted to the tower's base, where a tall, thin Orc waited.

"*What have we here, Garag?*" she asked.

"*Outsiders, Minister. Discovered in the eastern reaches. This is Kargen, Chieftain of the Red Hand, and his shaman, Shaluhk.*"

*"Greetings to you,"* she replied. *"I am Thusha, the Second Minister of Ard-Gurslag."* Her nose wrinkled. *"You brought Humans, I see."*

*"This is Athgar, High Thane of Therengia,"* said Garag, *"and his companion is Nat-Alia, master of water."*

*"They are members of my tribe,"* added Kargen, *"and deserve the respect given to all Orcs."*

Thusha gave a slight bow of her head. *"It shall be as you wish, Chief Kargen. Word of your arrival has swept through the city, and the queen is eager to meet you. If you follow me, I shall take you to her."*

Garag stood to one side.

*"You are not coming with us?"* asked Kargen.

*"It is not my place to be in the queen's presence unless summoned."*

*"He is correct,"* said Thusha. *"The audience chamber is not for everyone. Now come, before Her Greatness grows bored of the delay."* She went through the doorway into a richly appointed hall with a thick carpet and wood-panelled walls decorated in battle carvings. They passed by openings on either side, while ahead of them sat a large door painted with a colourful depiction of a dragon soaring through the air.

*"This,"* she said, *"is where Her Greatness, Queen Urgash, presides over the affairs of Ard-Gurslag."* She pressed her right hand upon the door, which glowed slightly before it swung open to two heavily armoured Orcs armed with golden glaives.

*"Who disturbs the queen's council?"*

*"Thusha, Second Minister to Her Greatness."*

*"Enter, Thusha, Second Minister of Ard-Gurslag."* The guards stepped aside, revealing a large, circular chamber with two steps leading to a raised platform. A bench sat along each side of the platform, while the other end held a throne, an immense wooden construction with a huge dragon skull mounted atop it. The queen's advisors, ten in total, sat on either side, their necks craned to see who had entered.

Thusha advanced to stand in the middle of the platform. *"I bring the outsiders, Greatness, as you requested."*

*"Bring them forward," said the queen, "that I might see them better."*

Thusha turned, waving them forward. *"This is Kargen, Chieftain of the Red Hand, and his shaman, Shaluhk."*

*"And the Humans?"*

*"Athgar, High Thane of Therengia and Nat-Alia, master of water."*

Urgash stood, then stepped closer, leading to a chorus of murmurs from her advisors. The first object of her scrutiny was Kargen. *"It has been eons since we welcomed outside Orcs to our city. Two thousand years ago, we shut our doors to outsiders to preserve our way of life. Now, millennia later, we find two of them at our very doorstep. How did you come to be in our land?"*

*"We are travelling north to Ruzhina, a Human realm."*

*"It must be a journey of considerable importance to take you through this region."*

*"We are going there to destroy the power of the Volstrum."*

*"Volstrum? That name is unfamiliar to me."*

*"It is an academy where they train masters of water,"* replied Kargen.

*"Ah, yes,"* said Urgash. *"Masters of water. We have had troubles with them in the past."*

*"You have?"* said Natalia.

The queen turned at the interruption. *"Why are you so surprised?"*

*"I was unaware the family had any contact with Orcs."*

*"It was centuries ago when the realm to the north was first founded. There were several incursions into our territory, although none survived to tell the tale."*

*"How did you know they were users of Water Magic?"*

*"They used their magic when we attacked them. Does it surprise you that we are familiar with magic?"*

*"Not at all,"* replied Natalia. *"We have mages back in Therengia, many of them Orcs. I was, however, under the impression the Stormwinds were powerful casters."*

*"Stormwinds? Another term I am not familiar with."* She looked at one of her advisors, a pale Orc of advanced years. *"Would you care to comment, Throgar?"*

*"They never revealed their names, Greatness, and even if they had, we would have been unable to understand them."*

A middle-aged Orc stood. *"With all due respect to the Keeper of History, that is incorrect."* He bowed his head at the queen. *"As you know, Greatness, our Enchanters are capable of casting the spell of tongues, even if there has been no requirement for it in recent years."*

*"Also true,"* said a younger female, *"yet here we are with Humans amongst us able to speak our language. Perhaps your Enchanters might wish to re-evaluate their choice of spells, Morgal?"*

*"You must forgive the outbursts,"* said the queen. *"I encourage all of my advisors to speak their minds."*

*"As we do back in Runewald,"* replied Kargen.

*"You say you are a chieftain. Do you have a monarch?"*

*"In a sense, yes. We Orcs, along with the Humans who live in our land, elected a High Thane."* He nodded at Athgar.

*"Elected? How curious."*

*"It is a tradition going back centuries."*

*"Tell me more,"* said Urgash. *"I find this most interesting."*

*"Shaluhk has much more knowledge on the subject than I do."*

*"Ah, yes. This shaman of yours."* She stepped closer to Shaluhk, looking her up and down. *"I must admit to some surprise. We lost our last shaman more than a thousand years ago."*

*"Fifteen hundred,"* corrected Throgar, bringing a withering glare from his queen.

She continued. *"It has been many generations since a shaman trod the streets of Ard-Gurslag. What do you know of Orc history?"*

*"The Ancestors tell of the Great War that enveloped the entire Continent. Both sides suffered horrendous losses, leading to the destruction of all the Orc cities, save for this one, it would seem. Those who survived became a wandering people, constantly moving to avoid being hunted down by the woodland folk. After centuries of such fear, our people settled down, building villages and becoming tribes rather than small enclaves. But by then, the Humans had arrived, claiming much of the Continent and driving us to increasingly dangerous lands to avoid them. Eventually, the Kingdom of Therengia was founded, and Orcs were welcomed to settle there, but it was not to last."*

*"Why was that?"*

*"The other Human kingdoms sought to destroy Therengia, what we now call the Old Kingdom. With its demise, our people were once more scattered to the far reaches of Eiddenwerthe."*

*"Yet you are here in the company of Humans. How did that come to pass?"*

*"The Red Hand settled in an area south of the Grey Spire Mountains. Athgar's people, descendants of the Old Kingdom, had a village nearby. My bondmate, Kargen, traded with Athgar, who is a master at making bows and arrows. Later, when Humans attacked our village, he and Nat-Alia came to our aid, along with others."*

*"What others?"*

*"There are many Humans who wish only to live in peace and harmony."*

*"Peace? The only way to achieve peace is by showing strength."*

*"Yes,"* said Shaluhk. *"Unfortunately, that has been our experience as well. Under Athgar's leadership, Therengia has become a great military power, rivalling the strongest of the Petty Kingdoms."*

*"Which are?"*

*"It is the collective name given to the Human realms of the Continent. We have had dealings with several of them and count a few as allies."*

*"Allies?"* said Urgash. *"What a strange thing to contemplate."* She looked around the room, gathering her thoughts. *"After two thousand years of isolation, much has changed across the Continent. This is a lot to absorb."*

Throgar stood, his age causing him to wobble slightly. *"With all due respect, Greatness, we have no way of authenticating any of this. She could be lying."*

Shaluhk turned on the old-timer. *"How dare you! I am a shaman of the Red Hand—to lie would be unconscionable."*

*"You have insulted my bondmate,"* added Kargen. *"By our customs, she could challenge you to a duel."*

*"You must forgive him,"* said Urgash. *"Throgar is a doddering old fool and meant no insult. Were I to punish all my advisors for speaking thus, I would have no counsellors left."*

*"I shall forgive him,"* said Shaluhk, *"providing he apologizes."*

The old Orc looked stunned. *"Apologize? To you? Who do you think you are?"*

*"She is a shaman,"* replied the queen. *"You, of all people, should understand the respect due a person of that status. Or do you no longer read the records you so studiously care for?"*

*"Then let her prove her magic."*

Shaluhk moved up to stand before Throgar. *"Your vision is dimmed,"* she said. *"I see it in your eyes."*

*"That is not magic. Every Orc of advanced years could be so diagnosed."*

*"True, but I can cure you."* She turned to face the queen. *"With your permission, Greatness, I shall repair the damage to Throgar's sight."*

*"Do so, and you and your companions will have free rein of the city."*

Shaluhk addressed the council members. *"I can heal flesh, but the advances of age are more difficult to counter. To restore Throgar's eyesight, I will use a spell of regeneration, but it requires casting over multiple days to completely heal him. There will, however, be a noticeable difference after the first."* She looked at her new patient, recognizing the fear in his eyes. *"Do you consent to be the object of this spell?"*

*"I do."* His voice betrayed his nervousness. *"Will it hurt?"*

*"My hands will glow before I place them on either side of your head, and then a slight warmth will flood into you, briefly lingering in your eyes. It is a strange sensation, even a little unsettling, but you will experience no pain."*

*"Then you may begin."*

As Shaluhk drew upon her magic, her hands glowed, and then she placed them on her patient. The light drained into him, lingering in his eyes. She stepped back, her spell complete.

*"Remarkable,"* said Throgar, looking around the room. *"I can see everything! Are the effects of this spell permanent?"*

*"The spell has done its job, but age will still cause your eyesight to deteriorate. Repeated castings would prevent that."*

*"How often does this spell need to be repeated?"*

*"In your case, likely only once a year."*

*"Remarkable,"* echoed the queen.

*"It is capable of much more than simply restoring eyesight,"* said Shaluhk. *"I used it to regenerate Nat-Alia's lost arm."*

*"How does one lose their arm?"*

*"She was attacked by a large flying creature whose talons inflicted a necrotic rot. We had no choice but to remove her arm lest the infection kill her."*

*"How interesting,"* said Throgar. *"How large was this creature? Was it dragon-sized?"*

*"Do you have records of such things?"*

*"Attacks, no, but some of our patrols have reported sighting a large creature far off to the east occasionally. Perhaps it was the same beast you encountered?"*

*"All that is interesting,"* said the queen, *"but let us return to the matter of this regeneration spell of yours, Shaluhk. How long did it take to replace the limb?"*

*"A ten-day."*

*"Your services would be most welcome in Ard-Gurslag."*

*"Given time,"* said Shaluhk, *"I can train others to perform this spell."*

*"But we have no shamans,"* replied Urgash.

*"True, but we have several gifted shamans amongst the tribes of Therengia, with more being trained every day. We could arrange for some to visit here, providing a safe route is found."*

*"This is a momentous occasion. I promised you the freedom of the city, and I am an Orc of my word. We shall house you in the great tower, and from this day hence, you and your companions are welcome throughout the city."*

# A LESSON IN HISTORY

## SPRING 1110 SR

(IN THE LANGUAGE OF THE ORCS)

"Here it is," announced Throgar, throwing his arms wide. "The great archive of knowledge. Every record of our people can be found on these shelves."

Shaluhk admired the view. They stood two floors above the council chambers in a room encompassing the entire floor. With no windows to light the area, glowing orbs hung from the ceiling, flooding the space with a brightness that made it feel like a midsummer's day. Shelves lined the outer walls, each packed with scrolls and arranged chronologically.

The Keeper of History continued his tour. "Each scroll has a ribbon affixed to it indicating the date the document refers to and the scholar who wrote it."

"I assume they were preserved with magic?"

"Correct. The city is blessed with spellcasters, particularly Enchanters. Morgal could tell you more, for he oversees their training, but you must trust me when I say we have dozens."

"Except for shamans, it would seem."

"You are quite right." He moved to a shelf, plucking a scroll from it. "This tells the story of our last shaman, Grishal. She died in the year 536 AC."

"AC?"

"After the Calamity—the name we scholars give to the period after the Great War."

"You say you possess numerous Enchanters; would they be opposed to training Humans?"

Throgar looked at her in surprise. "Why would we train Humans?"

"Amongst our people is a young girl named Greta who shows potential as a possible Enchanter, but there is no one to train her."

"I do not believe we have ever trained a Human, but I see no reason why it could not be done. You expressed an interest in sending us shamans, so we can at least do you a favour in return."

"What do you know about the Great War?"

He indicated a shelf packed with scrolls. "Quite a lot, as you can plainly see. What did you want to know?"

"How did you hide Ard-Gurslag?"

"A powerful enchantment was cast upon the top of this tower, a variation of the blend spell. Thankfully, the spell has endured for over two millennia, for none of us living today know how it was cast. Oh, we can cast a blend spell on individuals, but the sheer scale of that spell boggles the mind."

"Was this spell cast during the war?"

"Yes. After we learned Ard-Uzgul had fallen, we knew the Elves would come for us. The best scholars of our time gathered to discuss how to safeguard our people. In the end, the great Enchanter, Grom, devised a solution, but in casting the spell, he forfeited his life. Now it seems the threat exists no longer."

"That spell saved your people," said Shaluhk, "by keeping you from the eyes of Humans for centuries."

"We are blessed by our location. Beneath us are the iron mines which allowed us to equip our army. We no longer mine them, so we converted them into growing caves ages ago."

"Is the mine depleted?"

"No," replied Throgar, "merely unnecessary. We dig occasionally, but only to facilitate repairs or to fashion replacement armour and weapons. Equipment rusts, and we are unable to preserve everything with a spell, for that would be too impractical."

"So you are completely self-sufficient?"

"We are, though perhaps the term stagnant would be more fitting. We focused so heavily on protecting ourselves that we never considered the possibility of other Orcs out there needing our help. Your arrival here compels us to look outside these walls for the first time in over a thousand years. That is a good thing."

"How large is your army?"

"That is not my area of expertise. The person to ask would be Zorga. You might remember her from the council meeting—she argued with Morgal's choice of spells."

"And she commands the army?"

"No. That is the duty of the First Glaive. Zorga is the administrator for our military. She has a sharp mind despite her relative youth. She knows exactly how many warriors are in each glaive, as well as the number of bows we keep in reserve. Speaking of which, I could not help but notice your bondmate's large bow. I do not recall ever having seen its like before."

"It is an Orc warbow," replied Shaluhk. "A variation of the Therengian longbow Athgar adapted for our people."

"The same Athgar in your group? How curious. He must be a most exceptional Human. I should make a note of this for our records." He moved to a table, pulling a blank parchment from the top of a stack. "Have you such records back home?"

"Ours is primarily an oral history, but since the rebirth of Therengia, we have been assembling scholars to increase our knowledge of the past."

Throgar nodded. "A most sensible approach. A kingdom should always be aware of where it came from." He plucked a quill from the table and dipped its nib in ink. "This is remarkable. I can see the tip of this feather quite clearly. I must thank you again for your spell of healing."

"It is called regeneration," replied Shaluhk. "You should be accurate when you record recent events."

He chuckled. "So I should. Thank you." He touched quill to paper, then looked up again. "It would serve both our purposes to exchange scholars. Your people can learn about the distant past while we, in exchange, learn about the outside world."

"I am certain our High Thane would be most agreeable to such an arrangement." She moved closer to the shelves lining the outer wall as her host made notes. "Where would I find the section concerning the Stormwinds?"

"The who?"

"The Stormwinds, the Human Water Mages who troubled you some time ago?"

"Ah, let me think. That would be during the reign of Thorga the Strong-Willed. You want the blue shelf to your left, though I must warn you, there is limited information concerning the intruders. Look for a scroll with a green tag—that denotes a military account. If I recall, the glaive in charge had a long report on the subject."

"You have read it?"

"I have read every record here, though it has taken my lifetime to do so."

"You possess a remarkable memory."

"Thank you," replied Throgar. "That is nice to hear. Many feel I offer nothing of value to this city."

"You are a most gracious host," said Kargen.

Queen Urgash reached across the table, spearing a sizeable chunk of meat. "And you, a most polite guest. Since outsiders have not visited our city in many lifetimes, we were unsure how to properly feed you."

"You have provided us with a feast worthy of the Ancestors."

"It is interesting you mention them, for they have been on my mind since your arrival." She looked at Athgar. "Do you worship the Ancestors as well?"

"My people worship the old Gods," he replied, "but we heed the words of the Ancestors on occasion."

"According to our history, Humans are a bloodthirsty lot, taking what they desire by force."

"Those men came here seeking fame and fortune. Such folk are not representative of the general population."

"This I understand," said the queen. "Even amongst our own, we have some who are hotheaded. Have you seen much of the Continent other than your own lands?"

"Natalia and I have travelled south to the Shimmering Sea and west to Reinwick. Aside from that, our group has collectively visited the duchies of Krieghoff and Holstead, Andover, Carlingen, and even Abelard, although we didn't see much of it. Oh, and I suppose we should add Ruzhina to the list."

"How familiar are you with our northern neighbour?"

"What specifically would you like to know?"

"I am curious whether they would respect our boundaries if we revealed ourselves."

"Am I to assume you intend to make your existence known?"

"It is time," replied Urgash. "From your accounts, the Continent is far different than when we went into hiding. My chief concern is if we reveal our location, Humans might take it upon themselves to attack us."

"We had the same problem," said Natalia. "Only by displaying the might of our armies did we win the respect of the Petty Kingdoms. Not all, mind you, but enough to make the others think twice about coming after us."

"Can we convince them to do the same for us?"

"I believe so. I may be speaking out of turn, but if Therengia recognizes you, it might assist you in gaining some legitimacy in the eyes of the Petty Kingdoms."

"Enough to prevent an attack?"

"We cannot promise that," replied Athgar, "but we would agree to come to your aid if you requested it."

"Why would you do that?"

"We want stability in the region, which is why we march on Ruzhina. For too long, the Stormwinds have interfered in the politics of the Human realms. We aim to break their control over the courts of the Continent, once and for all."

"War is our history," said Urgash. "When we heard about the destruction of Ard-Uzgul, we vowed to never surrender. We have spent the last two thousand years training our army to be the finest warriors ever created. It is a heavy boast, especially considering we have not seen war for ages, but I assure you, we are ready for whatever threatens our home."

"What if you expanded beyond these city walls?" asked Natalia. "We refer to the area you live in as Zaran. Ruzhina sits on its northern border, while Carlingen lies to the south. It has the Great Northern Sea as its western coast and unexplored wilderness to the east. No person in living history has a claim to this region other than you. I suggest you declare it your own and spread out, forming a true kingdom of Orcs rather than just a city."

"I have difficulty believing the Human realms would permit this."

"The King of Carlingen is our ally. As for Ruzhina, the entire idea of attacking the Volstrum came from their king, so we can safely assume he is on our side. If both of those recognized your claim, who would say otherwise?"

"What of the sea?"

"The western coast is the Temple Fleet's domain, and we've worked with them before. Their only concern is keeping the peace and preventing piracy, so long as your warriors do not become sea marauders, I see no problem. I could set up a meeting with their admiral once we are done with the Volstrum."

"I like the idea," said the queen, "but worry about the cost to my people. Never in our history has another power made an offer without expecting something in return."

"We ask only for your friendship and that you stop outright killing anyone who enters your territory. If you want to do more, such as exchanging mages, we are open to the possibility."

"I like the idea of having friends outside of our walls. Perhaps I shall send some of my people to visit your land."

"I can have them there before the sun sets," replied Natalia.

"You can?"

"Yes. I know a spell that creates a portal between my present location and the standing stones back in Therengia. It's a few day's travel from there to Runewald, but we can arrange a guide."

"I have not heard of that spell before."

"It is a Water Magic spell called frozen arch. I found it hidden in the Volstrum's archives."

"The very place you seek to destroy?"

"Yes. I was held prisoner there for months and discovered a few things."

"Most interesting," said Urgash. "Might I ask why they imprisoned you?"

"The Stormwinds have been breeding powerful mages for centuries. I once served them, but when they tried to force me to bear a child, I fled, meeting Athgar along the way. Eventually, we found a home and now have a daughter, Oswyn."

"Orc friend? What an interesting name."

"The Ancestors named her."

"I assume these Stormwinds wished to steal away the child?"

"They did," said Natalia. "We stopped them, then decided we'd had enough. Athgar and I travelled to Ruzhina to finish it once and for all. Needless to say, it didn't go the way we expected."

"And now you return with an army. Or do you? I can't imagine the four of you, powerful as you may be, fighting an entire country?"

"You'd be correct. Our army in Therengia is ready to march at a moment's notice. We intend to cross into Ruzhina and open a portal to let the army come through."

"And how large is your army?"

"Eight hundred souls," replied Athgar, "with three hundred coming from the Orc tribes, along with several spellcasters, most of them rather powerful."

"Eight hundred is not a large number to launch an invasion with," said the queen.

"We've managed more with less."

"Our history reports the Elven cavalry was the bane of our existence. It's why our warriors are trained in the glaive, a weapon particularly suited against mounted opponents."

"The Volstrum won't employ cavalry," said Natalia, "and even if they did, our Temple Knights are capable of dealing with them."

"Temple Knights? Your arrival here has brought a myriad of new terms."

"Temple Knights are Holy Warriors, dedicated to their Saint."

"More Gods?"

"The Saints were living, breathing Humans who espoused a way of life that included acceptance of others. They were not Gods, merely wise men and women who helped guide others with their words. We work closely with two orders: the Temple Knights of Saint Mathew and those of Saint Agnes, which counts only women amongst its numbers."

"You seem to know a lot about military matters."

"I am the Warmaster of Therengia," explained Natalia, "trained as a battle mage by the very people we seek to destroy."

"I would be interested in hearing your opinion of our warriors. As I indicated earlier, many centuries have passed since we went to war, and I am concerned our training methods may no longer be effective against outsiders."

"I'd be delighted to observe them whenever it's convenient."

"Excellent," said Urgash. "I will let our First Glaive know you desire a demonstration. Shall we say tomorrow morning?"

"Most certainly."

"As for visiting Therengia," said Athgar, "I suggest postponing it until after we've dealt with our little problem in the north. Although it's easy enough for Natalia to get your people there, I'm afraid the return journey would be more difficult with us in Ruzhina."

"Nat-Alia," continued the queen, "could you teach the frozen arch to others?"

"Of course, but it requires a casting circle to target it properly, either that or a set of standing stones."

"We have a casting circle, but I am more concerned about our mages' ability to understand the magic. They are not as powerful as they once were, though I cannot explain why. Morgal is the expert in such things. Perhaps I shall have him talk with you."

"The frozen portal is a Water Magic spell."

"This I understand. We have several masters of water, although their services are seldom required these days."

"Then, with your blessing, I shall meet with them right after the demonstration tomorrow morning. I can assess their strength and determine if they are able to learn the spell." She grinned. "You have just made it much easier to travel to Therengia and return, providing you don't mind us using your magic circle?"

"The circle is guarded day and night by sentinels, but the mages have the final say over its use." She glanced up at the ceiling. "It lies above us at the top of the tower. It also gives a most impressive view of the area, for the walls are crystal clear, at least from the inside. I do not pretend to understand the magic behind it, but it is wondrous to behold." She stood. "I have much to prepare for tomorrow. I shall bid you good night." With that, she left, leaving the servants to clear away the table.

"I like her," said Athgar. "I feel we understand each other."

"As do I," added Kargen. "But she is right; it will be a busy day tomorrow. Let us retire."

"Shouldn't we wait for Shaluhk?" said Natalia.

"She has discovered their archives and will not emerge until the sun rises."

# DEMONSTRATION

## SPRING 1110 SR

(IN THE LANGUAGE OF THE ORCS)

The warriors moved forward in a solid block, their steps in unison. At the command of Garag, they lowered their glaives, presenting a wall of steel.

"Impressive," said Natalia. "I'd wager they could best any company in the Petty Kingdoms. Have they any experience against cavalry?"

"Unfortunately, no," replied the queen. "We have no cavalry, and although we have practiced the manoeuvres for generations, we have no actual knowledge if the tactic actually works."

"We have some experience fighting horsemen," said Athgar. "Perhaps you could have them show us their defence?"

"Most certainly."

Urgash whispered to one of her aides, who then ran over to Garag. The First Glaive gave the order, and the Orcs formed into a hollow square, their glaives now sticking out in all directions.

"We call it the porcupine," said the queen. "According to our records, it was used to great effect at the Battle of the Green River."

"When was this?" asked Natalia.

"Back before the fall of Ard-Uzgul. Their warriors conducted a delaying action to slow the Elven advance. It proved most effective, buying enough time to evacuate those in the outlying lands. According to the accounts of survivors, the Elven horses would not dare approach the porcupine for fear of impalement."

"And Ard-Uzgul?"

"It was eventually destroyed, with many of the survivors fleeing here to Ard-Gurslag."

"What do you think, Athgar?"

"It's a useful tactic," he replied. "It wouldn't stop a tusker, but I doubt a warhorse would willingly approach."

"Tusker?" said the queen. "I am unfamiliar with such a creature."

"They are massive," replied Athgar, "with cloven hoofs and large tusks."

"Ah, yes. I believe I know what you speak of. They can be found in the wildlands to the east. We call them magants."

"Our Orcs ride them," added Natalia. "Our masters of earth convinced them to work with us."

"We, too, have masters of earth, but I never would have believed there would be an advantage to having tuskers as mounts."

"Understandable, considering your present situation. Tuskers are not what you want roaming a city."

The queen turned back to the demonstration. "Are our warriors equal to those in the Petty Kingdoms?"

"Most definitely, but I'd like to see them gain some experience facing horses. Knights can be a frightening prospect in battle, and it takes nerves of steel to stand up to them."

"Like the Temple Knights you spoke of yesterday?"

"Exactly."

"Then we will invite them here, to Ard-Gurslag. I am eager to see them for myself."

"Much as I'd like to oblige," replied Natalia, "we still have our own matters to attend to in Ruzhina."

"Can I convince you to delay your plans in exchange for us offering you some help?"

"What did you have in mind?"

"This northern kingdom needs to feel the bite of the Orcs if only to discourage them from ranging into our territory. This expedition of yours could benefit from the addition of some of our warriors."

"I'm sorry," said Athgar. "Perhaps I misunderstood. Did you just offer to loan us warriors?"

"That was certainly my intent. The Orcs of the Continent need a power that can inspire them. I do not mean to imply that Therengia is not on friendly terms with our people, but others will always view it as a Human-run realm. Ard-Gurslag could show the Continent that Orcs are a power to be reckoned with, and demonstrating our fighting prowess would go a long way to convincing others of our might. Was that not your experience?"

"I'm sorry to have to admit it was. All we ever wanted was to be left in peace, but the Petty Kingdoms sought to eradicate us. On behalf of the people of Therengia, I gratefully accept any aid you wish to render."

"I am pleased to hear this," replied Urgash. "I will convene a council meeting this evening to discuss the arrangements, and I would appreciate it if you two were both there."

"Certainly," said Athgar. "I suggest you invite Kargen and Shaluhk as well. I find their advice to be most insightful."

"I shall inform the others of their attendance. Nat-Alia, I believe you have a meeting with our masters of water. They are expecting you at the casting circle."

Natalia nodded. "At the top of the tower, correct?"

"Yes. I shall have someone show you the way."

"I'd like to stay here awhile," said Athgar. "I'm most curious to hear Garag's opinions on military matters."

"I shall inform him that he may speak freely. Now, I must go. The life of a queen is a busy one." She turned, heading back towards the tower, all save one of her servants following in her wake. The remaining Orc walked over to Garag, exchanged a few words, and then abandoned him, rushing to catch up to his mistress.

The First Glaive wandered over. "You wanted to speak with me?"

"I did," said Athgar. "Your warriors are very well-trained and highly disciplined; they are a credit to you."

The Orc bared his teeth in a grin. "They practice diligently, but we have never fought in battle, only skirmishes. What about you? Have you seen battle?"

"Yes. More times than I care to admit."

"Then you and I should find a nice seat in the Armoury and discuss things over a pot of ale."

"The armoury? That's a strange place to drink."

Garag laughed, a deep, rumbling sound. "The Armoury is a tavern down the street from the tower and is a common place for our warriors to meet when they are not on duty. Have you ever had Orc ale before?"

"I have, although your descendants brewed it. I'm curious to see how it compares to a two-thousand-year-old recipe."

"Challenge accepted. Let me dismiss the glaives, then I will show you the way."

"The glaives? Is that what you call that formation?"

"What else would we call it?"

"We call them companies, a term dating back to the old Kingdom of Therengia."

"You must tell me more, but first, duty calls."

Kargen released the arrow, and it flew downrange, striking the target dead centre, burying itself halfway to the fletching.

The Orc beside him stared in disbelief. "A most powerful weapon. Are all your archers armed thus?"

"No, Lurka. Only our most experienced hunters. Superior strength is required to wield such a bow, and not every Orc can use it to its full potential."

"How long have you had them?"

"Only a few years," replied Kargen. "Athgar made the first Orc warbow seven years ago. Since then, it has proven itself again and again in battle."

"The archers of Ard-Gurslag have weak bows."

"That stands to reason. The terrain in these parts is not suitable for long-range archery, and the thick underbrush makes carrying a larger bow cumbersome."

"If we are to fight the Human kingdoms, we need weapons capable of penetrating their armour."

"Ard-Gurslag does not need to go to war with the Petty Kingdoms. The best way to assure peace for your people is through alliances."

"Aside from your people, who would consider allying with Orcs?"

"You might be surprised," said Kargen. "The Ashwalkers proved most effective in Andover. As a result, the kingdom of Reinwick is now considered an ally of Therengia. Many kings do not care what race you are so long as your objectives align with theirs. There are exceptions, but people of that ilk tend not to be trustworthy enough for any worthwhile cooperation."

"Do your archers loose arrows in volleys?"

"The fyrd does, while we Orcs prefer to pick our targets. Our role is generally on the flanks, where we take advantage of rough terrain."

"What is a fyrd?"

"Every Therengian between the ages of eighteen and forty is expected to help protect the realm during war. To that end, they practice weekly."

"And do all Human realms do this?"

"Many call on their people to defend the land in times of war, but their skill level is usually limited. Therengia also differs in that females serve."

"A sensible approach. None serve in the glaives, however, many of our archers are females, including those in charge. I am told you have shamans."

"We do. Several, in fact. Aside from healing, their magic lets them communicate over large distances, useful on the battlefield."

"I can well imagine."

Kargen held out his bow. "Would you like to try my warbow? I must warn you, it takes much strength to use it properly."

Lurka took hold of it with a firm grip, then tested the string. "A most powerful weapon. Any advice on how to best employ it?"

"First, stand with your feet well apart…"

"This is most fascinating," said Shaluhk. "According to this, you once had your own horsemen."

"That was long ago," replied Throgar, "before the founding of Ard-Gurslag."

"This wasn't your original home?"

"The origin of the Great War is lost to history, but we know it lasted for centuries. Ard-Gurslag was founded after it began when we were building strategic locations for our war against the Elves. It is said we are the last city of the Orcs. I assumed that was because we, alone, survived the war, but perhaps it was meant to signify this is the last city built by our people?"

"What has that to do with horses?"

"We came from the west, where land was more accommodating to such creatures. Once we arrived here, it proved difficult to utilize the cavalry, so we concentrated on small patrols designed to discover any intruders early before they could locate our city. Patrols were aggressive initially, but over the centuries, it became apparent we had been forgotten, so they grew less frequent to hide our existence. These days, we still patrol the area, but only sporadically."

"Yet you found us."

"That was no accident," said Throgar. "That was Morgal's magic."

"Are you suggesting he has a spell that can detect others?"

"Atop this tower, beside the giant gem that protects the city, sits the scrying tube of Throkar, our greatest mage."

"His name is very similar to yours."

"That is because I was named after him."

"But yours is slightly different," noted Shaluhk.

"That is a more recent affectation, meant to reflect the present rather than the past."

"And this tube allows you to see intruders?"

"No, but campfires give off smoke, which is readily apparent when your point of view is high above the treetops."

"How far can this device see?"

"It uses a variation of the far scrye spell. On a clear day, it reveals many leagues in all directions, but the person using it must be skilled in its operation."

"I assume that means it is always controlled by one of your mages?"

"It is."

"There are no buildings like this in Runewald. None of our huts are higher than a single storey, although Ebenstadt boasts taller structures."

"Is that a city?"

"The largest in all of Therengia, if you do not count the annexed territories."

"The outside sounds like a fascinating place."

"It is," replied Shaluhk, "but your city has its own interesting features."

"I understand how you might believe that," said Throgar, "but to me, it is as unchanging as the mountains, a place where time stands still, and we exist in a never-ending fear of invasion."

"Now that we found you, that time is at an end. We shall guide you as you take your rightful place amongst the powers of the Continent."

"Just how many powers are there?"

"I do not have an exact count, but I have been told there are over fifty Petty Kingdoms, though that does not include Therengia or Ruzhina."

"Which are considered the most powerful?"

"The Northern Alliance, a coalition friendly to us, commands a sizeable army, while Hadenfeld is believed to employ the largest single-nation army, but I know little about it except that it is centrally located."

"And Therengia?"

"We would be considered one of the more powerful realms due to our military success rather than the actual size of our army."

"I wonder where the forces of Ard-Gurslag would find themselves, power-wise."

"That depends on your numbers," said Shaluhk. "The larger Petty Kingdoms can field two or three thousand warriors in times of war."

"We could do that," replied Throgar, "although it would strip our defences. A more realistic number would be one thousand: fitting, considering our heritage."

"Meaning?"

"The founders of Ard-Gurslag were known as The One Thousand. More arrived later, fleeing the destruction of other cities and swelling our numbers. To this day, descendants of The One Thousand still wield enormous influence."

. . .

Natalia entered the room to see eight Orcs standing around the magic circle. Behind them, the transparent walls bathed the room in the afternoon sun—a breathtaking sight. Had she more time, she would have stopped to admire it. Instead, she regarded the spellcasters of Ard-Gurslag.

"Good day to you," she said in greeting. "My name is Natalia Stormwind. Queen Urgash asked me to evaluate those of you who are masters of water to determine if you can employ advanced spells."

"We are all masters of water," replied a darker-skinned female, "though some have yet to master the art." She cast her gaze around, giving several a look of contempt.

"And you are?"

"Nakthar."

"You don't look very old. How long ago did you pass your ordeal?"

"Ordeal?"

"Where I'm from, when Orcs come of age, they undergo a test of both mental and physical strength. Have you no such tradition here?"

"And if they fail, do they remain younglings for the rest of their lives?" The rest chuckled.

"No, they usually die. The ordeal involves surviving on their own for a ten-day with only rudimentary weapons."

The room sobered.

"My apologies," said Nakthar. "I meant no offence."

"Yes, you did," replied Natalia, "or you wouldn't have said it. I know you view me as a mere Human, but I am a member of the Red Hand. Insulting me insults the entire tribe." She stared at each in turn, noting their look of shame as they all studied their feet. "Perhaps a demonstration might convince you of my abilities." She stepped into the circle and then began casting, feeling the power held within almost instantly. Far more magic resided here than in Carlingen, and she wondered if a power node lay beneath them. She slipped back to casting her spell, and soon the familiar arches appeared. She let the top connect them, then closed her eyes to concentrate on the circle of stones back home.

She couldn't see the arch on the other side of the connection, but she felt it. A loud snap occurred in her mind as they connected, and then she opened her eyes, watching for everyone's reactions.

The Orcs in the casting room moved around, excited by her spell. A familiar figure waved from the other side, then moved closer, revealing it to be Kragor. "Nat-Alia," he said. "This is a surprise. I did not expect the army to move so soon."

"This is not for the army," she replied, "merely a demonstration of my magic. Would you be so kind as to step through and greet the masters of water here in Ard-Gurslag."

The Orc did as he was bid, then stood straighter as his gaze swept the room. "I am Kragor," he announced. "Hunter of the Red Hand."

"He is being modest," said Natalia. "He is one of our finest hunters and the best archer in all of Therengia."

"This is a trick," said Nakthar.

"This is no ruse. I assure you."

Kragor blushed slightly. "Who is this who brightens my day so?"

Nakthar's own face darkened, a sign she found the hunter appealing. "I am Nakthar."

"Then come, Nakthar. Let me show you the standing stones unless you would rather not?"

She looked at Natalia.

"Go ahead," she replied. "I'll hold the gate open, but don't be too long; we have more to do."

Kragor held out his hand, and Nakthar grasped it, then stepped gingerly through the arch. They wandered over to one side, out of everyone's sight.

"Remarkable," said an older Orc, her hair a mixture of grey and green. "I never thought such a thing possible."

"Are you the senior master here?" asked Natalia.

"My name is Zorith, and yes, I bear that honour." She glanced at the arch. "It must take a huge amount of power to sustain that connection."

"The other end is anchored by a power node, an area where ley lines intersect. Are you familiar with such things?"

"I am. One lies beneath us, which is why this site was chosen for the construction of Ard-Gurslag in the first place."

"I thought as much. I detected considerable power when I began casting my spell."

"You must take care; too much power can damage the wielder."

"I'm well aware. Now, might I ask that you perform a little favour?"

"If I am able."

"Can you pass through and convince Nakthar to return? Although I possess enough power to maintain this connection for some time, other priorities need our attention this day."

# ALLIES

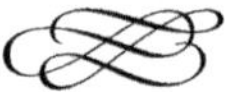

## SPRING 1110 SR

(IN THE LANGUAGE OF THE ORCS)

They gathered in the queen's council chambers, making for two very crowded benches. It was an informal affair, the queen waiving their usual rules of conduct to allow for a freer exchange of ideas.

"I gathered you here," she began, "because I have decided to aid our new friends in their expedition to the north. I know that goes against millennia of tradition, but we cannot remain hidden from the Continent forever. Eiddenwerthe has changed greatly during our seclusion. If we do not adapt, we risk becoming a relic of the past. We must emerge while we can still project strength, and the best way to do that is by demonstrating our commitment to aid an ally. Let me be clear on our purpose this evening. We are not here to discuss whether or not to help but to determine the details of that aid."

She paused, gathering her thoughts. "Anyone wishing to speak will be given the chance, but I thought it best we begin by discussing the current state of our army." She locked eyes with the youngest of her advisors. "I believe that would be your responsibility, Zorga."

"It is, Greatness." The administrator stood, moving to the centre of the circle. "I shall attempt to keep this as brief as possible, but I do not wish to confuse our new friends."

She addressed Athgar. "We have two armies in Ard-Gurslag: the professional glaives and archers who protect our territory and the citizenry who take up arms in the event of an attack. I will address only the first in this report, as we are not currently concerned about an attack on our city. The one thousand warriors under Garag's command are organized into fourteen glaives and six arrows of archers, which are, I am told, equivalent to Therengian companies in size, thus making things simpler. Each archer is equipped to loose thirty volleys, with double that in reserve. They could draw on further stores for a more prolonged campaign, but that would reduce our stocks for defending the city. As for the glaives, they are ready to march once their travel rations are issued."

"Thank you," said the queen. "Have you any questions, Athgar?"

"I watched them training," he replied, "and have no doubt they would acquit themselves well in battle. My concern is not their quality but who would command them. It is difficult to lead an army when multiple voices give contradictory commands."

"This is your expedition," the queen assured him. "Garag commands the Orcs of Ard-Gurslag, but would be responsible to you or your warmaster, who, I am told, typically commands your army."

"That's true. My other concern is getting your warriors to where they can be utilized. There is a lot of thick forest between here and the Volstrum."

"That largely depends on what Nat-Alia discovered about our masters of water?"

"Most are capable of learning the frozen arch spell," replied Natalia, "but to bring them north, they would either need to travel with us, or you permit me to commit your magic circle to memory, thus allowing me to cast my spell from Ruzhina. Then, your mages can step through and assist with further arches."

"This is no simple request," said Zorith. "Your knowledge of our circle puts us all at risk. How do we know you would not use that knowledge against us?"

"We have no reason to attack your fine city. In fact, we have multiple reasons to further good relations with you, especially as you offered to send us warriors to help."

"I still do not like the idea of outsiders gaining this knowledge."

"Would it calm your fears if, in return, your spellcasters committed the standing stones back in Therengia to memory?"

Zorith nodded. "That would be a suitable compromise, though I am surprised you trust us so quickly."

"You are Orcs," said Kargen. "Why would we not? It also allows the free exchange of ideas, not to mention trade."

"Both our peoples benefit from this arrangement," added the queen, "but it requires our spellcasters to learn the frozen arch spell. How much time do you need to teach this to our people, Nat-Alia?"

"I could teach the three strongest casters in a day or two. A few others could eventually learn it, but I fear they will require more time. Committing the standing stones to memory does not take long, so they could be ready by tomorrow afternoon, should you wish."

"That soon? You surprise me. Very well. You may begin the process first thing tomorrow morning. Now, as to numbers, I would like to hear from Garag."

The First Glaive stood, taking the centre position. "We must not abandon our responsibility to protect the city. I therefore propose we send only ten companies—to use the Therengian term. I talked with Athgar at length, and he assured me the Army of Therengia has sufficient archers. However, the assault on the Volstrum will be a close-in affair, more akin to seizing a fortress, something our glaives are particularly well-suited for."

"Have you any concerns?" asked the queen.

"I have. The enemy we face will be strong in magic, making it imperative we bring spellcasters of our own. Perhaps Morgal would like to give us his thoughts?"

The Enchanter remained sitting while he spoke. "Ard-Gurslag has always prided itself on its number of masters of magic. We count masters of earth, fire, water, and even air, not to mention Enchanters. In fact, the only magic we lack is that of life. That is not to say we can afford to commit them all to this enterprise. No, far from it. Those in training are not ready, while our seasoned casters are needed to ensure the continuation of their craft."

"Are you suggesting," replied the queen, "that we do not send any?"

"Battle is not the domain of those seeking to further their understanding of the arcane arts."

"That is unacceptable. You yourself took an oath to protect this city."

"And protect it I will, Greatness, but attacking another kingdom is not keeping our people safe."

Natalia stood. "May I speak?"

"Most certainly," replied Urgash.

"I understand your desire to keep your people safe. We are of a similar mind, yet the Petty Kingdoms wait on no one. Whether you like it or not, Humans will push eastward, claiming that which is not theirs. You can no longer afford to hide; you must make a stand, announcing to the Continent you are a power to be reckoned with. When we did that in Therengia, it allowed our people to prosper. Indeed, when news spread of our victories, Therengians from across the Petty Kingdoms came east, seeking a new life in our lands. Many Orc tribes are scattered throughout the lands of men; your emergence would be a guiding beacon for them the same as Therengia is for the descendants of the Old Kingdom."

"Your words inspire," said Morgal, "but at what cost? How many Orcs must die to establish us as a legitimate kingdom in the eyes of the Human realms? And would our emergence only fuel hatred against those Continental Orcs?"

"There is no simple answer," replied Natalia. "Athgar and I have travelled extensively and done much to help both Therengian and Orc alike. If you are worried about reprisals against the Orcs scattered throughout the Continent, then displaying your military might is even more important. The Petty Kingdoms respect strength, and although they may dislike the concept of an Orc Kingdom, they are not so foolish to take on such a powerful foe."

"How does that help our brothers and sisters?"

"You help them by sending diplomats to ensure their safety."

"Are you suggesting Humans would welcome Orcs at their courts? I find that hard to believe."

"Some will," said Natalia, "and those who don't will have no objection to receiving Human envoys from Carlingen or Ruzhina, who might be convinced to speak on your behalf."

"Ruzhina?" said Morgal. "That is the kingdom we are about to invade!"

"We are not invading the realm, merely destroying the rot infesting its court. We did not decide on our own to march to Ruzhina; its ruler, King Yulakov, invited us."

"Your objection is noted, Morgal," said the queen, "but you are still required to answer the question. How many of our spellcasters can you provide for the expedition?"

"I do not command them as Garag does the glaives. Each is entitled to choose whether they will assist in this endeavour."

"Then order them to assemble this evening, and we shall see who answers the call."

"As you wish," replied the Enchanter. "But I caution you against being overly optimistic, Greatness. The vast majority have spent years perfecting their respective fields of study. I highly doubt they will wish to risk their lives in battle."

"That," said Queen Urgash, "is not your concern."

Morgal simply bowed.

"Now, on to other matters. How are our food stores?"

. . .

It was late when Athgar fell into bed. "That meeting went on far longer than I anticipated. And then I had to spend most of the evening making plans with Garag. How did things go with the mages?"

Natalia chuckled. "We're alone; you don't need to speak Orcish."

"I can't help it. I've been using their language all day long. In any case, what does it matter? We're both fluent."

"I suppose that's true. As to my evening, it went better than expected, perhaps a little too much."

"Meaning?"

"Many mages wanted to volunteer, which makes my job much tougher."

"How?"

"I must choose whom to accept. It was one thing working with the masters of water, but now I have to evaluate masters of fire, earth, and air, not to mention Enchanters. Then there's still teaching them how to cast the frozen arch. What we really need is more time."

"Nothing is saying we must leave right away."

"True, but every day we delay is another day the family might get wind of our plans. If you recall, Yulakov has Stormwinds at his court. How long before they become suspicious? Especially since Piotr never came back from Abelard?"

"I can't argue with that," said Athgar, "but you could leave the selection process to Shaluhk. She's more than capable of assessing someone's magical potential."

"Yes, of course." She smiled. "I knew I kept you around for some reason."

"Glad to hear it. Now, we should get some sleep. It's going to be a long day tomorrow."

"It will for me," said Natalia. "What are you up to?"

"I'll be working with Garag, letting his glaives know what to expect." He paused. "It's strange calling them glaives."

"Why? It's their weapon of choice."

"Yes, but they use it to refer to their foot troops."

"And why would that be strange? Don't you sometimes refer to the number of axes you command?"

"I suppose I do, but we still use the term 'company' and, as the person in command, I'm not the first axe."

"True, but you know the Therengians of the Old Kingdom were the originators of the term 'company'. You can't expect the Orcs of Ard-Gurslag to have heard of it when they've been isolated for two thousand years."

"I suppose that's true. Tell me, and be honest now, do you have any reservations about this?"

"You mean getting help from the Orcs? No. Why?"

"It's just that we are essentially unleashing a new power upon the Continent. That's likely to upset people."

"That's a good thing, surely? Remember, the Halvarian Empire is out there, waiting to conquer the Petty Kingdoms. You trust the Orcs, don't you?"

"I trust the Orcs of the Continent, but these are direct descendants of city dwellers, which gives them a completely different perspective."

"What does your gut tell you?"

"That there's good people here, along with bad."

"You mean Morgal?"

"He didn't want to help us," said Athgar. "He made that quite plain."

"Yet he did what he was told. Not everyone likes the idea of going to war."

"Yes, you're right. I should learn to be more trusting, but I can't help but remember Gorlag. He was the Chieftain of the Red Hand before Kargen."

"You duelled him if I recall."

"I did."

"Look," said Natalia. "I'm not sure if this helps, but remember when we first found Runewald. The king was prepared to go to war with the Orcs, but you got them through that hatred. We must strive to do the same thing here. Orcs are a lot like Humans in one respect—we both fear what we don't understand. The more the Orcs of Ard-Gurslag interact with Therengians, the more they'll get used to us. Kargen and Shaluhk are also influences on them, along with all those tribal Orcs they'll meet during the campaign. Not everything will be perfect, but at least this relationship is off to a good start."

"You were always the wise one."

"You are as wise as I am. I just happen to have training in court politics. That's all this is—a royal court with all the usual players."

"I'm not sure I follow?"

"Ignore that they're Orcs, and look at this from the point of view of personalities. We have the queen who wants to do what's best for her people, the mage, whose only concern is his magic, and then there's the dedicated warrior, Garag, who wants a chance to prove his mettle. We've seen people like this before in Reinwick, Andover, and Carlingen."

"I wasn't with you in Andover."

"I was making the point that Orcs are not so different from Humans when you get right down to it. If you think about it, what is a society other than a collection of individuals? It matters little whether they be Human, Orc, or even Dwarves—they're still people."

She rolled over to lay on top of him, her face pressed close to his. "Now, how about we come up with a way to take your mind off all of this?"

The next morning, Athgar made his way downstairs, where Kargen and Shaluhk sat eating their breakfast.

"I was wondering when you might join us," said Kargen. "Nat-Alia awoke some time ago."

"I assume," replied Athgar, "she's gone off to train the mages?"

"She has."

"And what are you two up to today?"

"I am going out with a patrol," replied Kargen. "Garag tells me his men can safely escort us to the border, but I want to recover our umak. I expect I shall be back by nightfall."

"That's quite the trip."

"Not as far as you might think. It seems our escort did not take us on the most direct path when he brought us here."

"Why not?" asked Athgar.

"To keep the location of Ard-Gurslag a secret."

"But we have no maps of the area."

"True, but he did not know that."

"I suppose that makes sense. What about you, Shaluhk? What are you planning?"

"I shall inform those back home about the recent developments. I am told we are only a short distance from the border of Ruzhina, so our army must begin its march to the standing stones in readiness. After that, I shall assess the other spellcasters."

"It's strange," said Athgar. "We saw very little change for days on end, but now everything is coming together so quickly. Are we doing the right thing?"

"Of course," replied Shaluhk. "Why would you even suggest otherwise?"

"It is natural," said Kargen. "Great leaders always have doubts; it is what makes them so endearing."

"Is it? Do you ever have doubts?"

"No. Of course not, but I have the wisdom of a powerful shaman to guide me."

"A good answer. You thought that through carefully."

Kargen grinned. "I have been thinking about it for some time. I only waited for the perfect moment."

"Then there is nothing wrong with your timing."

# LESSONS

SPRING 1110 SR

Agar swung his axe while Zaruhk, his sparring partner, parried the blow, following up with an attack of her own that struck his axe handle, almost knocking the weapon from his grip.

"Very good," he said, backing up slightly. "You have grown much in my absence."

She grinned, showing her ivory teeth. "As have you, Agar, but I wonder why you speak the common tongue when fighting. Is it because of him?" She nodded her head towards Piotr, watching off to one side.

"It is."

Zaruhk looked at the young prince. "What do you think of our sparring?"

"Not much. The axe is a crude weapon, especially compared to the sword."

"Not so," said Agar. "In the right hands, an axe is deadly."

"Perhaps if you're fighting peasants, but trained swordsmen are superior." Piotr glanced at the nearby fyrd, practicing their shield wall, then shook his head. "I will never understand why you arm your women. It would be seen as disgraceful back in Ruzhina."

"I am female," Zaruhk reminded him.

"You are, which only proves my point. Females, whether Orc or Human, are not suited to the role of warrior."

"The Temple Knights of Saint Agnes might argue with you."

"Possibly, but you know as well as I, they're primarily ceremonial."

"That is not true. They fought at Ord-Kurgad."

"You witnessed this yourself, did you?"

Zaruhk shook her head. "I was too young then."

"It's not your fault," replied Piotr. "You're simply the victim of someone else's stories."

"You have a… What is the Human expression? Ah, yes. A big mouth. Perhaps you would care to prove your claims?"

"How does one prove an untrue story?"

Zaruhk's flesh darkened, a sign her temper was in danger of flaring. "If you think the sword is superior to the axe, then prove it."

"What are you suggesting?"

"That you fight me."

"Here?" replied Piotr. "Now?"

"Why not? You are not scared, are you?"

A smile crept across the prince's face. "Stand back, Agar, while I give this young woman a lesson in swordplay." He paused. "Do I refer to her as a woman? I'm never certain with your people."

"If you intend to duel," said Agar, "I must insist you both use wooden weapons. I do not want to be the one to inform my uncle there has been a death in the village."

"That is fine with me," said Zaruhk. She walked over to a small chest sitting nearby and rummaged through it. "I have not used a wooden axe for years. It will be interesting to see how I fare." She tossed a wooden sword at Piotr's feet. "Will that suffice?"

"It will," replied the prince. He strolled over, looking confident as he picked up the weapon.

Someone amongst the fyrd must have noticed their activity, for the shield wall disbanded, its members wandering over to watch. Zaruhk swung her wooden axe a few times before taking up a position at one end of the practice circle.

"What are the rules?" asked Piotr.

"There is a tradition of duelling in the Red Hand," replied Agar. "It does not happen often, but when it does, we follow strict rules. Where we are standing, you will notice a ring of small stones that define a circle. You fight until one of you submits or is driven beyond those stones."

"Is that all?" Piotr glanced at the gathering crowd. "Don't get too comfortable; this will be over before you realize it."

Zaruhk stood patiently, the axe resting in her right hand.

"Come to the centre," said Agar, waiting until they did as he commanded before continuing. "This is a friendly duel to prove who is better at fighting, not a fight to the death."

"I understand," said Piotr.

"As do I," added Zaruhk.

Agar stepped back, sweeping his right arm down dramatically. "You may begin."

Piotr rushed forward, his wooden sword held out as he stabbed. Zaruhk easily avoided the attack, countering with a blow of her own, the head of her axe scraping up his blade to rest against its crossguard.

"A lucky swing," said the prince, backing up. "You won't succeed with that a second time."

"You talk too much," replied the Orc, stepping closer and hitting him with small, efficient chops. The whirling axe drove Piotr back as he tried to block.

"Careful," warned Agar. "You are close to the edge of the circle."

The Prince of Ruzhina struck back, desperately going on the offensive, but his opponent was ready. As his sword came down, she blocked, using her axe handle to tug the weapon from his grasp, unbalancing him, and he stumbled forward. Zaruhk stepped to one side, allowing him to move past, then tapped the head of her axe onto his back.

"You are defeated," she said.

"I'll admit you're the superior fighter," he replied, "but I still maintain the sword is better than the axe."

"How can you say that when you failed to achieve a victory?"

"While I know how to handle a sword, I don't claim to be an expert. Were you facing a knight, this fight would have ended differently."

"You forget," said Zaruhk. "I am only a youngling. Adult Orcs are much more adept at axe play than me."

"Let us settle the argument in a different way," suggested Agar. "Wait here, both of you." He ran off towards the great hut.

"What's he up to?" asked Piotr.

Zaruhk smiled. "I am not certain, but knowing Agar, I can only assume it is something unusual."

"What does that mean? Are you suggesting he's strange?"

"Not strange, no, merely full of surprises. He has learned much on his travels and delights in bringing that knowledge back to share with others."

Agar emerged from the great hut carrying something. As he got closer, it became apparent he had taken a breastplate from a suit of plate armour.

"Where did you get that?" asked Piotr.

"It is a relic from the Battle of the Standing Stones, taken from a Cunar."

"A Temple Knight?"

"Yes. The Therengians and Orcs worked together to defeat the Holy Army. It was a day of great rejoicing."

"Why have you brought it out here?"

"For a demonstration." Agar laid it on the ground. "Go ahead. Hit that as hard as you can with your sword."

Piotr looked down at the dented and scratched piece of armour. "I can't penetrate that with a sword, and I doubt your axe will do any better."

Agar held up his axe. "This was a gift from my father. It has seen many battles, but Kieren made some improvements."

"Kieren?"

"A Dwarven smith found here in Runewald. Notice the spike on the back of the head, opposite the blade?"

"What's that for?"

"Watch and see." Agar lifted the axe and struck with all his might, the blade denting the breastplate slightly but not penetrating. He then reversed his grip and brought the weapon down spike first. It made a dull ringing noise as it penetrated the steel.

"Impressive," said Piotr. "Perhaps there is merit to your claims."

Agar went to pull the axe out, but the spike was stuck fast. In desperation, he put one foot on the breastplate to steady it, yet a second tug proved as unsuccessful as the first. Zaruhk stepped closer to lend a hand, and together, they grasped the handle, but it still wouldn't budge.

The prince soon joined them. "On the count of three," he said, then began counting. They pulled on the handle at three, and the spike wrenched free, the sudden release sending all three tumbling, leaving them convulsing in fits of laughter.

"Congratulations," said Piotr, trying to catch his breath. "You've discovered a very interesting way to disarm yourself."

"I must agree," added Zaruhk. "Though I doubt a Temple Knight would sit still for such an attack."

"I apologize. I was out of place when I suggested females were not suited to fighting."

"Thank you. I imagine that was hard for you to admit."

"It was," replied Piotr. "I don't mean to make excuses, but my tutors back in Ruzhina were very persuasive."

"It is easy to be so when only presented with one side of a story."

Piotr turned to Agar. "She's smart, this one. Where did you find her?"

"She is a member of the Red Hand. She grew up in Runewald."

"That is not completely true," replied Zaruhk. "Like you, I was born before we left Ord-Kurgad, although I was too young to remember much of it."

"It must've been difficult to flee your home," said Piotr.

"As I said, I remember little of it. What of your home?"

"Mine? What's there to tell?"

"Is it like Runewald?"

"No, not in the least. It's an immense city with buildings several stories taller than what you have here, not that I saw much of them."

"I am not sure I understand," said Zaruhk.

"I spent most of my time at the Palace. On those rare occasions when I was allowed out, I was heavily guarded."

"So, you have never hunted?"

"No. Never."

"Can you use a bow?"

"As long as we're only loosing arrows at targets."

"Then it is time we organized a hunt."

"Sounds like fun," replied Piotr. "And while we're at it, could you show me how you wielded that axe?"

"The army is restless," said Raleth. "It's been weeks since the High Thane left on this expedition of his, and we have yet to receive the order to march."

"You must be patient," said Laruhk. "We always suspected the going would be rough, and my sister's reports confirm that. And now there is the matter of these new Orcs."

"New Orcs?" said Durgash. "Why was I not told about them?"

"You were visiting the Stone Crushers, no doubt to see Varag again."

"Do not tease him," said Ushog.

"Why not?"

"Did he tease you when we were bonded?"

"Yes."

"Then you should strive to be the better Orc. Kargen left you in charge during his absence. Would you want him to know you are teasing his hunters?"

"No," said Laruhk, turning a slightly darker green. "My apologies, Durgash. I did not mean to upset you."

The hunter laughed. "Bonding has served you well, my friend. I might try doing the same."

"With Varag?"

Durgash grinned. "Is it that obvious?"

"Only to us," replied Ushog. "If you bond with her, which tribe will you settle in?"

"I had not considered that. Which do you believe she would prefer, Stone Crusher or Red Hand?"

"I will not answer that for her, nor should you. It is a discussion best held in private."

"But I was raised as a Red Hand."

"And she, as a Stone Crusher. Do you now claim your tribe is better than hers?"

"No," replied Durgash. "I suppose not."

The door opened to Oswyn.

"Yes?" said Laruhk.

"Agar is coming," she replied. "He's bringing the boy prince."

"Thank you for letting us know."

"He's going to be in big trouble," she shouted, then ran off without a word of explanation.

"Trouble?" said Durgash. "What is he up to now?"

The sound of running feet approached, and the hut door opened to the two younglings. Agar stopped short. "My pardon. I did not mean to interrupt."

"Yet you did," replied Laruhk. "What was your purpose in coming here?"

"I wanted Piotr to see how our realm was governed."

"Could you not have told him?"

"I did," said Agar, "but he insisted on seeing for himself."

Laruhk glanced at the other council members.

"We have nothing to hide," said Ushog. "I say we let him take a seat." The rest nodded their agreement.

"Come in, Piotr," said Laruhk. "Join us."

"Don't you mean, Your Highness?" replied the youth.

"There are no titles in the Thane's Council. All voices carry equal weight."

"Even the son of a king?"

"Tell me," said Ushog. "What makes a king better than his subjects?"

"His birthright."

"And what does that mean, exactly?"

"The blood of kings flows in my veins."

"Your blood is no different from that of anyone else. If you do not believe me, then ask Voruhn."

"Who is?"

"I am a shaman. In Human terms, I would be called a Life Mage."

"And you support the claim that my blood is no different from anyone else's?"

"It is not a claim; it is fact. If you spilled your blood on the battlefield, it would be indistinguishable from a commoner's. You are a prince because you had the good fortune to be born a king's son. That does not make you better, merely privileged. If you wish to become a wise king one day, I suggest you remember that."

"This is all so hard to understand," said Piotr. "My tutors told me I was destined to be a great king."

"And would these tutors be the ones telling you what to do?"

"I…"

"While it is advisable to listen to the opinion of others," said Voruhn, "you must learn when to make your own decisions."

"Is that how the High Thane rules?"

"You could learn a lot from Athgar," replied Laruhk. "He was not born to be High Thane; he earned that right through his actions on behalf of the Therengian people. Life in the Petty Kingdoms would be far better if they ruled similarly." He rose, moving closer to the young prince. "Look around you. What do you see?"

"A large hut with a firepit running down the middle. Is this what you use as your council chambers?"

Laruhk pointed to a door at the far end of the room. "That hut belongs to Kargen, Chieftain of the Red Hand"—then nodded towards the opposite end, where another door stood—"and that is where Athgar, our High Thane, lives."

"Are you suggesting you're so poor, you can't afford a regular meeting place?"

"No. There is no permanent meeting place. The council chambers, as you call them, are anywhere the council gathers. The thane and chieftain take turns hosting the gathering."

"Yet you're all here, in your capital."

"You are correct, but not for the reason you think. We do not gather here because Runewald is more important than other villages. Rather, we are here because the Army of Therengia has come together to aid your father."

A worried look flashed across Piotr's face. "But Ruzhina is hundreds of miles away. Shouldn't they already be marching?"

"The first companies are headed to the standing stones, where they will be transported to Ruzhina by magic."

"Impossible!"

Laruhk shrugged. "It matters not whether you believe us. The army is already marching."

"Perhaps," said Agar, "we might accompany it as far as the standing stones? Then he can witness Nat-Alia's magic for himself?"

"You oversee the army, Raleth. What is your opinion on this matter?"

"I'm willing to allow it," replied the commander, "provided the young prince keeps well out of our way."

"I shall make sure of it," insisted Agar.

"Then you'll need to move quickly to get there in time."

"I can dispatch some hunters to keep him safe," offered Laruhk.

"Perhaps he would like to ride a tusker," added Ushog. "I can take him."

"I thought the tuskers were remaining here?" said Agar.

"We are not going to Ruzhina, merely escorting the army to the standing stones."

"Then it is settled," said Laruhk. "Agar will ride with me."

"What about me?" piped up Oswyn.

"Where did you come from?"

"I was outside, listening."

Laruhk winked at Ushog. "It appears we have another passenger."

"She can travel with you," said Agar. "I will walk."

"Nonsense," replied Ushog. "There is plenty of room on Laruhk's tusker." She smiled. "At least until our own youngling comes into the world."

Oswyn beamed. "You're going to have a baby?"

"I am, though it will be awhile before she is born."

"I'm confused," said Piotr. "Are you saying you're carrying a child?"

"I am. Why does that surprise you?"

"I never considered Orcs as having children."

"Where do you think Agar came from?"

"I… I suppose I really hadn't given it much consideration. You must accept my apologies; my tutors gave little thought to such things."

"How fascinating," said Voruhn. "Perhaps it is time you learned about how creatures reproduce?"

Piotr's cheeks were ablaze. "I know the differences between a man and a woman."

"Yet you never gave any thought to where our younglings come from. You and I should have a little talk."

"Can I talk too?" asked Oswyn.

"No," said Agar. "You are still too young. Come. You and I will feed the tuskers while Prince Piotr chats with Voruhn."

# RUZHINA

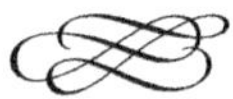

## SPRING 1110 SR

"We are here," announced Garag. "*You now stand in the land claimed by the Kingdom of Ruzhina.*"

"*That's it?*" said Athgar, looking over his shoulder. "*That's hardly even a river.*"

"*It's been a dry spring,*" replied Natalia.

"*How could you possibly know that? We've only just arrived.*"

"*Look at the riverbanks, and you'll see the erosion from previous years.*" She smiled. "*I'm a Water Mage, remember? I notice things like that.*"

Athgar nodded at Garag. "*We must thank you for your help.*"

"*We will see you soon,*" replied the Orc, though he did not turn away.

"*Is something wrong?*" asked Shaluhk. "*You seem troubled.*"

The Orc glanced around, then lowered his voice. "*I must warn you to be careful. There is great danger ahead.*"

"*Of course. We are in enemy territory.*"

"*That is not what I refer to.*"

"*Speak plainly,*" said Kargen. "*We shall not hold it against you.*"

"*Some view this as an opportunity to expand our borders.*"

"*Are you suggesting the Orcs of Ard-Gurslag would invade Ruzhina?*"

"*Our city boasts a formidable army, and the queen is eager to erase the shame of the past.*"

"*We're only bringing through five hundred glaives,*" replied Athgar.

"*True, but you are also relying on our masters of water to help transport them. By teaching them the frozen arch, you enabled them to bring additional warriors when the time is right.*"

"*Who's behind this?*" asked Athgar.

*"I regret to admit it is the queen."*

*"That explains a few things,"* said Natalia. *"I should have seen this coming."*

*"Why would you say that?"* replied Athgar.

*"Queen Urgash was too easily convinced to help us."*

*"You had no reason to mistrust her,"* said Shaluhk. *"Orcs do not lie."*

*"That was our mistake,"* added Kargen. *"We took them at their word. We should have realized they would not share the same beliefs as us."*

*"I shall say no more on the matter,"* warned Garag. *"I wish you well."* With that, he turned and waded across the river.

"This throws the entire expedition into danger," said Athgar, reverting to the Human tongue. "I suppose we could abandon it?"

"No," replied Natalia. "It's too late. We were so eager to gain allies that we gave them the same advantage as us: the ability to move warriors great distances. All they have to do is send their mages north, and then they can use magic to bring the rest of their people."

"Perhaps," said Shaluhk, "but their contingent is only a part of a much larger army, including Therengians. I doubt they would try anything while in the midst of our army. The danger comes later, once the Volstrum falls."

"She speaks the truth," said Kargen. "When that time comes, we must be ready to act."

"Garag had misgivings," said Natalia. "How likely is it that others feel the same?"

"What are you suggesting?"

"That we make every effort to encourage friendship between us."

Shaluhk grinned. "It is harder to turn on a friend."

"Precisely."

"I'm all for this," said Athgar, "but it puts us in a precarious position. By allowing them to commit the standing stones to memory, we've given them the keys to the kingdom."

"I shall send word to my brother," said Shaluhk. "He can have the tuskers remain there to oppose any potential attack."

"I doubt it will come to that," said Kargen. "I understand the queen's desire to conquer, but I do not believe she would turn on her own race."

"Even if we oppose her?" said Natalia. "We can't take that risk."

"Is there a way to disrupt the casting of a frozen arch?"

"I can think of several, but they require the mage to be visible to the person attempting to stop them."

"What if the destination arch were attacked while it was forming?"

"I imagine it would shatter if you did enough damage. The problem is any arch formed near the standing stones would be reinforced by the power of the ley lines."

"Is that necessarily true?" said Athgar. "You can channel it, but to any other mage, wouldn't it act like a magic circle?"

"I hadn't considered that."

"It would be easy enough to determine," said Shaluhk. "We must arrange for Katrin to cast the spell and target the standing stones. Then the hunters there can attempt to damage it."

"Would that not hurt Katrin?" asked Kargen.

"It shouldn't," replied Natalia. "Theoretically, it would just break the connection."

"Theoretically?"

"I doubt anyone ever tried attacking a frozen arch; it's not a commonly known spell." She paused, surveying her surroundings. "Let's give it a try here. I shall create a pair of arches, and then you can use your axes on them. That would show us if they're fragile enough to be disrupted."

Kargen drew his weapon and then moved into a small clearing. "Will this do?"

"That's perfect," said Natalia. "You'd best get over there as well, Athgar. I'm reasonably confident destroying a gate will take more than a single axe." She focused on her surroundings, calling forth the magic within her. The air frosted slightly as an arch formed in front of her. Natalia shifted right, giving her a better view of her next target. "Here it comes," she warned. Her concentration grew more intense as the second arch took form.

Kargen swung at it, his axe digging deep. A chunk of ice slewed off but was soon replaced. Athgar added his weapon to the task, carving off more of the arch, but Natalia's magic replaced what was lost.

The arch finished forming, linking together with the first one. "Keep going," urged Natalia.

The two of them kept hacking at it, sending ice flying, gradually chopping it away until a final blow from Kargen broke through and shattered the entire thing.

Natalia dismissed the spell. "That proved most effective."

"Did you feel any pain?" asked Athgar.

"No. Only the link being broken, almost as if I was pouring water from a full bucket that suddenly became half-empty. If anything, it was a relief."

"At least we know we can stop it if necessary. However, those on the receiving end would not know if friend or foe was casting the spell."

"The solution to that is simple," offered Shaluhk. "We keep archers standing by to repel any unwanted visitors. As for the arch itself, it took Kargen and Athgar considerable effort to destroy it, but I doubt a tusker would find the task too difficult."

"We will need a permanent garrison at the stones," said Kargen. "Perhaps even an entire village."

"I shall let Voruhn know of our concerns."

"Once that's taken care of," said Natalia, "we must get going. We need to locate a place to bring our army through, and we don't even know where we are."

"No need to worry," said Athgar. "Garag told me about a road west of here."

"Can we trust him?"

"He warned us about the queen's plans. If he supported her, he would have remained quiet."

"We have to trust someone," added Shaluhk. "And Garag's warning enabled us to take precautions."

"True," agreed Natalia. "But before we go any farther, let's bring in some help."

"Who did you have in mind?"

"I'd like Stanislav here. He's far more familiar with Ruzhina than us."

"We should also fetch some hunters," suggested Kargen. "They can keep an eye out for danger."

"Should we not find the road first?" said Shaluhk. "An open space is more convenient for Nat-Alia's spell."

"There's plenty of room here," offered Athgar.

"True, but a road provides better accessibility for horses."

"You make a good point. Come on, then."

Stanislav stepped through the arch, then halted, scanning the area. "This isn't much different from Therengia."

Belgast pushed past him. "If you're going to lollygag, then step aside so others can come through."

The mage hunter opened his mouth to object, then thought better of it. He moved closer to Natalia, who was concentrating on the frozen arch. "We're not bringing the entire army through, are we?"

"Not yet," she replied. "Just enough to provide a safe escort. The last thing we want is to alert our enemies we're here."

Kragor stepped through, followed by ten of his hunters, their warbows at the ready.

"Lower your weapons," said Kargen. "The area is safe." He waited until Kragor was closer, then lowered his voice. "Did Voruhn tell you everything?"

"You mean concerning Urgash's treachery? Yes." He shook his head. "I have a hard time believing it."

Kargen placed his hand on the Orc's shoulder. "Have you so easily forgotten the treachery of Gorlag?"

"I have forgotten nothing. I am merely surprised at the turn of events. Do not worry. I shall do what is necessary to keep the tribe safe."

"I am glad to hear it."

Herulf stepped through, along with Katrin, surprising everyone.

Natalia grinned. "How in the name of the Saints did you get to Therengia? I never got the opportunity to bring you to the standing stones."

"The old-fashioned way, by boat. You may not realize this, but you've been gone for some weeks."

"And what if I'd needed to contact you?"

"Don't worry. I brought the bowl with me, and I could've easily opened an arch to Beorwic if necessary."

Natalia turned to Shaluhk. "You didn't tell me Katrin went to Therengia."

"Voruhn did not see fit to inform me," replied the shaman.

"Is Greta with you?"

"No," said Katrin. "I thought it best to send her to Carlingen to keep her safe. I have further news, though."

"Which is?"

"Galina is with Svetlana. She arrived aboard the *Formidable* two days ago."

"Things are moving quickly."

"Shall I open an arch to Carlingen and bring her here? Her knowledge of the area might prove valuable."

"Yes, but let's finish transporting everyone from Therengia first."

"I brought six men," said Herulf, "all trained in woodcraft." He swept his hand, indicating the arch, then blushed. "Sorry. It appears my timing is not perfect." He waited until a line of Therengians came through, each leading a horse.

"The mounts are for you," he continued. "Voruhn indicated they might prove helpful."

"Thank you," said Natalia. "I'm certain we'll put them to good use." She waited until they were all through. "I assume that's everyone?"

"It is," said Katrin. "Raleth has the companies standing by, but there's no point bringing them here till we know where we are."

Natalia dismissed the spell, and the arch cracked, then shattered into chunks of ice. She turned to Katrin. "I'll leave it to you to collect Galina. In the meantime, we'll organize a camp and scout the area. Come nightfall, we should gather to go over our plans. What does Galina know of our current situation?"

"She knows nothing of Ard-Gurslag, but Svetlana told her of our initial plans regarding the Volstrum."

"Can you bring her up to date?"

"Certainly."

"Thank you. Now, you must excuse me. I need to brief Kragor's hunters on what to expect now that they're in Ruzhina."

They met that evening in a forest clearing.

"This is all quite remarkable," said Galina. "I always knew you were powerful, Natalia, but you've redefined what it means to be a mage with your accomplishments. How do you see us proceeding?"

"Our priority is to determine where precisely we are in Ruzhina. We don't know how far away Karslev is, or Zurkutsk, for that matter, but a nearby road may provide some clues. If we ride ahead, we should find a village. After all, all roads lead somewhere."

"This one runs roughly east-west," said Stanislav. "Which way do we search?"

"In most Petty Kingdoms, villages are usually a day or two apart. Wouldn't the same be true here?"

"Usually, and on the few occasions where they're not, you'd expect to find a roadside inn. That doesn't answer my question, though."

"We'll start by going west, but no more than a day's ride."

"And by 'we', you mean?"

"Galina, Katrin, and I."

"Pardon me," said Herulf, "but wouldn't it make more sense to have an escort?"

"We are Stormwinds. Do you really believe we need one?"

"Actually," said Galina, "I'm known as Galina Marwen now. Still, I can use my old name if needed. Regarding Natalia's idea, I agree it would be best if we travelled alone. After all, we're in Ruzhina, the heart of the family's power. In fact, the presence of an escort might raise questions concerning the ability of the family to protect itself. We are known to be the most powerful casters on the Continent."

"Even so," said Athgar, "I'd feel a lot better if help was close by."

"In that case," replied Natalia, "you and Stanislav can tag along, but when we encounter a village or an inn, you two remain out of view. Agreed?"

"I can accept that."

"Kargen will look after things here at camp, but everyone should be ready to move quickly. We must also watch the road in case someone approaches from the east."

"My hunters are already in position," replied Kragor. "And Herulf's men will be ready to come to our aid if needed."

"I'm curious," said Stanislav. "When do we intend to bring the rest of the army through?"

"Not until we're closer to Zurkutsk," replied Natalia. "Having everyone here complicates our supply line considerably. As for the mine, it could be ten miles away or a hundred; we have no idea. It's not as if we possess any maps of the area."

"True," said Galina, "but there's a road to follow, so I doubt it'll take more than a day to get our bearings. Even someone in the most remote village will know the route to the capital."

"Once we've determined our location, we'll begin moving, but I'd like to avoid civilization as much as possible. We can't risk word reaching the Volstrum that we're here."

"Easy enough," said Kargen. "Our hunters will lead the way. If they spot anything, they can send a warning."

"Won't that give them away?" replied Galina.

"They will sound no different from the local wildlife."

"Ah. I should've realized."

"Is the army ready?" asked Natalia.

"It is," replied Belgast. "At least the contingent coming from Therengia. Have you considered how to utilize the warriors of Ard-Gurslag?"

"I thought we'd contact them once we're in Karslev. We need them for the assault on the Volstrum, not the mine."

"Speaking of which, what's our plan with Zurkutsk?"

"I was considering a very old tactic," said Natalia.

"That being?"

"Shock and awe. There are two companies of Temple Knights at our disposal. I can't imagine the guards there offering much in the way of opposition, can you?"

"Likely not," replied the Dwarf, "but we should back them up with some foot troops, say a company of the Thane Guard?"

"Agreed."

"I'll lead them," offered Athgar. "I can't wait to see the look on the guards' faces when we march through their gates."

"Our primary concern is liberating those held within. Once that's done, I'll need Galina and Katrin to help us sort friend from foe."

"Are you suggesting we won't be able to tell the guards from the prisoners?"

"That won't be a problem," replied Natalia, "but not every member of the Disgraced will be prepared to assist us in overthrowing the Volstrum."

"I doubt they'd turn on us."

"Even if it helps put them back in the good graces of the family? We can't take that risk, Athgar. Remember, the Stormwinds are a powerful family. We trusted Stanislav's first wife, and she betrayed us."

"Sorry about that," said the mage hunter. "I should've known better."

"I mention it not out of blame but to illustrate the sway they hold over the local populace."

"What I don't understand," said Belgast, "is why we want these people? They're Disgraced. Doesn't that mean they don't know how to use their magic?"

"It's not their magic that will serve us; it's their knowledge of the Volstrum. Yes, Galina is well-versed in its layout, but she can't be everywhere. Once we breach the walls, we need people to guide our warriors. Of course, we have more immediate concerns before we worry about that."

Natalia looked around the campfire. They were deep in unknown territory, about to launch a campaign against the most powerful mages on the Continent; did they have the wherewithal to carry this out to its conclusion? She soon realized it wasn't their abilities she doubted; it was her own. Had her desire for revenge consumed her to the point she'd failed to see the possible danger the Orcs of Ard-Gurslag presented?

A part of her wanted to cry out, to return home and hide away from the terrors of the family. Panic bubbled up inside, and then Athgar placed his hand on hers, calming her.

"Everything will be fine," he soothed, sensing her fear.

"How are you so certain?"

"We've seen a lot, you and I. If there's one thing I know, it's that we can overcome anything as long as we have each other."

# THE ROAD

## SPRING 1110 SR

A stiff wind blew in from the north, not unusual in this part of the country, yet it made Luka Morozov reconsider continuing his work.

"This is impossible," he grumbled, although no one was there to hear him. "If Lord Rostov wants the field sown, he can do it himself." He gazed across the street at the Mage's Delight, the thought of a pot of ale making his mouth water. Thirst consumed him due to this morning's labour, but he would have no new source of coins without finishing his work.

"Just one cup," he said, desperately trying to convince himself of the necessity of slaking his thirst. Luka set down his hoe and then crossed the road. Kolovsky, a small village, consisted of ten houses, an old collapsed barn, and the Mage's Delight tavern, the only one in the area. He fished out a coin, content to purchase a drink, but halted before he reached the door. Three horses were tied up out front, a sure sign visitors were inside. Perhaps, he thought, he might persuade them to ply him with ale in exchange for information.

He tucked away his meagre funds before entering. Three women, high borne if their clothing were anything to go by, sat at a table. He edged closer. "Pardon my asking, but are you lost?"

The palest of the trio replied, "Why would you think that?"

Luka grinned. "It's not very often we get people of quality visiting Kolovsky, excepting His Lordship."

"Did you say Kolovsky?" asked the oldest, turning to her companions. "I was here many years ago to visit an uncle who lived in these parts."

"Was he a mage as well?" asked the pale one.

"No. He was a noble—a baron, I think."

Luka paled. "Are you mages?"

"Yes," replied the pale one. "My name is Valentina Stormwind, and these are my companions, Katherine and Galiana."

"Galiana?" said the oldest. "I suppose that's close enough. She shifted her attention to Luka. "And who might you be?"

"Luka Morozov."

"And do you live in Kolovsky?"

"I do, mistress. I am intimately familiar with the entire region."

"How far away is the capital?"

"Four days, or three, if you've got a fast horse. Take the road west, and you'll soon come across a fork. Go north, and it leads straight to Karslev."

"And if we were to go east?"

Luka scratched his head. "Didn't you come from that direction?"

"We did," replied Valentina, "but I'm afraid we somehow wandered off the road."

"East is the old border road. It runs east for a day, then turns north, until it crosses over the Mitchutskin."

"Ah, yes," said Galiana. "That's the river that runs through Karslev."

"Eventually," continued Luka, "but it meanders north for a while before it cuts west."

"How do you know this?"

"I do all sorts of odd jobs for His Lordship, including delivering messages. I could hardly do that if I didn't know my way around. Where are you looking to go?"

"Zurkutsk," said Mistress Katherine. "Do you know it?"

"Can't say I do. Is it a village?"

"No, a mine."

"A mine? Around here? Let me think." He turned to the woman working behind the bar. "Hey, Marta. Ever heard of a mine in these parts?"

"Never, unless you mean the old quarry."

"Quarry?" said Lady Valentina.

"They built a stone bridge over the Mitchutskin last year, replacing a broken-down wooden one. I remember the workers saying they brought the stone from a place called Zurkutsk."

"That's it," said Mistress Galiana. "Any idea how we might find it?"

"Cross that bridge," replied Marta, "then keep going. The road meanders a bit, but you'll get there eventually. At least that's what I've been told."

"Thank you. You've been most helpful."

"What about me?" said Luka. "It was my idea to ask Marta about the mine."

"So it was." Galiana produced a coin and placed it on the table. "Anything else you can tell me about the area?"

"That depends: what are you looking for?"

"Our superiors sent us into the region to gather information, but none of us are proficient at navigating the wilderness. Are there any other villages in the area?"

Luka chuckled. "Afraid not. Kolovsky is the arse end of the kingdom. You must be lost indeed to find yourself here."

"Yet you indicated you served a baron."

"I do, but he lives in the capital. I am merely one of his agents."

"No, you're not," said Valentina. "You're a farmer. Your boots are covered in mud, and you've blisters on your hands from working a rake or hoe. Not only does that identify you as a common labourer, but it also makes it doubtful your description of the area is entirely accurate."

"I'm a farmer, but that doesn't mean I lied about the bridge. You heard Marta; she confirmed its existence and told you about the quarry."

"Very well, take the coin, but if I hear about you telling anyone of the family's interest in these parts, you shall receive a rude awakening."

He snatched up the coin. "Of course, mistress. My apologies for exaggerating the truth." He tucked it away before heading out the door, eager to escape their presence.

---

"Most interesting," said Galina.

"When were you here?" asked Katrin.

"Before I was inducted into the Volstrum. My mother was a Stormwind, while my father, a Sartellian, returned to Korascajan. I think he detested her, but they were both very loyal to the family, so neither was willing to argue with their pairing." She saw the frowns. "It all turned out for the best. My uncle was very good to me."

"Would he still be around?"

"No. He died shortly after my unleashing, a fever, I was told, but that doesn't help us with our current situation."

"Are you familiar with this bridge she spoke of?"

"The old one, yes. My uncle's estate was near it."

"Did you have any cousins?"

"I know what you're thinking," said Galina, "but the estate was abandoned after my uncle's death." She paused, looking around to ensure no one was within earshot. "The buildings are most likely run-down by now, but the fields would make an excellent spot to assemble the army."

"They would," said Natalia. "It seems the trip to Kolovsky was useful after all. How far away would this estate be?"

"A few days, at least. That labourer was right about where the road leads, but I'm afraid his estimate of distance was nowhere near accurate."

"And how much farther would Zurkutsk be?"

"Difficult to estimate without knowing the conditions of the roads, but I'd say another week."

"Then maybe the estate grounds aren't the best choice after all."

"We don't have a lot of options. The land between my uncle's old estate and the mine is nothing but thick forest, hardly the terrain suitable for assembling an army."

"Then we'll bring through only those we need to take Zurkutsk. The rest will come once we've taken the mining camp."

"Sounds like we have a plan," said Katrin, "although I must admit to some hesitation in returning there."

"I can understand that," replied Natalia. "You don't have to set foot in that place if you don't want to."

"No. I must face my past head-on, or I'll never get over it."

"Good. Then it's settled. Now, let's find the others, shall we?"

They were more of a collection of adventurers than an army, yet Athgar felt safe in their company. Kragor's hunters led them east, staying at least a hundred paces ahead to give ample warning lest danger threaten. The road turned north after two days, and by the end of the third, they encountered the bridge the innkeeper had mentioned. The slightly arched roadway was barely wide enough to hold one wagon at a time, but Athgar immediately recognized the stone.

"Now we know what they did with the stone the magerite was buried in," he said. "There must be bridges like this throughout the kingdom."

Belgast stood at the riverbank, examining the bridge from below. He shook his head. "Shoddy work. Why can't you Humans take greater care? Why, you'd be lucky to get a century out of this." When no one responded to his remarks, he looked back up the road. "Oh yes. You Humans have brief lives compared to us mountain folk. Still, you'd think you might at least appreciate the artistic nature of stone."

"I suppose that means we'll have to hire Dwarves to build any bridges back in Therengia?"

"It certainly wouldn't hurt."

"What's your assessment of the bridge? Can it support the weight of two companies of knights?"

"Definitely, though if you wait fifty years, I couldn't make the same claim."

"That's a little longer than we're willing to stay here," replied Athgar.

Kragor stepped closer. "I will spread my hunters out on the other side of the bridge. Herulf and his men can secure what's left of the manor house.

"I'll go find Natalia," said Belgast. "She and her fellow mages were looking for the best spot to open their gates."

"They are arches," insisted the Orc.

"Arches they might be, but they still connect two locations, and in my book, that makes them gates."

"Never argue with a Dwarf," warned Athgar.

"Because they are always right?" replied Kragor.

"No. They like to argue. If Belgast had his way, you'd be discussing the topic till the break of dawn, two days hence."

"And what's wrong with that?" said the Dwarf. "Discussion is an essential part of living in a civilized manner."

Athgar shrugged. "See what I mean?"

The Dwarf shook his head, wandering over to the run-down buildings behind them.

"The forest in these parts is thick," noted Kragor. "It will slow our progress considerably."

"Once the knights come through, we'll have them lead. Let's hope the locals think they belong to the king."

"Does King Yulakov have any knights?"

"Not that we know of. They have cavalry, but according to His Majesty, they're lightly armoured. I doubt they'd present any obstacles to your bows."

"Still, we must take precautions. If we stumble across a patrol and even one rider escapes, it could ruin our plans."

"You make an excellent point. What have you got in mind?"

"I suggest the knights ride in single file, with my archers on either side. My hunters will disperse into the trees at the first sign of trouble."

"I'll pass that on to Temple Captain Cordelia. I imagine she'll be the one leading her knights. Be aware, though, she doesn't speak Orc."

"That matters little," replied Kragor. "The hunters I brought all know the Human tongue." He grinned. "It is a skill they acquired from working closely with the Thane Guard." He paused, looking down the road. "When do we expect to resume the march?"

"Tomorrow morning. Natalia will want to fully recover from her spell before we continue."

"One more question, if I may?"

"By all means."

"What should we do if we encounter anyone on the road?"

"I hadn't considered that. If they're locals, we can ignore them, but travellers are another matter. As you said earlier, we don't want someone riding off to give warning of our approach. I suppose we shall be forced to take prisoners."

Kragor nodded. "I suspected as much, but that presents us with a new challenge."

"That being?"

"We need additional people to guard them."

Athgar grinned. "I can think of another, easier solution."

"Surely you do not intend for us to kill them?"

"No, of course not. I was going to suggest we open a connection to the standing stones and hand them over to our army. We'll return them once we're done in Ruzhina, but it gets them out of the way without complicating things."

"Perfect."

"I'll bring it to Natalia's attention once she's done casting for the day. I don't want to interrupt her."

A rider came up the road.

"Greetings," called out Kragor. "I am Kragor, hunter of the Red Hand."

"Ah, yes," replied Temple Commander Cordelia. "Kargen told me I might find you by the bridge."

"I assume your knights are following?" asked Athgar.

"They are. They'll assemble in that field behind us for now. While that's happening, I thought I'd come here and check things out." She glanced at Kragor. "Is that one of those warbows I've heard so much about?"

"It is," replied the Orc, handing it over.

Cordelia examined it with great interest. "I'm told they have quite the pull to them, enough to puncture a knight's armour."

"They did at the Battle of the Standing Stones," replied Kragor, "although admittedly, they had to be close."

"Have you trained with knights before?"

"Not yet. With the acquisition of Novarsk, Therengia acquired an order of knights called the Mailed Fist, but we have yet to see them on our training fields."

"Secular knights are an odd group," said Cordelia. "Individually, they are skilled but lack the discipline of Temple Knights."

"That would be my experience as well."

"Kragor suggested his hunters accompany your knights as they advance," said Athgar.

"I'd be happy to have them nearby," replied Cordelia. "Does that mean you intend for us to lead the way?"

"Yes, though it was Natalia's suggestion. She is, after all, the warmaster."

"Are you saying you don't agree?"

"Not at all. It's a fantastic idea, but I didn't want you to think I was in charge. I'm the High Thane, but any military matters should be taken to Natalia."

"Understood." She glanced across the bridge. "I assume this is the way we'll be riding?"

"Yes. Kragor's hunters have already crossed and taken up positions several hundred paces to the north. They'll warn us if anything shows up on the road."

"My knights are coming from Carlingen. Once Natalia brings them here, she'll open another arch to the standing stones to bring through Gabriel's company. I imagine it'll be dark by the time everyone gets here."

"I'd agree."

"Good. The Temple Knights will secure the estate's perimeter until the Thane Guard arrives. Speaking of which, how many do you intend to bring?"

"Only one company for now; the rest will come once we've secured Zurkutsk."

"Are we certain fifty will be enough?"

"Trust me. I was there, back in oh-eight. I doubt we'll see much resistance between my Thane Guard and your knights. Have you considered how to proceed?"

Cordelia smiled. "I thought we could ride to the gate and ask them to let us in. The sight of Temple Knights should be enough to convince them it's in their best interest to do so."

"And if it isn't?"

"That's why we wear armour. My only real concern is whether we'll find mages amongst the garrison."

"There were none there while I was a prisoner," said Athgar, "but it's possible they've made changes, especially since we led an uprising."

"I assume that's how you escaped?"

"It was."

"How were the guards armed?" asked the Temple Knight.

"Most used clubs and wore light armour, nothing like the plate armour your people have."

"That may have changed, particularly considering your escape."

"We need further information," said Kragor. "Once we are within range, I shall send my hunters to investigate. Do not worry. They will remain concealed, but their keen eyesight will give us an idea of what to expect."

"And how far away is this mine?"

"We don't have the exact distance," replied Athgar, "but Galina thinks it's likely a week's travel."

"And between us and them?"

"We're in the easternmost reaches of Ruzhina. I'd be surprised if we came across anything noteworthy."

Cordelia looked behind her. "This estate is here."

"Was," corrected Athgar. "It's been abandoned for over a decade."

"There's a serviceable road here and a relatively new bridge. You don't build something like that for no reason."

"You make a good point. Do you wish to change tactics?"

"We'll still take the lead," she replied. "We'll just be a little more cautious."

"Welcome to Ruzhina."

She chuckled. "I never imagined seeing so much of the Continent when I joined the order. I've been to the Shimmering Sea, and now you've brought me to the northernmost Petty Kingdom."

"I don't think Ruzhina considers themselves a Petty Kingdom; at least the family doesn't."

"Then we shall remind them they are."

"Why would that be important?"

"It builds a sense of community," replied the Temple Captain. "After all, we're trying to unite the Petty Kingdoms against a common enemy, not encourage them to fight amongst themselves."

# ZURKUTSK

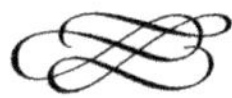

## SPRING 1110 SR

Cordelia crouched on the hilltop overlooking Zurkutsk. "Not much down there," she said. "What's that tall structure?"

"The lift," replied Belgast. "If you look closely, you'll see the horses that work the mechanism."

"Fascinating."

"That's only half of it," added Athgar. "Inside the building is a large room they raise and lower to transport the prisoners to the mine."

"It must be of Dwarven construction."

"It most certainly is not!" declared Belgast. "No Dwarf worth his stone would consider such a crude way of working a mine. We'd use gears instead."

"What's a gear?" asked Cordelia.

The Dwarf shook his head. "Never mind. I'll explain it later. Now, if memory serves, that long building to the right of the lift is the barracks."

"No," said Athgar. "That's a prisoner hut."

"Is it?" Belgast squinted. "So it is. I beg your pardon. The barracks must be the building on the left of the lift." He looked at Athgar and shrugged. "We broke Athgar out nearly two years ago, and things developed quickly. You can't blame me if I don't remember every little detail."

Athgar pointed. "There's a guard."

Cordelia surveyed the entire mining area. "You weren't far off the mark when you said they were lightly armoured. That one is wearing a leather vest; I'd hesitate to call it a jacket. Are you certain there aren't more heavily armoured men inside?"

"We could continue to watch and find out."

"I doubt that will add anything." She looked skyward. "It's almost noon. Are there set mealtimes?"

"The prisoners earn their meals by digging out magerite. I have no idea what they supplied the guards with in the way of food or how often they ate."

"Anything else you can tell me?"

"The man in charge of the mine works out of that building near the entrance."

"Two guards are standing outside its door."

"That's new," said Belgast. "I don't recall seeing them on my last visit."

"They've taken down the palisade," replied Athgar. "It used to encircle the prisoner's huts. I wonder why they might have done that?"

"Likely to keep a closer eye on them," replied Cordelia. "Were the hut doors padlocked when you were here?"

"No, they most certainly were not."

"That means we'll have a little more work ahead of ourselves once we've taken the place."

"Now that you've seen it," said Athgar, "what do you think?"

"It's designed to keep people in, not out. From our perspective, there's not much to stop us from entering the camp. However, there's more to this than overpowering the guards. We must also ensure no one runs away, or we could end up facing a relief force. Did that happen when you escaped?"

"I presume so, but I didn't stick around long enough to find out."

"They have more horses than last time," noted Belgast. "When Stanislav and I came to rescue Athgar, only a dozen horses were in that pen. There appears to be double that now." He snapped his fingers. "Corderis! I forgot about him."

"Corderis?" said the Temple Captain.

"Yes. Corderis Stormwind, the man in charge. If his name is any indication, he's a Water Mage."

"Might there be other mages present?"

"I couldn't say," replied the Dwarf. "However, during the uprising, Corderis was nowhere to be found. Perhaps he used his magic to keep himself safe? Could he know the frozen arch spell?"

Athgar shook his head. "Natalia thinks only the most advanced Stormwinds are given access to it, and I can't imagine one of them being tasked with the responsibility of a mine. That would be like a noble getting his hands dirty with planting crops."

"He's still a Stormwind. We shouldn't dismiss his spellcasting abilities."

"I'll detail six knights to rout him out," said Cordelia. "The main column will come from the west, riding straight to that entrance. Temple Captain Gabriel will work her way around to the east, moving in from there."

"And Kragor's hunters?" asked Athgar.

"We'll split them half and half. They're not required to take down any guards unless they look like they're running away or casting a spell."

"Please be careful not to target prisoners trying to escape."

"That shouldn't be too hard," said Belgast. "I imagine they'll all be wearing those belts."

"Oh yes," replied Athgar.

"Belts?" said Cordelia.

"Yes. Leather belts with loops used to chain them together whenever they move between the huts and the mine."

"What about the mine itself? Are we expecting to attack it?"

"No. Anyone down there has to come up in the lift. I can't imagine the guards would try to fight their way out."

"There's also the matter of those bellows," said Belgast. "If they refuse to surrender, we'll stop blowing air down there."

"He makes a valid point, but I'd prefer not to do that. Our main objective is to rescue those prisoners. If a few guards die in the fight, then so be it. I have no sympathy for them."

"I understand that completely," said Cordelia. "I was once a prisoner of the Halvarians, and they treated me abysmally. I doubt I'd let them surrender if I found myself amongst them now." She took a deep breath, letting it out slowly. "Rest assured. My people will do all they can to help those prisoners down there."

"Good. Then we'd best get moving. I'd like this over and done with by nightfall."

Slavil Yenkov halted. "My feet are sore."

His companion, Igor, was not sympathetic. "What do you want me to do? Carry you?"

"You could let me sit down and rest."

"Are you mad? The captain would slap us both in irons!"

"Easy for him. He sits in a nice comfy chair all day long." He gazed over at the small hut standing off to one side.

"Keep your voice down, you fool, or he'll hear you."

"And what if he did?"

Igor moved closer, grabbing Slavil by the front of his tunic. "Listen, you ungrateful goat. Do your job and keep your mouth shut, or we'll both face the lash. Understand?"

Slavil opened his mouth to respond, then his gaze locked on something in the distance.

"What are you looking at?" Igor turned, noting the approaching horsemen. "What's this?"

"Horsemen," said his companion.

"No, really? Go inform the captain we've got visitors."

"Why do I have to do that? You know he doesn't like me. You do it."

"Listen, you little turd. Do what you're told, or so help me, you'll be complaining about more than just sore feet."

Slavil walked over to the hut and disappeared inside while Igor moved closer to the gate. It was more akin to a garden fence, stretched between two low stone walls, hardly much of an obstacle, but despite this, the riders slowed. They wore armour, yet he had difficulty determining who employed them: the king or the Stormwinds?

"Trouble?" The captain's voice startled him.

"Knights, sir," Igor replied.

"I can see that. Go find out who they are."

"Yes, sir." Igor opened the gate and proceeded towards the riders, holding his hand up. The knights halted while one advanced, a sash presumably denoting rank of some sort.

"Who commands here?" came a woman's voice.

Igor let out his breath. The family must employ them, for the king would never consider women for such a role. "Corderis Stormwind," he replied.

His captain moved up beside him. "What's going on here?"

"Stand aside," the knight commanded, then urged her horse forward. Igor moved aside, eager to avoid being crushed beneath its hooves, but the captain stood his ground.

"You hold no authority here," he said.

The knight ignored him, her horse forcing him out of the way as she drew her sword and raised it on high, then swept it down, and those following her advanced.

The captain swore, then tried to yell out a warning, but the knight's sword took him in one clean, efficient swing, and he fell to the ground, motionless.

Igor turned and ran, almost tripping in his haste to escape. He raced for the trees, certain Zurkutsk was doomed. He assumed the family had decided to erase the mine from existence, killing everyone in the process. As he neared the treeline, an arrow hit him square in the chest. His legs lost their strength, and he fell to his knees, staring down as blood trickled out of his mouth. Another arrow struck beside the first, and then he toppled over, quite dead.

---

The Temple Knights flooded into the mining camp. A few brave souls tried organizing a defence, but a charge by six heavily armoured knights soon had them throwing down their weapons.

Cordelia lifted her visor, the better to survey her surroundings. Ten knights had dismounted and entered the barracks, searching for any resistance. It appeared this would be over in a matter of moments, and then a searing pain lanced through her leg. Her horse collapsed beneath her, screaming in agony, the frost encasing her leg evidence of what had happened.

She rolled as she'd been trained and came up into a crouch, sword in hand. Another streak of ice shot past her, knocking a knight from the saddle.

Cordelia hobbled towards the source of the magic, a man with snow-white hair and a beard preparing to cast another spell. She dropped just as he pointed at her, narrowly avoiding yet more flying ice.

She pushed up, ready to launch herself at him, but her pain-laced leg buckled, and she collapsed. The mage came closer, staring down at her with pure hatred.

"Pray to your blessed Saint," he said. "It is time for you to die."

He threw out his hands, ready to cast, and then an arrow pierced his neck. His eyes widened, focusing momentarily on something behind Cordelia before he collapsed.

Kragor pushed past her, bending to retrieve his arrow, then nocked it and scanned the area. "It is safe," he said at last. He moved closer. "Are you hurt?"

"He took out my horse with that spell of his," replied Cordelia. "I'm afraid it damaged my leg."

"Shaluhk will be here soon and can heal it."

"I must see to my command."

"Then lean on me, and I shall support you."

A Temple Knight drew closer, then dismounted. "Take my horse, Captain."

Cordelia hauled herself into the saddle. "Thank you, Sister Carmen. Go to Temple Captain Gabriel and find out how their attack is progressing."

"Yes, Captain." The knight ran off.

"Would you do me a favour, Kragor?"

"If I can."

"Unless I'm mistaken, that's Corderis Stormwind over there. He should have a set of keys that will prove useful."

The Orc grinned. "I shall see what he has in his possession."

Natalia wandered through the camp. The fight had been vicious but short, with none of her people suffering serious injuries, but it wasn't over. With control of the surface, they must now see to securing the mine. To that end, they prepared to lower the lift.

"I shall go down," announced Belgast. "They might see me as less threatening. We're trying to convince the guard down there to surrender, not fight to the death."

"I'll accompany you," said Athgar.

"Are you certain that's wise?"

"We need to convince the prisoners we have their best interests in mind. My presence may help."

"I suggest taking a Temple Knight or two."

"I'll go," offered Cordelia.

"You're wounded," replied Athgar.

"I cured her," said Shaluhk, "and I assure you, she is still capable of defending herself."

"And who in their right mind," said Belgast, "will offer resistance to a mail-clad knight?"

"Into the lift with you," said Natalia, "but I want you out of there at the first sign of trouble."

Once they were ready, the platform lifted slightly and swayed. Men moved forward to remove the large timbers holding it in place, and then the ropes and pulleys lowered them into the mine.

"Quite the contraption," said Cordelia. "I don't believe I've seen anything similar before."

"What, this?" replied Belgast. "Far too crude for my liking. It sways like an apple about to fall from the tree. If this was Dwarven-made, it would be solid and dependable."

"What can we expect when we reach the bottom?"

"There will be a rough-cut tunnel," replied Athgar, "leading into a larger chamber where they remove the chains and issue tools. At least they did when I was here; things may have changed since then."

"It's very bright down here," noted Cordelia. "I wasn't expecting that."

"They use magical orbs," said Belgast. "At least these people managed to get that right." The lift bumped to a halt. "Come on. Let's get this over with before these tunnels collapse."

"Would they really do that?"

"No," said Athgar. "Belgast just likes to complain about anything not built by Dwarves."

"Can you blame me?" grumbled his companion.

An enormous fellow greeted them as they emerged into the chamber.

"I don't remember you," said Athgar.

The man grinned, showing yellowed teeth. "The name's Giliad. I suspected something was happening up there, so I prepared a little surprise for you." He stepped to one side, sweeping his arm to indicate those behind him.

A large group of prisoners huddled together, still bound by chains looped through their belts. Their pale faces held a haunted look that was the stuff of nightmares. A handful of guards stood watching over them with naked blades, ready to strike.

"This is how things are going to go," continued Giliad. "Me and my friends will ride that lift to the surface, then walk away as free men."

"And what makes you think we'll let you do that?" Athgar asked.

"If you don't, these people are dead."

"I presume," said Cordelia, "you intend to take them with you?"

"Only until we're safe, then we'll let them go."

"I cannot permit you to do that."

"Who are you to make such a statement?"

"Temple Captain Cordelia of the Order of Saint Agnes."

"What makes you think I won't order these people killed?"

"Do that, and you no longer possess anything to bargain with." She stepped forward, drew her sword, and, in a flash, held it at the man's throat.

"Now," she continued, "release the prisoners, and I'll ensure you're not condemned to death."

"I was only doing my job."

"There is no excuse for the treatment these people have endured."

Giliad raised his hands. "I give up. Release them, boys. It's over."

His men obeyed, tossing their swords to the ground. Belgast moved in, snaffling a ring of keys from Giliad. He began releasing the prisoners.

"Athgar?" said a familiar voice. "Is that you?"

The Therengian moved closer. "Felix? I thought you dead?"

"No. Simply recaptured."

"Is Alfie here?"

"I'm afraid he's no longer with us."

"What happened?"

"He died of starvation."

"But I showed you how to find magerite."

"Aye, you did, but none of us realized there is only so much to pull from the ground. The mine's nearly depleted, and without enough magerite, we've received little food."

As Athgar was about to respond, a glint of steel flashed off to his right. Before anyone could react, a prisoner had picked up a discarded sword and attacked a guard. The rest quickly followed suit.

Belgast pulled Athgar out of harm's way. Cordelia stepped forward, only to be halted by the Dwarf's words. "No," he called out to her. "Let them settle this."

The Temple Captain stood, stunned, as the prisoners exacted their revenge. Giliad was the last to go down, pummelled to death by more than a dozen fists. She looked away, sickened by the sight.

Athgar conjured flames as the prisoners drew closer, causing them to halt their wild onslaught. He let the fire die down. "We came to liberate you. Gather your companions and make your way to the lift." He singled out Felix. "Are there more guards down here?"

"A handful."

"We'll take care of them," said Belgast. "Come along, Cordelia. We've got some work to do."

# ROOM TO BREATHE

## SPRING 1110 SR

Save for the perimeter guards, everyone else gathered outside the office of Corderis Stormwind, the only place large enough to address them all.

"It's time we collected the rest of the army," said Natalia. "With Zurkutsk as a base, we can assemble all our forces here for the march on Karslev."

"What about the prisoners we released?" asked Galina.

"Shaluhk healed those she could, but I'm afraid it will take time and plenty of food to restore them to their former health. I thought we might send them to Carlingen to recover."

"And the mine guards who survived?"

"We will intern them here at Zurkutsk," replied Natalia, "until this campaign ends. Their ultimate fate is up to King Yulakov. For now, they're in the old prisoner huts, under the watchful eyes of the Thane Guard."

"Who will you bring first?" asked Cordelia.

"I've given that considerable thought. The rest of Kragor's archers will come through first, then the remaining Thane Guard, and Hilwyth's archers will follow. Last to arrive will be the hunters of the Red Hand. There are also our masters of magic and shamans, but that shouldn't present a problem since there's only seven. The real challenge comes later when we open the arch to Ard-Gurslag."

Natalia took a deep breath before continuing. "As most of you are aware, we learned Queen Urgash has designs on conquering Ruzhina. Our only intention here is to destroy the Volstrum, thereby breaking the Stormwinds' power. We must take steps to ensure we achieve this without giving our new allies the opportunity for conquest."

"How do we accomplish that?" asked Herulf.

"By keeping them well away from the Palace."

"Easy enough," said Athgar. "We'll only use them to isolate the Volstrum."

"Agreed, which brings me to my next point. Our army will soon assemble here in Ruzhina. Once we hit the city's outskirts, we must move quickly to surround the Volstrum, cutting off any possible help they might receive from the outside. To that end, we shall split the army into three groups."

Natalia glanced around, trying to get a sense of their mood. These people appeared eager to move ahead with the plan, yet the prospect of taking on powerful mages in a defensive position was terrifying. "Raleth will lead the Thane Guard to the front entrance, isolating the Volstrum as quickly as possible. Kragor, you and Kargen will secure the back entrance. I must warn you, though, the stables are extensive, so it will be significantly more difficult to secure."

"And the third group?" asked Kargen.

"The Temple Knights will ensure no outside forces attempt to gain entry. The last thing we need is to be attacked from behind while fighting in the hallways. I'll leave it up to Cordelia to decide how best to employ her people. We'll discuss the order of march once we've assembled the rest of the army. Any questions?"

"How big will this army be?" asked Temple Captain Gabriel.

"Thirteen hundred souls," replied Natalia. "That's more than we had at the Battle of the Standing Stones. The difference here is we're not seeking to conquer a kingdom, merely root out a nest of rats."

"I'm certain you have more questions," said Athgar, "but they are best left until the army is fully assembled. Now, go get some rest." He waited as everyone dispersed. "They're nervous."

"They're not the only ones," replied Natalia.

"You have misgivings?"

"It's easy to talk about capturing the Volstrum, but quite another thing to carry out the attack. I fear we shall fail to take the building, or outside forces will launch a counterattack."

"There are always risks in battle," said Athgar, "but I doubt the family would willingly settle for a diplomatic solution."

"True, but what about all those students? How many young lives will be lost because of our assault?"

"I tell you what," said Athgar. "Once we've sealed that place up, we'll offer them the chance to surrender. An amnesty, if you like."

"We can try, but I doubt it'll do any good. The family has an iron grip on its students. I should know—I was one of them, remember?"

"'Was' is the key word. Your presence alone demonstrates it's possible to have a life outside of the family's influence."

"And suppose we do succeed in capturing the Volstrum? Then what? Do we take over and continue training mages? Wouldn't that make us just as bad as them?"

"How can you say that!" said Athgar. "We're not the ones working with the empire."

"How do we ensure future generations don't use the Volstrum to expand their power base like the family did?"

"If you wish to continue training Water Mages there, then make sure they understand there are no requirements for them to serve the family or whatever we call those in charge. We don't need to rewrite history, simply make a few changes to the training. Personally, I'd start by getting rid of changing everyone's name to Stormwind. You also might want to consider less-rigorous methods."

"Meaning?"

"Well, for one thing, how about letting family members visit or allowing students the time they need to master their magic?"

"Both excellent ideas," replied Natalia, "but we've yet to capture the Volstrum. Let's take this one step at a time, shall we? The rest will fall into place later."

Raleth ordered the advance, then stepped through the arch with the remainder of the Thane Guard following him. Hilwyth was off to his left, leading her archers through Galina's arch, while Master Rugg and the remaining Orcs came through Katrin's.

Raleth spotted Athgar. "This is much more efficient, my lord."

"How long have we known each other?" replied the High Thane.

"Almost six years."

"Then I think it's high time you went back to using my given name?"

"That wouldn't be right, Lord. You're the High Thane now."

Athgar shook his head as he stepped closer, grasping the fellow's hand. "Good to see you. I trust there were no problems on your end?"

"None whatsoever."

"And Voruhn got word to you concerning our little problem with Ard-Gurslag?"

"She did. Laruhk's tuskers will guard the standing stones in our absence. Unfortunately, with all our shamans in Ruzhina, we cannot contact him."

"One way or another, this will be a short campaign."

"Have you any doubts?"

"That we'll win? No, but the Volstrum is an imposing structure, and it's guarded by experienced casters. I don't imagine they'll step aside and just let us walk in. We can assume we'll see significant casualties—that's one of the reasons we brought the shamans here."

"The Thane Guard will not waver, my lord."

"I never thought they would."

"What can you tell me about the Orcs of Ard-Gurslag?"

"They'll be in mail," said Athgar, "much like your warriors. However, they use spears equipped with a cutting blade called glaives."

"Do they employ shields?"

"Not as far as we're aware, but you'll see them this evening; that's when Natalia plans to open an arch to Ard-Gurslag. I advise you to study them carefully. We may one day find ourselves on opposite sides of a battle."

"Understood."

"How are Hilwyth's archers?"

"Keen to prove themselves, Lord. They've seen battle before, but never with so many of them armed with Therengian longbows."

"I hate to disappoint her, but they'll have little to do if all goes according to plan. The archers aren't going into the Volstrum, they'll be helping to secure the surrounding streets."

"She'll do her duty."

"I never doubted she would," replied Athgar. He spotted a familiar face stepping through the arch. "Please excuse me. I must speak with Master Rugg."

Raleth returned to organizing his men.

"Greetings," said the Orc. "I believe you have met Urumar and Gahruhl."

"Yes," replied Athgar. "They're your apprentices, if I recall."

"No longer. They are both now accomplished masters of earth. No doubt their skill will prove valuable in the coming days."

"Agreed. Now, I have a question for you. Can you provide us access to the Volstrum by opening a hole in the outside wall? I know you can bring walls down like you did in Novarsk, but we're trying to gain entry, not destroy the place."

"Without observing it, it is difficult to give an accurate answer, but I know of no reason why it could not be done. The bigger question is how fast the warriors can go through the opening. We will accomplish little if we only send in one at a time."

"Can't you make a bigger hole?"

"We use our magic to manipulate stone, not blast holes in it."

"I'm not sure I understand."

"Our spell softens the stone in the hands of the caster, who then shapes it like clay."

"But if that's the case, couldn't we use a battering ram to knock our way through?"

"No. The wall remains in its natural state to anyone other than the caster. Softening the stone does not take long, but the caster needs to shape it by hand, which makes it dangerous, for when so engaged, the master of earth is at the mercy of those on the other side of the target."

"I see what you mean. Could I offer a suggestion?"

"By all means."

"If your masters made smaller holes, large enough for an archer to use, they could protect you while you worked."

Rugg grinned. "An excellent idea. I shall discuss it with my fellow masters of earth."

Natalia's arch dulled, then shattered into chunks of ice.

"It appears the transition is complete," said Rugg. "When do we expect to contact Ard-Gurslag? I am eager to meet these new Orcs."

"Later this evening," replied Athgar, "after Natalia's had a chance to recover her strength. I should warn you, however, they're not the same as the Therengian tribes."

"Nor would I expect them to be," said Rugg. "Unlike our people, they never lived off the land or had to compete for space to settle. Despite this, we have a shared history, one which I am eager to learn more about."

"Even if they ultimately prove hostile?"

"We Orcs have had our fair share of disagreements. Need I remind you of Kargen's first attempt to seek aid from the Stone Crushers?"

"I am familiar with the tale," said Athgar, "but your tribes eventually worked everything out."

"We did, but it could have ended in much more serious consequences had it not been for Shaluhk. We Stone Crushers owe her much."

"Just as we owe you for getting us into Ebenstadt. Without your magic, we would never have recovered Oswyn."

"Indeed. In the words of the Ancestors, 'Our people are bound together, each individually strong, yet stronger still by our bond of friendship.'"

"I couldn't have said it better myself."

Natalia took a deep breath, letting it out slowly. Casting her frozen arch was now so familiar, it was almost instinctive, yet at the same time, the drain on her inner magic was substantial.

She imagined herself floating in a pool of water, letting the waves wash over her. Her energy built, and she called it forth, watching in satisfaction as the archway formed before her. Once complete, it allowed her to concentrate on the distant circle of Ard-Gurslag.

It took time to find it due to the enchantment protecting the city, but she finally locked the image into her mind. The magic channelled through her, and though she couldn't see it, she felt the distant arch forming. Then came the satisfying click as the two arches connected, and she looked through to see Garag waiting.

*"You may come through,"* she said, effortlessly switching to the language of the Orcs.

The First Glaive of Ard-Gurslag crossed the magical threshold, stepping closer to Natalia. *"Where do I form up my warriors?"*

*"Over there,"* she replied, pointing. *"Kargen waits to show you where they'll be camping."*

The Orc looked around, taking in his surroundings, then lowered his voice. *"You remember my warning?"*

*"I do,"* she replied. *"We can discuss the matter later if you wish, but right now, you must get your glaives through that arch before I expend all my power."*

*"Of course."* He went towards the gate, yelling a command for his warriors to advance, then thought of something and turned back to Natalia. *"I must warn you, in your absence, there has been much discussion regarding our presence here. Some suggested we take the lead in the assault on the Volstrum despite our promise to follow your orders."*

*"What is your opinion?"*

*"I shall uphold my promise to you and Athgar. I fear, however, Morgal may cause problems."*

*"Is he aware that you warned us?"*

*"I am not certain,"* replied Garag. *"Morgal, despite his misgivings about the use of our masters of magic, is still one of the queen's most loyal followers. Which means he may take measures to prevent a threat to her rule."*

*"Do you mean to suggest she suspects you of plotting against her?"*

*"It would not be the first time in our history such a thing has occurred."*

*"Is she in danger of being overthrown?"*

*"I do not believe so. Her grip on the Throne is too tight, but if I am suspected of plotting against her, I could vanish."*

*"You would always be welcome in Runewald."*

*"I shall bear that in mind, but I hope it will prove unnecessary. I assume we will meet later to discuss strategy?"*

*"Yes,"* agreed Natalia. *"I'll send someone to fetch you once we're ready to begin. In the meantime, I suggest you look after your glaives."*

*"It shall be as you wish, Warmaster."* Garag bowed before going back through the arch to gather his warriors.

It was one thing to fit Athgar, Natalia, Kargen, and Shaluhk inside the office of Corderis Stormwind, quite another to add Cordelia, Gabriel, Katrin, Galina, and all the other commanders into such tight quarters.

Meeting outside would've been a better option, but Natalia needed to reference a crude map they'd found of the area.

"Sorry for the cramped conditions," began Natalia, "but I wanted everyone to see this." She indicated the map laid out on the small table. "If you look here, the main road goes right into Karslev, making it easy to follow. The problem is what we do once we arrive. I've already talked to some of you and explained the basic strategy, but I'd like to discuss individual tactics once we arrive."

She took a breath, using the delay to gather her thoughts. "I previously regarded the guards at the Volstrum as the biggest obstacle, but I have since reconsidered. Even a minor mage can freeze doorways, and that will prove hard to overcome."

"Is there a way to break the ice?" asked Kragor.

"In time, but a dedicated caster could keep casting the spell, effectively creating a never-ending supply of ice."

"But surely even a mage grows tired."

"Yes, and that's their weakness. The key for us will be striking quickly and spreading out, forcing them to defend more and more corridors. I won't lie to you; the Volstrum can be a maze at times, but Galina has cobbled together some maps to help you reach your targets."

"What about the students?" asked Hilwyth. "Surely you're not suggesting we kill youngsters?"

"Not as long as they surrender, but make no mistake, any student who's undergone their unleashing can do a lot of harm."

"Unleashing?"

"They give the younger students something called magebane to suppress their inner magic. Once they come of age, the dose is reduced so they can learn to control their magic."

"So you're saying anyone young enough will be incapable of spells?"

"Yes," replied Natalia. "Students typically undergo the ritual of unleashing when they turn twenty, so anyone younger than that should not prove a threat."

"How many are we talking about?"

"A few dozen at least, some likely as young as thirteen. I'm afraid we don't have exact numbers."

"And instructors?" asked Raleth. "Are they all accomplished battle mages?"

"Some will be, especially the senior instructors, and most will have spells at their disposal, but not ones useful in a battle. I expect they'll be more interested in escaping than putting up a fight, so make sure you're prepared to take prisoners."

"And if they find Marakhova?" said Athgar.

"She is the single most powerful mage in the entire Volstrum. If you come across her, end her life before she ends yours."

# THE PALACE

## SPRING 1110 SR

Stanislav Voronsky halted at the gate. "There it is," he said. "The Palace of His Majesty, King Yulakov of Ruzhina."

"Have you been here before?" asked Belgast.

"No."

"Weren't you one of the more successful mage hunters?"

"Don't be ridiculous," said Galina. "Stanislav was the best mage hunter we had, but that was family business; it had nothing to do with the Royal Court."

"Isn't it common courtesy to visit the court of the appropriate king when on the hunt for new students?"

"Not in Ruzhina. The family has always enjoyed a close working relationship with the ruling line here." Galina forced a smile. "I know we're here to end that, but I find myself wondering of late what good could they have accomplished had the Stormwinds been more sensible."

"Sensible?" said the Dwarf.

"Yes. Think of all they could have done had they chosen benevolence over working with the empire."

"Too late for that now." Belgast nodded at the guard coming towards them. "Looks like they've spotted us." The warrior wore the king's colours, along with a fine suit of mail. An officer, if his sash was any indication, although Belgast couldn't be certain. "Why can't you Humans use the same dress code for your warriors?"

"Sorry," replied Stanislav. "Shall I send word to all the courts of the Petty Kingdoms and admonish them?"

"There's no need to get testy."

"Says the complaining Dwarf."

"Now, now," said Galina. "That's enough of that."

The king's man drew closer, then halted, peering through the front gate at the new arrivals. "Who are you?"

"I am Galina Marwen, aide to His Grace, Fernando, Duke of Reinwick. I am here to speak to His Majesty, King Yulakov."

"And who are these two?"

"This is Stanislav Voronsky, a mage hunter of some renown, along with Belgast Ridgehand, advisor to the Dwarven Realm of Kragen-Tor."

"His Majesty is not seeing anyone today."

"And you are?"

"Captain Duvarov, Commander of the Royal Bodyguard."

"Please convey to His Majesty that we are here at the invitation of King Rordan of Abelard. I believe that might convince him to see us."

Duvarov stared back, not moving.

"For Saint's sake," said Belgast. "Are you deaf, man, or is this a special occasion?" He stepped closer to the gate, pressing his face against the bars. "If I were you, I'd run off and tell your master we're here. I doubt he'll appreciate the thought of us waiting!"

"Stay here," said the captain, who turned and marched off to the front door of the Palace.

"He's taking his sweet time," grumbled the Dwarf. "And what does he mean by that remark? Stay here? In the name of the Gods, where else would we stay?"

Stanislav looked at Galina. "He's not known for his patience."

"Clearly," she replied.

"What about you? Ever been here before?"

"Once. Tatiana brought me right after I joined the Volstrum as an instructor."

"Whatever happened to her?"

"Marakhova removed her as Grand Mistress of the Volstrum. As to her ultimate fate, that remains a mystery. She wasn't at Zurkutsk.

"She likely knew too much," said Belgast. "I expect they killed her to keep the family secrets safe. After all, the last thing they want is all this internal strife leaked."

"I suspect she's still alive," said Stanislav.

"What makes you say that? Wouldn't it be safer for them to kill her?"

"They locked me up after I helped Natalia escape, and I'm only a mage hunter. By your reckoning, getting rid of me would've been more expedient."

"I didn't say I agreed with the decision, merely that it made sense from a certain point of view." Belgast's voice choked up. "You are my dearest friend. I would never wish you such ill will."

"Let us focus," said Galina. "We can speculate all we like later. We must tend to the business at hand right now."

Belgast cleared his throat. "Yes, of course."

They waited in silence, their eyes glued to the front door of the Palace. After what felt like an eternity, Captain Duvarov returned, followed by four men.

"I hope he hasn't come to arrest us," said Belgast. "I didn't bring my pick."

Galina gave him a withering glare, then focused on the captain.

"His Majesty has agreed to see you," he said, nodding at one of his men who, in turn, produced a ring of keys. "My apologies," Duvarov continued. "I was unaware His Majesty expected such esteemed dignitaries."

"That's understandable," replied Galina. "Our visit was meant to be kept quiet, as it could hold huge political ramifications if the other Petty Kingdoms discovered we were here."

The guard finished unlocking the gate and then swung it open.

"If you'll follow me," said Duvarov. "I'll take you to His Majesty."

"By all means," said Galina.

The captain led them through the front door of the Palace into a large entrance hall packed with people.

"Is His Majesty holding court?" asked Stanislav.

"No," replied the captain. "The Royal bureaucracy awaits orders for the day."

"Do they gather like this every morning?"

"They do."

Belgast shook his head. "What a strange way to run a kingdom."

"Strange, Master Dwarf? What makes you say that? Do your own people not follow the orders of your king?"

"The bureaucrats of Kragen-Tor are capable of doing their jobs without the vard's direct orders. I would think the same true here?"

"Ah," said Duvarov. "You seem to have misconstrued my meaning. They await His Majesty's directives, which are handed down through the Royal Ministers, not directly from the king."

"Then why gather here?"

"This building serves as the seat of government, allowing the Royal Advisors to receive their orders directly from the king when needed."

"How strange."

"Is it? I think it common practice amongst the Petty Kingdoms."

"This is not the time to discuss politics," interrupted Galina. "If you would be so kind, Captain. We must speak with His Majesty."

"Yes, of course." Duvarov continued, leading them down the entrance hall and through a set of double doors. His men, trailing behind, closed them and took up positions, blocking the exit.

"What's this, now?" said Belgast. "Surely you're not arresting us?"

"No," replied the captain, "but if you wish to see the king, you must surrender your weapons. Place them over there." He nodded at a nearby table. "You can retrieve them when you leave."

Stanislav unbuckled his sword and set it down. Belgast hesitated, then did the same with his knife.

"And you, Lady Marwen?" asked Duvarov.

"I am unarmed."

"I'm afraid I'm not permitted to take your word for it. You will have to be searched, as will all of you."

"But we just gave up our weapons," said Belgast.

"So you claim, but we're tasked with ensuring His Majesty's well-being, and to do that, I must insist we search you. Of course, if you'd prefer not, you're more than welcome to leave."

"Fine," said Belgast. He pulled another knife from his boot and then slowly placed it on the table. "That was from my father."

"It will be safe. I promise you."

"It better be."

Three guards moved closer and patted them down for weapons.

"I apologize for the inconvenience," said the captain, "but there have been threats against His Majesty of late."

"Threats?" replied Galina. "What types of threats?"

"I'm afraid I'm not privy to that information, and even if I were, I wouldn't share it with outsiders."

"Let me guess," said Stanislav. "This came from one of the king's advisors?"

"How do you know that?"

"It is common amongst the Petty Kingdoms for the king's advisors to deal with such things."

With the search complete, Captain Duvarov indicated the far end of the room, where another set of double doors waited. "That's where the king is. If you wait here, I'll find out if he's ready to see you."

A guard opened one of the doors, admitting the captain, then closed it again.

"I sense a Stormwind is behind this," muttered Galina.

"To what end?" replied Belgast, keeping his voice low. "They're already at court."

"True, but Yulakov is relatively new to the Throne. I suspect the family is using this pretense to isolate him from outside influences."

"Yet he agreed to meet us."

"He did," said Galina, "but I imagine we'll see one or two Stormwinds once we go in there."

Captain Duvarov returned. "His Majesty will see you now." He nodded at the two guards who pulled the doors open, then swung his arm wide to indicate the trio should enter.

Stanislav went first, with Belgast following on his heels. Galina stayed back a couple of paces, eager not to draw too much attention until she discovered who was present.

The throne room's floor was set in alternating black-and-white marble squares. At the far end stood the throne of Ruzhina, an overly large, ornate wooden chair with a high back that dwarfed the king. Two guards flanked His Majesty, while off to his right, three robed individuals sat watching.

Stanislav moved closer, halting ten paces from the throne, then bowing. "Your Majesty, we bring you greetings from King Rordan of Abelard."

"Rordan, you say?" the king replied. "How fares my son?"

"He is well, sire, and sends his regards. You won't know me, but I believe we have a mutual acquaintance whom you met in Abelard. She suggested your son spend time at His Majesty King Rordan's court."

"Ah, yes. And who are these other individuals?"

"Representatives from Reinwick and the Dwarven Realm of Kragen-Tor, here to discuss the return of the Stormwinds to the Reinwick court."

One of the robed individuals shifted slightly. "Wouldn't the Volstrum be more suitable for such a visit?"

"Indeed," said Stanislav. "That is their ultimate destination, but it's common practice amongst the Petty Kingdoms to pay a visit to court when in foreign countries."

"He's got you there, Veris," said the king.

"My apologies for the outburst," the fellow replied, "but something about these visitors doesn't ring true. Perhaps it might prove useful if they introduce themselves?"

Galina stepped forward. "You know full well who I am, Veris, or is your brain addled with age?"

"Galina Stormwind? I thought you dead."

"No. Merely away on family business. I came from Reinwick."

"The family no longer has a presence in Reinwick."

"That's why I'm here. I have a strategy for us to return to court."

"I'm listening."

Galina glanced briefly at the king before continuing. "As you stated earlier, this is not the place to discuss the family's business. However, if you are willing, we could arrange a private meeting."

Yulakov looked bored. "There are rooms available for that sort of thing. Captain Duvarov can take you to one, although I'm not done with Veris yet."

"Thank you, Majesty. My companions and I will happily wait in whatever room you deem suitable."

"Is this to be a long meeting?"

"Likely not," replied Galina. "Though it might prove beneficial for your treasurer to be present, and even your chancellor, if possible. I understand they are all members of the family?"

"You would strip my court of my most trusted advisors?"

"Only when you're done with them, Majesty. I don't mean to intrude on the business of state."

"Very well. Take them away, Captain, and find them something to eat. I will need Veris and Yaleva for a while longer."

Duvarov bowed. "As you command, Majesty."

Belgast paced. "Are you confident this will work?"

"You agreed to this mad plan," replied Stanislav. "I did warn you it might have some element of risk."

"This is far more than an element. If Yulakov suspects foul play, he'll set his guards on us."

"Nonsense. We're perfectly safe. The king understands what's at stake here."

"How can you be so certain?"

"Two things. First of all, he's posted guards outside that door rather than in here with us."

"And secondly?"

"He's given us another attached room where Galina can do her part in private."

"Yes, but will it be enough? I might remind you these Stormwinds are powerful mages."

"I'm fully aware of that," said Stanislav, "but there can be no ultimate victory without some risk."

"I'd feel better if Natalia were with us."

"As would I, but she's needed elsewhere."

A knock interrupted their discussion. The door opened, revealing their guard. "Lord Veris Stormwind is here."

"Ah. Please send him in," said Stanislav.

The Water Mage entered and looked around the room. "Where is Galina?"

"She'll be along shortly," replied Belgast. "She's answering a... call of nature."

"This is a waste of time," said the mage.

"If you bear with us, Master Veris, I'm certain you'll see what a tremendous opportunity we're offering." Belgast glanced at the door. "Are your companions coming?"

"They'll be along shortly. What's this all about?"

Belgast took a deep breath. He must keep Veris busy until the other two arrive, or the plan would be for naught. "As I understand, the family was dismissed from the court of Reinwick. Can you shed any light on that?"

"You're already familiar with the story, otherwise you wouldn't be here."

"Ah, but we've only heard Reinwick's side, and you know how the rulers of the Petty Kingdoms like to exaggerate."

"Some years ago, Larissa Stormwind was implicated in a plot to foment war."

Belgast nodded. "Yes, that's what I've heard. There was mention of the Halvarians being involved. Was that true, or was Reinwick looking for a scapegoat?"

"You tell me; you claim to be from the Reinwick court."

"I'm afraid you're under a misconception," replied Belgast. "I come from Kragen-Tor. Galina sailed from Korvoran, but she's not here, else I'd ask her."

"You're wasting my time," said Veris. He opened his mouth to say more, but the door opened, admitting two individuals. "Ah, at last," he snapped. "I wondered when you were going to show up." He returned his attention to Belgast. "This is Yaleva Stormwind, the king's treasurer, and Irinushka Stormwind, his chancellor."

"Pleased to meet you both. Am I to assume you are the sole representatives of the family here at the Palace? I shouldn't like to have to repeat ourselves."

"Yes," replied Veris. "Now get on with it, will you? We haven't got all day."

Belgast made an exaggerated bow. "My apologies. Galina will be with us momentarily. While we wait, would you like some wine?" He moved to a small table by the other door and lifted a bottle to examine it. "Ah, ninety-five, a good year." He filled six glasses, then passed them around, saving one for Galina. "To the king," he said, then downed his glass.

"The king," they all chimed in.

Belgast looked at Stanislav, who shook his head.

"I say," continued the Dwarf. "This is fine, very fine indeed. I must compliment His Majesty on his wine cellar."

Veris stood, holding his empty glass. "Can we get on with this?"

Belgast looked at Stanislav once again.

"A moment longer," replied the mage hunter.

"For what?" said Veris. "What's going on here?" He stared at his glass, a look of panic crossing his features. "You've poisoned us!"

"No, we haven't," replied Stanislav, downing the rest of his drink. "There. You can plainly see there's nothing in that bottle that would kill you."

"Magebane!" said Yaleva. She turned, ready to bolt from the room, but the door behind Belgast opened, and Galina entered, followed by a group of archers, each with arrows nocked.

"Yes," said Galina. "We found a lot of it when we captured Zurkutsk."

"Those are not the king's archers!" shouted Veris.

"No, they're not. They're Therengians. We brought them here just for you."

"Impossible. There's no way they entered the Palace without being discovered."

"Quite the contrary," said Galina. "Now, if you come this way, we'll take you somewhere nice and quiet." She indicated the door that she'd entered through.

Yaleva bolted for the other door, two arrows thudding into her as her hand touched the handle. She fell to the floor, blood staining the stone.

"My apologies," said Stanislav. "I should have warned you. Those are Therengian longbows, particularly lethal to those of us who choose not to wear armour."

Veris stooped to examine his companion. "She's dead!"

"As you will be if you don't follow orders."

"This way," motioned Galina.

"Where are you taking us?" asked Irinushka.

Galina stepped aside. "The frozen arch in that room leads to Therengia. Laruhk will be waiting."

"Laruhk?"

"It's a long story," said Stanislav. "He'll explain everything. Thankfully, he speaks the common tongue well."

"What's that supposed to mean?"

"It's simple. You see, he's an Orc. Oh, and I wouldn't recommend you try escaping; tuskers don't take kindly to that sort of thing."

"Tuskers?"

Stanislav smiled. "I'll let you discover them for yourself."

# KARSLEV

## SPRING 1110 SR

Natalia felt the arch connect to the one at the standing stones, then Galina stepped through, followed by Stanislav and Belgast. Natalia broke the connection, letting the arches shatter. "All went according to plan?"

"It did," said Belgast. "Though I was a little worried for a moment. Veris Stormwind showed up without his companions, and I had to keep him occupied so he wouldn't suspect a trap."

"What he means," added Stanislav, "is he had to continue talking, hardly a difficult task for a master storyteller like him."

"And they're now prisoners?" asked Natalia.

"Veris is, as is Irinushka, but I'm afraid Yaleva tried to make a run for it. She was killed by arrows."

"You did what you could. Now the court of Rhuzina is free of their influence. Just out of curiosity, how did you convince them to take the magebane?"

"We toasted the king. Who could possibly refuse that?"

"It was a terrible gamble."

"Nothing ventured, nothing gained," said Belgast.

"He's being modest," replied Galina. "The entire escapade was quite frightening."

"They couldn't have done it without you," said Natalia. "Did you meet with the king afterwards?"

"We did, then I opened another arch to the standing stones, though I'm afraid I have little energy left."

"And did His Majesty have anything to pass on to us?"

"Yes. He's issued orders for the Army of Ruzhina not to interfere with us in any way, and those stationed in the city are to keep at least five blocks away from the Volstrum until further notice. Naturally, it will take time for those orders to trickle down to the companies, but everything should be in place by morning. How are things going here?"

"We halted within sight of Karslev. I thought it best not to proceed until we heard back from you."

"Will you march tonight?"

"No," replied Natalia. "Better to leave that for first light. It'll let us enter the outskirts while people are still asleep."

"Wouldn't that be true if you marched in the dark?"

"It would, but our people are unfamiliar with the city's layout, so I can't risk them getting lost. We have a few volunteers showing us the way, but they're still weak from their time in Zurkutsk, so I don't want to push them."

"Did you bring the mages from Ard-Gurslag here while we were at the Palace?"

"No. I thought it best we leave them where they are for now. If we need them later, then so be it, but I'd prefer to limit their knowledge of Ruzhina, just in case."

"You still think they'll turn on us?"

"On us?" said Natalia. "No, but once we're gone, there's a good chance they might try taking Ruzhina. Did Yulakov mention an alliance?"

"I'm afraid not," said Galina. "To be honest, I don't think he likes mages."

"He needs to understand the danger Ard-Gurslag represents."

"I tried to impress that upon him, but he wouldn't listen. Perhaps he'll be more receptive once our army is no longer within his border."

"Let's hope so," replied Natalia. "The last thing we need is to find ourselves in the middle of another war."

"Isn't that where we are now? I know it's not a war in the traditional sense, but let's face facts; you've been at war with the family ever since you left the Volstrum, not that anyone's blaming you."

"It feels like I've been pushing back at them since I ran away. It's hard to believe it's almost over."

"I have my doubts about that," said Galina. "Can we truly destroy the power of the Stormwinds by capturing the Volstrum? Couldn't they set up an academy elsewhere?"

"Certainly, but it would take years, and by then, word of their treachery will have spread throughout the Continent. I'll make sure of it."

"That's always assuming there are still Petty Kingdoms to warn. Who knows, the Halvarians might have conquered the entire Continent by then."

"They won't go down without a fight," said Natalia, "and I can't imagine Athgar letting the Petty Kingdoms fight a threat that large without sending aid."

"You'd help save the very kingdoms that condemned the descendants of the Old Kingdom?"

"If it ends the cycle of hate, yes. We will never see peace if we seek to punish those who oppressed us. We must forgive our enemies and work to build a better, more secure Continent where the threat of war no longer hangs over everyone's head."

"A noble sentiment," said Galina, "but I fear one that will only lead to disappointment. The Petty Kingdoms are driven by greed and a never-ending quest for power; very few kings would see it otherwise."

"Still, we must try, if only for the sake of our descendants."

"We've certainly made a good start, assuming we capture the Volstrum. I have some doubts about that."

"We will win because we have to," said Natalia.

"But at what cost?"

Cordelia led her company through the early morning mist, riding two abreast, leaving scant room on either side in the narrow confines of the city streets.

"Are you certain we're heading in the right direction?" she asked.

"I am," replied Felix, following behind her on a much smaller horse. He was so weak he had difficulty remaining upright in the saddle. "Another block, and we'll come across a considerably wider street, which will take us directly to the front entrance of the Volstrum."

"And you're absolutely certain?"

"Most definitely. Although I've been away from Karslev for a few years, I spent my childhood amongst these streets. I know them like the back of my hand."

The Temple Knights rode on, keeping the horses at a steady walking pace to preserve their strength. It made for slower progress but ensured they'd arrive ready to fight, should that be necessary.

The streets remained eerily empty as they drew deeper into the city, but once the mist dissipated, it revealed people staring out of windows at the sight of the knights.

Cordelia wasn't worried, at least not about the city folk. The actual danger lay in the mages waiting at the Volstrum. Would word reach the Stormwinds before her knights could trap them? She berated herself for her lack of faith. Natalia was one of the most skilled generals in the entire

Continent, and she knew what she was doing. Cordelia said a silent prayer to Saint Agnes and kept riding.

"They're nervous," noted Sister Carmen.

"Wouldn't you be if the situation were reversed? We are an outside army marching down the streets of their capital. Hardly the type of thing that endears us to the population."

"But we are Temple Knights of Saint Agnes. Surely they're happy we're here?"

"Our order has never had a presence in Ruzhina, nor any of our brother orders, for that matter. These people mistrust outsiders. To them, we represent a threat to their way of life."

"But we're here to protect them!"

"They don't know that."

"Then we should take pains to ensure they understand."

"Well-spoken," said Cordelia, "but I fear that takes considerable time, time which we can't spare."

"And after we've rousted the Stormwinds from their fortress?"

"It's not a fortress, it's a school, and as far as the future goes, that's not our concern. I intend to rebuild the order in Therengia, then help spread our message across the Continent."

"Even if we're the only ones left?"

"Have faith," said Cordelia. "We may be isolated in the east, but we are not alone. All across the Continent, others seek safety in the hopes of building a better future for our order."

"How do we accomplish that without the Church's approval?"

"By working with those realms friendly to our cause."

"Even if it means war with the other Temple Knights?"

"You may not be aware of this," said Cordelia, "but Carlingen wasn't the first time we were in conflict with the Cunars. Years ago, we fought them in Krieghoff. I even arrested a father general—not that much happened to him. They sent him to the Antonine, but you know how it is with the orders; they always protect their own."

"It's Human nature," replied Carmen. "Any time you gather over ten people, you enter the realm of politics."

"Spoken like a true pessimist. Don't you want to bring about change?"

"That's why I joined the order, but that doesn't change how things work."

"There are advantages to being free from the Church's jurisdiction."

"Those being?"

"We are no longer bound by their rules of non-intervention."

"That's why we're here, isn't it?"

"We're here to eliminate a threat to the Petty Kingdoms."

"We're almost there," called out Felix as they reached the crossroads. "The front entrance of the Volstrum will be on the right."

"I don't see it," said Carmen.

"That's because these buildings block your view. You'll see the place as soon as we turn."

Cordelia wheeled the column to the right, and there it was, a massive building with six towers, almost as big as the Palace. She'd been told it was hexagonal, though you wouldn't know it from her current point of view. It was set back from the road with marble steps leading up to two statues, a man on one side of the entrance and a woman on the other, although Cordelia didn't recognize them.

Unlike the road they'd come from, people on foot went about their business. As the column proceeded towards the Volstrum, the sound of their hooves drew attention, and someone shouted a call of alarm. The pedestrians quickly cleared the street, rushing for the safety of nearby shops and closing the doors.

Cordelia gave the order, and the column split into two, Carmen taking half the sisters to secure the side streets while the rest remained with Cordelia, blocking the entrance to the Volstrum.

Temple Captain Gabriel was doing the same around the back, isolating all within the enormous structure. A pair of guards stood beside the two statues as if they, too, were anchored by stone.

"You there," called out Cordelia. "Surrender in the name of Saint Agnes!"

The guards stared back, aghast at the sight of armoured knights riding towards them. She couldn't hear what they said, but they exchanged words, then turned and ran, rushing into the building and slamming the doors shut behind them.

Cordelia slowed her horse, letting her knights take up their assigned positions. "No windows," she noted. "I thought this was a school. This place looks harder to assault than a commandery."

"And so it is," replied Felix. "They built it to withstand attacks by magical forces, or so we were all told."

"And the students study with no windows?"

"Yes. It was designed to force them to look inwards instead of out."

Cordelia shook her head. "This does not bode well."

Kargen peered around the corner at a locked iron gate blocking the entrance to the Volstrum's stables, the target of their attack. He pulled back, avoiding the gaze of the distant guards who wandered back and forth across the cobblestones.

"This is unexpected," he said. "I had hoped to get through the gate before they raised the alarm."

"Do not worry about what is done," replied Garag. "Concentrate on what needs to be done. We must take the gate if we are to proceed." He glanced back at his glaives, standing ready to launch their attack. "I need your warbows to keep those guards busy while we bring down the gate."

"It is made of iron," replied Kargen.

"Even iron will bend if you apply sufficient force."

"True, but give me a moment to think. We have masters of magic at hand; one might provide a solution." He spotted Shaluhk waiting in the rear, ready to provide healing, and beckoned her over.

"Is something wrong?" she asked.

"We must get through that gate," replied Kargen, "but it is locked. Have you any spells that might help us?"

"The magic of a shaman is of no use here. What you need is a master of earth to manipulate the stone."

"How will that help us?" replied Garag. "The gates are made of iron."

"True, but they are attached to posts."

"Also of iron."

"Iron set in stone. Soften that, and the gate will collapse under its own weight."

"Have we a master of earth to spare?"

"Wait a moment, and I shall see," replied Shaluhk. She moved back, giving herself room to cast.

"I thought her magic was of no use," said Garag.

"She is contacting Voruhn, who is with the Stone Crushers and, amongst their numbers, are masters of earth."

Shaluhk stood there, engaged in a one-sided conversation, then the magic in her eyes faded, and she turned her to her bondmate. "It is done. Urumar will be here shortly."

"I thought he was only an apprentice," replied Kargen.

"That was ages ago. He has been a master for many seasons."

Kargen shrugged. "I am far too busy looking after the Red Hand to worry about such things."

"That is why you have me. Now, listen to me, Garag; this is most important. Urumar requires access to the stonework on either side of that gate for the best chance of success. Your glaives must keep him safe while he casts his spell."

"It is not me you should tell, it is Kragor's archers. My glaives cannot touch the men in that courtyard unless they are foolish enough to come within reach of our weapons."

"I shall keep them busy," said Shaluhk. "You need only worry about Urumar's safety."

"I thought you said your magic was of no use?"

"You should pay better attention. My magic will not help open that gate. It is, however, more than capable of keeping those guards busy."

"How?"

"Wait and see."

The young master of earth appeared, his face smeared with mud, giving him a grey complexion. "I am here," he announced. "Voruhn tells me a gate is giving you trouble?"

"It is," replied Shaluhk, "although we do not want you to use your magic on the gate itself. If you soften the ground on either side, the posts will no longer support the gate's weight, is that not so?"

"Let me take a look." Urumar peered around the corner of the building as Kargen had done. He stood that way for the count of ten before pulling back. "Your idea has merit, but I would need to be closer."

"Have you no range to your magic?" asked Garag.

"Most certainly, but this particular spell requires me to manipulate the stone directly."

"Those guards carry bows," replied Garag. "My glaives would be slaughtered trying to protect you."

Shaluhk sighed. "I told you I would take care of them. Now, prepare your people to attack." She closed her eyes as words of power tumbled forth. The air buzzed as if a swarm of bees had been summoned, and then Shaluhk stepped around the corner of the building and pointed.

In the distant courtyard, a faint mist arose, coalescing into the form of Orc warriors. In appearance, they were much like Garag's glaives but wielded axes and spears rather than the polearms of Ard-Gurslag. They surged forward as one, charging towards the Volstrum's guards.

"What magic is this?" said Garag.

"Warriors of the past," replied Kargen. "Now go, while the enemy is distracted."

The First Glaive gave the command, and his glaives advanced, Urumar rushing to catch up. Weighed down by the heavy mail armour, they were not the quickest of Orcs, but they kept a tight formation, their weapons presenting a wall of steel. They were soon at the gate, formed in a line, behind which Urumar weaved his magic.

"Will this work?" said Kargen.

"It should," replied Shaluhk.

"But how can he view his target?"

"He only needs to see part of it. He will soften the ground, then begin pushing the gate over. Its own weight will do the rest."

"Would Garag's Orcs be able to help?"

"The magic of the earth does not work that way. The stone is softened, but only to the hands of Urumar."

"But you said the gate's weight would work against it."

Shaluhk nodded. "It will, although I am unable to explain why. Our knowledge of magic is still lacking in many ways."

"You are the most powerful shaman I know."

"You are kind to say so," said Shaluhk, "but my magic will not get us through that gate. Look!" She pointed.

Urumar finished his spell and stepped up to the pole supporting the right-hand side of the gate. He knelt, scraping away stone like mud, then grabbed the pole and pushed with all his might. A groaning sound echoed through the courtyard as the gate tilted at an obscene angle.

The master of earth then moved to the other side, repeating the process. Another groan rang forth as the entire gate fell, clanging as it struck the cobblestones.

"He has done it," said Kargen. He sought out Kragor. "Send in the warbows to support the attack; we shall soon be inside!"

# PARLEY

## SPRING 1110 SR

"Well, this is an unexpected turn of events." Belgast shook his head. "I thought the Orcs were supposed to seize the stables?"

"They were," replied Natalia. "They captured the rear courtyard, but the Volstrum's guards fought a successful delaying action until they'd secured the doors from within."

"So what do we do now? Send in the Thane Guard?"

"We can't," piped up Galina. "There are students in that building, some only thirteen years of age. We should give them a chance to surrender."

"Galina is correct," said Natalia. "We'll see if we can arrange a truce before the bloodbath begins. Where's Athgar?"

"Over there," replied the Dwarf. "Giving the Thane Guard a little encouragement. It's not easy convincing someone to attack a prepared position. Shall I fetch him?"

"No. It's best we don't both offer the enemy a target." Before anyone could object, Natalia began ascending the steps to the front door of the Volstrum. Belgast rushed after her, his pick in hand lest danger threaten.

She looked back at him. "I don't remember inviting you."

"We've been friends a long time, Natalia, but you can't have all the fun."

"Then we shall likely die together."

"That's hardly reassuring. Here I thought I was the only pessimist."

"Hush now," said Natalia. "We have a job to do."

They halted ten steps from the door.

"You there," she called out. "Who is the current headmistress?"

"Who wants to know?" came the reply.

"Natalia Stormwind, Warmaster of Therengia."

"And who's your friend?"

"Belgast Ridgehand, Hero of Kragen-Tor and Slayer of Dragons."

"Slayer of dragons?" said the Dwarf, his voice low. "Laying it on a bit thick, don't you think?"

"It's not like they know anything about Dwarves, and it will serve to unsettle them."

"Oh, aye, and make me a target for their arrows—"

"Go away! You're not wanted here."

"Tell your grand mistress I have returned, or I shall make it known to the matriarch that one of her guards was disrespectful to a member of the family."

"That will take time."

"Is she in the building?"

"Yes."

"Then send word I am here. Trust me, she'll want to talk to me."

They heard grumbling, even from their position outside the door.

Belgast chuckled. "He didn't like the idea of getting into trouble."

"You think he'd know better, serving the Stormwinds."

"I assume they don't want their guards thinking for themselves?"

"Not in the slightest."

"Far different from Therengia, then."

"Most definitely."

They stood waiting, the silence growing too much for the Dwarf. "Who do you suppose rules the Volstrum these days?"

"I really couldn't say," replied Natalia. "The only name that springs to mind is Gregori Stormwind, but considering his failure in Andover, I can't imagine him being put in charge."

"Could it be someone you knew from your training days? A fellow student?"

"Anything's possible, but I might remind you, the Stormwinds can call on the most powerful mages from across the Petty Kingdoms. It could be any one of those."

"Well, whoever it is, let's hope they see reason and release those children. I'd hate for them to get caught up in all this."

The morning wore on, and still they waited. Belgast took to sitting on the steps and examining the head of his pick to pass the time.

"Something's happening," said Natalia.

The Dwarf quickly got to his feet. "What makes you say that?"

"I hear people moving around behind that door."

"You don't suppose they're readying an attack, do you?"

"We'll find out soon enough."

"Natalia Stormwind," called out a woman's voice. "What brings you back to the Volstrum?"

"I've come to give you a chance to surrender. Who am I talking to?"

"Voltana Stormwind."

"Do you know her?" asked Belgast.

"Yes. We learned how to cast together. Katrin knows her, too, and Galina, as well."

"Small world. Is she as powerful as you?"

"That doesn't matter," replied Natalia. "We're here to negotiate, not duel."

"You never should've returned, Natalia," said Voltana. "You could've lived out your life in safety."

"Safety? You people came for my daughter. I cannot let that stand."

"So you arrive here at the head of an army? What do you hope to achieve?"

"The time of the Stormwinds has come to an end."

"Hah! Far from it. We grow ever more powerful with each passing day."

"You could've fooled me. You're banned from the court of Reinwick, not to mention Carlingen, and I hear even the Kingdom of Hadenfeld is no longer safe for members of the family."

"Get this over with," said Voltana. "I grow bored with your prattling."

"Release the children," replied Natalia. "They are too young to help you defend the Volstrum and would only get in the way. Their deaths serve no one."

"You make a compelling argument, but how do I know this isn't an elaborate plot to get us to open the doors?"

"If I wanted the door open, it would already be so, if not by magic, then by force of arms. I have a large army at my disposal, Voltana, more than sufficient to force our way in there."

The two of them stood outside the door, waiting for an answer.

"She's gone quiet," said Belgast. "Does that mean she's considering it?"

"Either that, or she's consulting with Marakhova."

"Are you suggesting the matriarch is in that building?"

"The guard said so, didn't he? And besides, it makes sense, considering Stormwind Manor burned to the ground."

"I don't see the connection."

"What could possibly be more secure in the eyes of the family than the Volstrum?"

"Oh, you mean the very building we are about to assault?" Belgast shook his head. "Sometimes your logic completely astounds me, but I'm with you, one way or the other."

"Thank you. I greatly appreciate that."

Marakhova peered out the window from the northwest tower, looking down at the army surrounding the Volstrum.

"This is intolerable! I should've sent Natalia to Zurkutsk when I had the chance." She whirled on the prisoner chained to the wall behind her. "This is all your fault."

"Mine?" replied Tatiana. "You sent her husband to the mines. You could've avoided all this if you'd welcomed her with open arms."

Marakhova stiffened. "How dare you speak thus to the matriarch! I could have you killed for your insolence."

"Yet you've chosen to keep me chained here, a witness to the great machinations of the all-mighty Marakhova Stormwind. The family's power is broken. The sooner you accept that, the better."

The matriarch stepped closer, staring at her prisoner. "Do you think that rabble out there poses a serious threat to us? We shall destroy them and, in so doing, break Therengia's power for all time."

A woman's voice followed a swift knock at the door: "Matriarch? I bear a message from the grand mistress."

A flicker of annoyance crossed Marakhova's face before she turned towards the door. "Enter." It opened to one of the Volstrum's newer instructors. "What is it, Lydia? Can't you see I'm busy?"

"Natalia Stormwind is down there, at the door, Matriarch."

"I know, you fool. What is it you want?"

"She asks that we allow the students to leave before the assault."

"All of them?"

"Only those yet to undergo the unleashing. At least, that's what we assumed; she referred to them as children. She claims they are of no benefit to us, and their staying would only lead to needless death."

Marakhova turned her back on the messenger, wandering over to the window. "I wonder..."

Lydia waited but dared to speak when no answer was forthcoming. "Have you an answer, Matriarch?"

"How many children have we here at the Volstrum?"

"I... I'm not sure."

She turned her wrath on her prisoner. "You know, don't you?"

"Before you arrested me, we had thirty-six students yet to complete their unleashing."

"Is that all? I would've thought more. When I was the headmistress, we had triple that."

"That was before you lost your most successful mage hunter."

"Ah, yes. The traitor, Stanislav Voronsky. His loss had further-reaching consequences than we expected. Still, we must work with what we have."

"So you'll release them?" asked Lydia.

"I shall consider it."

"They are children," said Tatiana, "and that army out there is set to storm our halls. How can you even think of endangering them?"

"Those children are the future of this family," snapped Marakhova. "We need them to retake our rightful place as rulers of the Petty Kingdoms."

"You mean in service to the empire?"

"Don't lecture me. We ARE the empire!"

"So, you finally admit it!"

"You never understood what we're trying to do here," the matriarch continued. "Imagine a Continent where we are free to explore magic to its fullest potential. Why, who knows what secrets we might unlock?"

"You're mad."

"Is it mad to imagine a better world?"

"Better?" replied Tatiana. "For whom? You'd enslave an entire continent to achieve your goals."

"I don't deny it," said Marakhova. "The weak serve the powerful. It's been that way since the dawn of civilization."

"So has conflict. Do you truly believe the Sartellians would allow you to rule without them?"

"Sartellians? You think a bunch of Pyromancers are a threat to us Stormwinds? As far as I'm concerned, they can be consumed by the very flames they conjure." Her gaze settled on Lydia. "Ah, yes, the children. What to do, what to do. I had a mind to let them perish in the attack, but they may still prove useful."

"You mean to release them?" said Lydia.

Marakhova smiled, though it was far from comforting. "Why, of course. We should be able to drag this out all day, allowing us time to prepare our defences. Tell Voltana we agree to Natalia's request, but she must make it last as long as possible."

"Yes, Matriarch."

"And when you're done, return to me, Lydia. I have further need of your services."

The younger woman bowed, then fled through the door, her footsteps receding down the stairs.

"You won't survive this," warned Tatiana. "Not after all you've put Natalia through."

"Perhaps," the old woman replied, "but before this is over, Natalia Stormwind will no longer be a threat to the family."

"All right," yelled out Voltana. "We agree to let the children go."

"Thank the Gods for that," said Belgast. "How do you want to do this?"

"I'll send them out in threes," came the reply, "but you must agree to keep your people away from the doors."

"Understood," said Natalia.

"It'll take a while to assemble them. I shall let you know when we're ready to commence."

"They're wasting time," said Belgast.

"It can't be helped," replied Natalia. "I'll not order the attack with the children still at risk."

"But wouldn't it work to their advantage to keep them inside the Volstrum, making it more difficult for us to take the building? Not that I'm complaining, mind you. I want these children freed as much as you do; it's just that I can't imagine the family being so accommodating without getting something in return." He glanced around the area. "You don't suppose they're waiting for someone to come to their rescue? There must be hordes of Stormwinds in the city, not to mention Sartellians."

"I doubt they'd try anything while we have the Temple Knights guarding our perimeter."

"They're trained battle mages, aren't they?"

"No doubt the more powerful ones are, but they've learned to work in conjunction with an army, not attack an enemy by themselves. I imagine most are sitting back, waiting to see what happens."

"Still, we must be on our guard."

"I trust Cordelia to watch our backs."

"Something's happening," said Belgast.

The door to the Volstrum opened, and someone pushed out three children, the fear on their faces obvious.

Natalia took a step towards them, but Belgast grabbed her arm. "No," he said. "That could be what they want. You get within range of that door, and there's a good chance they'll try killing you. I'll go."

"Please be careful."

"I will." He slowly climbed the remaining steps, fearful an arrow might come flying out. He paused at a point between the two statues. "This way," he called out, beckoning.

The children were frozen in place, looking back and forth between the Dwarf and the door behind them.

"It's all right," Belgast soothed. "No one's going to hurt you. You see that woman back there?" He pointed at Natalia. "She went to the Volstrum, just like you."

A dark-haired girl made the first move, taking a tentative step towards him.

"That's it," said Belgast. "A little farther, and you'll be safe."

She took another step, then another, each slowly bringing her closer to the Dwarf.

"What's your name?" he asked.

"Nika," she replied.

"Hello, Nika. My name is Belgast Ridgehand, and that lady over there is Natalia Stormwind." He turned, nodding at the last two children. "Who are your friends?"

"Aleksei and Hedy, but she's not from around here."

He held out his hand, and she took it. He guided her down a few stairs, letting her walk the rest of the way on her own. Once Natalia had her, he climbed back to his previous position.

Emboldened by their companion, Aleksei and Hedy ran forward, their fear driving them onward. They raced past Belgast, clinging to Nika as if their lives depended on it.

"Send us the next group!" called out Belgast.

"In time," came the reply. "We need to collect them."

He sat down on the steps once again. This was going to take all day.

A lone lantern lit the room, shadows flickering across the walls. Around a table stood the leaders of the alliance, as Natalia liked to call them, making for a crowded space, but everyone needed to be aware of what the night would bring.

"What I don't understand," said Belgast, "is why we aren't waiting till morning? Surely you don't want everyone fighting in the dark?"

"It won't be dark," said Galina. "The halls of the Volstrum are magically illuminated. The defenders will prefer things well-lit, enabling them to see who's coming."

Raleth shifted slightly. "What can we expect in terms of magic?"

"Frozen shut doors," replied Natalia, "and it's not unreasonable to assume ice will block some hallways. They'll likely try to lure you into a killing room, so you must resist the temptation to take the easiest path."

"Perhaps I should go with them," said Athgar. "My mastery of flames might prove useful."

"No," insisted Kargen. "Until you train a successor, you are the sole master of flame in all of Therengia. We must not risk losing you."

"I agree," said Natalia. "Besides, you can only be in one place at a time. We'll use the Thane Guard's axes to batter down doors and break the ice, a time-consuming endeavour, but it forces the defenders to fight on our terms."

"We will do the same in the stables," said Garag, "providing we get past their doors. We tried taking axes to them, but they resisted our efforts."

"That's to be expected," said Belgast. "They're made of shadowbark, and that stuff resists even the keenest blades."

"Then how do we get in?"

"You should not concern yourself with the door," said Rugg, "but the stone forming the frame. We masters of earth shall use our magic to clear away the anchor points for the hinges, then the weight of the door will cause it to fall."

"As Urumar did at the gate?"

"Precisely, although I imagine the stone supporting that door will be thicker, thus requiring additional time."

"A good idea," said Natalia, "but does that leave you with enough magic to make an entrance along the side of the building?"

"That largely depends on how thick the Volstrum's walls are."

"Would they be thicker than a commandery?" asked Athgar.

"I doubt it," replied Natalia.

"Good," said Rugg. "I am familiar with the Mathewite commandery in Ebenstadt. Based on that assumption, I can promise you that the Volstrum's walls do not present a significant problem. However, I must warn you, making a hole large enough for warriors to enter the building will take time."

"You contradict yourself," said Garag. "You say it is not a problem, then complain it will take time."

"You are not a master of earth, so I will forgive your ignorance. The spell we use is not difficult to master, but one can only manipulate small sections at a time. We must create a hole large enough for Orc hunters to pass through."

"Can we knock a hole in the wall?"

"With what?" said Athgar. "We have no catapults, and the building is made of stone, not wood, else we'd go at it with axes. We also have the advantage that magic is relatively quiet, at least from the point of view of those inside the building."

"Then it is settled," said Garag. "When are we to begin?"

"As soon as our masters of earth are in position."

# THE ASSAULT BEGINS

## SPRING 1110 SR

Raleth stood ready, his men lined up behind him. The assault on the Volstrum's front door would commence with an initial charge that would encounter the same issue as those facing the stables: a shadowbark door, the hardest wood in all of Eiddenwerthe. The Thane Guard couldn't cut their way through even if they wanted. To that end, they intended to win through by using magic, the same way the gate had been overcome in the rear.

Gahruhl stood waiting, ready to rush to the door once she received the signal all was safe. To keep her alive, Raleth's men would use their shields, protecting her while she moved up. They need not fear arrows, for there were no windows, save for those adorning the six towers atop the Volstrum, but magic was an unknown variable.

Natalia had informed them that no Water Magic spell could target the master of earth if she couldn't be seen, yet Raleth wasn't willing to take any chances. Should Gahruhl fall, his only recourse would be to retreat.

He took one more look at the Thane Guard, men and women from all across Therengia, united in their desire to keep the land safe. The High Thane himself requested only volunteers come to Ruzhina, but as soon as Raleth asked, they all stepped forward.

As far as the Petty Kingdoms were concerned, they were not the best-armoured warriors, wearing coats of mail rather than plate armour, but what they lacked in equipment, they more than made up for with their ferocity. These men and women could be counted on to do their part regardless of cost.

For some, it was fulfilling their oath to serve their High Thane, while for others, it was payback for the attack on Runewald two years ago, when two mages had attempted to kidnap Oswyn. The time had come to take revenge and punish the family for their insolence.

Athgar appeared out of the dark, pausing before Raleth and putting his hand on the fellow's shoulder. "Ready?" he asked.

"We will not fail you, Lord."

"You face a tough foe, my friend. They will do anything and everything in their power to stop you."

"My people will not waver."

"I'm sure they won't. Begin the assault when you are ready. Good luck, and may the Gods be with you." With that, Athgar departed, vanishing into the dark of the night.

Raleth regarded the Volstrum. It was little more than a gigantic shadow, yet he knew what he faced. They must advance up a set of steps, then assault a door that couldn't be opened until the master of earth finished her work.

The thought made him turn to Gahruhl. "*Ready?*" he called out, using the Orcish tongue.

She nodded in reply.

"Forward!" he shouted, his voice calm despite his fears. As he advanced, he heard the footfalls of the men and women following him. He kept up a moderate pace, staring at the ground, waiting for the steps to appear lest he stumble in the dark. The torchlight from behind flickered on the first step, and he began the climb towards the front door.

Something whizzed past his ear, and a grunt came from behind him. Another two steps and something flickered as it flew through the air. Raleth focused on the door until he drew close enough to see movement amongst the shadows. Someone held up a crossbow, and then a bolt flew forth, narrowly missing him.

He gave the order to charge, breaking into a run. The defenders melted into the shadows, and then the door slammed shut.

The Thane Guard reached the door and began chopping, but their efforts could neither penetrate the wood nor mar it. However, their assault prevented defenders from opening the door to loose additional bolts.

Gahruhl advanced, then shifted to the left, placing herself against the outside wall of the Volstrum: her objective, the hinges, which were protected by stone. She motioned over a Thane Guard, who held a torch, illuminating the area. Based on her earlier observations, she knelt, counting stones to estimate where the bottom hinge should be found. Then she cast, the magic pouring out, her hands glowing with yellow light as she plunged them into stone that parted as if it were no more than clay.

Raleth moved up to her left, his axe ready should it prove necessary. "Any luck?" he asked.

She worked silently for a count of ten, then smiled, her ivory teeth glowing in the torchlight. "I found the hinge." She drew back her hands, pulling loose a handful of stone. Two further scoops exposed the hinge anchored into a wooden beam.

"Tell your men to be careful," she warned. "Shadowbark is a dense wood. Once we pry the hinges loose, its own weight may bring it crashing down." She adjusted her position, reaching higher to plunge her hands back into the stone for the upper hinge.

"I have it," she said, then pulled more stone away from the doorway. She jumped back. "It is up to you now."

Two of Raleth's warriors moved in, jamming spears into the hinges, attempting to wrest them loose from the timber. The door groaned as the metal snapped, dropping slightly, no more than a finger's width. They shifted their spears higher, working on the second hinge. As they struck wood, the bolts holding the hinge to the beam popped loose, and the door fell outward.

The Thane Guard stepped back, desperate to avoid being crushed. The heavy door struck the ground, and they surged forward, yelling as their axes reached out.

The doorway led to a small entrance hall where the defenders had set up a barricade, using tables, barrels, and even a few chairs to block the way. Crossbow bolts flew, taking down two of Raleth's warriors, and then the Thane Guard was atop the barricade screaming as they lashed out with axes and spears.

---

Garag waved his Orcs forward to the stable doors. The massive things swung out on either side under normal conditions, yet today, they were barred shut, the Volstrum's defenders taking refuge inside. Unlike the door out front, these were built into a shadowbark wooden frame, making Urumar's spell of shaping stone useless. He needed to use a different approach.

The Orcs of Ard-Gurslag reached their target and began hitting the door. This was not an attempt to destroy it but to cover the noise of Urumar's casting.

Garag was soon amongst them, Urumar just behind. *"You know what to do?"* he asked.

*"I do,"* replied the master of earth. *"But I need some space to operate."*

Garag barked out a command. *"Fall back, but continue making as much noise as possible, and pay close attention to the door. It will crush the life out of you if you are in its way when it falls."*

Urumar cast his spell, calling on his inner magic to do his bidding. The air buzzed, small lights circling the master of earth as if a swarm of fireflies had been summoned. He pointed, and the lights floated forward, disappearing into the ground just before the door.

The ground shook ever so slightly as slender tendrils protruded through the dirt. Urumar concentrated, and they thickened into vines that crawled up the doorway, curling around the steel bars that held the wooden planks together.

Thicker and thicker, they grew, the door groaning with the strain of their weight. The shadowbark planks remained in place, but the steel bars holding them were crushed under the onslaught. A stray bolt popped, flying over Urumar's head, but his gaze stayed fixed on the door. *"Get ready,"* he warned. *"It will not be long."*

*"Back! Back!"* shouted Garag. He formed his glaives into a double line, their weapons held before them, ready to charge.

A metal strip suddenly broke free, the vines clutching at it in vain as it fell to the cobblestones. The groaning grew louder as the rest of the metal strips were ripped free, no longer securing the shadowbark planks.

Urumar waved his hands, dismissing the spell, and the vines suddenly went limp, releasing their grip. The planks fell with a heavy crash, and then Garag ordered his glaives forward, the Orcs letting out a war cry not heard in over two thousand years.

*"We are in!"* shouted Garag, chasing after his warriors.

---

Rugg placed his hand against the outside wall of the Volstrum. *"I am about to begin, but there is no telling what lies on the other side."*

*"My bows stand ready,"* said Kragor. A distant roar echoed through the night air. *"The assault has begun,"* he added. *"Let us hope it is enough to mask our own attack."*

The master of earth cast his spell. Like Gahruhl, he would use his magic to soften the stone, but instead of exposing hinges, he would attempt to create a hole for the Orcs of the Red Hand to enter the Volstrum. It was a gamble, for they knew not where such an opening would lead.

His hands glowed as he plunged them into the stone. It was a quick action, designed to create an arrow slit rather than a door, the better to protect him as he worked on a larger opening.

Kragor moved up, pressing his eye to the newly made hole. *"I see light beyond,"* he said, *"but no movement."*

Rugg repeated the action, creating another hole four paces to his right. He waited as Grundak pressed his eye to it, then moved between the two holes to work on a larger opening.

The process was slow, for only the master of earth could scoop out the stone; to everyone else, it was cold, unyielding rock.

*"It remains quiet,"* said Grundak, *"but you must hurry before the enemy discovers what we are about."*

Rugg, working at a feverish pace, was not amused. *"It is no simple task to make an opening fit for an Orc, let alone dozens of them. This would be faster if you were not so large."*

*"Me? Large?"* said Grundak. *"I will have you know I was the smallest in my family."*

*"Shhh. Someone is coming,"* whispered Kragor. He nocked an arrow, lining it up with the hole before him, then let fly, to be rewarded by a gasp and then a thud as a body fell to the floor.

*"You got them,"* said Grundak.

*"Let us hope it was a mage. It means one less for us to face."*

Urumar stumbled forward as a large section of the wall collapsed. *"It is done,"* he announced.

*"That was faster than I expected,"* said Kragor.

*"Rather than creating a hole, I dug around in a circle, the middle of which has fallen into the room beyond."*

*"Attack!"* shouted Grundak, charging through the opening, bow in hand. The rest of the hunters followed, the majority carrying axes.

They entered a room with desks lined up facing one end. The sole occupant was a man lying in the doorway, Kragor's arrow protruding from his chest.

*"Secure the door,"* said Kragor, *"then, when we have gathered enough hunters, we shall push farther into the building."*

Grundak stood in the doorway, peering out. *"The corridor heads left and right,"* he said. *"Which direction do we go?"*

*"Any sign of defenders?"*

*"No."*

*"Then left, which takes us towards the front of the building."* He faced the hunters piling into the room behind him. *"You six remain here, along with Master Rugg. We shall send for you if we require his magic. The rest follow me."*

With that, Kragor moved into the hallway, his axe replacing his bow. He set two hunters to watch the corridor to the right, then led his Orcs farther into the Volstrum.

The corridor continued straight but presented Kragor with a problem, for doors were on either side, likely leading to other classrooms. He selected the one to his left, opened the door a crack and peered within. *"Empty."*

Grundak, meanwhile, positioned himself across the hall. At Kragor's nod, he opened the other door to a class of young men, their attention focused on someone at the front of the room. He closed the door as quietly as possible, then turned to his comrade. *"This is full of students."*

*"How many?"*

*"Eight, and presumably an instructor, although I could not see him directly. What do you want us to do—charge in and kill them all?"*

*"No,"* said Kragor. *"We must give them the option to surrender peacefully. Open the door and stand with weapons ready. I shall speak to them."*

*"Are you certain that is wise?"*

*"If we are forced to fight every single student within these walls, we shall soon find ourselves bogged down. However, if we convince them to surrender peacefully, we may succeed."* He opened the door, stepping into the room.

Those within were focused on the man at the front, but one student noticed movement out of the corner of his eye and turned his head to see an Orc standing in the doorway. The surprise on his face was quite evident, and he almost fell out of his chair.

"W-w-who are you?" he stammered.

His remarks drew everyone's attention, and they turned, staring at Kragor.

"What is the meaning of this?" demanded the man at the front.

"I am Kragor of the Red Hand," the Orc replied in the common tongue. "Surrender, and we will spare your lives."

The fellow's eyes darted around, though whether that was to check on his students or seek a means of escape was unknown. "Close your books, students. It seems we are to be escorted from the building."

"Out in the hallway are Orcs who will escort you to the breach. You will be safe amongst them."

The students lined up, their instructor moving in front to lead them. "Thank you," he said, though he did not appear very pleased.

Kragor went farther into the room, allowing everyone else to exit. He intended to follow along behind the Humans, ensuring none remained, but no sooner had they left than the air turned frigid, and an Orc cried out.

Kragor rushed from the room, axe in hand, to find the instructor in the midst of casting a spell. His students, obviously more experienced than the Orcs suspected, had let loose with a barrage of ice shards. Three of his hunters were down, their black blood splattering the walls.

Kragor struck out, feeling the axe bite into the instructor's back. With his concentration broken, the fellow could only turn in shock, his features paling as he collapsed. The Orc polished him off with an efficient strike to the throat.

Grundak, lying on the floor, raised his arm in a vain attempt to protect himself. Ice shards dug into him, shattering his arm and sending bits of bone flying. A sigh escaped him as he went limp.

Fury built within Kragor, and he leaped to the attack, his axe swinging out, seeking revenge. A shard of ice clipped his arm, drawing blood, and then he was amongst them, his blade digging deep. It all became a blur, a tightly packed corridor where the smell of blood and death mingled as if this were the Underworld.

Swing after swing, blow after blow, he attacked until his muscles ached with the strain. As the last student fell under his onslaught, Kragor collapsed to his knees. Eight Humans lay dead, nine if you included their instructor, but he felt no sorrow. He'd offered these people an escape from the family's control, and instead, they had turned on him, slaughtering his fellow Orcs with their magic.

Additional hunters arrived, drawn by the sound of battle. They picked their way through the dead, and then Durgash was there, lifting him to his feet. "*You are injured,*" he said. "*Let us get you to a shaman.*" He passed him into the care of a pair of hunters.

"*His wounds will heal,*" said Urag.

"*His physical injuries will,*" replied Durgash, "*but his soul is another matter.*"

# DESPERATION

SPRING 1110 SR

Tatiana watched as a distraught Marakhova paced. There could be only one reason—the defence of the Volstrum was not going according to plan.

"This is taking far too long," fumed the matriarch. She turned from the window to regard Voltana. "Why haven't we repulsed the attacks?"

"We are trying, Matriarch, but their warriors are too numerous. We have, however, halted their advance."

"How much of the Volstrum do they control?"

"Only a few corridors and a handful of rooms captured in their initial assault this morning. They've made no further progress since."

"It's not enough! If we are to win this day, we must push them back into the streets." She moved to a nearby table and picked up a goblet, but as she raised it to her lips, she noticed it was empty. "Lydia. Get me another bottle of the Radetsky Red."

Tatiana smiled. In the rush of the attack, they'd forgotten her morning's dose of magebane. She remained manacled but felt her magic returning. The question now was how to stop her captors from realizing their mistake. She decided the best course of action was to keep Marakhova angry. "You won't win. Natalia will press on until no one is left standing. You made a mistake sending people after her child."

"Do not speak to me of mistakes, Tatiana. I trusted you with the Volstrum while you worked against me the whole time."

The matriarch returned to the window, staring at the enemy watching from across the street. Natalia was amongst them, distinctive with her pale skin and jet-black hair.

"Surely she doesn't believe she can take the Volstrum?" Marakhova muttered.

"Why not?" said Tatiana. "She burned down Stormwind Manor easily enough."

"That was a fluke. She surprised us then, whereas we are fully prepared now." She looked at Voltana. "Tell our warriors to prepare for a counterattack."

"You mean to drive them from the building?" asked the grand mistress.

"In time, but I will be content with bleeding them dry for now. I want all senior instructors to the front of the building; we'll begin there."

"And the other points of attack?"

"Tell them they may fall back if necessary, but only if they make our attackers suffer for every step."

"This would be easier if we had some Sartellians. Is there some way to contact them?"

"Fool. Don't you think I've already tried? Our cousins refused to come to our aid, hoping to enrich their standing at our expense. Now go, Voltana, and carry out my orders, or shall I replace you too."

The grand mistress fled.

Lydia took a hesitant step forward.

"What is it?" snapped Marakhova.

"Your wine, Matriarch."

"Put it on the table. I shall see to it myself."

Lydia backed up, remaining near the door.

Again, Marakhova stared out the window, her gaze fixated on Natalia. "What is she up to? She must realize the futility of this attack?" Suddenly, she turned, staring off to the left as if a realization had just hit her. "She's not after the Volstrum!"

"Matriarch?" said Lydia.

"Natalia is not after the Volstrum. She's after something far more valuable."

"Which is?"

"The Baroshka."

"I don't know what that is," replied Lydia.

"It is a secret repository of our most powerful spells; its existence is known to only a few." Her gaze snapped to her prisoner. "And that includes you, doesn't it? I should've realized it when I discovered you were helping her."

"I'm surprised you know of it," said Tatiana. "Illiana told me it was a carefully guarded secret."

"You forget. I was grand mistress here before you. Did you truly believe a mage of my power wouldn't know?"

"But she cannot reach it; you control the Volstrum."

Marakhova's eyes bored into her. "Unless you allowed her to commit the magic circle to memory. That's it, isn't it? At last, your true treachery is revealed." She wagged her finger. "You shall pay for this with your life, I assure you, but I must act quickly to prevent this mad scheme of Natalia's. Call my guards, Lydia."

Lydia stepped outside the room, summoning the guards.

"I may die," said Tatiana, "but I'll have the satisfaction of knowing you've been beaten."

Sounds of boots drew closer, and a warrior appeared at the door. "We await your command, Matriarch."

"Lydia, you stay here and keep an eye on our… guest. I'll deal with her on my return. Come along, Captain."

She strode through the doorway, her footsteps heavy.

"She wasn't lying about killing me," said Tatiana. "Do you really want to be implicit in murder?"

"You betrayed the family," replied Lydia.

"Did I, or did I serve it?"

"Don't try to confuse me with your false sense of loyalty. You betrayed the matriarch."

"I served Illiana. She wanted to save the family."

"Save it? How?"

"By turning it from a dark path. Look around you—see what's happening. Marakhova will be the ruin of us all."

"She is a powerful mage," insisted Lydia.

"Remember how powerful Natalia was? You were in the same class. Can you stand there and tell me you believe Marakhova is her equal?"

"Natalia may be more powerful, but she turned her back on us."

"Wouldn't you, given the same circumstances? They tried to kidnap her child, Lydia. You, of all people, should understand that. What would you be willing to do to save the life of your son?"

---

Athgar watched as they carried Raleth out of the Volstrum on a litter. He moved to intercept, looking down on the injured warrior. Blood soaked his mail, and a deep gash on his chest was evidence of the ferocity of the fight.

"Take him to the healers," said Athgar.

The young commander reached out, grabbing his arm with blood-soaked fingers. "It's no use," he said, his breathing laboured. "We've only captured three rooms and a section of corridor. Every time we launch a fresh attack, they respond with magic. They were casting ice shards but tried a different tactic this time."

"Which was?"

"They flooded the floor by conjuring water, then froze it, making it impossible for us to move. Their warriors advanced, and we only defeated their counterattack thanks to Hilwyth's archers. We took heavy casualties." He lifted himself up partway, watching as more of the Thane Guard hobbled past, victims of severe frostbite. "I'm sorry, Lord, but we can't keep this up."

"I hear you," said Athgar. "I'll bring this news to Natalia." His attention shifted to the bearers. "Take him to Shaluhk."

He watched them carry off Raleth. This was not the news he'd hoped for. It was now late afternoon, and their assault had ground to a halt. He spotted Kargen and wandered over.

"You have news?" he asked.

"Nothing good, I am afraid. Garag's glaives got inside the stables, but I fear they will make no further progress, for the Stormwinds have carefully prepared their defences."

"Any news from Kragor?"

"Yes, though it is also not good. They got farther inside than the rest of us but were driven back to their entry point in a fierce counterattack. They only hold one room and a section of corridor, and I doubt it will be long before they are overwhelmed. I sent additional hunters to relieve those from the latest assault, but I fear it is a losing proposition."

"We must do something," said Athgar.

"I agree, but what?"

They made their way over to Natalia, but she wouldn't meet Athgar's gaze.

"We are failing," he called out. "At this rate, we'll be out of warriors by nightfall."

"It's all my fault," replied Natalia. "I never took the family's resolve into account." Their eyes finally met, and he saw the sorrow behind hers. "What have I done?" she asked. "Hundreds are going to die, and to what end? It would have been better to ignore them."

"Yes, we'll suffer heavy losses," said Athgar, "but that pales in comparison to how many will die if we do nothing."

"Why do only our people have to pay the price?"

"We could always call on the masters of magic from Ard-Gurslag."

"We can't do that, not after Garag's warning. It only supports their plans of conquest."

"Would it not be better to sacrifice Ruzhina to ensure the safety of our home?"

"If the Orcs of Ard-Gurslag go to war," said Natalia, "I doubt they'd stop at Ruzhina."

"Then perhaps we should abandon this campaign and go home?"

She sighed. "We can't. If we withdraw, we'd only be inviting the family to come after us."

"With what? We have an army to defend us."

"Despite recent events, the family still holds sway over most of the Petty Kingdoms. The last thing we need is another crusade marching into our lands."

"What other option do we have?" said Athgar. "Our attacks are failing, our losses mounting, and we have no surprises left to spring on our enemies. Any way you look at it, we're losing this battle."

She stared at the Volstrum, her face tightening.

"What are you thinking?" he asked.

"We need a way to finish this, once and for all."

"That way being?"

"I'm open to suggestions. Gather the others; we'll meet here, out in the open. The fresh air will help us think."

"I shall find them," offered Kargen.

They met across the street from the Volstrum's front door. Galina and Katrin were there, along with Cordelia and Kargen, but Shaluhk was busy caring for the wounded. Belgast rounded out the group, though he looked none too pleased with their current circumstances.

"Have you a plan?" asked Cordelia.

"Not at present," replied Natalia. "I thought, between us, we might devise some way of salvaging this assault."

"I could send in my Temple Knights?"

Belgast shook his head. "No offence, but I doubt that would do any good. It's not as if you could squeeze your horses into those corridors, and they would freeze your knights to the floor as easily as they did our warriors."

"What if we tried breaking through another wall?" asked Kargen. "Perhaps on the opposite side from Kragor's attack?"

"We would still have the same problems. We need a different approach, something they wouldn't be expecting."

"How about a tunnel?" said Katrin. "Didn't you use that to get into Ebenstadt?"

"We did," replied Kargen, "but it was a long process, taking days."

"Yes," added Belgast. "By the time we broke through, no one would be left to fight."

"Hang on," said Galina. "What about the Baroshka?"

"What's that?" asked Cordelia.

"A spell repository beneath the Volstrum."

"How does that help us?"

"There's a magic circle there. We could use it to get people inside."

"That doesn't help us," said Belgast. "Yes, we'd get some of our warriors inside, but as soon as they're discovered, we'd be bogged down, just like our other attacks."

"I might have a better way to deal with this," said Natalia. "I'm just not sure if it would work."

"Go on," urged the Dwarf.

"If I'm not mistaken, a tributary of the Mitchutskin runs beneath the Volstrum."

"Yes," said Galina. "That's right. We used its waters in some of our rituals. You're not suggesting we use an underground river to enter the building?"

"No. I propose we use the river to destroy the Volstrum on our behalf."

"That would require a tremendous amount of power," said Katrin. "I doubt even you could accomplish that."

"Ah, but if we were in the Baroshka, I could use the magic circle to amplify my power."

"To do what? Flood the lower floors? You'd only be drowning yourself."

"Yes," said Athgar, "but she can breathe water with the proper spell."

"Perhaps," said Galina, "but using a spell to breathe underwater does not let one cast a spell. The words of power are precise; any mispronunciation would result in failure."

Athgar's shoulders slumped. "Then we're back to the beginning."

"There must be something we can do?" said Belgast. "Does this repository hold a lot of paper?"

"It does," replied Natalia.

"Could we set fire to it and burn them out?"

"The building is made of stone."

"True," said the Dwarf, "but smoke makes breathing difficult."

"The Volstrum is too large," noted Athgar, "and even if it wasn't, we'd be smoking out our own people."

"Hold on," said Katrin. "I just thought of something."

"Which is?"

"When we were in Beorwic, Natalia used the standing stones to create a great storm."

"Yes," replied Athgar, "but there are no standing stones here, and even if there were, how does a rainstorm hurt those safely ensconced inside a building?"

"Ah, but I doubt every confluence of ley lines has standing stones above it. Could there be a node deep beneath the Volstrum?"

"I hadn't considered that," replied Natalia. "What do you think, Galina?"

"It would explain why the family chose this particular location to build. If I recall my history, they levelled several blocks of houses. Surprising, when they could have easily built on the outskirts of the city."

"Assuming that's true," said Katrin, "how does that help us?"

"I can use an arch to get to the Baroshka," replied Natalia. "Then, I can harness the power of the ley lines to weaken the building from below."

"Are you suggesting you'll collapse it in on itself?"

"Quite possibly," replied Natalia, "though I can't say for certain. It depends on how much water is in the underground river."

"But if this works, the weight of the building will crush you too."

"A small sacrifice to defeat the family."

"No!" shouted Athgar. "I won't hear of it."

"Not so fast," said Galina. "I know the circle of which she speaks. I can create an arch out here, allowing her an escape route."

Natalia turned to her husband. "I know you don't want to hear this, but it's our only chance to stop Marakhova."

"There must be another way!"

"This is our best option."

He gritted his teeth. "Then I'm going with you."

"You can't; someone has to look after Oswyn."

"I'm not losing you. If you're meant to travel to the Afterlife, I'll be there, holding your hand."

Kargen gently touched Natalia's arm. "He has made his choice, Nat-Alia. You must respect it. Should you both perish, Shaluhk and I will look after Oswyn. I give you my word."

"This is madness," said Belgast. "Even if you use your magic to enter this Babooshka place..."

"Baroshka," corrected Galina.

"Whatever it's called, has it occurred to you it might be guarded? You could appear in that circle only to be cut down by swords."

"That is a risk I'm willing to take," said Natalia.

"As am I," added Athgar.

"Well, if you're so determined to throw your lives away to defeat the Stormwinds, I'm going with you."

"So am I," said Katrin. "I may not be the most powerful Water Mage in these parts, but I can use my magic to help keep a few guards at bay. I owe them that much for sending me to the mines."

"Very well," said Natalia, "but we must make arrangements before we go. The last thing we want is to bring the building crashing down with our people inside."

"When do you wish to carry out this plan?" asked Kargen.

"The sooner, the better."

"I shall inform Garag he needs to withdraw his glaives."

"I will tell Kragor," offered Cordelia. "What about the Thane Guard?"

"Hilwyth commands them now," replied Athgar. "I'll send word."

"This will be difficult to coordinate," said Natalia. "If we go too soon, we risk killing our own people, too late, and the defenders could swarm us in the Baroshka. You must keep them busy until the very last moment."

"We shall coordinate using the shamans," replied Kargen. "We will watch your progress through Galina's arch."

"We'll spread the word," said Cordelia. "Galina, you'd best come with me. We need to find a safe place to cast your spell. If this works, we can't predict how much of the ground will collapse."

They all left Athgar and Natalia, heading out to inform the others of their plan, save for Kargen and Belgast. "It is not easy to say farewell, my friends," started Kargen, his voice choking up. "You are both family. I understand your reasoning, but your loss will be felt throughout the tribe, perhaps even the entire Continent. The world of Eiddenwerthe will not be the same without you."

"You've done great things for the Red Hand," said Athgar, "and I hope you and Shaluhk continue to prosper. I'm not eager to die, but it will be easier with the knowledge our sacrifice gives the tribe a safe and secure future." He turned to Belgast. "And you, my friend. How can words ever express our gratitude at having you by our side during our final moments?"

"Now you've done it," said Belgast. "You've gone and made me cry."

# SACRIFICE

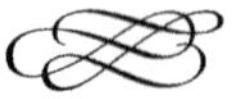

## SPRING 1110 SR

"It is time," announced Natalia.

Galina cast her spell, concentrating on creating the first arch. They'd picked a building down the street from the Volstrum, enabling them to remain unobserved by the family. The first arch formed quickly, and then she closed her eyes, picturing the magic circle in the Baroshka.

"Will this work?" asked Athgar.

"She knows the circle as well as I do. Having her cast the initial arch preserves my magic for the cataclysm."

"Cataclysm?" said Belgast.

"It's what I've decided to call this spell," replied Natalia.

"I'm still not certain I understand how it will work," said Katrin.

"I shall divert the underground river to flow upwards, into the Volstrum, instead of downstream where it joins the Mitchutskin. The ley lines should provide sufficient power to create a great flood, drowning those within, or at the very least washing them out the doors."

"A horrible way to die," said Belgast, shaking his head, "but I suppose they brought this upon themselves."

"How is it any worse than killing them with axes?" said Athgar. "That's the only alternative, and we'd lose a lot of good people doing that."

"Aye, you're right, although if it were me, I'd much prefer to be killed by falling stones than submerged in water."

"It's ready," announced Galina. She motioned towards the arch, which now offered them a way into the Volstrum's lower floor. "Good luck."

Athgar turned to Natalia, who nodded in response. He grasped her hand, and they walked side by side through the arch. They emerged into a large, circular room with columns that supported a vaulted ceiling and murals decorating the walls. Athgar's attention, however, focused on the floor, for the white marble reflected the light coming through the arch, bathing the room in a soft, yellow glow. Beneath them stood a circle of gold, with gold and silver runes set within it.

"This must've cost a fortune," noted Athgar. "Why use all that gold? The standing stones don't."

"Precious metals are better able to hold magical energy," replied Natalia.

"I know that, but this uses significantly more gold than the one in Carlingen."

"This is a more powerful circle. Those runes boost the power of anyone casting within it."

"I can't feel a thing."

"Not surprising. Fire and Water Magic are opposites, thus you are unable to tap into its power, just as I could not harness the power of a circle of flame."

"What does that mean for Oswyn? She'll be able to call on both?"

"I don't know. Perhaps it will amplify her Water Magic while hindering her inner spark, but I doubt she'll have the opportunity to learn. This circle will be broken by the time I'm done here."

They moved aside as Belgast and Katrin stepped through.

"Which way to the books?" asked Belgast.

Natalia pointed. "A door between those two pillars leads to the arcane library."

"We'll save all we can," said Katrin, then hurried off, ready to haul every book, scroll, and parchment out of the library and toss it through the arch, where others stood by to receive them.

"Don't waste time trying to pick and choose," said Natalia. "Just start grabbing whatever's closest to the door."

"Understood," replied the Dwarf as he disappeared into the library.

"What do I do?" asked Athgar.

Natalia nodded to her right. "Up those stairs is a secret door. If anyone comes to stop us, that's the route they'll take."

"Couldn't they use the circle?"

"Not while this arch is using it."

"Are you certain we have no other options?"

She nodded. "Too many people have already died. I must put an end to this." She moved closer. "I…"

"I know," he replied. "I love you too." He kissed her, knowing it would be for the last time. "I'll see you in the Afterlife."

"We'll escape through Galina's arch," insisted Natalia.

"You know the arch will disappear once the circle is destroyed. This was a one-way trip—we all understood that. Now, you'd best get started. We can't risk being interrupted."

Natalia closed her eyes, her innate magic tapping into the power of the circle as she reached out with her mind, feeling the river rushing beneath them. She pushed farther still until she sensed the immense power of the ley lines coursing below her feet. In Beorwic, she'd tapped into this with the help of the standing stones, but here, she had only her innate magic to help her focus. She hesitated, knowing it would be difficult to control once the process began. Back in Carlingen, Shaluhk helped keep her physical form intact, but there was no such safeguard here. Once the spell started, it would consume her.

She fought back the tears, blinking her eyes open to take one last look at Athgar standing at the bottom of the stairs, his bow in hand, his gaze glued to the top step. She hesitated, her mind not yet able to accept this would be her final act.

All she ever wanted was to be free of the family. She'd fled this place, seeking safety, only to fall into the arms of a Fire Mage. She chuckled at the thought, for she'd done exactly what the family had wanted: birthed a child with a powerful Fire Mage. Her mind shifted to Oswyn. Both she and Athgar had dreamed of a grown-up daughter running through the forest, and her heart broke at the realization that she'd never live to see it herself.

In that moment, her heart closed. The family was responsible for this, and she'd ensure they paid the price! Anger built inside her, and as she unleashed her magic, she felt the power coursing through her.

---

The arch shattered, leaving Galina momentarily stunned. She staggered back, her mind trying to adapt to this new development.

"What happened?" asked Herulf.

"My connection to the circle was broken. Natalia must've started her spell."

"But how will we get them back?"

"That's just it. We can't, not until she completes her casting."

"You can't both use the circle at the same time?"

"No. Natalia had to be there to draw upon the power of the ley lines, but she wasn't supposed to utilize the circle."

"What went wrong?"

"I can't say. I can only surmise the ley lines flow directly through it."

"You mean they're trapped?"

"It would seem so."

"Gods preserve them," said Herulf.

---

The arch shattered. Athgar looked at Natalia, concerned for her safety, but she was in the throes of channelling her magic. The air around him buzzed, the hairs on his arms stood on end. He hadn't been with her when she'd used the ley lines in Beorwic, but now he understood just how much power lay beneath them.

Belgast stepped out from the arcane library, a stack of books between his arms. He stopped abruptly, staring at the circle. "Where's the arch?"

"Gone," said Athgar. "We should've predicted this."

"So we're stuck here?"

"We are."

"That's annoying. I don't mind dying, but I hoped we could've at least saved some of these books."

"What's happening?" asked Katrin as she stepped from the library, almost knocking over the Dwarf.

"The arch has shattered," muttered Belgast. "I'm afraid we're not going anywhere. Best pile the books off to one side of the circle. We might be able to restore the arch later once Natalia's done her thing."

"Her thing?"

"Yes, you know, her cataclysm—whatever that ends up being."

"I don't think you quite grasp the seriousness of our situation."

"You and I both knew there was no coming back from this. Now, what I think we should do is—"

"Someone's coming," interrupted Athgar. He stepped back from the stairs and aimed his bow towards the top. A crease of light appeared, and then a figure stood there, bathed in the glow of the hallway above.

He let fly and had the satisfaction of hearing his arrow hit, and whomever it was fell forward, limp. Two figures behind retaliated by loosing crossbow bolts, luckily missing Athgar, but he couldn't remain in the open. He ducked behind a pillar and tossed his bow aside, determined to use his magic instead.

Belgast dropped the books and pulled the pick he'd slung on his back. He ran over to Athgar and joined him, crouched behind the pillar. "How do you want to do this?"

"Wait until they come halfway down the stairs. It'll make them a better target."

"Easy for you to say. I don't have a ranged weapon."

"You know, you really should learn to use a bow."

"I've used an arbalest plenty of times," said Belgast. "I just don't happen to have one here."

"In that case," replied Athgar, "I'll rely on you to hit anyone who reaches the bottom step."

"Aye. That I can do."

Athgar could no longer see the top of the stairs from their current position. Not that he had to, for everyone heard the approaching footsteps as the two warriors came down, one behind the other. Athgar leaned around the pillar and thrust out his hands, sending a streak of fire flying towards the lead guard, striking him in the chest and setting his tabard aflame, but it failed to penetrate his mail.

The man ran down the remaining stairs, screaming in defiance, his eyes stung from the smoke pouring up from his tabard. Belgast rushed forward, his pick penetrating the fellow's leather boot, chipping away at the stone step beneath. A horrible wail emanated from the warrior as he pitched forward. Unable to halt his quick descent, he fell on top of the Dwarf, knocking him to the ground.

Katrin sent an ice shard into the second warrior's shoulder, immobilizing his arm, his shield dropping to the stairs and rolling into the room.

Athgar readied another spell, but the floor beneath him rumbled, interrupting his casting. It started with small vibrations, then water shot out as cracks appeared in the marble, sending a spray to the ceiling.

The second warrior lost his balance and fell, his face striking a step as he went. Additional men followed, moving slower lest they suffer the same fate.

Belgast hauled himself out from under his victim, struggling to his feet. His back hurt, his bones, too, and he found it hard to breathe. He looked about, not quite believing his eyes. The water from the fissures bounced off the ceiling, splashing all around, filling the room with a mist that was growing thicker by the moment.

Athgar let loose with another fire streak, taking down a guard and burning away some of the mist, if only temporarily. In that moment of clarity, he noticed a woman of advanced years following the warriors. He instantly knew who it was. Marakhova Stormwind herself had come to end this. He yelled a warning, but it was like standing at the base of the waterfall back in the forest, the sound of escaping water drowning out all else.

Belgast glanced at Natalia, standing with her eyes closed, her arms outstretched. A whirling mist surrounded her, and then her feet left the ground, bearing her aloft as the power of the ley lines coursed through her.

He tore his gaze from her, only to spot a woman on the stairs preparing to cast. With no doubt as to whom she was targeting, the Dwarf sprinted, jumping the last little bit to put himself between Natalia and the incoming spell.

A streak of ice so large it looked like a ballista bolt struck him mid-air, piercing his stomach, agonizing pain lancing through him. Cold, wet marble was the last thing he felt as he landed.

Seeing Belgast go down, Katrin turned towards Marakhova, ignoring the guards in a vain attempt to take down the Stormwind Matriarch. Ice shards shot from her hands, but a flick of the old woman's wrist produced a shield of ice that blocked the attack.

Water flowed over Athgar's feet and was rising quickly. He stepped back as another crack appeared, and a wall of water surged upward, blocking his view of Marakhova and her men.

A tremendous explosion rocked the room, throwing him to the floor. Behind him, the now-shattered magic circle, its runes exploded, had sent chunks of gold flying in all directions. Natalia was a blur, surrounded by a vortex of water rising to the ceiling.

Something grazed Katrin's arm, and she looked down at blood seeping from a cut. She cast about, trying to make sense of things, but all she could see were sheets of water, endless rain, and Athgar lying prone, blood covering his back. She moved towards him, the floor uneven and getting worse by the moment. Her foot slipped, and she fell to her knees, pain lancing up her leg, but she fought on and grabbed Athgar, pulling his head above the rapidly rising water. She pushed him into a seated position, leaning him against a pillar, then directed her attention to Belgast.

The Dwarf lay on his back, his nose, for the moment, still above water. She was slogging her way over to him despite her injury when Marakhova threw another spell. This time, the spear of ice struck the vortex surrounding Natalia. Rather than penetrate, the spell shattered, fragments of ice flying out, one striking Katrin's shoulder and sending her splashing to the floor.

Marakhova ignored her, advancing on Natalia, who continued her spell, oblivious to what was happening around her. A crack widened, and suddenly, it was as if a backward waterfall was lifting up from the floor, defying all logic. The surge of water pushed Katrin across the room, slamming her into a wall. Her chest hurt, blood poured from her shoulder, and she struggled to keep her head above the water.

Natalia's magic filled the room, the amount of power she was funnelling made everyone's skin crawl. From a detached portion of her mind, she saw it all unfolding: Athgar falling, chunks of gold puncturing his skin, the death of Belgast, a spear of ice through his chest, and now Katrin, crushed beneath the very magic Natalia had summoned. With all hope of success fading, she surrendered herself to the power of the ley lines.

Katrin clung to life, unwilling to admit defeat. She'd survived the mines of Zurkutsk and found love with Herulf; she had too much to live for! Someone approached, and she glanced up, expecting to see Marakhova coming in for the killing blow, but instead, Tatiana was speaking to her. The rush of water was too loud, so Katrin nodded, hoping it was enough to convince her friend she clung to life.

Tatiana began casting. At first, Katrin thought she might be offering a painless death, but then a frozen arch appeared. The waist-deep water was rapidly growing deeper, yet she somehow managed to get to her feet. Even Marakhova struggled, clasping the railing to stop from being tossed about by the inverted waterfall.

A loud crack rose above the noise as part of the ceiling dropped with a splash. The pillars wobbled, the overwhelming force of water crashing into them, and then they, too, cracked and fell.

The water swirling around Katrin's waist suddenly developed a current, carrying her off towards the frozen arch. To her amazement, light shone from the other side, and then she was swept through and deposited on a burned wooden floor. Belgast's body came next, and then another woman stepped through, someone Katrin didn't recognize.

Athgar rose unsteadily, soaked through and through, aching all over. When a body floated by, sucked towards the frozen arch, he realized it was his only chance of escape. Safety lay no more than three paces off to his left, but he couldn't leave without Natalia. His gaze whipped to the centre of the room, where a tornado of water engulfed his wife while she remained oblivious to the outside world, the raw power of the ley lines twisting her about as if she were a rag doll.

He summoned his inner spark, desperate to protect himself as he tried to reach her. The Ashwalkers had taught him to absorb fire; he now called on that same technique to create a wall of flame to envelope him.

Athgar took a step, the current pulling at him, trying to keep him from his beloved. With another step, his legs weakened. He was so close, yet he couldn't reach her; the terrifying vortex blocked his way.

He caught a movement off to one side and turned, witnessing Marakhova, her face twisted in a mask of rage, reaching out, using her magic to call forth all her remaining power, her eyes bleeding even as her hands glowed.

Athgar concentrated, letting loose with all the magic he had left to draw upon. His spark roared to life, and he tasted blood as he willed his fire shield to flare up.

The vortex exploded, sending steam and water hurtling everywhere. Natalia dropped to the floor while Athgar, held back by the spell, was sucked into the centre of what used to be the magic circle.

Athgar blindly reached out to Natalia, catching her arm. He clung to her with a death grip as the current washed them through the frozen arch. Moments later, Tatiana appeared, carried out of the Baroshka by the same rush of water.

Katrin sat up, gasping for air. She briefly glimpsed Marakhova, struggling towards the arch as a pillar collapsed, crushing her under its weight, then the arch shattered, the flood of water ceasing.

---

Kargen heard a rumble.

"Everyone back!" he shouted.

The ground shook as one of the Volstrum's towers toppled over, stones and dust flying into the air.

"It's collapsing," said Hilwyth, a look of awe on her face. "They did it!"

Two more towers cracked, tumbling to the ground, and then a great fountain of water and stone soared skyward. All anyone could do was watch, awestruck by the raw power unleashed. The water reached high into the sky before collapsing in on itself, sending brick and stone tumbling onto the roof of the Volstrum.

The street shook with another groan before the entire building collapsed. Men and Orcs struggled to get out of the way as a tremendous chasm opened up, devouring the building until all that remained was an immense gaping hole filled with water and rubble.

---

Someone grabbed Katrin's arm, pulling her to her feet.

"W-w-who are you?" she stammered, still struggling to understand what had happened.

"Lydia," came the reply. "Tatiana and I went to the Baroshka to stop Marakhova."

"Where are we?"

"I can answer that," offered Tatiana. "I brought us to what's left of Stormwind Manor."

"I don't understand," said Katrin. "I thought it burned to the ground."

"It did, but I gambled on the force of all this water clearing enough space for us to safely travel here. Now, let's see to the wounded, shall we, while they still have lives left to save."

# THE END

## SPRING 1110 SR

Athgar opened his eyes to see Shaluhk staring down at him. "Where am I?"

"You are back in Karslev."

"And Natalia?"

"She is here, though it will be a while until she can unleash her magic."

"What happened?"

"Tatiana saved you."

"Tatiana? Where did she come from?"

"She will tell you all that later, once you rest."

He tried to sit up but was too weak.

Shaluhk smiled. "My magic cured you, Athgar, but you lost a lot of blood."

"I hear noises. What's happening?"

"The Army of Therengia is preparing to return home."

"So soon?"

"Soon? It's been two days since Natalia destroyed the Volstrum. At first, we thought you were all dead, then Tatiana appeared from the south."

He closed his eyes, trying to recall what had happened. "I remember being washed through a gate."

"Yes. Tatiana opened a frozen arch, but it acted like a hole, sucking water from the room and all of you with it."

"Belgast?"

"He's fine, though, like you, he will be resting for some time. Katrin, as well."

"I can't believe it. I thought we were all going to die." He looked at Shaluhk. "Please take me to Natalia."

The Orc shaman moved his right hand until he felt flesh. He grasped Natalia's hand, crushing it in his own. He tilted his head to see her staring back at him from the bed beside his.

"We knew you two would want to be together," said Shaluhk.

"Ah," came Kargen's voice. "I see our friends have finally awoken. It is about time!" His face loomed large as he stared down at Athgar. "I have good news and bad. What would you like to hear first?"

"Let's start with the good, shall we?"

"The Volstrum is no more, sucked into the very river that flowed beneath it."

"Any survivors?"

"A few, mostly younger, less-fanatical students who had the good sense to surrender. I am told Marakhova is dead."

"Are you certain?"

"Katrin saw it with her own eyes."

"Thank the Gods for that. What's the bad news?"

"King Yulakov banned all magic from his kingdom. Spellcasters will no longer be welcome in Ruzhina."

"It's not surprising, considering how things turned out. Anything else I should know about?"

"Garag decided not to return to Ard-Gurslag. He wishes to live in Therengia, as do most of his glaives."

"They would be more than welcome."

"I already told him as much."

"Is that all?"

"Prince Piotr was returned to his father. He enjoyed his time in Runewald, but I doubt that will be enough to sway his father's opinion regarding magic or the possibility of rebuilding the Volstrum."

"I don't want to rebuild," said Natalia. "We'll start a new school in Ebenstadt, one that doesn't harbour ulterior motives. I had hoped Tatiana might agree to look after the running of it."

"There is something else you should know," said Kargen. "We had a visit from someone named Dagor Sartellian. I let Stanislav deal with him."

"What did he want?"

"He seemed almost relieved the Volstrum was destroyed. It appears there was no love lost between the Sartellians and the Stormwinds. Stanislav passed on the king's wishes regarding mages within his borders, and that family members have a month to leave."

"A month? That's very generous."

"That was Yulakov's decision. As for Dagor himself, we have him under guard. Stanislav told me he ordered the death of your mother, Nat-Alia. I thought it best to hold him until you decide his fate."

"There's been enough death here," she replied. "Extract a promise from him that the Sartellians will never threaten Therengia again and send him on his way."

"And if he refuses?"

"Then he can join Queen Rada as a prisoner in Ebenstadt."

# EPILOGUE

## AUTUMN 1110 SR

Natalia smiled as Oswyn ran past, bow in hand.

"She has a restless spirit," said Athgar. "One day, she's going to change the world."

"Like her father?"

"Me? You broke the power of the Stormwinds, not me."

"If it hadn't been for you, I would never have found the courage to even attempt to destroy the Volstrum."

"She is correct," said Shaluhk, who sat across the fire from them. "Combined, you two are more powerful than the sum of your individual selves."

"As are you two."

"What is next for Therengia?"

"Yes," added Kargen. "Tell us what future you foresee for this home of ours."

"Peace, hopefully, though there are already rumours from the west. They say the empire is causing trouble."

"There will always be another war," said Natalia. "It is the way of the Petty Kingdoms, but for now, let's concentrate on ruling a land of peace."

"And the future?"

Natalia watched as Oswyn ran towards her. She crushed her daughter to her and gave her a big hug. "The future lies with our children."

---

Thus ends The Frozen Flame

. . .

<<<<>>>>

Review Cataclysm

---

On to The Duality of Magic: Voices From the Past
The Legacy of Athgar and Natalia continues
Coming Spring 2025

If you liked *The Frozen Flame* series, then *Servant of the Crown,* the first book in the *Heir to the Crown* series awaits.

Start Servant of the Crown for FREE

# CAST OF CHARACTERS

**Main Characters:**

Agar - Son of Shaluhk and Kargen, Red Hand Tribe
Athgar - Fire Mage, High Thane of Therengia, bondmate Natalia
Belgast Ridgehand - Dwarf Entrepreneur, friend of Natalia and Athgar
Cordelia - Temple Captain of Saint Agnes
Galina Marwen - Water Mage, Reinwick
Greta - Young girl, Katrin's ward
Herulf - Fyrd commander, Beorwic, Carlingen
Kargen - Chieftain, bondmate to Shaluhk, Red Hand Tribe
Katrin Stormwind - Water Mage, former student of the Volstrum
Maksim IV - King of Carlingen
Natalia Stormwind - Water Mage, Warmaster of Therengia, bondmate Athgar
Oswyn - Daughter of Athgar and Natalia
Shaluhk - Shaman, bondmate to Kargen, Red Hand Tribe
Skora - Friend of Athgar and Natalia, Therengian
Stanislav Voronsky - Former Mage hunter, friend of Natalia
Svetlana Stormwind - Water Mage, Queen of Carlingen

**Orcs of Ard-Gurslag:**

Garag - First Glaive
Grisha (Deceased) - Last shaman
Grom (Deceased) - Enchanter during Great War
Krogal - Gate guard
Lurka - Archer captain
Morgal - Head Enchanter
Nakthar Nakthar - Master of Water
Thorga the Strong-Willed (Deceased) - Former ruler
Throgar - Keeper of History
Throkar (Deceased) - Shaman
Thusha - Second Minister
Urgash - Queen
Zorga - Administrative head of army
Zorith - Senior Master of Water

**Orcs of Therengia:**

Artoch (Deceased) - Master of Flame, Athgar's mentor, Red Hand
Durgash - Hunter, Red Hand
Gahruhl - Master of Earth, Stone Crushers
Gorlag - Former chieftain, Red Hand
Grundak - Hunter, Red Hand
Khurlig (Deceased) - Ancestor
Kragor - Hunter, Red Hand
Kraloch - Shaman, Black Arrows
Laghul - Shaman, Black Axe
Laruhk - Tusker rider, brother to Shaluhk, Red Hand
Ogda - Hunter, Black Axe
Rotuk - Master of Air, Cloud Hunters
Rugg - Master of Earth, Stone Crushers
Tonfer Garul - Scholar, Ebenstadt
Uhdrig (Deceased) - Shaman, Shaluhk's mentor
Urag - Hunter, Red Hand
Urgon - Chieftain, Black Arrows
Urumar - Master of Earth, Stone Crushers
Uruzuhk - Shaman, Cloud Hunters
Ushog - Tusker rider, Bondmate to Laruhk, Red Hand
Varag - Hunter, Stone Crushers
Voruhn - Shaman, Stone Crushers
Zaruhk - Youngling, Red Hand
Zharuhl - Chieftain, Stone Crushers
Zhura - Ghostwalker, Black Arrows

**Stormwinds in Rhuzina:**

Anushka (Deceased) - Former Volstrum student
Corderis - Master of Zurkutsk
Gregori - Water Mage
Illiana (Deceased) - Former head of family, Natalia's Grandmother
Irinushka - Chancellor, Court of King Yulakov
Larissa Stormwind - Water Mage
Lydia Stormwind - Instructor, Volstrum
Marakhova - Stormwind Matriarch
Tatiana - Former head of Volstrum
Veris - Military Adviser
Voltana - Current head of Volstrum
Yaleva - Treasurer, Court of King Yulakov
Yereva - Tutor, Court of King Yulakov

**People of Ruzhina:**

Aleksei - Young boy, Volstrum
Alfie - Prisoner, Zurkutsk mine
Duvarov - Captain
Felix - Prisoner, Yurkutsk mine
Galiana - Name used by Galina Marwen
Giliad - Guard, Yurkutsk mine
Hedy - Young girl, Volstrum
Igor - Guard, Zurkutsk mine
Katherine - Name used by Katrin Stormwind
Luka Morozov - Labourer
Marta - Proprietor, Mages Delight, Kolovsky
Nika - Young girl, Volstrum
Nikolai (deceased) - Mage Hunter
Piotr - Son of King Yulakov
Slavil Yenkov - Guard, Zurkutsk mine
Valentina - Name used by Natalia Stormwind
Yakim - Warrior in service to King Yulakov
Yulakov the Eight - King of Ruzhina

**Others:**

Aelfric - Therengian fyrd member, Carlingen
Carmen - Temple Knight of Saint Agnes, Carlingen
Wulfwyn - Therengian fyrd member, Carlingen
Aubrey Brandon - Life Mage, Baroness of Hawksburg, Merceria
Dagor Sartellian - Fire Mage, Korascajan
Denise - Temple Knight, Temple Ship *Formidable*
Dorkin - Captain, Grim Defenders, Abelard
Eugene - King, Ostrova
Farin Greybeard - King, Kragen-Tor
Fernando Brondecker - Duke of Reinwick
Gabriel - Temple Captain, Abelard
Grazynia - Temple Captain, Temple Ship *Vigilant*
Karis - Temple Knight, Saint Agnes, Abelard
Karzik - Self-proclaimed King of Zaran, disappeared a century ago
Kieren Brightaxe - Smith, cousin of Belgast Ridgehand, Runewald
Melethandil - Dragon, Merceria
Rada - Former Queen of Novarsk, Ebenstadt
Raleth - Commander of the Thane Guard, Therengia
Hilwyth - Commander of the Therengian Archers, Therengia
Carl Dotterfeld (Deceased) - Founder of Carlingen

Rordan - King, Abelard
Rostov - Baron, Ruzhina
Satira - Sea Cow, Zaran
Valeria - Temple Captain, Temple Ship *Formidable*
Vicavia - Enchanter, said to have experimented on children
Wynfrith - Governor of Novarsk, Therengia
Yaromir - Temple Captain of Saint Mathew, Ebenstadt

**Places**

**Petty Kingdoms:**
Abelard - Kingdom, Northern Coast
Andover - Kingdom, South of Reinwick
Arnsfeld - Kingdom, Northern Coast
Braymoor - Kingdom, West of Carlingen
Carlingen - Kingdom, North of Therengia
Eidolon - Kingdom, Northern Coast
Erlingen - Duchy
Hadenfeld - Kingdom, Central Continent
Holstead - Duchy, South of Grey Spire Mountains
Ilea - Kingdom, Southern Coast
Krieghoff - Duchy, South of Grey Spire Mountains
Ostrova - Kingdom, North of Novarsk
Reinwick - Duchy, Northern Coast
Rhuzina - Kingdom, Northeast Continent
Ruzhina - Kingdom, Northeastern Coast
Talyria - Kingdom, West Central Continent
Zalista - Kingdom, West of Novarsk
Zaran - Region between Ruzhina and Carlingen

**Cities:**
Ard-Gurslag - Orc city, Zaran
Ard-Uzgul (Destroyed) - Orc city destroyed during the Great War
Ashborne - Village, Therengia
Athelwald (Destroyed) - Therengian village, Holstead
Beorwic - Ruins of ancient Therengian city, Carlingen
Carlingen - Capital, Carlingen
Corassus - City-state, Southern Coast
Ebenstadt (Dunmere) - City, Therengia
Karslev - Capital, Ruzhina
Kienenstadt - Capital, Abelard
Korascajan - City, Home of Sartellian Academy

Korvoran - Capital, Renwick
Ord-Kurgad (Destroyed) - Orc Village, Red Hand Tribe, Holstead
Porovka - Port city, Ruzhina
Raketsk - Barony, Carlingen
Runewald - Village, Therengia

**Other Places:**

Adlinschlot - Barony, Carlingen
Antonine - Head of the Church of the Saints, Regensbach
Baroshka - Secret repository of knowledge, Volstrum, Ruzhina
Great Northern Sea - Northern Coast
Grey Spire Mountains - Mountain range, South of Therengia
Khasrahk - Orc Village, Stone Crushers, Therengia
Kragen-Tor - Dwarf Kingdom, Grey Spire Mountains
Kurathian Isles - Island ruled by princes, far to the south
Magpie - Inn, Kienenstadt, Abelard
Northern Alliance - Reinwick and Andover
Novarsk - Province, Therengia
Old Kingdom - Original Therengia
Pillars of Truth - Kragen-Tor
Shimmering Sea - Southern Coast
Stormwind Manor - Ancestral home of Stormwinds, Ruzhina
Teeth of Karamir - Shimmering Sea
Temple Bay - Home of the Temple Fleet
The Darkwood - Elven Realm, near Merceria
Thornwood - Home of the Ashwalkers, Reinwick
Volstrum - Stormwind Academy, Karslev
Windrush River - Orc name for the Carlsrun River
Zurkutsk - Mine, Ruzhina
Mages Delight - Inn, Kolovsky, Ruzhina
Kolovsky - Village, Ruzhina
Mitchutskin River - River running through Karslev, Ruzhina

**Other Information**

**Orc Tribes:**

Ashwalkers - Masters of fire, Reinwick
Black Arrows - Merceria
Black Axe - Therengia
Cloud Hunters - Masters of Air, Therengia
Red Hand - Masters of Fire, Therengia
Stone Crushers - Masters of Earth, Therengia

Night Dreamers - Enchanters, Talyria

**Ships:**

*Bergannon* - Carlingen
*Faithful* - Temple Fleet
*Fearless* - Flagship of the Temple Fleet
*Fervent* - Temple Fleet
*Formidable* - Temple Fleet
*Furious* - Temple Fleet
*Triumphant* - Flagship of the Holy Fleet, Corassus

**Battles:**

Battle of the Standing Stones (1104 SR) - Therengian/Orc defeat Holy Army
Battle of Krosnicht (1090 SR) - King of Abelard defeats rebel army
Battle of the Green River (date unknown)- Battle during the Great War
Great War - War between the Elves and Orcs two thousand years ago

**Gods:**

Akosia - Goddess of Water
Hraka - God of Fire
Tauril - Goddess of the Woods

**Terms:**

After the Calamity (AC) - Calendar years since the end of the Great War
Charc - Dried and salted meat
Disgraced - Failed Volstrum student
Fyrd - Therengian levy
Grim Defenders - Mercenary company
High Thane - Ruler of Therengia
Kingdom of Shadows - Mythic kingdom, East of Ruzhina
Ley lines - Magical lines of energy flowing underground
Magerite - Rare gem, indicates magical power
Master of Air - Orc term for an Air Mage
Master of Earth - Orc term for an Earth Mage
Master of Flame - Orc term for a Fire Mage
Master of Water - Orc term for a Water Mage
Ordeal - Orc coming of age rite
Order of the Mailed Fist - Novarsk order of chivalry
Standing Stones - Built atop ley line intersections
Successor States - Precursor to Petty Kingdoms

Thane - Elected ruler of a Therengian Village
Thane Guard - Elite Therengian warriors
Thane's Council - Ruling council of Therengia
Tusker - Huge animal ridden by Orcs
Umak - Orc boat, similar to a canoe

# A FEW WORDS FROM PAUL

With the completion of Cataclysm, Athgar and Natalia's journey comes to an end. Their story began with each of them discovering the power within them, and while there can be no doubt both would have pursued a life of magic had they not met, their chance encounter in Draybourne set them on the road to greatness.

Natalia was always a powerful Water Mage; her time at the Volstrum only confirmed that, but it wasn't until Athgar taught her how to harness her inner spark (or, in her case, water) that she learned the most valuable lesson of all, that of restraint. This, in turn, led her to a far greater understanding of magic, where she could harness the raw power of Eiddenwerthe to accomplish the impossible.

Athgar's journey was no less impressive, from his humble beginnings as a poor hunter to his mastery of flame under the tutelage of the Ashwalkers. Even more important, however, is their unwavering support of each other, a bond that, while forged in misfortune, led to them becoming even stronger as a team.

Now that their struggle with the Stormwinds is complete, Athgar and Natalia can look forward to a life of relative ease in their new home, Therengia—a realm that never would have existed had it not been for Athgar's belief in his people and Natalia's refusal to bow down to their enemies.

I had fun writing these series, but it's time to allow them the rest they so justly deserve. Though their story is over, their legacy lives on.

This story, indeed, this entire series, would not have been possible without the hard work of my wife, Carol, who, in addition to being editor, marketer, and social media coordinator, was instrumental in helping me bring these characters to life. Her encouragement and support helped me start this writing journey, and I shall ever be thankful.

I would also like to thank Stephanie Sandrock, Christie Bennett, and Amanda Bennett for their support throughout my career, along with my beta team, which consists of the following: Rachel Deibler, Michael Rhew, Phyllis Simpson, Don Hinckley, Charles Mohapel, Debbie Reeves, Susan Young, Anna Ostberg, Joanna Smith, James McGinnis, Jim Burke, Lisa Hanika, and Lisa Hunt.

Last but most assuredly not least, I owe a debt of gratitude to you, my readers, who've embraced these characters. Your comments and reviews inspire me, and I encourage you to tell me what you think of Cataclysm.

# ABOUT THE AUTHOR

Paul J Bennett (b. 1961) emigrated from England to Canada in 1967. His father served in the British Royal Navy, and his mother worked for the BBC in London. As a young man, Paul followed in his father's footsteps, joining the Canadian Armed Forces in 1983. He is married to Carol Bennett and has three daughters who are all creative in their own right.

Paul's interest in writing started in his teen years when he discovered the roleplaying game, Dungeons & Dragons (D & D). What attracted him to this new hobby was the creativity it required; the need to create realms, worlds and adventures that pulled the gamers into his stories.

In his 30's, Paul started to dabble in designing his own roleplaying system, using the Peninsular War in Portugal as his backdrop. His regular gaming group were willing victims, er, participants in helping to playtest this new system. A few years later, he added additional settings to his game, including Science Fiction, Post-Apocalyptic, World War II, and the all-important Fantasy Realm where his stories take place.

The beginnings of his first book 'Servant to the Crown' originated over five years ago when he began running a new fantasy campaign. For the world that the Kingdom of Merceria is in, he ran his adventures like a TV show, with seasons that each had twelve episodes, and an overarching plot. When the campaign ended, he knew all the characters, what they had to accomplish, what needed to happen to move the plot along, and it was this that inspired to sit down to write his first novel.

Paul now has four series based in his fantasy world of Eiddenwerthe, and is looking forward to sharing many more books with his readers over the coming years.

Printed in Great Britain
by Amazon

42050958R00169